KB137778

셰익스피어와 여성
성, 권력, 그리고 여성의 몸

김미경

서울대학교 영어영문학과에서 학사와 석사학위를 취득하고 영국 에섹스 대학교(University of Essex)에서 문학 박사학위를 취득하였다. 현재 백석대학교에서 부교수로 강의하고 있다. 박사학위 논문으로 "The Politics of Body Images in Shakespearean Drama: Sexuality and Nation-building in the History Plays and *The Tempest*"가 있다.

셰익스피어와 여성:
성, 권력, 그리고 여성의 몸

초판 1쇄 발행일 2016년 8월 25일

지은이 김미경
발행인 이성모
발행처 도서출판 동인 • 서울시 종로구 혜화로3길 5 118호
　　　　 TEL 02-765-7145 / FAX 02-765-7165 / dongin60@chol.com
등 록 제1-1599호
I S B N　978-89-5506-726-2
정 가 22,000원

셰익스피어와 여성
성, 권력, 그리고
여성의 몸 Sexuality, Power, and Female Body in Shakespearean Drama

김미경 지음

도서출판 동인

셰익스피어와 여성: 성, 권력, 그리고 여성의 몸을 내면서

이 책은 영국 르네상스시기의 셰익스피어 드라마와 당대 식민주의 시대의 글들, 웹스터의『말피 공작부인』, 그리고 스토파드의 <사랑에 빠진 셰익스피어>를 주로 다루고 있다. 이는 본인이 페미니스트적인 시각이나 젠더에 대한 관심에서 작품을 주로 연구하는 과정에서 특히 관심을 가지게 되었던 주제로, 이와 관련된 작품들을 하나로 모아 책을 출간하게 되었다. 이 책은 3부로 구성되어 있다.

1부는 영어 논문들로 구성되어 있으며 주로 셰익스피어 드라마를 다루고 있다. 셰익스피어 드라마로『폭풍』과『베니스의 상인』,『한여름 밤의 꿈』, 역사극 등을 다루고 있으며 콜럼부스의『일기』와 랄리의『가이아나의 발견』, 웹스터의『말피 공작부인』 등도 함께 다루고 있다. 1부의 중심 주제는 식민주의(1장), 여성의 몸의 재현과 시각적 욕망(2장), 성적 인종적 차이의 재현(3장), 셰익스피어 드라마의 한국적 재현(4장), 마녀사냥과 여성의 재현(5장), 여성의 성적 몸과 정치적 재현(6장), 남성의 성적 몸과 동성애(7장) 등이다. 기본적으로 성과 민족주의의 재현이라는 관점에서 여성의 몸이 어떻게 형상화되고 재현되는지에 관심을 가지고 작품을 연구하였다. 2부는 한글 논문들로 구성되어 있다. 초기 식민주의 담론에 나타난 여성의 몸이라는 주제가 2부 1장의 제목이며 1부 1장에 대한 한글 번역본인데 조금의 수정을 가하였다. 2장은 톰 스토파드의 <사랑에 빠진 셰익스피어>라는 영화를 분석하여 집필한 논문으로 복장전도라는 기제를 통하여 바이올라가 주체성을 추구하고 시대적 한계를 극복하는 과정을 분석하였다. 3장은 『오셀로』, <저녁 식사하러 누가 왔나 보세요> 그리고 <정글 피버>에 나타난 인종차별적 이분법과 백인 남성의 집단 불안심리'라는 제목으로 세 개의 영상물을 분석했다. 이 장의 기본 주제는 인종과 성 파워이며 흑인 대 백인의 인종구조에서 『오셀로』에 나오는 백인 남성 이아고와 <정글 피버>의 다수의 백인 남성들, 그리고 <저녁 식사하러 왔나 보세요>의 조이의 아버지 맽 등 백인 남성의 흑인 남성에 대한 인종차별적 시각들과 이러한 편견과 심리적 대응 방식이 어떻게 형상화되고 재현되는지에 주목하였다. 4장은 셰익스피어의 희곡 『안토니와 클레오파트라』를 다루고 있으며 이 희곡에 나타난 '안토니의 과도함과 클레오파트라의 이국성'이라는 주제로 작품을 분석하였다. 3부는 최근에 필자가 학회에서 발표한 글들로 아직 미완의 글들이며 수정 보완하여 완성된 글들로 미래에 학회지에 수록할 예정의 글들이다. 1장은 셰익스피어의 『베니스의 상인』과 영화 <베니스에서의 죽음>이라는 두 작품을 비교 분석하였으며 두 영화에서 공통으로 등장하는 베니스라는 공간에 주목하여 세계 시민주의, 그리고 노마디즘(유목주의라는 뜻으로 어디에도 속하지 않음을 뜻함. 적절한 번역어를 찾을 수 없어 영어 원문대로 기재하였음)에 대하여 분석하였다. 2장은 영화 <베니스의 상인>과 <가장 따뜻한 색, 블루>에 나타난 성과 인종에 대한 이분법적 인식과 소외된 문화의 상징으로서의 색의 이미지의 상징성에 대한 분석을 시도하였다. 3장은 셰익스피어의 『코리올레이누스』에 나타난 폭력의 대상으로서의 몸과 노마디즘에 대하여 분석하였다. 4장은 필자가 영국 에섹스 대학교에서 석사 과정 학생들 수업을 진행하면서 사용했던 리딩 리스트이다. 셰익스피어 공부와 드라마 연구에 재미를 느꼈던 필자가 박사 학위 취득 후 나의 딸 유진이와 함께 영국에 머물면서 얻은 귀한 기회였던 석사 과정 학생들과의 만남을 감사하며 박사 과정에서 공부했던 내용을 정리해서 수업했던 셰익스피어 연구과정 학생들 수업 리딩 리스트이다.

　박사 논문 이후 처음으로 한국에서 책을 출간하면서 기쁨과 설렘을 함께 느낀다. 책 출판에 도움을 준 이가은, 박수경, Shaka Richardson, Mike Song, 딸 이유진, 그리고 바쁜 일정 가운데서도 이 책을 출간하게 해주신 동인 출판사에 깊은 감사의 말씀을 전하며 항상 격려해 주고 동기 부여를 해주는 가족과 제자들에게 이 책을 빌려 감사의 말을 전한다.

2016년 7월
태조산 자락에서
김미경

차례

1
장
—

The Female Body on the Margin of Colonialism:
Diario, *The Discovery of Guiana*, and
The Tempest

The ideology of otherness which is achieved by differentiating and discriminating others is articulated in the discourse of colonialism. Within the apparatus of the colonialist discourse, sexuality and race are related in a process of differentiation and discrimination. In this context, I will examine the discourse of incipient Western colonialism and its manipulation of sexuality, by focusing on the texts of Christopher Columbus's *Diario*, Walter Ralegh's *The Discovery of Guiana*, and William Shakespeare's *The Tempest*. The travel narratives of emergent colonialist discourse represent the desire and anxiety of the colonialist to exploit the virgin land and manipulate sexuality by means of the inscription of the gendered exchange between Western male and Amerindian female. In this context, *Diario* and *The Discovery of Guiana* provide us with good examples of the emergent colonialism and its manipulation of sexual economy. Based on the contemporary cultural background of these travel narratives, I will focus on *The Tempest* in terms of the representation of the other land as the demonised female body of Sycorax, and the manipulation of Miranda. Also, I will deal with the dramatization of Claribel's ill-starred marriage to the African king of Tunis which demonstrates the geographical difference and the otherness of North Africa. Manipulation of female subjectivity and sexuality by an imperial patriarchal control is dramatized as the conquest over race and gender in the case of Sycorax and Miranda. Prospero's inexorable will to power is manifested through his deliberate demonization of Sycorex, the queen of the island, and the exploitation of his own daughter's sexuality.

1. Columbus's *Diario* and the feminisation of the new land

Columbus's *Diario* can be regarded as non-literary, thus incongruous with the discussion of literary texts. But it may be said that it is not written by historians. Its status as a non-literary text is put into suspension in the sense that it represents the emergent colonial anxiety in a subjective and imaginary way. I would like to quote Peter Hulme's explanation for the use of literary texts in the discussion of non-literary colonialist discourse.

> What should follow is a careful examination of the claims and assumptions implicit within different statements, an examination that would involve attention to such elements as ganre, rhetoric, pragmatics and so verification—seemingly made irrelevant by the universality of 'fiction' as a discursive mode—return in a minor key where a statement claims veracity. These somewhat abstract issues take on considerable importance in the colonial context since certain of the particular discourses involved—narrative history, historical linguistics, ethnography—stand or fall by their trutha - claims. It is therefore in the first instance politically dermine their claims; and ideological analysis remains an essential tool for Marxism because it enables us to say not just that a particular statement is false, but also that its falsity has a wider significance in the justification of existing power-relations. (Hulme 7-8)

The issue of genre takes on ambiguity in the colonial context because travel narrative and colonial romance can be either historical or imaginary. Particular statements of travel narratives may be false and their falsity may be based on existing power-relations between the West and the East. In particular, with regard to Diario and The Discovery of Guiana, there is much debate on the question of whether the stories are complete fabrications or not. For Diario, Las Casas not only summarizes and paraphrases Columbus, he insinuates himself as a new subject into the text by imposing on it an editorial rhetoric that could not have existed in the original journal. Through a selective process of transcription and omission, "these editorial interventions altered the original text's content and, perhaps even more fundamentally, also altered the way in which the context can be read" (Zamora 43). Las Casas published the palimpsest as the Diario. Because the missing Diario of the first navigation remains lost to us, Las Casas's editorial manipulations affected the fictive and imaginary aspect of the Diario to a large degree.

The drawing by Jan Van der Straet (refer to Hulme xii figure 1) exuberantly represents the inaugural scene of erotic encounter between a full-clothed European male and a naked Amerindian female, an image that has been firmly established in the Western cultural imagination. This erotic encounter is much more than simply sexual because "cultural values that privilege the European male are embedded in this gendered exchange, rendering the Indian female extremely receptive, open, and empty" (Zamora 154). It can be recognised in the drawing that the reclining nude women is greeting the European man who stands before her, armored and bearing a staff with crucifix, contrasting the want implied in Amerindian female's gesture—empty hand beckoning—and the fullnes noted in the European male's hands and cloth. These gendered cultural values and exchanges are embedded and inscribed in the sexual economy embodied in the question of gender and in the discourse of discovery. The stategy of feminization and eroticization uncannily renders gendered difference a fixed characteristic of the 'Indies', with the difference a fundamental basis of the representation and the essential component of the process of interpretation. Strategically, the representation of the land as feminine is closely connected with the issues of power and economic exploitation which were carried out by inscribing 'the Indies' in a coordination of beauty, fertility, and ultimately, possession and domination. The idealized feminizing description of the Indians and the land can be demonstrated through Columbus's *Diario.*

They were well bulit, with handsome bodies and fine features. Their hair is thick, almost like a horse's tail, but short. They wear it down over their eyebrows except for a few strands behind which they wear long and never cut. Some of them paint themselves black, though they are naturally the colour of Canary Islanders, neither black nor white; and some paint themselves white, some red and some whatever colour they can find. (Ife 29)

The Indian is ideologized in terms of a masculine-faminine contrast and articulated through the rhetorical feminization. Effeminate characteristics are ascribed to the Indians such a Arawak physical attributes (long hair, the painting of the body), their cowardice, and their explicitly spontaneous and natural subservience to the Spaniards.

In this process, cultural dichotomies—courage/cowardice, activity/passivity, strength/weakness, intellect/body —are applied to the justification of the difference between Europeans and Indians, and "gender difference is ideologized and inscribed onto a cultural economy in which gender is a question of value, power, and domonance" (Zamora 173-4). This feminization and even eroticization can be endorsed through the startling interpretation of the shape and location of paradise as a nipple and a woman's breast. In the recounting of his third voyage, Columbus makes a striking observation that the globe is not round at all and it is shaped like a pear, or a women's breast; moreover, he claims that he was actually moving upward on the slope of the breast toward the location of the Earthly Paradise. He writes:

> Now, as I have already said, I have seen so great irregularity, that, as a result, I have been led to hold this concerning the world, and I find that it is not round as they discribe it, but that it is the shape of a pear which is everywhere very round except where the stalk is, for there it is very prominant, or that it is like a very rounball, and on one part of it is placed something like a women's nipple, and that this is the highest and nearest to the sky, and it is beneath the equinoctial line and in this Ocean Sea at the end of the East. (Jane 30)

From Columbus's viewpoint, the Paradise is situated on the nipple and the new land is the paradise itself. Interestingly, the territorial appropriation is eroticized through the feminisation of the land. This contradiction and ambivalence—the contradiction between evangelizer and colonizer, desire and disdain—in colonial discourse can be detected in the discourse of incipient colonialism. This text interprets the central issues of power, dominance, and appropriation in terms of sexual dichotomy. This idiosyncratic dichotomy assumes its full sociocultural significance and structural dominance in terms of masculine power. The Indies are inscribed into the colonial exchange as a feminine value intended for consumption in a cultural economy where femininity is synonymous with exploitability. Therefore, the difference is interpreted in the political and economic terms and the gendered cultural values are inscribed in the discourse of discovery. Interestingly, the feminization and eroticization of the new found land is idiosyncratically found not only in Columbus's Diario, but also in Walter Ralegh's The Discovery. The two texts share a common feature in the sense that they are travel narratives and that in both texts we can find strong similitude of the new land and the eroticized female body. Their attitude as a colonizer and the representation of the new land as a virgin female body reinforce the ideology of gendered cultural values in the discourse of discovery.

2. Ralegh's *The Discovery of Guiana* and the representation of the new world as a virgin female body

Walter Ralegh's frustrated inquiries after an island Guinia, and his writing, represent the social fantasy of colonialism and commercialism. His textualization of the body of the other is neither a mere description nor a genuine encounter but rather an act of symbolic violence, mastery, and self-empowerment. For example, the New World isitself gendered feminine and sexed as a virgin female body:

> To conclude, Guiana is a countrey that hath yet her maydenhead, never sackt, turned, nor wrought, the face of the earth hath not bene torne, not the vertue and salt of the soyle spent by manurance, the graves have not bene opened for glode, the mines not broken with sledges, nor their Images puld downe out of their temples. It hath never bene entred by any armie of strength, and never conquered or possessed by any Christian Prince. (Ralegh 428)

The metaphor of Guiana's maidenhead activates and embodies the similitude of the land and a woman's body, of colonization and sexual mastery. His discription of Guiana conveys a proleptically elegiac sympathy for the unspoiled world, and it arouses excitement at the prospect of deflowering it. By subsuming the New World and Amerindian men in the metaphor of the female body, the English intent to subjugate the indigenous peoples of Guiana is paralleled to and justified as the male's mastery of the female. The hierarchical structures of colonial discourse rely on generalized understandings of the so-called natural relatioships between male and female. As Joan Scott notes, "power relatioships among nations and the status of colonial subjecta have been made legitimate in terms of relations between male and female" (Scott 42). Indeed, "the ideology of gender hierarchy sanctions the English-men's collective longing to prove and aggrandize themselves upon the feminine body of the New World" (Montrose 188). At the same time, the incipient hierarchical discourse of colonial exploitation and domination reciprocally confirms that ideology's hegemonic force.

This similitude of the earth and the female body is reinforced through various textual plays of travel literature. For instance, in A Relation of the Second Voyage to Guiana, Laurence Keymis justified the gendered violence of the colonialist project as provoked by the animated land's own desire to be possessed: "Fruitfull rich grounds, lying now waste for want of people, do prostitute themselves unto us, like a faire and beautifull woman" (Keymis 487). In this discourse, masculine desires for possession have been subjected to a form of reversal. That is, Englishmen have been rendered not as territorial invaders but rather as passive beneficiaries of the animated land's own desire to be possessed. This is a real imposition of the fantasy of 'self-prostitution,' which strategy is employed to justify the exploitation of the new land. We can observe how gender and sexual conduct are figured into the complex textual play of otherness in the colonialist discourse. The linkage between sexuality and power is activated through the cooperation with the cultural fantasy of exploitation and domination. Undeniably, gender is reciprocally related to other modes of cultural, political and economic organization in terms of a multivalent ideological process. As Louis Montrose argues, "the gendering of the protocolonialist discourse of discovery has existed in Western Europe since 16C and with it the articulation of the European representations of gender with new projects of economic exploitation and geopolitical domination"(178). However, the paradoxes and contradictions are foregrounded and interrogated in the process of protocolonialist "othering" of the Indians. By means of foregrounding the rupture and contradiction, it is imperative to expose the appropriation and the effacement of the experience of both Native-Americans and women.

The appropriation of the newly found land was subtly carried out through the feminization of the land and the exploitation of the sexual economy. The new land was named 'Virginia' in honour of an English monarch Queen Elizabeth. She employed the gender-specific virtue as a means of self-empowerment and played her role of participant in an emergent colonialist discourse. The name "Virginia" confirms the verbal and symbolic reconstitution of the land as a feminine place unknown to man and has the effect of effacing the indigenous society that already physically and culturally inhabits and possesses the land. England's first American colony was so named in honour of queen Elizabeth, a virgin. Indeed, 'the Virgin Queen Cult' was a collectively sustained political fiction and a mystery of state. As Roy Strong sugests, "the phantasmagoria of obscure and often extremely bizarre images were used to celebrate the queen's glorious presence, and certainly they established a way of thinking about a monarch, a psychic structure in which images were not merely fanciful flattering labels but embodied attributes of the person concerned, a comprehensiveness in multiplicity matched only in religious cults" (Strong 52). For example, the "Ditchley" portrait of queen Elizabeth represents queen Elizabeth standing as an empress on the globe of the world, her feet planted on a cartographic image of Britain. This representation of queen Elizabeth suggests "a mystical identification of the inviolate female body monarch with the unbreached body of her land, at the same time that it affirms her distinctive role as the aggrandized female monarch" (Montrose 190). This imperial blazon of the virgin queen Elizabeth and the representational strategies of the trope might well serve to ingratiate oneself with the queen and to formulate 'the Virgin Queen Cult.' It is certain that to the masculine readership of Elizabethan England, "a feminized space was an escape valve for the frustrations of disaffected or marginalized groups, and a solution to endemic socioeconomic problems at home" (Montrose 206). These 'compensatory tactics' reposition woman as an object of rape physical or metaphorical.

It is through the symbolic display and manipulation of these feminized spaces of the new found land that cultural fantasy of expansionism was conducted in the discourse of incipient Western colonialism. It is intriguing to note that cultural anxiety and desire of the colonialist to exploit the virgin land was achieved by the representation of the other land as the female body and the similitude of colonization and sexual mastery. The female body functions here as the crucial locus in the cultural fantasy of colonialism and expansionism. As we examined through *The Discovery of Guiana*, the images of carnal desire and sexuality are subtly deployed to justify the colonizer's desire to possess the new found land. *Diario* and *The Discovery of Guiana* explicitly articulate incipient colonial discourse and its manipulation of sexual economy. Based on the contemporary cultural background of these tavel narratives, I will focus on the geographical images of the other land as the female body in *The Tempest* through the analysis of the representation of Sycorax. The manifestation of colonial desire is inscribed through the metaphoric representation of the island as the native female body of Sycorax.

3. Shakespeare's *The Tempest* and the Representation of the other land as the female body

The problem of the female representation and subjectivity within colonial discourse is due to an imperial patriarchal control which is dramatized as the conquest over race and territorial space, and is inscribed in various ways as an inexorable will to power. The manifestation of itself as the conquest over native "female" space demonstrates the violence of a conquering masculine sexuality exposes the experience of conquest as rape, and inextricably links power and sexuality to the landscape of the colonial encounter. Questions of gender and principles of sexuality sanction access to power; and frequently women, both European and Native, act as indices of the status of the conquering, authoritarian males. *The Tempest* provides us with the good examples of these Native and European women; Sycorax and Miranda.

Firstly, I will focus on the representation of Sycorax. Prospero never saw Sycorax and everything he knows about her he has learned from Ariel. Nevertheless, she is insistently present in his memory—far more present than his own wife—and she embodies to an extreme degree all the nagative assumptions about women that he and Miranda have exchanged. The name "Sycorax" is glossed by Stephen Orgel as "an epithet for Medea, the Scythian raven", largely on the basis of the roots "Sy" (Scythia) and

"Korax"(raven) (Orgel 115). Furthermore, by worshipping the god "Setebos", "Sycorax is identified with the most remote, God-forsaken and degenerate of 16C Amerindian types". She is one of the text's three absent women (Alonso's daughter, Miranda's mother, Sycorax). Her impregnation by an incubus, her banishment from Algiers, her casting away on the island, the birth of Caliban, her imprisonment of Ariel, and her death, all information relayed by Ariel, marks her degraded status. But Ariel is hardly considered an impartial witness in the matter, because he had spent a dozen years confined in a cloven pine by Sycorax. The nature of her "charms" is determined "in the context of the power struggle that takes place between Prospero and Ariel" (John 243). Thus Prospero's obsessive invocation, indeed conjuration of "the foul witch Sycorax", or of "that dam'd witch Sycorax" and her "most unmitigable rage", is calculated to aggrandize, almost to immortalize his freeing of Ariel, but only retains him in an often exasperatingly frivolous servitude.

Ariel: My liberty.
Prospero: Before the time be out? No more.
Ariel: I prithee,
       Remember I have done thee worthy service,
       Told thee no lies, made no mistakings, served
       Without or grudge or grumblings. Thou did promise
       To bate me a full year.
Prospero: Dost thou forget from what a torment I did free thee?

Ariel: No.

Prospero: Thou dost; and think'st it much to tread the ooze
    Of the salt deep,
    To run upon the sharp wind of the North,
    To do me business in the veins o th' earth
    When it is baked with frost?

Ariel: I do not, sir.

Prospero: Thou liest, malignant thing! Hast thou forgot
    The foul witch Sycorax, who with age and envy
    Was grown into a hoop? Hast thou forgot her?

                                 (I. ii. 246-58)

A dominant class or culture's power to declare certain objects or activities self-evidently valuable is an essential measure for "reproducing social differentiation" (Bennett 3-21). The process of "reproduction" is carried out through Prospero's incessant remembering of foul witch Sycorax to Ariel; "O, was she so – I must/ Once in a month recount what thou hast been,/ Which thou forget'st. This damned witch Sycorax,/ For mischiefs manifold and sorceries terrible/ To enter human hearing, from Algiers/ Thou know'st was banished – for one thing she did/ They would not take her life. Is not this true?" (I. ii. 262-68).

Even though Prospero exerts himself to draw the line between his white magic and Sycorax's black magic, some similarities are found between them. There are some basic biographical similarities between Prospero and Sycorax; both rulers are magicians, both have been exiled. Prospero and Sycorax; both rulers are magicians, both have been exiled because of their practices, both have nurtured children on the isle. Sycorax's black, female magic is remembered as viciously coercive, yet Beneath the apparent voluntarism of the white, male regime iles the Threat of precisely the same coercion. From Caliban's point of view, and even at times from ariel's and Ferdinand's Prospero looks very much like Sycorax. The rage, the demand for unwilling servitude, the continual threats of constriction and painful imprisonment are characteristic of both. And late in the play, Prospero reminds us of Sycorax with a speech of Ovid's Medea (V. i. 33-50). The effort to draw the line between him and Sycorax is foregrounded and interrogated in a contradictory way to Prospero's original intention. His effort could be regarded as a representation of his anxiety about Sycorax's power, "for she is so strong/ That could control the moon, make flows and ebbs/ And deal in her command without her power," (V. i. 269-71) and of his fantasy about manoeuvring and manipulating other people's minds. It would be essential to raise a question about the issue of his power. How extensive is Prospero's magical power? The answer is that "Prospero can not, or will not, chop wood, make dams to catch fish or Do the washing up, all tasks for which Caliban's services are required. . . . Prospero's magic . . . can do anything at all except what is most necessary to survive"; "a precise match" can be found "in the situation of Europeans in

America during the seventeenth century, whose technology . . . suddenly became magical when introduced into a less technologically developed society, but who were incapable . . . of feeding themselves" (Hulme 128).

What ever happened to Caliban's mother? She is only abstractly involved in the seeming comprehensiveness of what Caliban and his revolt, as metaphor and praxis, mean. She is make visible not in her own right, but only in the light of such crucial patriarchal contests of wills. Her attributes are urgently fashioned and deployed to terrorize: "All the charms of Sycorax – toads, beetles, bats, light on you," or else become the basis for an agonized claim to patrimony: "This island's Mine, by Sycorax my mother,/ Which thou takest from me." Fiedler suggests:

"Sycorax, along with Claribel . . . remains offstage throughout, the one already dead, the other lost to Africa as far removed as Arcturus. They exist as memories only, as if to make clear that the Africa-Europe axis exists only in the remembered past; for after Prospero's arrival, the island becomes a point on a new line joining not only East and West but also a past behind the past of Africa to a present beyond any which present Europe could conceive." (172)

As Ania Lumba suggests, the juxtaposition of Miranda and Sycorax is deployed by patriarchal ideology which contrasts and evaluates "Sycorax's licentious black femininity" and "the passive purity of Miranda" (151-52). This ideology defines Sycorax as a white devil, whore and witch, Miranda as a virgin and goddess. Thus, construing non-European and colonized women as promiscuous served to legitimize their Sexual abuse and to demarcate them from white women.

Sycorax is invoked quite insistently throughout the play, but only as the disembodied symbol of the men's most terrible fears. Prospero's recounting of her story (I. ii. 262-68) represents a deliberate unvoicing, or silencing of the African woman rather than any intrinsic absence of speech on her part. In the imperial and colonial context, it is the despised body-as-land/land-as-body of the native woman which must be possessed; not as an object of desire but as the conquered object; in order to signal dominion and establish "civilized" order. The loss of Sycorax's language is endorsed through Caliban who curses in the language of the master rather than in his 'mother tongue'; it demonstrates "how the black woman's voice has been made to disappear" (Busia 94).

As suggested by Louis Althusser's definition of ideology, "it is not their real conditions of existence, their real world, that men represent to themselves in ideology, but above all it is their relation to those conditions of existence which is represented to them there" (Althusser 154). In this way, Sycorax is defined and demonized through Prospero's ideology and the power struggle between Prospero and Ariel. Paul Brown asserts that "The

Tempest is not simply a reflection of colonialist practices but an 'intervention' in an ambivalent and even contradictory discourse" (Brown 48). In this context, the rereadings of master texts are required as an interpretive strategy, to understand and consider the implications of the manipulation of the voices and images of black women within these colonial discourses. The voices and images of Sycorax are manipulated and interpreted by the strategy of Prospero Which aims at the colonization of the new land and the demonization of the queen of the island. Prospero's discursive strategy, however, is foregrounded and interrogated in process of his manipulation of the Voice and images of Sycorax within the colonialist discourse.

In addition, the representation of the other land is explicitly dramatized through ill‐starred marriage of Claribel to the Tunisian king and the symbolism of geographic difference. The ideology of otherness is apparently represented by the emphasis on the remoteness of Tunis which was topographically not so far from Southern Europe. The pictorial symbolism of geographic difference and female body is delicately represented in the debate on the relative locations of modern Tunis and ancient Carthage in The Tempest:

> Adr. Tunis was never graced before with such a paragon to their Queen.
> Gon. Not since widow Dido's time.

. . . .

Adr. "Widow Dido" said you? You make me study of that:
       She was of Carthage, not of Tunis.
Gon. This Tunis, sir, was Carthage.
Adr. Carthage?
Gon. I assure you, Carthage. (II. i. 71-82)

The typology of place is more concerned with 'loci' than with area as such. Hence, "the deeper irony of this rather pedantic discussion is that modern Tunis recapitulates ancient Carthage in moral-geographical terms." This, in turn, provides an exemplary context for reading the curious marriage of Alonso's reluctant daughter, Claribel, to the 'African' king of Tunis. Because modern Tunis recapitulates ancient Carthage, the marriage of Claribel to the African recapitulates the illstarred relationship of Dido and Aeneas. Indeed, it is potentially more ominous, because it represents the mischief of a consummated stranger marriage which Aeneas was piously able to avoid. Even though we are not told of the fate of Claribel's marriage to the 'African' king of Tunis in The Tempest, it seems ominous enough, and neither appears onstage in any case. Hence, the cartographic symbolism of geographic difference is endorsed through the widow Dido's legend and the ill-starred marriage of Claribel, for they demonstrate moral-geographical difference and otherness. The companions of the King of Naples remind the king of their original objections to the match:

Seb. Sir, you may thank yourself for this great loss,
    That would not bless our Europe with your daughter,
    But rather lose her to an African,
    Where she, at least, is banished from your eye,
    Who hath cause to wet the grief on't. (II. i. 121-25)

In fact, Claribel herself had only reluctantly agreed to the marriage: "and the fair soul herself/ Weighed between loathness and obedience. . . ." (II . i. 128-29). The king came to regret that he had compelled Claribel to marry the African King of Tunis against her will, and grew to believe that the presumed death of Ferdinand is a punishment for this enforced marriage.

Alon. . . . Would I had never
    Married my daughter there, for coming thence
    My son is lost, and, in my rate, she too,
    Who is so far from Italy removed
    I ne'er again shall see her. (II. i. 105-109)

As Fiedler notes, "this insistence on the remoteness of North Africa from southern Europe may seem a little absurd, not only in the light of actual geography. . . . But such exaggeration is important to all the meanings of the play, including its suggestion that to succeed, the black-white marriage must be removed as far as possible from the world in which Shakespeare had previously demonstrated its inevitable failure"(170). The representation of the ill-starred marriage of Claribel to the Tunisian King foregrounds and interrogates the cultural differentiation of 'the other,' social anxiety about the mischief of the black-white marriage, and the remotedness of the unknown territory. The representation of the other land is explicitly embodied not only in the exaggeration of the remoteness of Tunis and Claribel's ill-starred marriage but also in the depiction of Caliban as a fish monster which reminds us of the Indians of the American Continent.

Shakespeare must have been familiar with accounts of the famous Somers's shipwreck and rescue in the Bermudas (1609-1610), or compendia of explorers' narratives such as Richard Eden's History of Travaille in the West and East Indies, or even with Montaigne's reflections on the alternative life-style of the savages in Antarctic France (Brazil). As fiedler notes, "at the moment when The Tempest was being shown for the first time, bazaars were in progress to raise money for the imperiled Jamestown Colony" (192). Within the play itself, Shakespeare refers to Caliban as a fish - monster, which must be the result of the impingement on the popular consciousness of the adventures of various groups of settlers on the American Continent, particularly their encounter with Indian cultures. Indeed, "the making of money by the display of Indians in Elizabethan London" (Lee 263-301) was not uncommon and Trinculo's subsequent words refer directly to the practice;

A strange fish! Were I in England now, as once I was, and had but this fish painted, not a holiday fool there but would give a piece of silver: there would this monster make a man; any strange beast there makes a man: when they will not give a doit to relieve a lame beggar, they will lay out then to see a dead Indian. (The Tempest, II. ii. 27-34)

The citizens proved enormously curious, in fact. In this respect, Shakespeare's vision of the stranger and his vision of geography are necessarily related. According to John Gillies, "renaissance maps are considered less as individual scientific documents than as a collective and evolving cultural text characterized as much by their pictorial and often ancient ethnographic symbolism as by their geographic content" (Gillies 44). The difference between the medieval and Ortelian constructions of geographic space is that the one is "a space of emplacement" characterized by "localization," and the other is "an open space" Characterised by amorphic "extension." Perhaps for the first time in the history of world cartography, world maps post-1492 began to privilege the unknown and unpossessed over the known and possessed. This is the 'semiosis' of desire. The very emptiness of the New World, its nakedness, perhaps, relative absence of graphic density and verbal inscription, invites the eye to rove over the continent in the way that Donne imagines his hands roving over his mistress's body:

Licence my roving hands, and let them go,

Before, behind, between, above, below,

O my America, my new-found-land.

(John donne, Elegies, 19; To his Mistress Going to Bed)

As we can see in this poem, the images of carnal desire and sexuality are the crucial locus in the cultural fantasy of colonialism and expansionism. The overlapping of America and the Mistress is subtly deployed to impinge of the consciousness of the colonizer's desire. Donne's erotic conceit and the geographical image shows the representation of the new land as the female body and the eroticization of the new found land.

As we examined above, Donne's eroticization of the new found land shows the colonizer's consciousness to possess the new land through the erotic imagery, and the similitude of the female body and the land. The representation of the other land as the female body in The Tempest is mainly embodied through the images of Sycorax. In Columbus's Diario, and ralegh's The Discovery of Guiana, the new land is depicted respectively as a woman's nipple and a virgin land which invite the colonizers' eye to deflower them. The eroticization mainly functions for the colonizer to justify the desire to possess the new found land by imagery of sexual mastery. In the same way, The Tempest represents the other land as the female body of Sycorax but as the demonized female body not as an attractive and enchanting body. The images of Sycorax are manipulated by the strategy of Prospero which aims to justify the colonization of the island. The voices and images of Sycorax is interpreted from the negative point of view. Thus, She embodies all the negative assumptions about women. She became pregnant by an incubus and banished from Algiers, cast away on the island, gave birth to Caliban, and cruelly imprisoned Ariel. This negative representation of Sycorax is conducted to demarcate his white magic from her black Magic, and to legitimize the cause of his colonization.

It is interesting to note that Prospero's strategy to restore his political power is practiced not only by the demonization of sycorax but also by his deliberate manipulation of his daughter's virginity which is a crucial nexus of the play. Prospero's power to control his subjects' sexuality, particularly that of his slave and his daughter, is repeated as he halts the potentially truant or subversive erotic desires in Caliban and Ferdinand. Prospero's reintegration into the political world of Milan and Naples is represented as an elaborate courtship, a series of strategic manoeuvres with political as well as erotic intentions and effects. Paul Brown notes, "Miranda is represented as just such a virgin, to be protected from a rapist native and presented to a civil lover, Ferdinand. The 'fatherly' power of the colonizer, and his capacity to regulate and utilise the sexuality of his subject 'children,' is therefore a potent trope as activated in The Tempest and again demonstrates the crucial nexus of civil power and sexuality in colonial discourse" (62-63). Prospero has acted the stern father just long and hard enough to confirm the love which propinquity has bred. And as the marriage he has hoped for is now assured, he delivers to the not-quite bridegroom two frenetic sermons against pre-marital sex.

> Pros. Then as my gift, and thine own acquisition
> Worthily purchased, take my daughter. But
> If thou dost break her virgin-knot before
> All sanctimonious ceremonies may
> With full and holy rite be ministered,
> No sweet aspersion shall the heavens let fall
> To make this contract grow; but barren hate,
> Sour-eyed disdain, and discord shall bestrew
> The union of your bed with weeds so loathly
> That you shall hate it both. Therefore take heed,
> As Hymen's lamps shall light you. (IV. i. 13-23)

> Pros. Look thou be true; do not give dalliance
> Too much the rein. The strongest oaths are straw
> To th' fire i' th' blood. Be more abstemious,
> Or else good night your vow. (IV. i. 51-54)

Prospero deploys manual work as a negotiable instrument by whose means his power can be ratified and reinforced. Ferdinand's acceptance of the work ethic and its restraining function, and his commitment to harmonious social order which it signifies, is both rewarded and symbollized by his winning of Miranda's hand. But "Caliban's rejection of work and thus of the subservience to which the relationship with Prospero condemns him smoulders throughout as a disturbing threat until it irrupts into actuality at a crucial moment in the play" (Hawkes 6). Intriguingly, Prospero's fashioning of Miranda's identity is practiced through the techniques of arousing and manipulating "anxiety" (Greenblatt 142). Keeping the subjects in a salutary anxiety serves the ideology, for it shapes their loyalties into a proper fashion. Miranda's emotional suffering reveals the cruelty of this strategy in so far as she did not notice the meaning of the tempest and suffered with the sufferers. Prospero's technique of arousing and manipulating anxiety is the demonstration of his power, and this technique is powerfully applied to Miranda. Miranda's sweet words to Prospero satisfy his need for admiration, indeed for reverence, and they mold the audience's sense that other relationships ought to do the same.

> Pros. Obey and be attentive. (I. ii. 38)
> Pros. Dost thou attend me?
> Mir. Sir, most heedfully (I. ii. 78)
> Pros. Thou attend'st not?
> Mir. O, good sir, I do.
> Pros. I pray thee, mark me (I. ii. 87-88)
> Pros. Dost thou hear?
> Mir. Your tale, sir, would cure deafness (I. ii. 106)

Prospero's marvelous powers of nurture, of design and his invisibility In the lover's first meeting are so absolutely deployed that Ferdinand Confesses his reverence for Prospero: "Let me live here ever: so rare a Wonder'd father and a wise/ Makes this place Paradise." IV. i. 122-24). Ferdinand's confession displays the supreme validation of the father's creating power. Miranda is his creation, exclusively nurtured, tutored, and controlled by him on the island. Her sexuality is firmly allied with the divine order behind nature. But it is Prospero who defines and guards that sexuality, subsuming it into his larger project for the settling of old scores and the resumption of his role in Milan. As John Gillies suggests, "the relationship between Prospero and Miranda is patently colonial, because she is nurtured, worked, troped, translated, idealized and commodified by Prospero" (143). This may sound too politicizing of father/daughter relationship, but it is true that his educational strategy makes her obedient to her father and the colonial venture. This relationship is embodied in an "Afro-Cuban dance in which the female dancer represents the she-ass, while the male dancer portrays the smith who is shoeing her hoofs" (Johnson 247). Just as woman is nothing but a submissive and impregnated body in shoeing the mule in Afro-Cuban dance, Miranda is a lyrically proffered exchange commodity, effectively shaped into a fertile crescent of kings in a lyrical and hegemonic rite.

Eric Cheyfitz defined Caliban's attempt to rape Miranda as the need for power, paralleling Miranda with property and land; in turn, Prospero's need to secure Miranda's virginity is analysed as "a political effort to attain an alliance with naples that will restore his old world power, an activity of appropriation for the purpose of gaining power" (cheyfitz 162). Caliban's attempt to "people the isle with Calibans" and his revolt boomerang to confirm the shaping power of dominant culture. However, as Stephen Orgel notes, "the practice of free love in the New World is regularly treated as an instance not of the lust of savages but of their edenic innocence; and this free love helps to explain why Caliban is not only unrepentant for his attempt on Miranda but incapable of seeing that there is anything for which to repent" (Orgel 42). Caliban's (I. ii. 348-50), however, is not the only dangerous sexuality to be feared in the play. Prospero's repeated warnings to Ferdinand against pre-marital sex are not prompted by anything we see of Ferdinand's behaviour. Prospero's strategic deployment and manoeuvring of Miranda and Ferdinand shadow the lyrical meeting of the lovers, making it their illusion. Thus, there is "much business appertaining" (III. ii. 97), and there is a need to admit and project an impediment to this marriage: "They are both in either's powers; but this swift business / I must uneasy make lest too light winning / Make the prize light." (I. ii. 45-53). The restoration does call for a strate-gic positioning of Miranda's awakening sexuality (she is now only 15) where it will be available to the shipwrecked Ferdinand's libidinal willingness, or better, compulsion to serve. Claribel's and Miranda's political marriages seemed the likeliest means of resolving European power struggles, as in the marriages of Mary Tudor to Philip II of Spain, and of james's daughter to the Protestant prince Frederick, through a consolidation of power. In so far as the marriage of Ferdinand and Miranda is desighed to resolve inveterate territorial enmities (I. ii. 121-22), it has more in common with James's plans for his children than with the actual wedding The Tempest was called upon to help celebrate. In this context, "Prospero can be understood as a predominant mode of

royal authority" (Orgel, "Introduction" 39). Shakespeare did not represent king James as Prospero, but the figure of Prospero embodies the predominant modes of conceiving royal authority in the period.

4. Conclusion

Columbus's Diario and Ralegh's The Discovery of Guiana are travel Narratives which represent the emergent colonial anxiety in a subjective and imaginary way. They share a common feature in the sense that there are strong elements of feminization and eroticization of the new found land in both texts. In Diario, this feminization and even eroticization is embodied through the representation of the shape and location of paradise as a nipple and a woman's breast. Interestingly, cultural anxiety of the colonizer is inscribed through the feminization of the land. Sexual imagery and erotic desire can be detected in the discourse of incipient colonialism. The feminization and the erotic representation of the new land is idiosyncratically found not only in Columbus's Diario, but also in Walter Ralegh's The Discovery. In Ralegh's The Discovery of Guiana, colonial anxiety is expressed in more subjecttive and imaginary ways. For example, the New World is itself gendered feminine and sexed as a *virgin* (italics are mine) female body.

Guiana's maidenhead is conveyed through metaphors like 'never sackt,' 'hath not bene tome,' 'never bene entred,' 'never conquered or possessed.' The acting words, such as sack, rear, enter, conquer, and possess strongly embodies the act of deflowering the female body. Sexual imagery is more actively and strongly expressed than in Diario. In Diario, the shape of the New World is depicted as a woman's breast or Pear and the location of the paradise as a nipple in a quite realistic and simplifying way. But in the Discovery, all the acting words strongly remind us of the action of sexual mastery and the metaphor functions to justify the colonization of the indigenous peoples of Guiana. Indeed, the ideology of gender hierarchy sanctions the ideology of race hierarchy, and the colonizer's cultural desire has been made legitimate strengthened by the hierarchical structures of male and female. This gendered cultural values and exchanges are embedded and inscribed in the sexual economy in the discourse of discovery.

The representation of the other land as the female body in The Tempest is mainly inscribed through the images of Sycorax. In Columbus's Diario, and Ralegh's The Discover of Guiana, the new land is depicted so enchanting as to invite the colonisers' eye to deflower them. The eroticization mainly functions for the colonizer to justify the exploitation of the new land through the metaphoric representation of the new land as the concrete female body. In the same way, The Tempest represents the other land as the female body of Sycorax but as the demonized female body not as an attractive and enchanting body. The images of Sycorax are manipulated by the strategy of Prospero which aims to justify the colonization of the island. The voices and images of Sycorax is interpreted from the negative point of view. Thus, She em-Bodies all the negative assumptions about women. The negative representation of Sycorax is deployed to demarcate the colonizer from the colonised to legitimize the cause of his colonization. This ideology of otherness which is achieved by differentiating and discriminating others is articulated in the discourse of colonialism. Within the apparatus of the colonialist discourse, sexuality and race are related in a process of differentiation and discrimination.

Miranda is a crucial locus of Prospero's vision and of his plans for the future. Prospero is so devoted to the welfare of his daughter and to an extension of his authority which may be achieved only so long as Miranda remains a virgin, a potential bride for the husband of his choice. The underlying assumptions here are not unique to Prospero, or to this play, or to Shakespeare. They are implicit, too, for example, in Ralegh's selection of the name Virginia for his new colony. The naming acknowledges the extent to which virginity had become, in Elizabeth's reign, "a crucial attribute of royal power," and had become For James, striving like Prospero and Alonso for political alliances Through the marriage of his children, "an essential royal bargaining chip" (Orgel, "introduction" 49). The potential of virginity lay not only in civilization but in the promise of infinite bounty within a hegemonic order. This myth is predominant in both Prospero's compulsive anxiety for Miranda's virginity and the Elizabethan Cult in which virginity is a crucial attribute of royal power. This myth of the female body is projected into and served for the colonial project which adroitly deploys a colonial romance as a means of imbuing a cultural fantasy of expansionism. Uncannily enough, the whole struggle fought for in the name of social and national cohesion was interestingly conducted in relation to the female body.

Works Cited

Althusser, Louis. "Ideology and Ideological State Apparatuses" in *Lenin and Philosophy and Other Essays.* Trans. Ben Brewster. London: NLB, 1971.

Barker, Francis and Hulme, Peter. "Nymphs and Reapers Heavily Vanish: the Discursive Contexts of *The Tempest*" in *Alternative Shakespeare.* Ed. John drakakis. London and New York: Routledge, 1985.

Bennett, Tony. "Formalism and Marxism Revisited." *Southern Review* 16 (1982): 3-21.

Bhabha, Homi. *"The Other Question: Difference, Discrimination and Discourse of Colonialism"* in *Literature, Politics and Theory.* Ed. Francis Barker et al. London and New York: Methuen, 1986.

Brown, Paul. "This Thing of Darkness I Acknowledge Mine" in *Political Shakespeare.* Eds. Jonathan Dollimore and Alan Sinfield. Manchester: Manchester UP, 1985.

Busia, Abena P. A. "Silencing Sycorax: On African Colonial Discourse and the Unvoiced Female" in *Cultural Ceitique* 14 (Winter 1989-90): 81-104.

Cheyfitz, Eric. *The Poetics of Imperialism: Translation and Colonization from the Tempest to Tarzan.* New York: OUP, 1991.

Cixous, Helene. & Clement, Catherice. *The Newly Born Woman.* Trans. Betsy Wing. Minneapolis: U of Minnesota P, 1986.

Columbus, Christopher. *Journal of the First Voyage.* Ed. and Trans. By B. W. Ife. Warminster: Aris and Phillips Ltd., 1990.

_____. *Select Document Illustrating the Four voyages of Columbus*, Vol. II. Trans. And Ed. with additional material, an introduction and notes by Cecil Jane. Oxford: Oxford UP, 1932.

_____. *The Four Voyages of Christopher Columbus.* Ed. And Trans. By J. M. Cohen. Harmondsworth: Penguin Books Ltd., 1969.

Eden, Richard. *The History of Trauayle in the West and East Indies.* London, 1577.

Fiedler, L. *The Stranger in Shakespeare.* St. Albans: Paladin, 1974.

Gillies, John. *Shakespeare and the Geography of Difference.* Cambridge: Cambridge UP, 1994.

Greenblatt, Stephen. "Martial Law in the Land of Cockaigne" in *Shakespearean Negotiations: The Circulation of Social Energy in Renaissance England.* Oxford: Clarendon Press, 1988.

Hawkes, Terence. "Playhouse - Workhouse" in *That Shakespearean Rag.* London & New York: Methuen, 1986.

Hulme, Peter. *Colial Encounters: Europe and the Native Caribbean, 1492-1797.* London and New York: Routledge, 1986.

Johnson, Lemuel A. "Shoeing the Mule: 'Caliban' as Genderized Response" in *Latin America and the Caribbean: Geopolitics, Development & Culture.* Ed. Arch R. M. Ritter. Ottawa: CALACS, 1984.

Kahn, Coppelia. "The Providential Tempest and te Shakespearean faminly" in *Eepresenting Shakespeare.* Eds. M. M. Schwartz & Coppelia Kahn. Batimore & London: The Johns Hopkins UP, 1980.

Keymis, Laurence. *A relation of the Second Boyage to Guiana: Performed and Written in the Yeere 1596.* London, 1956.

Lee, Sidney. "The American Indian in Elizabethan England" in *Elizabethan and Other Essays.* Ed. F. S. Boas. London: Oxford UP, 1929.

Lumba, Ania. *Gender, Race, Renaissance Drama.* Manchester: Manchester UP, 1989.

Montrose, Louis. "The Work of Gender in the Discourse of discovery" in *New World Encounters.* Ed. Stephen Greenblatt. Berkeley: U of California P, 1993.

Niederland, William G. "The Naming of America" in *The Unconscious Today: Essays in Honour of Max Schur.* Ed. Mark Kanzer. New York: International UP, 1971.

Nixon, Rob. "Caribbean and African Appropriations of The Tempest" in

Critical Inquiry 13.3 (1987): 557-78.

Orgel, Stephen ed., *The Oxford Shakespeare: The Tempest.* Oxford and New York: Oxford UP, 1987.

_____. "Shakespeare and the Cannibals" in *Cannibals, Witches, and Divorce: Estranging the Renaissance.* Ed. Marjorie Garber. Baltimore and London: the Johns Hopkins UP, 1987.

Ralegh, Walter. *The discoverie of Guiana from Principal Navigations, Voyages and Discoveries of the English Nation.* Compiled by Richard Hakluyt. Volum X. London, 1955.

Sundelson, David. "So Rare a Wonder'd Father: Prospero's Tempest" in *Representing Shakespeare.* Eds. M. M. Schwartz & Coppelia Kahn. BaltiMore & London: The Johns Hopkins UP, 1980.

Virgil. *Aeneid. Book IV.* Trans. C. Day Lewis. London: The Hogarth Press, 1961.

Zamora, Margarita. *Reading Columbus.* Berkeley: U of California P, 1993.

2
장
—

The Ocular Impulse and the Politics of Violence in *The Duchess of Malfi*

1. the ocular impulse to inspect and control the female body in *The Duchess of Malfi*

There are the articulations of the desire to see, inspect and control the female body in Webster's *The Duchess of Malfi*. This desire is intimately connected with the "ocular impulse" which emerges within coeval anatomical and gynaecological discourses. This ocular economy is a regulatory production of the body; but it also problematizes the position of the subject of the gaze. Moreover, it presents the privatized body of the conjugal couple. The Duchess's body is invested with the principle of "fixed order," so as to sustain the proper boundaries of class, gender and eroticism. It is articulated in Antonio's picture of the Duchess as the normative and inaccessible lady of courtly love, a high-born virginal being whose "countenance" is liable to be misinterpreted as erotic provocation and yet remains, fundamentally, nothing but the em-bodiment of "continence" and denial.[1]

> For her discourse, it is so full of rapture,
> You only will begin then to be sorry
> When she doth end her speech: and wish, in wonder,
> She held it less vainglory to talk much
> Than your penance to hear her: whilst she speaks,
> She throws upon a man so sweet a look
> That it were able to raise one to a galliard
> That lay in a dead palsy; and to dote
> On that sweet countenance: but in that look
> There speaketh so divine a continence
> As cut off all lascivious and vain hope. (1.1.200-210)

In this statement, the Duchess is presented not only as a woman but also as a way of making statements about the body politic and as a yardstick against which the political activities of her two brothers can be gauged. However, Ferdinand regards his sister's body as potentially non-transparent, threateningly

---

1 All quotations from the play are taken from John Webster, *The Duchess of Malfi, Drama of the English Renaissance II: The Stuart Period*, ed. R.A. Fraser and N. Rabkin (London: Macmillan, 1976).

predicated upon the discrepancy between a public face and a secret inner part (1.1.317-320): "be not cunning, For they whose faces do belie their hearts Are witches ere they arrive at twenty years, Ay, and give the devil suck." He aims to bring to light what is hidden and "private," so as to reinforce visibility as a modality of power over the body of the Duchess. It is Bosola who is charged with the task of inspecting and controlling the young widow. According to Patricia Parker, there is the close relation between the delator's activity of bringing something hidden before the eye and the "voyeuristic" drive of early modern anatomical and gynaecological discourses that seek to expose the "secret place" of women (Parker 64-7). One of the many masks Bosola puts on in his role of "intelligencer" is that of the physician detecting the signs of the transformation of the Duchess's body.

> Bosola. I have other work on foot: I observe our Duchess
>   Is sick a-days, she pukes, her stomach seethes,
>   The fins of her eyelids look most teeming blue,
>   She wanes i'th'cheek, and waxes fat i'th'flank;
>   And, contrary to our Italian fashion,
>   Wears a loose-bodied gown: there's somewhat in't.
>   I have a trick may chance discover it,
>   A pretty one; I have bought some apricocks,
>   The first our spring yields. (2.1.70-78)

The role of physician seems at the center of the debate about his role of "intelligencer." He takes part in the vital process of revealing the signs of the pregnancy of the Duchess. As described in the above passage, vomiting, stomach-agitation, blue eyelids, wane cheek and fat flank are the most typical signs of pregnancy. The scrutinous analysis and voyeuristic intrusion of the irreducible private body were carried out to exhibit the secrets of the female body and the Duchess's pregnancy. After tempting her with some dainties, he concludes that "her tetchiness and most vulturous eating of the apricocks are apparent signs of breeding" (2.2.1-3). Bosola's reading of the Duchess's body took place in the Duchess's belly where a knowledge of the reproductive body is inscribed with its act of examination and discovery. It has little to do with a gradual understanding of its thereness and much to do with relations of domination. The analysis of the signs of pregnancy is just the beginning of Bosola's work as an intelligencer. Bosola's scrutiny of the body reveals the gynaecological discourse's ocular impulse to see and know, to lay bare and exhibit the secrets of the female body: A whirlwind strike off these bawd farthingales, for, but for that, and the loose-body'd gown, I should have discover'd apparently the young springal cutting a caper in her belly (2.1.156-159). Bosola's scrutiny of the Duchess's body certainly has echoes and elements common to the gynaecological discourse's ocular impulse to lay bare the female body. William Kerwin argues that the *Duchess of Malfi* has an explicitly medical frame, not only in its characters and language, but also in the historical context of Jacobean medical politics (96). He examines that the play's use of medical theater repeatedly connects the authority of educated physicians and the attenuated legitimacy of the court at Malfi. According to Kerwin, in connecting the problems of doctors and royalty, Webster was echoing in very directed ways historical parallels in his own city. The numerous challenges to their authority which London physicians faced were inseparable from their culture's challenges to king and bishop. Galenic medicine, in both its technical knowledge and its organizational structures, was incapable of meeting the needs facing a country of new social problems and arrangements. Most healers were non-physicians who did not aspire to professional status, and the physicians' attempts to create such a status involved a radical centralization of power, and with it a new representation of their own role. In connection with Kerwin's argument, it is interesting to note the important role of Bosola who is charged with the task of inspecting the Duchess's body like a physician. Bosola's scrutiny of the Duchess's pregnant body seems inseparable from their culture's understanding of the general female body and there is a trace of distrust toward this kind of inspection and Bosola's attempts to create power through inspecting the Duchess's body and giving information to Ferdinand. The distrust to his role can be analysed through the representation of the Duchess's pregnancy, childbearing, and the representation of the bliss of the conjugal couple in the text. Moreover, those elements are understood to be the subversive potential against the attempts of

Bosola and Ferdinand to control the irreducible female body of the Duchess. As Michel Foucault has argued, in the context of a discussion of the body's involvement in the exercise of power, "there is no power relation without the correlative constitution of a field of knowledge, nor any knowledge that does not presuppose and constitute at the same time power relations" (27). In this sense, the "objective" status of the pregnant body of the Duchess emerging from Bosola's inspection can be taken as symptomatic of a realistic knowledge of the body. Yet, this realism needs to be conceived as one of the effects of the anatomical and gynaecological discourse which engenders the female body as an object subjected to the male gaze. As Coddon points out, the Duchess of Malfi projects a discovery of her body as the "private" locus of authenticity and self-determination (8-11). The Duchess addresses Antonio in the wooing scene.

> Duch. You do tremble.
> Make not your heart so dead a piece of flesh
> To fear, more than to love me. Sir, be confident,
> What is't distracts you? This is flesh, and blood, sir,
> 'Tis not the figure cut in alabaster
> Kneels at my husband's tomb. Awake, awake, man,
> I do here put off all vain ceremony,
> And only do appear to you, a young widow
> That claims you for her husband, and like a widow,
> I use but half a blush in't. (1.1.457-463)

The body disclosed by the Duchess is made of "flesh and blood." This palpable body functions as a self-evident, essentialist construct from which heterosexual desire seems to flow spontaneously, breaking down social boundary and dispelling class and gender tensions. Antonio is torn between the traditional hierarchy of rank, which enjoins his submission, and the traditional gender hierarchy, which enjoins him to dominate. But the Duchess's insistence that Antonio should avert his eyes and explore the depth of his inner self is undoubtedly an affirmation of personal merit and interiority. Thus, the Duchess interrogates the regulation of gender and sexuality implemented through the exchange of women's bodies under the "dynastic" version of patriarchy. The heterosexual desire established and instigated by the "flesh and blood" body of the Duchess is sanitized as soon as it is brought to light. It finds its proper meaning in the sedate, monogamous and reproductive merging of bodies sanctified by matrimony:

> Duch. Bless, heaven, this sacred Gordian, which let violence
>   Never untwine.
> Ant. And may our sweet affections, like the spheres,
>   Be still in motion.
> Duch. Quickening, and make
>   The like soft music.
> Ant. That we may imitate the loving palms,
>   Best emblem of a peaceful marriage,

That ne'er bore fruit, divided. (1.1.481-8)

The Duchess and Antonio's embracing bodies are subjected to the sinister incarnations of the dynastic version of marriage. They are within the dynastic and the liberal version of marriage impinges upon each other, inducing those class, gender and erotic anxieties supposedly alien to such private realm. The survey of the realm of the self suggested by the Duchess is consistent with the path she follows in her own voyage of discovery of the true self and bodily identity lying behind the dreams of those that are born great (1.1.445). Yet, the bourgeois authenticity she represents is only one of the subject-positions from which she speaks in this scene. Antonio underlines this multiplicity as he articulates his regret about not having played an active role in the wooing: "These words should be mine, / And all the parts you have spoke" (1.1.475-6). They seem to register a partial incorporation of the patriarchal values of the old and new regime. In spite of the fact that the Duchess has already converted Antonio's bosom into the repository of her heart—"You have left me heartless; mine is in your bosom" (1.1.453), the consummation of the marriage and the fulfillment can only take place offstage, in another secret place by definition absent. However, their marriage life is represented as utter happiness and based upon complete integrity even though it can not be displayed to the public and attained in the secret place. As I examined, there is the deliberate efforts to scrutinize the Duchess's pregnant body projected by Ferdinand and his agent, Bosola. However, in defiance against this persistent ocular impulse, the Duchess projects her subject position, and originally articulates her heterosexually oriented flesh-and-blood body she uncovers. The Duchess protests against Ferdinand's logic that she should be remained as a widow (3.2.136-39). Her body natural is understood to be threatening to the integrity of the body politic. Therefore, Ferdinand defines her a notorious strumpet and her partner as a strong-thighed bargeman (2.4.4). However, Ferdinand is sexually obsessive and incestuous; the Cardinal has broken his vow of chastity and carries on with Julia. This overt display of sexual passion pervades the court.

Moreover, Ferdinand's behaviour toward his sister is disturbing. He desires to violate his sister by having her "darkest actions, nay your privatest thoughts, . . . come to light" (1.1.324-25). His desire to delve into her sexual behaviour climaxes when he exposes his father's poinard to her and notes that "women like that part which, like the lamprey, / Hath never a bone in't" (1.1.338-344). The sword he shows to the Duchess incarnates violent male oppression and a symbol of patriarchal power. This desire, then in addition to being incestuous, figures him as an effeminized male, the same term used to describe homosexual men. According to Behling, Ferdinand's extreme interest in his sister's sexuality has less to do with political ambitions than with fear that he is losing his own masculine identity (7). In other words, Ferdinand's fear is to be cuckolded. As Orgel states, "the fear of losing control of women's chastity, a very valuable possession that guaranteed the legitimacy of one's heirs, and especially valuable for fathers as a piece of disposable property is a logical consequence of a patriarchal structure" (18). Antonio is perceived as threatening to Ferdinand's masculine identity because Antonio cuckolded him both sexually and also economically by robbing him of the Duchess, the Duke's method of securing economic or political bounty. But the Duke is threatened also by the Duchess, who he feels is capable of castrating his power, or subsuming his power, by re-establishing the bloodline (Behling 7). Though perhaps paranoid, the Duke must definitely have understood that the Duchess has the power of disrupting his authority and her political identity would undoubtedly have been regarded by him and the Cardinal as genuinely masculine. Therefore, the brothers' desire to sustain their political and economic power reinforces their logic that the Duchess's body should be inspected and controlled. This desire is intimately related with the ocular impulse which projects the ideology of exposing the secret part of the female body.

2. secret places, abject bodies, the politics of violence

In Helkiah Crooke's 1615 anatomical treatise *Microcosmographia*, Crooke defines "the orifice of the necke [of the womb] as a part too obscene to look upon" (239). The desire to see and to avert the eye are inextricably related to each other. Crooke described that "those parts which in some creatures [i.e., men] are prominent and apparent, should in others [i.e., women] be veyled and covered" (216). It seems that it is only by visually unfolding and penetrating a woman's secrets that what is "veyled" by nature is finally given a proper shape and therefore actualizes its potential status. A woman's "privy" thus remains a bodily excess which cannot be properly categorized within the anatomical discourse's ocular production of bodies that matter; a discourse in which it is nonetheless inserted as an "object" and in the form of a "masculinized" morphology.

Patricia Parker linked this paradoxical place "too obscene to look upon" to the hidden place of Desdemona's sexuality in *Othello* (71). This is described as a site that is impossible to see (3.3.408) and as a locus which is too hideous to be shown (3.3.112). The place is nonetheless situated at the center of the play. It cannot be brought to light and yet is endlessly displayed, as in the bedroom scene at the end of the play. In *The Duchess of Malfi*, the Duchess is defined as the "infection" rather than the "infected," as the assertive widow playing an active role in that which her two brothers forcefully categorize as transgression.

> Card. You may flatter yourself,
>   And *take your own choice: privately* be married
>   Under the eaves of night.
> Ferd. Think't the best voyage
>   That e'er you made; like the irregular crab,
>   Which though 't goes backward, thinks that it goes right,
>   Because *it goes its own way.*
>   (1.1.316-21; italics are my emphasis)

In this passage, there is the emphasis on the discrepancy between the Duchess's "outside" and "inside" and Ferdinand described her potential assumption of such a role as the figure of the witch, one of those cunning women whose faces do belie their heart (1.1.308-10). He adds that "a visor and a mask are whispering-rooms that were ne'er built for goodness" (1.1.335). In his remark, the Duchess's threatening depth is represented through a double disguise, a visor and a mask, and Ferdinand announces to detect the Duchess's "darkest actions" and her "privat'st thoughts" (1.1.315). This is the articulation of the desire to see, inspect and control the female body and this desire is intimately connected with the "ocular impulse" which emerges within coeval anatomical and gynaecological discourses. Helkiah Crooke's *Microcosmographia*, like most sixteenth- and seventeenth- century anatomical and gynaecological treatises, is marked by anxiety towards the ambivalent interior fold of the female body, veiled and covered by nature to register a woman's proper place. In addition, the anxiety easily turns into violence. Ferdinand assures that he will "hew" his sister "to pieces," after threatening to dispense mixed doses of cure and punishment:

> Ferd.   Apply desperate physic:
> We must not now use balsamum, but fire,
> The smarting cupping-glass, for that's the mean
> To purge infected blood, such blood as hers. (2.5.23-6)

As for Ferdinand, the exposure of the Duchess's "whispering-rooms" as something remote from a "private" reservoir of chastity undoubtedly intensifies the voyeuristic pleasure of discovery. It seems that it is only by visually unfolding and penetrating a woman's secrets that what is "veyled" by nature is finally given a proper shape and therefore actualizes its potential status. A woman's "privy" remains a bodily excess which cannot be properly categorized within the anatomical discourse's ocular production of bodies that matter; a discourse in which it is nonetheless inserted as an "object" and in the form of a "masculinized" morphology. In the coeval anatomical and gynaecological discourses, there are strong traces of the desire to see and to avert the eye from the female "privy." In *The Duchess of Malfi* it is mainly the position of Ferdinand that is fraught with such ambivalent desire to see and not to see; a desire which finds an emblematic articulation in relation to the Duchess's corpse. He responds to the abjectified corpse of the Duchess by saying, "Cover her face: mine eyes dazzle" (4.2.264). The gesture of covering the Duchess's face is nonetheless followed by his request to uncover it once more: "Let me see her face again" (4.2.270). Whereas these lines are consistent with the play's dominant drive to see, inspect and control the female body, they also anticipate the speech in which Ferdinand announces another discovery, that of the murder of his sister: "The wolf shall find her grave, and scrape it up / Not to devour the corpse, but to discover / The horrid murder" (4.2.307-309). The Duchess's murder is carried out in a private space – her lodging – by a number of nameless executioners who use strangling rather than dismemberment as a mode of reinscription of power over her body. Moreover, her prolonged torture, which reaches its apogee when Ferdinand decides to "remove forth the common hospital / All the mad-folk, and place them near her lodging" (4.1.127-8), a resolve whose underlying logic is that she'll needs be mad to confirm the madness of her transgression, does not seem to achieve the desired effect. The Duchess ironically comments as follows: "Indeed, I thank him: nothing but noise and folly / Can keep me in my right wits" (4.2.6-7). There is also no confession to seal the violence of execution. Furthermore, the Duchess's last dying speeches repeatedly focus on the monotony of the spectacular display which requires her subjection. Just before her death, she associates the tediousness of the spectacle with the "whispering" and clandestine maneuverings of Ferdinand and his acolytes, which *reverses* the connotation of "whispering" as *her* "secret" and illicit sexuality:

> Duch.　I know death hath ten thousand several doors
> 　　　　For men to take their exits; and 'tis found
> 　　　　They go on such strange geometrical hinges,
> 　　　　You may open them both ways: −any way, for heaven-sake,
> 　　　　So I were out of your whispering. (4.2.219-223)

Whispering, in short, like the revolving doors of death, goes both ways. The "Whispering-rooms" is represented in the play as "intimate, private closets," a site containing and becoming the sign of one of the Duchess's most "privy" places. There is the strong homology between a woman's secret parts and her intimate "private" closet or "cabinet." However, according to Ferdinand, depth is achieved in this privy places "not in the figure of interiority by which the concealed inside is of another quality from what is external, but by a doubling of the surface" (1.1.315). This "doubling" can be related to the anatomical and gynaecological discourses in which Ferdinand's position participates. According to these discourses, as Thomas Laqueur points out, there is only one body, a one-sex or one-flesh teleologically male body, whose colder, less perfect and inverted mirror image is gendered female (5-6). The "concealed inside" represented by the female sex-organs is thus not "of another quality" or essentially different from the "exterior surface" signified by the male sex-organs. Therefore, we need to point out that early modern anatomy and gynaecology articulate "an assertion of male power to know the female body and hence to know and control a feminine Nature." In the death scene, however, the Duchess articulates and problematizes Ferdinand's attempts to inspect and control the female body. The Duchess made no confession to seal the violence of execution. Furthermore, the Duchess's last speeches put emphasis on the secret manipulating of the female body deployed by Ferdinand and Bosola. Just before her death, she relates the weariness of the spectacle with the "whispering" and clandestine maneuvering of Ferdinand and Bosola. It definitely reverses the connotation of "whispering" as her "secret" and forbidden sexuality.

3. uncanny specular reversals

As we examined, it is interesting to note the important role of Bosola who is charged with the task of inspecting the Duchess's body like a physician. Moreover, Bosola's scrutiny of the Duchess's pregnant body seems inseparable from their culture's understanding of the general female body. In the text, the brothers' desire was to sustain their political and economic power by reinforcing their logic that the Duchess's body should be inspected and controlled. This desire is intimately related with the ocular impulse which projects the ideology of exposing the secret part of the female body. However, the position of the subject of the gaze is problematized and there is a trace of distrust toward this kind of inspection on the female body and the privatized body of the conjugal couple. The distrust to the inspection can be attained through the representation of the Duchess's pregnancy, childbearing, and the representation of the bliss of the conjugal couple in the text. Moreover, those elements are understood to be the subversive potential against the attempts of Bosola and Ferdinand to control the irreducible female body of the Duchess. In the bed-chamber scene it is the "private" economy of pleasure of this body that articulates itself.

Duch. Bring me the casket hither, and the glass: –
      You get no lodging here tonight, my lord.
Ant. Indeed, I must persuade one: –
Duch. Very good:
      I hope in time 'twill grow into a custom
      That noblemen shall come with cap and knee,
      To purchase a night's lodging of their wives.
Ant. I must lie here.
Duch. To what use will you put me?

Ant. We'll sleep together: –

Duch. Alas, what pleasure can two lovers find in sleep?

(3.2.1-10)

The casket and the glass, later on, the kissing, Antonio's reference to the Duchess and Cariola as two "faces so well form'd," the Duchess's concern about her hair and its colour: all these elements contribute to naturalize the pleasures of the conjugal couple. In this scene, the bodies of the conjugal couple are invested with an erotic charge. Those elements put emphasis on the privatized body of the conjugal couple and they are understood to be the subversive potential against the attempts of Bosola and Ferdinand to control the irreducible female body of the Duchess.

According to Frank Whigham, Ferdinand's is a desire to evade degrading association with inferiors. He even redefines Ferdinand's "incestuous inclination toward his sister" as the irredeemably social narrowing of his kind from class to family, with the Duchess coming to stand for "his own radical purity," conceived in class terms (Whigham 169). The Duchess's body, construed by Ferdinand as a body in which his blood "his rank" flows uncontaminated, functions as a specular image, conferring an "ideal unity" on his body. Put another way, Ferdinand's "possession" is simultaneously an appropriation of another body and a construction of his own body, which is inseparable from the process of demarcation of class boundaries. The threat to Ferdinand's "body proper," for instance, is most often signified through a signifier such as "blood" as passion and desire. Blood as passion is a signifier bringing an intolerable effect of sameness to bear on blood as lineage, which is one of the privileged points of identification around which the contours of the "body proper" attempt to establish themselves. This is perhaps nowhere more apparent than when "blood" as the cherished signifier of Ferdinand's "rank" uncannily turns into a "rank blood": "Her witchcraft lies in her rank blood" (3.1.70). Ferdinand presents an uncanny and distorted counterpart between two bodies:

> Ferd. Methinks her fault and beauty,
>   Blended together, show like leprosy,
>   The whiter, the fouler. (3.3.62-4)

The ambivalence of the specular image corresponds in many ways to the ambivalence of the double described by Freud in his paper on the "uncanny." In this paper, Freud argues that in specific circumstances the double as "insurance against the destruction of the ego" "reverses its aspect," so as to become "the uncanny harbinger of death" (235). For Freud, this reversal is a sign of the return of the "surmounted" stage of "unbounded self-love," of "primary narcissism," a return which transforms the once so familiar interchangeability between the ego and its image into something too familiar to be endured. As far as Ferdinand is concerned, the salutary interchangeability between his body and that body of hers, which appears so familiar, represents itself as a hostile, uncanny image, an image whose effect is one of fragmentation. Needless to add, this fragmentation instantaneously makes way for an active will to punish. What Lacan would call "aggressivity" is in the play a desire on the part of Ferdinand to "hew her to pieces" in order to grasp his always precarious, imaginary sense of unity. Yet, the estranging and foreign image which keeps on returning from without is nothing but one's own projected image. It makes perfect sense for Ferdinand to declare, speaking to his brother: "I could kill her now, / In you, or in myself, for I do think/ It is some sin in us, heaven doth revenge / By her" (2.4.64-6). Yet, once Ferdinand comes into close proximity to the rival "who leaps his sister," the desire of aggressivity is deferred.

> Ferd. Whate'er thou art, that hast enjoy'd my sister,
>   For I am sure thou hear'st me—for thine own sake
>   Let me not know thee: I came hither prepar'd
>   To work thy *discovery*, yet am now persuaded
>   It would beget such violent effects
>   As would damn us both:—I would not for ten millions
>   *I had beheld thee*; therefore use all means
>   I never may have knowledge of thy name.
>
>   (3.2.90-7; italics are my emphasis)

These lines immediately follow an exchange between the Duchess and Ferdinand in which the latter ironically claims that he would accept to "see her husband" only if he "could change eyes with a basilisk" (3.2.86-7)—with a reptile whose eyes were imagined to strike people dead. Short of this metamorphosis, it is the antagonist that seems to embody something "too obscene to look upon": "I would not for ten millions I had beheld thee." This "something" is identifiable with the threatening reversibility of the look.

After the murder of the Duchess, typically effected through the intermediary of a double, the problematic of the double is given a further twist by Ferdinand's confession: "She and I were twins: / And should I die this instant, I had liv'd / Her time to a minute" (4.2.267-9). Once more, Ferdinand's plenitude appears only as lost. Moreover, by linking the elimination of his double to his own death, he implicitly remarks that his proper being is out there, in the other. In the last act of the play Ferdinand presents himself as follows:

Ferd. Leave me.
Mal. Why doth your lordship love this solitariness?
Ferd. Eagles commonly fly alone: they are crows, daws, and starlings that flock together:—look, what's that follows me?
Mal. Nothing, my lord.
Ferd. Yes:—

Mal. 'Tis your shadow.

Ferd. Stay it, let it not haunt me.

Mal. Impossible: if you move, and the sun shine: —

Ferd. I will throttle it. [*Throws himself down on his shadow.*]

(5.2.28-38)

Moreover, he is reported to be affected by lycanthropy and to have been found behind Saint Mark's church, with the leg of a man upon his shoulder. The doctor says, "He howl'd fearfully; / Said he was a wolf, only the difference / Was, a wolf's skin was hairy on the outside, / His on the inside" (5.2.15-8). Ferdinand represents himself as a turned-inward version of himself and he is spurred on to compulsively return to the same place. By the end of the play, Ferdinand is the deformed embodiment of haunting, situated at the point where absolute 'singularity' and absolute "otherness" uncannily coincide with each other without neutralizing each other. As such a disfigured figure of haunting, he cannot but haunt that by which he is haunted — the grave, where the scene of discovery as well as its violence are endlessly reenacted in an occluded form.

Works Cited

Behling, Laura L. "'She scandles our proceedings': The Anxiety of Alternative Sexualities in the *White Devil and the Duchess of Malfi.*" *English Language Notes* 33 (1996): 1-11.

Belsey, Catherine. *The Subject of Tragedy: Identity and Difference in Renaissance Drama.* London: Methuen, 1985.

Borch-Jacobsen, Mikkel. *Lacan: the Absolute Master.* Trans. Douglas Brick. Stanford: Stanford UP, 1991.

Coddon, Karin S. "*The Duchess of Malfi*: Tyranny and Spectacle in Jacobean Drama." *Madness in Drama.* Ed. James Redmond. Cambridge: Cambridge UP, 1993. 1-17.

Crooke, Helkiah. *Microcosmographia. A Description of the Body of Man.* London, 1615.

Desmet, Christy. "Neither Maid, Widow, nor Wife: Rhetoric of the Woman Controversy in *Measure for Measure and the Duchess of Malfi.*" *Another Country: Feminist Perspectives on Renaissance Drama.* Ed. Dorothea Kehler and Susan Baker. Methuchen: Scarecrow, 1991. 71-92.

Foucault, Michel. *Discipline and Punish: The Birth of the Prison.* Trans. Alan Sheridan. New York: Pantheon, 1977.

_____. *The History of Sexuality.* Vol. 1. Trans. Robert Hurley. Harmondsworth: Penguin Books, 1981.

Freud, Sigmund. "The Uncanny." *The Standard Edition of the Complete Psychological Works of Sigmund Freud.* Vol. XVII. Ed and trans. James Strachey. London: The Hogarth Press, 1953-74. 217-52.

Kerwin, William. "'Physicians are like Kings': Medical Politics and *The Duchess of Malfi.*" *English Literary Renaissance* 28 (1998): 95-117.

Laqueur, Thomas. *Making Sex: Body and Gender from the Greeks to Freud.* Cambridge, Mass.: Harvard UP, 1990.

McLuskie, Kathleen. "Drama and Sexual Politics: The Case of Webster's Duchess." *Drama, Sex and Politics*. Cambridge: Cambridge UP, 1985. 77-91.

Orgel, Stephen. "Nobody's Perfect: Or Why Did the English Stage Take Boys for Women?" *South Atlantic Quarterly* 88 (1989): 7-29.

Parker, Patricia. "Othello and Hamlet: Dilation, Spying, and the 'Secret Place' of Woman." *Representations* 44 (1993): 60-95.

Webster, John. *The Duchess of Malfi. Drama of the English Renaissance II: The Stuart Period*. Ed. R.A. Fraser and N. Rabkin. London: Macmillan, 1976.

Whigham, Frank. "Sexual and Social Mobility in *The Duchess of Malfi.*" *PMLA* 100 (1985): 167-86.

3
장
—

Difference, Territory, and Body in
The Merchant of Venice

1. Europe: the meaning of Venice

The Venetian myth of ethnic purity expressed the Elizabethan
ambition for London. John Gillies postulates this idea in his
study, *Shakespeare and the Geography of Difference*. Gillies
further asserts that Shakespeare found the Renaissance imperial
myth of Venice as alluring as the classical imperial myth of Rome.
The image of the maritime world in *The Merchant of Venice* goes
far beyond the concrete map presupposed by Antonio's obsession
with ports, piers, and roads. Shakespeare insists that Antonio's
network of maritime trade is world-wide in the full Renaissance

sense (Gillies, 66). Shylock mentions that Antonio "hath an argosy bound to Tripolis, another to the Indies . . . a third/ at Mexico, a fourth for England, and other ventures he/ hath squandered abroad" (1.3.17-21). Additionally, India, Lisbon, and Barbary are later offered by Bassanio when lamenting the apparently wholesale miscarriage of Antonio's ventures:

> What, not one hit?
> From Tripolis, from Mexico, and England,
> From Lisbon, Barbary, and India,
> And not one vessel scape the dreadful touch
> Of merchant-marring rocks? (3.2.265-9)

It is unreasonable to even suggest that Venetian ships would sail to Mexico, India, and the Indies. These routes required trans-oceanic navigation or blue water skills and those were not known in Europe at the time. Venice, even in its halcyon maritime era (about 1460) remained a coastal maritime nation as did the rest of Europe. The discovery and development of the trans-oceanic routes by the Iberians were the prime causes of the maritime decline of Venice in the early Sixteenth Century. As Gillies observed, what is suggested by the introduction of this geography into a play about the merchants of Venice, is not the Venetian reality, but of Elizabethan ambitions for London (Gillies, 66). Shakespeare presents such ambitions in a Venetian fantasy because Venice encapsulated the ideal world maritime capital which leading Elizabethan merchants hoped to achieve for London. For example, the ambiguity of the Elizabethan response to Venice is beautifully ensconced in Thomas Coryat's description of St. Mark's Square (Gillies. 124). In his essays concerning Venice, Coryat describes the riches and strangeness to such an extent that we, reading his works today, can easily see how he was inundated by a kaleidoscope of impressions. There were soaring cathedrals, the palaces of the wealthy, raucous hordes of people thronged the streets, and of course, they weren't speaking English but instead, Coryat's senses were assailed by a dozen different languages, skin colors, and likely to his chagrin, religions not his own. The initial hint of unease grows increasingly more pernicious in Coryat's account of visiting the Jewish ghetto and the synagogue. Coryat wants to be assured that Venice will be able to profit from barbarous "ethnickes" without compromising its integrity as a civilized and Christian state. Such assurance is not forthcoming as some parts of Europe had by that time been conquered by Islamic forces who had also injected themselves into Mediterranean trade. It is here that the full concept of geographical difference as promulgated by the northern and western Europeans is given full bloom. There were Mosques in many cities, bringing a different paradigm to reside next to that of Catholicism. Self-consciously imperial and a market place of the world, Shakespeare's Venice invites barbarous intrusion through the sheer exorbitance of its maritime trading empire. In *The Merchant of Venice*, the contradiction is expressed on a personal level in the opposition between Antonio and Shylock. This, however, is intended to be a metaphorical illustration of the racial and social differences as viewed through the Elizabethan eyes.

2. The other

Gerard Mercator's Atlas (refer to figure 14 in Gillies' *Shakespeare and the Geography of Difference*) depicts the ideological concept held by the west Europeans and British Isles of the contrast between civilized European and whom they considered barbarous savages through drawings of different figures wearing indigenous clothing. The costumes of these figures are, in fact, derived from the Renaissance ethnographic tradition. To the left of the stage is a group of some eight figures, all of whom are attired in recognizably European clothing. To the right is a group of nine figures, all of whom are attired in a variety of primitive garments. Some are almost naked, and some seem distinctly of African descent. Three wear feather head-dresses; two of whom are almost certainly New World, while the other is perhaps East Indian. The turbaned figure is Turkish, while the goateed spear-holder would appear to be Mongolian. All are distinctly reminiscent of the repertoire of exotics in the pages of seventeenth-century voyage publications, such as the "Great Voyages," effectively a serialized encyclopedia of discovery published by the de Bry family between 1590 and 1634. In the above cited picture, the exotic characters are represented as barbarians and innately aggressive. Geographically difference is homophobic. The farther one travels from one's own ethnic center, the more probable it is that one will encounter strangeness or otherness. Thus, all of the figures are grouped in a way that suggests an encounter between the civilized Europeans on the left and the barbarians (Turkish and Mongolian) and savages (African, East Indian and American) on the right. The prevailing logic of that period was that of the ancient poetic geography, the geography of difference that distinguished civilized people from barbarous ones could be delineated not by intelligence, but rather by location on the map. The scene might almost be emblematic of the drama of the exotic in Shakespeare. Expressing this cultural fantasy, in *The Merchant of Venice*, the contradiction between civilized Europeans and the barbarians is expressed in the opposition between Antonio and Shylock.

Antonio regards wealth as only a source by which goodness can be accomplished, rather than achieving the goal of amassing wealth. Thus, he refuses to "lend nor borrow/ upon advantage" (1.3. 68-9), and his philanthropy is well known as is his generosity, redeeming worthy debtors from the clutches of usury.

Antonio's abhoration of usury is exemplified in doggedly persecuting Shylock. It is important to realize that more than simple racial bigotry is involved here. Antonio's exclusion of Shylock, both as usurer and as Jew, is as much a social fact as his own idea of riches. Antonio's position on usury and Jews is supported by the symbolism of the "bond of flesh." This Caesaric law is both a parody and a negation of the reciprocal bond presupposed by the ideal Venetian body-politic. It is a parody to the extent that it echoes the flesh and blood symbolism of other forms of kinship bonding in the play: bonds between parents and children, and bonds between husbands and wives. It is a negation to the extent that Venetian law is shown as allowing the most barbaric practice (cannibalism) over the civilized ideal notionally represented by the commonwealth itself.

An ancient Roman law on debt stipulated that debtors were to be confined for sixty days, during which time they were to be produced before the Praetor on ". . . three successive market-days and on the third day . . . capitally condemned or sent to be sold abroad" (Gillies, 127). This barbaric statute on debt suggests the Aristotelian bias of Shakespeare's own conception of the Renaissance trading city. According to Gillies, that bias is underlined in the two legal caveats by which Portia denies Shylock's claim on Antonio. The first caveat ("Shed thou no blood, nor cut thou less nor more/ But a just pound of flesh" 4.1.322-3) symbolically denies the quasi-sacramental character of the flesh-bond as a rite of incorporation or kinship. Without blood, Shylock's pound of flesh cannot symbolize the iconic value of the blood-covenant, which is a sacramental assertion of kinship for the reason that ". . . there can be no kinship except by blood and no bond except by kinship". Even more essential to the quandary of Shylock, without blood being shed, it cannot function as the "flesh and blood" imagery operates elsewhere in the play, i.e., within a symbolic lexicon of kinship and marital incorporation. The second of Portia's caveats is also powerfully Aristotelian:

> It is enacted in the laws of Venice,
> If it be proved against an alien
> That by direct or indirect attempts
> He seek the life of any citizen,
> The party gainst which he doth contrive
> Shall seize one half his goods; the other half
> Comes to the privy coffer of the state,
> And the offender's life lies in the mercy
> Of the Duke only, gainst all other voice. (4.1.344-52)

The effect of this is to concretize the absolute distinction between alien and citizen. This is though, perversely blurred by the questionable practice of granting commodity to strangers. Instead of the *debtor* suffering death, dismemberment or alienation, it is here the *creditor* (an intruding alien) who suffers a version of dismemberment or death. Shylock's ducats - as intrinsic to his 'flesh and blood' as his daughter is - are here parceled out to Antonio and the Venetian state.

More than just a Jew, Shylock is a stranger, an alien and even more odious, an infidel. His Jewish otherness has a pandemic quality, and it is interesting to notice Shylock's mischievous facility with "voices". In the trial scene, Shylock is not merely embarrassing but also subversive:

> You have among you many a purchased slave
> Which, like your asses and your dogs and mules,
> You use in abject and in slavish parts
> Because you bought them. Shall I say to you,
> 'Let them be free, marry them to your heirs.
> Why sweat they under burdens? Let their beds
> Be made as soft as yours, and let their palates
> Be seasoned with such viands.' You will answer,
> 'The slaves are ours.' So do I answer you. (4.1.89-96)

Shylock's ability to accurately imitate the voices of other classes enables him to conjure up an entire underclass of slaves who are characteristically represented in the form of a hydra-headed rabble, the penultimate symbol of political confusion. In the above chastisement, Shylock subsumes the court's pretense to egalitarianism. Shylock's usury likewise identifies his social class as that of a barbarian. In Aristotle's terms, the usurer shares the unnaturalness of the barbarian. Just as the barbarian is excluded from the natural body of the *Polis* and of the family, so is the usurer is ostracized from the economy of the city. The city fathers believed that the management of a city should closely replicate that of the properly ran household, but only on a grander basis. Shylock then, in being placed outside the social structure is even more an alien, albeit one whose services are often sought by those who are inside the circle of citizens. In this sense, the confrontation between Antonio and Shylock amounts to more than a struggle between two individuals over personal creed, but rather the socio-struggle they represent over the political and economic heart of Venice. Just as Christ chased the money-changers from the temple, Antonio seeks to restore the more honorable stature of the city by exposing the abominations of interest and intrusion. Shylock's perceived greed and apathy towards the plight of those he deals with is cast into doubt by Shakespeare's depiction of him as a householder, a man dedicated to his family, and one of impressive piety. While lamenting the loss of his ducats and his daughter, Shylock surprises us by his indignant outrage concerning Jessica's exchange of the betrothal ring that he 'had . . . of Leah when . . . a bachelor'(3.1.111-13). As far back as Ancient Greece, but even more relevant, Roman society rings have always functioned as the eternal symbol of unbroken loyalty and in later times as religious symbols of human bonding, the implication is clear: Jessica has disposed of her heritage and has broken the family structure. Shylock decries this, but nonetheless does not totally denounce Jessica. This demonstrates that although he is distraught over the loss, he is willing to forgive if repentance is offered. There is also a compelling suggestion of Shylock's having compassion when he expresses a sense of pity for the wretched Gobbo. Shylock refers to Gobbo as 'that fool of Hagar's offspring' (2.5.43), meaning Ishmael (the mixed-race son of Abraham who was banished in favor of his pure-blooded brother, Isaac) yet he also allows that ". . . the patch is kind enough (45)." The very idea of an Ishmael being kind enough for the tribe-conscious Shylock proclaims more loudly his deeper philanthropy than does his apparent coldness. The significance of Shylock's being shown in the context of family and household is heightened by the apparent lack of both these qualities in the portrayal of Antonio. In the play, Antonio is effectively a friend rather than a kinsman, in which capacity he actually poses a danger to kinship by interfering in the fundamental bond between Bassanio and Portia.

With only a cursory examination, *The Merchant of Venice* seems to ascribe and confirm an ideological paradigm in which the interests of the state, Christianity, and capitalism are fused. At the same time, however, different viewpoints and efforts to schematize the play make it no easy matter to say what *The Merchant of Venice* is about. The degree to which the play leaves us, for example, feeling troubled over the treatment of Shylock, or appears to blur the distinctions upon which the polarities above depend, leads us, in effect, to ask with Portia, "Which is the merchant here? And which the Jew?" (4.1.170). Surely questions will arise from the academe whether the play invokes the ideologically sanctioned mythologies of the time only to query and subvert them. The increased involvement of the Merchant in the economic discourse of that era is the triumph of the play over usury in the figure of the usurer Shylock. In Shakespeare's time, usury was an accepted, although frowned upon practice that penetrated every class of society; from the wealthy merchants wishing to expand, to the scions of the rich, even to the nobles and included the Queen herself, and descending to the impoverished wretch trying to find shift to purchase succor for his family. Official records from that age reveal the extent of usury's ubiquity, so there is no challenge to its pervasiveness. (Moisan, 192). The importance of money lenders is emphasized here to accentuate the degree to which a work like *The Merchant of Venice*, indebted as it is to its Italian sources, could yet distill the concepts of the one social structure and present it in another thematic venue capitalizing on customs and mores more relevant to the audience to which the play is presented. Such a presentation opens an avenue by which the viewer can see the communal concerns of his own society, vent frustrations over similarities and engage in dialogue leading to resolution. Whether or not this was the intent of Shakespeare is moot, but one facet that has yet to be fully explored is that of the illusion, that regardless of the socio-economical status of the audience, and the disparity that might exist between themselves and those portrayed in the play, the viewers were led to the conclusion that they shared a common distaste for usury and the personification offered in the character of Shylock.

In Shakespeare's time, and for centuries prior to him, usurers were considered to be heretics, willful choosers of the wrong course and, therefore, most deserving of unqualified reproach. "One saith well," Henry Smith observes, "that our Vsurers are Hereticks, because after manie admonitions yet they maintaine their errours, & persist in it obstinately as Papists do in Poperie" (1591,2)(Moisan, 194). The wrongness of the choice is again pointedly a matter of difference of geography. The Jews chose not to accept the Christ of the Catholic church (and ergo the Church of England), but rather to remain steadfast in the Mosaic Law. That law emphatically states that it is not usury to ask interest on a loan to a gentile. Again, to the Jew, Christians are "outlandish" playing once more to the idea that geography is conceptual and as well as spatial. The Jews amassed wealth through intracommunal lending and support, while at the same time, denying Christ and charging the non-Jew burdensome interest. This association of usury with heresy and with making the choice dates as far back as the First Century to the misconception of Jews being responsible for the death of Christ and is of interest on several counts. On the one hand, the connection between usury and heresy might suggest that the rhetoric was emplaced and given validity so that the usurer could be singled out, not simply as an economic plunderer, but as an enemy of God and, therefore, a threat to the state. Pograms of Jews have occurred countless times and each time it was because they were considered as enemies of the state. Our recognition of this possibility deepens our perception of the audience's perception of Shylock. Conversely, the connection of usury with choosing enables us to see a link between Shylock and the unhappy choosers of the casket scenes and suggests a sense in which both elements of the rather exotic tradition behind the *Merchant-* the flesh-bond, and the caskets stories, could be in response to the domestic experience and economic concerns of Shakespeare's audience.

However, usury and trade existed in a relationship that was far more ambiguous than anti-usury tracts might imply, indeed, a relationship that might be said to have been more symbiotic than inimical.

This embarrassing interrelationship is a fact that not even avowedly anti-usury discourses can fully suppress. So it is that we hear the author of *The Death of Usury* labor to give the most moral, anti-usury, reading to the law enacted by Elizabeth which obviated the ban imposed by Edward VI upon the practice of usury, and which formally reinstated 10 per cent as the maximum interest rate (Moisan, 196). The law, the author maintains, could not be construed as condoning usury, but, instead, "leaves it after a sort to the curtesie and conscience of the borrower"-rather as if interest payments were to be regarded as something no more coercive than tipping! If it were not Elizabeth's intent to encourage the practice of usury, then to what purpose did she enact the statute? By rendering the usurer culpable for the failures of the system, the governing body is absolved of the blame. The common people were only too ready to cast the Jew in the role of the scapegoat. He embodies the enemy within that must be exorcised by being externalized and, literally, alienated. What better figure to fill this role than the Jew, whose vices can be familiarized. Shakespeare's Shylock is an appropriate focus for the domestic anxieties of Shakespeare's audience.

3. Female Body as Territory

For Morocco and Bassanio in *The Merchant of Venice*, Portia is represented as the four-cornered classical world. To Morocco, who recognizes his identity as a black man and mentions his skin color from the beginning of the first meeting "Mislike me not for my complexion, The shadowed livery of the burnished sun, To whom I am a neighbour and near bred," Portia is the epitome of womanhood, and the focus of a universal pilgrimage.

. . . All the world desires her.

From the four corners of the earth they come

To kiss this shrine, this mortal breathing saint.

The Hyrcanian deserts and the vast wilds

Of wide Arabia are as throughfares now

For princes to come view fair Portia.

The watery kingdom, whose ambitious head

Spits in the face of heaven, is no bar

To stop the foreign spirits, but they come

As o'er a brook to see fair Portia. (2.7.38-47)

Morocco is the exemplar of this ethnic migration, which represents both medieval pilgrimage and barbarian invasion. Bassanio also imagines Portia as the centre of universal desire.

Her name is Portia, nothing undervalued

To Cato's daughter, Brutus' Portia;

Nor is the wide world ignorant of her worth,

For the four winds blow in from every coast

Renowned suitors, and her sunny locks

Hang on her temples like a golden fleece.

Which makes her seat of Belmont Colchis strand,

And many Jasons come in quest of her. (1.1.165-72)

Bassanio's perspective on the four-cornered world differs from the foreigner, Morocco. Here, the direction of the quest is reversed (Gillies, 67). Bassanio is a second Jason, voyaging *outwards* from an imagined world-center to an imagined world-rim. The poetic geography of Portia is governed by the classical theme of limits: limits of geography, of desire, of marriage ability and of transgression. As mentioned in section 2, the symbolic contrast between Bassanio and Morocco as well as the contrast between Antonio and Shylock is sharply represented in Mercator's first volume of the 1636 edition of the *Atlas* (figure 1). The picture suggests an encounter between the civilized Europeans on the left and the barbarians (Turkish and Mongolian) and savages (African, East Indian and American) on the right. The logic is that of the ancient poetic geography, the geography of difference that distinguishes civilized from barbarous. Morocco in *the Merchant of Venice* is imagined in terms of a polluting sexual contact with a European partner. He is presented in terms of a scenario of miscegenation. As in the ancient poetic geography, all Shakespearean moors combine a generic exoticism or exteriority with an inherent proclivity for not following customs or laws. This undesirable trait is less a matter of immorality than of structure. Aaron in *Titus Andronicus*, Morocco in *The Merchant of Venice*, Othello, Cleopatra, and the king of Tunis who married Claribel in *The Tempest*, are all represented in a scenario of miscegenation. The pigmentation of the moor is intimately related to this scenario. Like their color, the exteriority of moors also has ethical significance. All Shakespeare's moors are associated with a generically "outlandish" geography; all are exotic in the comprehensive Elizabethan sense of being outlandish, barbarous, strange, and uncouth. None of them have any real existence independent of their fractiousness of those margins.

Next, I would like to examine the issue of equality or partnership within marriage. All counselors worthy of the name stress the necessity of intelligent equity between marriage partners. Such equity, however, was premised on what was then universally regarded as the self-evident natural inferiority of the female of the species. The standard scientific account of this inferiority in the period is still that which is found in Aristotle (Maclean, 42), the standard authority on natural scientific fact throughout the seventeenth century:

> The female is less spirited than the male . . . softer in disposition, more mischievous, less simple, more impulsive, and more attentive to the nurture of the young. . . . Woman is more compassionate than man, more easily moved to tears, at the same time more jealous, more querulous, more apt to scold and strike.

A compassionate and thoughtful approach to woman's place in marriage therefore incorporates some measured recognition of the woman's need to be guided by her husband, or in other words, a need for the willing submission of the wife to her husband's authority. Portia, in *The Merchant of Venice*, partakes of the chaste goddess/fierce warrior quality which celebrates and contains female achievement, and which is ultimately found wanting alongside the richer qualities of fulfilled womanhood-wifehood and motherhood. As Lisa Jardine mentioned, in spite of the wider range of opportunities which became available to some women during the Renaissance and Reformation, attitudes towards women did not perceptibly change (Jardine, 60). For example, Portia's abdication of her hereditary independence to Bassanio in *The Merchant of Venice* projects women's traditional roles.

You see me, Lord Bassanio, where I stand,
Such as I am. Though for myself alone
I would not be ambitious in my wish
To wish myself much better, yet for you
I would be trebled twenty times myself,
A thousand times more fair, ten thousand times more rich,
That only to stand high in your account
I might in virtues, beauties, livings, friends,
Exceed account, But the full sum of me
Is sum of something which, to term in gross,
Is an unlesson'd girl, unschool'd, unpractis'd
Happy in this, she is not yet so old
But she may learn; happier than this,
She is not bred so dull but she can learn;
Happiest of all is that her gentle spirit

Commits itself to yours to be directed,

As from her lord, her governor, her king.

Myself and what is mine to you and yours

Is now converted. But now I was the lord

Of this fair mansion, master of my servants,

Queen o'er myself; and even now, but now,

This house, these servants, and this same myself,

Are yours—my lord's. (3.2.149-72)

She supports the empty fiction that husbands are of their essence, economically superior to their wives, when she abdicates her rank and status in favor of Bassanio. The speech actually attempts to distort the perceived circumstance (the impoverished Bassanio fortune-hunting the hand of the wealthy lady by means of folkloristic solving of a riddle) into a 'dutiful' marital relationship. Here is a financial balance sheet, 'Too little payment for so great a debt'. Portia converts her hard financial currency into 'virtues, beauties, livings, friends'. Meanwhile the 'full sum of her' (her putative marital worth in the moral sphere) is fraught with disadvantages (unlesson'd girl, unschool'd, unpractis'd) all of which subsequently turn out to be fictions when Portia pleads as an accomplished advocate later in the play. She, however, engineers these disadvantages into total capitulation: Bassanio can claim a legitimate 'taming' of the independent woman, despite lack of means or real claim, because Portia has rhetorically contrived it.

Moreover, the use of legal methods to save Antonio alters Portia's initial obedient conformity with the patriarchal demands on her as a female heir into something close to unruliness. Her conception of her value as a person steps beyond her perception of herself as a female, bound by tradition, and it is to this truth she bridles. Portia's intervention into the iron-clad Brotherhood of law to bring justice to Antonio is followed by a piece of folk-tale misrule: in her disguise as the young lawyer Balthazar, she persuades Bassanio to give up to her the betrothal ring he promised never to part with, while her maid Nerissa, disguised as a clerk, similarly dupes her husband Gratiano into giving up his ring. As Jardine points out(Jardine, *Cultural Confusion*, 58), returning to Belmont, the two men find themselves severely compromised by the loss of their ring pledges, and the sorting out of the circulating rings fails to dislodge the two women convincingly from their position 'on top'. Portia pledges with the gift of a ring; "I give them with this ring, Which when you part from, lose, or give away, Let it presage the ruin of your love, And be my vantage to exclaim on you." The formality of this pledge befits the fortune she brings to the marriage, which carries its own contractual obligations and undertakings. If Bassanio doesn't keep his promise, she will be entitled to exclaim, to renounce her claim, to break the betrothal, to renounce the contract drawn up. Portia's maid Nerissa's betrothal ring is a traditional love-token- a pledge of sexual fidelity, in another social class: "For all the world like cutler's poetry/Upon a knife, 'Love me, and leave me not'". The terms of that bond are called into question by a piece of sophistry, when the two betrothed men are prevailed upon to give up their rings to misrule-to the very women who gave them, but now in breeches, unruly, free of speech. Through the deliberate 'ring trick', Bassanio and Gratiano face the consequences of having parted with their betrothal rings. Portia and Nerissa solemnly announce themselves contracted as sexual partners to the doctor and his clerk; and when the rings are produced as renewed pledges by Nerissa and Portia themselves, the two women repeat their threat of sexual infidelity to their husbands.

> Bassanio. By heaven[this ring] is the same I gave the doctor!
> Portia.   I had it of him: pardon me Bassanio, For by this ring the doctor lay with me.
> Nerissa.   And pardon me my gentle Gratiano, For that same scrubbed boy (the doctor's clerk) In lieu of this, last night did lie with me.
> Gratiano. Why this is like the mending of Highways. In summer where the ways are fair enough! What, are we cuckolds ere we have deserv'd it? (5.1.257-65)

As Jardine suggests, we have a reminder that Portia's learning is potentially translatable into knowingness into the sexual and as such has to be bridled by a vigilant husband, even if he depends upon her permanently for financial support (Jardine, *Cultural*

Confusion, 60). The poetic geography of Portia is governed by the classical theme of limits: limits of geography, of desire, of marriage-ability and of transgression. From the viewpoint of Bassanio, the female body is recognized as a land. Portia is represented as the four-cornered classical world. To Morocco, Portia is the essence of a desirable partner. To Morocco and Bassanio, the female body is represented as a desirable locus for the male expansionism and their financial fulfillment in the play.

Portia, however, is not content to fulfill the traditional role of a woman whose role is to serve her husband and generate male heirs. Her forceful intercedings into the traditional male realm demonstrate her active role and her social status as the Lady, the woman of independent means, the heiress. The first interceding is operated in the selection of her partner and the second one is when she saves her betrothed Bassanio's friend, Antonio. In the casket scene, as long as she primarily conceives of herself as a daughter, she never experiences herself as powerful, never owns her power, and never seriously questions the necessity of submitting to her father's dictates. The very fact, however, that Portia's dialogue with Nerissa takes place at all, and the way she problematizes her dilemma, establishes that her compliance is a matter of choice.

The second interceding is deployed when she saves Antonio and it is made in the strictly financial terms appropriate to her wealth power. When Bassanio confesses that 'he was worse than nothing, for he has engaged himself to a dear friend, and engaged his friend to his mere enemy to feed his means'(3.2.251-62), she takes it upon herself to intercede legally and independently. Portia's expertise in the law court scene comes from her cousin, the lawyer Bellario, although the magnitude of learning is her own. Her superiority is her rank and power over Bassanio (on his own admission, the penniless–powerless–suitor for her hand), Antonio and Lorenzo, all of whom are her social and financial inferiors, despite their gender superiority. As Jardine points out, for all of them her superior knowledge proves the instrument of good fortune; she announces the recovery of Antonio's lost ships, restoring his lost fortune; while Nerissa presents to Lorenzo, who has eloped with Shylock's daughter, Jessica, a deed of gift, entitling the couple to all Shylock's goods on his death (Jardine, 61). In spite of her legitimate entitlement to rule, it is the sexual subordination of women that closes the play. The sexual theme is deployed by means of the Gratiano/Nerissa couple and a final lewd pun on the woman's 'ring': "But were the day come, I should wish it dark/ Till I were couching with the doctor's clerk. / Well, while I live, I'll fear no other thing/ So sore, as keeping safe Nerissa's ring" (5.1.304-7). In the play, there are contradictory feelings about the value of education and the forwardness of female articulateness in the treatises and manuals of the period. The noble action of Portia, saving Antonio, also mobilizes a set of expectations of knowingness, of sexual unruliness and ungovernability. Portia acts with authority, and she retains full control of her financial affairs. Yet it is the husband's ownership and control of his wife's 'ring' that closes the play. In addition, the play defuses the tensions the rule of woman creates, in the witty verbal play on the theme of potential cuckoldry of the play's close. In this cultural confusion in the early modern attitudes towards the learned woman, it is interesting to note that the female body is categorized as a territory, which should be safely contained and subordinated to the male ownership.

4. Conclusion

In the first part, examination clarifies that Shakespeare's *The Merchant of Venice* shows Venetian myth as the expression of the Elizabethan ambition for London. Shakespeare found the Renaissance imperial myth of Venice just as alluring as the classical imperial myth of Rome. The image of the maritime world in *The Merchant of Venice* goes far beyond the kind of map presupposed by Antonio's obsession with 'ports and piers and roads'. Antonio's network of maritime trade is world-wide in the full Renaissance sense. What is suggested here is not the Venetian reality, but rather the Elizabethan ambitions for London. Shakespeare projects these in a Venetian fantasy because Venice represented the idea of a world maritime capital which exemplified those ambitions.

In the second part, the focus of the analysis is on the representation of the exotic characters as barbarians and innately unlawful. Venice will be able to profit from barbarous people without compromising its integrity as a civilized and Christian state. Self-consciously imperial and a market place of the world, Shakespeare's Venice invites barbarous intrusion through the sheer exorbitance of its maritime trading empire. In *the Merchant of Venice,* the contradiction is expressed in the opposition between Antonio and Shylock. At a glance, *the Merchant of Venice* seems to inscribe and affirm an ideological calculus that fused the interests of the state and the assertions of a providentialist Christianity with the prerogatives of an increasingly capitalist marketplace. At the same time, however, the considerable residue of qualification that attends even the most compelling efforts to schematize the play in this way has made it no easy matter to say what the *Merchant* is about, and in the degree to which the play leaves us, for example, feeling troubled over the treatment of Shylock, or appear to blur the distinctions on which the polarities above depend.

Finally, it is problematic that the female body is assessed as a territory which should be safely restrained and subordinated to the male's ownership. For Morocco and Bassanio in *The Merchant of Venice,* Portia is represented as the four-cornered classical world. Moreover, in spite of Portia's legitimate entitlement to rule, it is the sexual subordination of women that closes the play. The sexual theme is manifested by means of the Gratiano/Nerissa couple including a licentious pun on the woman's "ring": Throughout the play, ambivalent feelings are generated concerning the worth of education and the importunate manner of female articulation. Portia's noble act in saving Antonio, while opening her new insight into her sense of female equality, further expands her of expectations of knowingness, of sexual unruliness and irascibility. The demure state is abrogated. Now, Portia acts with authority, and retains full control of her financial affairs. Nonetheless, it is still the patriarchal husband's spousal dominance and control of his wife's 'ring' upon which the play closes that shows the audience that there is no real contention with the way things should be. In addition, the play defuses the tensions the rule of woman creates, in the witty verbal play on the theme of potential cuckoldry of the play's close. In this cultural confusion in the early modern attitudes towards the learned woman, it is interesting to note that the attitudes of the female body as property of the husband persisted until the early 20th Century.

Works Cited

Belsey, Catherine. "Love in Venice" in *Shakespeare and Gender: A History*. 196-213.

Eagleton, Terry. "Law: The Merchant of Venice, Measure for Measure, Troilus and Cressida" in *William Shakespeare*. Oxford: Blackwell, 1986. 35-63.

Gillies, John. "'The Open Worlde': The Exotic in Shakespeare" in *Shakespeare and The Geography of Difference*. Cambridge: Cambridge UP, 1994. 99-155.

Jardine, Lisa. "'She openeth her mouth with wisdom' The double bind of Renaissance Education and Reformed Religion" in *Still Harping on Daughters: Women and Drama in the Age of Shakespeare*. London and New York: Harvester, 1983. 37-67.

Jardine, Lisa. "Cultural Confusion and Shakespeare's Learned Heroines: 'These are old paradoxes" in *Reading Shakespeare Historically*. London: Routledge, 1996. 48-64.

Leventen, Carol. "Patrimony and Patriarchy in The Merchant of Venice" in *The Matter of Difference: Materialist Feminist Criticism of Shakespeare*. Ed. Valerie Wayne. London and New York: Harvester, 1991. 59-79.

Moisan, Thomas. "'Which is the merchant here? And which the Jew?': subversion and recuperation in The Merchant of Venice" in *Shakespeare Reproduced: The Text in History and Ideology*. Ed. Jean E. Howard and M. F. O'connor. London and New York: Routledge, 1987. 188-206.

Pequigney, Joseph. "The Two Antonios and Same-Sex Love in Twelfth Night and The Merchant of Venice" in *Shakespeare and Gender: A History*. 178-195.

Plax, Martin J. "Shakespeare, Shylock and Us" in *Culture and Society*

September/October 2004. 69-73.

Scott, William O. "Conditional Bonds, Forfeitures, and Vows in The Merchant of Venice" in *English Literary Renaissance* 34.3 (2004): 286-306.

Shakespeare, William. *The Merchant of Venice*. Oxford: Oxford UP, 1993

Traub, Valerie. "The homoerotics of Shakespearean comedy" in *Desire and Anxiety: Circulations of Sexuality in Shakespearean Drama*. 117-144.

Wilson, Scott. "Usure in The Merchant of Venice" in *Cultural Materialism: Theory and Practice*. Oxford: Blackwell, 1995. 104-118.

4
장
—

Yang Jung-Ung's Korean Adapted Version of *A Midsummer Night's Dream* and Its Localized Gender

1. Koreanized Shakespeare and its possibilities

During the winter of 2008, several Shakespearean plays were adapted and reinterpreted in a very Korean style (Jung Sang Young). In December, 2008, Oh Tae-suk ran *Romeo and Juliet* that he adapted into a Korean musical play for the first time in Korea in 1995. His production was invited to perform at The Barbican Theatre in 2006 and several international theatre festivals held in China in 2008. The play starts with a soft glow of candlelight of traditional Korean light, with a red-and-blue silk shade, and ends with a scene with a fluttering curtain of the five traditional Korean colors of yellow, blue, white, red and black. His play is filled with traditional Korean language, body movements, and colors.

Lear-Washing hands in a running river, Park Jang-ryol's adaptation of *King Lear*, was performed from December 10-28, 2008. It reinterpreted and recreated the play into a story after Lear's death based on a Korean fable. The location of the play is the Samdojon running river which is believed to be on the way to the other world by Buddhists. There he reflects on what has happened to him and meets dead people. Park's adaptation focuses on Lear's controlling his vehement feelings whereas Shakespeare's play centers on fierce feelings such as betrayal, conspiracy, curse, and rage. Director Park mentioned that the restoration of familial love which has been destroyed in the 21st century is the core theme of his play.

Twelfth Night which was performed by the Yohangja theatre group was on stage from the 22nd of December 2008 to the 11th of January 2009. Yang Jung Ung, who transformed Shakespeare's *A Midsummer Night's Dream* into a Koreanized Dotgabi chaos in 2006, directed this play. This play was in a form of a musical based on the story of twins, Chongasi(Sebastian), and sister, Hongasi(Viola) who succeed in their individual love relationships with Somchorong(Olivia) and Sanjago(Duke Orsino). A clown Kokdusoni(Feste) plays the guitar and sings romantic songs in a humorous and playful way which is uniquely Koreanized. These three productions of Shakespeare's plays show the possibilities of Koreanized Shakespeare and provide us with a fresh perspective. As I examined above, the Koreanization of Shakespearean play is very popular nowadays in Korean stage, and one of the successful examples of the case abroad is Yang Jung-Ung's *A Midsummer Night's Dream.*

In the next part, Koreanized version of Jung Ung Yang's *A Midsummer Night's Dream* will be examined and the limits of his production will also be analyzed. His production is meaningful because it is the first Korean production that was invited to perform at the Barbican theatre, one of the most famous theatres in England for the performance of Shakespearean plays. It is a remarkable experience that a Korean director's play was invited to the Barbican theatre and his production received critical acclaim because of its unique Korean characteristics. I watched the performance of Jung Ung Yang's *A Midsummer Night's Dream* in Korea in the summer of 2008, and I had a fantastic impression of the performance. The first production that I watched was in the summer of 1991 which was directed by Professor Hyong-In Choi and performed by the students of the department of film and theatre studies of Hanyang University. The round stage, the simple white long dress, and love and desire of the two couples still vividly remain in my mind. The visualization and representation of Shakespeare's play was quite consistent with the original play. After almost 20 years, I was faced with a quite different version of the same play. Jung Ung Yang's Koreanized version of the play was fantastically fresh and overwhelming to me because I was imagining Shakespeare's play only from the perspective of Western culture. The use of the stage, the costumes of the actors, the change of the charactors' names, Korean hospitality, and the music were uniquely Korean and the elements of Koreanness were appealing to me. In the next part, Jung Ung Yang's Koreanized version of *A Midsummer Night's Dream* will be analyzed.

2. Jung Ung Yang's Koreanized version of *A Midsummer Night's Dream*

Jung Ung Yang turned Shakespeare's *A Midsummer Night's Dream* into a Koreanized play in 2006. His production was invited to perform at the Barbican theatre, one of the most famous theatres in England for the performance of Shakespearean plays. It was a very meaningful performance because it was the first time that a Korean director's play was invited to the Barbican theatre. His production received critical acclaim because it has unique Korean characteristics.

As Shim Jung-soon, a professor in the English Literature department of Soongsil University and a theatre critic, said Korean plays were relatively unknown around the world, compared to the plays from other Asian countries such as Japan, China, and India. In an interview with the Korea Times (2006/12/11), professor Shim said that over the last 10 years, more than 60 theatre-related departments have been created at Korean universities. And about 1,000 students graduate each year from the theatre departments. She mentioned that This has a big potential for Korean contemporary theatre, which would lead to explosive growth in Korean theaters. That astounds many Japanese scholars, as Japan has only 10 theatre-related divisions nationwide(Chung, Ah-young. *The Korea Times*, 11 Dec. 2006). In her analysis, Korean theatre, including Korean adaptations of the Shakespearean plays, just started to become known on the world stage over the last few years.

In an article in *The Korea Herald* on 2007/08/16, Chung un Cho examined Korean musicals and a homegrown success story. Many musicals such as Saljaki Opseoye, The Last Empress, The Great Jangguem, Dancing Shadow, and Jump, according to the analysis, have become some of the most vibrant forms of theatre for Korean audiences. It also looked at the example of a unique adaptation of *A Midsummer Night's Dream* by director Yang Jung Ung of the Yohangza troupe. The fact that more than 70,000 people have seen the drama and that the production has been invited to 17 festivals around the world, is such a thrilling achievement in the history of Korean theatre on the world stage(Cho, Chung Un. *The Korea Herald*. 16 Aug. 2007).

Furthermore, the article brought to light the financial support from the Seoul City Government and the Ministry of Culture and Tourism as being the crucial factor for the theatre group members' participation in international theatre festivals, such as Edinburgh Fringe Festival. As Korea Arts Management Service said, this is the first time for the government to financially support Korean artists entering the European market through the annual Edinburgh Fringe Festival and this support will further promote Korean directors' accomplishments.

It is interesting to note some of the Korean characteristics in Yang's production. Peter Lathan summarized some of them as follows (Lathan, *The British Theatre Guide*, 2006). First, it is remarkable to note the use of stage. According to Yang, the stage is a living room. Thus, it is natural that members of the audience are beckoned into the living room, hence the open space. Pinewood was chosen for the frame because it is a natural material and gives an authentic oriental house image to the stage. Second, the use of the colors in characters' costumes on stage is unique. Each of the lovers is dressed in a different colored top when they approach the forest. The meaning of the colors is clear to a Korean audience. Blue, red, white, black. Third, the change of the names and characters is interesting. For example, Dotgabi is a Korean fairy equivalent to a goblin in the Western culture. In addition, Bottom is replaced by an old female herb collector. She is transformed into a pig by Duduri(Puck) and she awakes from her dream to find her fortune in a form of Sansam, a very rare hundred-year old ginseng, which is also based on Korean tradition. The fourth is Korean hospitality. The throwing of the florescent rings to the audience is a kind of gift to the audience. It is the way for Korean actors to express their thanks to the audience which is rooted in the Korean tradition of distributing a small token of appreciation to create a unity between cast and audience. Fifth, the music in this production is traditional Korean music in which four instruments are used. Kwaengwari, jing, janggu, buk, that is a drum, a gong, a small gong and an hour-glass drum are the traditional Korean percussion instruments.

One of the most attractive elements of the play was the way in which it weaves Korean legend and myth into its context. Combining elements of both cultures is a great way of reminding audiences how much we, as human beings really do have in common, inside, in our psyches, despite external differences. *Extra! Extra!,* one of the online theatrical publications, interviewed Yang and evaluated his production as one of the most delightful theatrical experiences (Couzens, *Extra! Extra!* 2006). Also, the interview summarized Yohangza Theatre Company's production of *A Midsummer Night's Dream* at the Edinburgh Festival, and anticipated the future production of it in Bristol, Germany, and Poland. Yang also recalled the performance in Japan in 2003, and he said he was very glad to hear from the Japanese theatre staff who said they were quite surprised to see those used-to-be-very-quiet-and-gentle Tokyo audiences react to the show by clapping and laughing. The strength of the show on the international stage, going beyond the cultural differences, was the way it combines Western and Oriental culture in such a comic way. Through the interview, we can understand that his work is having 'characteristic Korean Mis-en-scene' and that he has kept his passion for visual expression.

The Times reviewed Yang's production not so favorably, but it gave a positive review of the cast's physicality and Eun Jung Kim's percussive live music.

> The cast's physicality impresses and the production will please those who like their comedy broad. The lovers fight and woo with meticulously choreographed kicks and leaps as well as wistful songs; the Puckish twins tumble acrobatically and flash their bare buttocks. The goblin-like Dokkebi- jabbering and leering, in hemp robes and grotesque make-up- can be faintly irritating, but when they weave and twirl in ritualized dance to Eun Jung Kim's percussive live music, which is boisterous and eerie by turns, the spectacle is compelling. (Sam Marlowe, *The Times*, 3 July 2006)

Even though Sam Marlowe pointed out the lack of poetry and the problem of subtitles in Yang's production of the play, he praised Eun Jung Kim's traditional Korean music as enhancing elements of an intriguing folkloric quality and the cast's physicality as boisterous and compelling. This evaluation demonstrates that a Korean folkloric spin using traditional music can impress Western audiences with its fresh cultural perspective. The traditional Korean percussive live music harmonized well with the traditional Korean costumes and the stylistic movements of martial art. As stated previously, Yang's production of *A Midsummer Night's dream* and its Koreanized version was evaluated favorably.

3. Localized gender: Ajume and Dot

In addition to the Korean characteristics, I will focus on the concept of localized gender in my analysis of Yang's production. What I mean by 'localized' is the cultural, or in this case, Korean, aspect of gender in his directing, which is both significant and important. As I mentioned earlier, the replacement of Bottom by Ajume (an old woman who is a herb collector) is very original and creative in the sense that female character is projected as a crucial character in his production. The energies and festive spirit of the lower classes represented by Bottom and his fellows are substituted by the character of Ajume. She is transformed into a pig by Duduri(Puck), and after her dream she finds some very rare hundred-year old ginseng. It is interesting to note that she represents the romantic energies and folkloric spirit in this process. Koreans would certainly know the meaning of Ajume which is a married woman. In Yang's production, she is represented as a woman who is looking for a fortune in the form of Sansam (wild Ginseng) and accidentally meets with Gabi and finally mocked and punished by Dot. Gabi fell in love with Ajume by trick of Duduri and after a short dream of fantasy, Gabi is mocked and punished by his wife Dot. In the process, figuratively speaking, Ajume's body is invested with erotic desire, because Sansam and Ginseng represents male sexual power and she is charged with the task of being an object of the male erotic desire. Even though every situation is manipulated by Dot who is tracking her husband's love affairs with another woman, Ajume's energies and festive spirit of the lower classes are lingering on the stage even when she is out of the stage. In the end, she is transformed into a pig, which means she was once transgressive and now her power is contained. What is important in the story of Ajume's love affair with Gabi is that Yang in his directing, foregrounded the female erotic power and Koreanized style of comic elements.

Furthermore, the change of Titania and Oberon into Dot and Gabi is Koreanized and the role of Dot is emphasized in contrast to Shakespeare's original text. Dot controls Duduri and manipulates her husband, Gabi, through the messenger role of Duduri. In the original text, it is Oberon that intentionally mocks and punishes his wife, Titania. However, in Yang's production, it is a female character, Dot, who plays an active role and exerts herself in order to control the male body. The comic love happening between Titania and Bottom is switched into the playfully mocked love between Gabi and Ajume. In this process, the controlling power of Dot is emphasized and the female voice of Dot is empowered. As Judith Butler mentioned, 'performativity' is important in the sense that male and female identity is not fixed and ultimately is generated by the role of performing one's own identity (Butler, 8). In this context, the irreducibility of the private body of Dot is foregrounded and female form takes precedence over the normally emphasized male form in Yang's production. Gabi's will is frustrated in his attempt to manipulate Dot's body since the female body cannot be violated. Considering the specific context of 16th century and the male predominant society. Oberon's scrutiny of Titania's body seems inseparable from the 16th century's understanding of the general female body. His role is tied up with manipulating the female body and Dot has subversive power to frustrate that controlling and to articulate the female voice. As Yang explained through the 21st century Korean context, male sexual predominance in the family and love affair with another woman is reflected in the role switching of Titania and Oberon to Dot and Gabi(UP stage, Minkyong Yoon, 2). In the original text, it is Titania who is deceived by her husband and playfully mocked because of the love affair with Bottom. However, ironically speaking, in the transformation of the story, Koreanized version foregrounds Dot's manipulating the male body and her power to articulate the female voice. Director Yang said that cheating female fairy(Titania) is transformed into cheating male Dotgabi(Gabi) because it is more convincing in Korean culture, and Dotgabi has an image of drinking, dancing, and womanizing. It was natural for the director to transform in that way. Combining general Korean culture and character, natural Korean festive expression and spirit become merged in the play. Language is the center of Shakespeare's play. It is newly created with the power of energy and dance without the heaviness of language. As Barbican director, Lewice Jeffreys, remarked, newly born *Midsummer Night's Dream* follows the basic storyline and each scene has its essence and power. Among many attractive elements, the foregrounding of female characters like Dot and Ajume is intriguing in the sense that they have the subversive power to frustrate male controlling and to articulate the female voice.

4. The limits of Yang's Koreanized version

There also a cynical criticism of Yang's production of the Shakespeare's *A Midsummer Night's Dream*. In an interview with *Joins* on 2006/08/11, Minwoo Choi, a Joongang daily newspaper journalist, raised several questions that were critical of Yang's production (Choi, Minwoo. *Joongang Daily Newspaper*, 11 Aug. 2006). The first criticism was on the sarcastic review of *The Times* that 'there was a lot of laughter but the play couldn't represent Shakespeare's philosophical depth.' Yang explained that the problem was caused by English subtitles. He said, Originally, there were no subtitles because they decrease the rhythm of Korean words. It was my mistake to accept Barbican's request for subtitles. But it is nonsense to talk about philosophical depth. The original play is a romantic comedy. I tried to focus on the aspects of love and life which are momentous and evanescent in a humorous and Koreanized way.

The second criticism was on the existence of the players. It is criticized that in his production there are no players. He answered that it's right in the sense that the essence of a play is the players. But I don't think that way. Light, music and Mis-en-scene are very important to me. The professional players should reveal their presence with the harmony of these factors. I don't want to sacrifice players but I also don't want to overemphasize players at the sacrifice of these elements. Finally, it was argued that Yang is obsessed with visual elements and that his production exposes the weakness of the story. In addition, it is mentioned that Yang emphasizes the adaptation of the plays, and thus he has no original work. On that criticism, he replied that I am against the imitation of the Western style of storytelling.

Oriental and Korean style is without beginnings and endings, and without conflict and conclusions. I sometimes imagine 'a play without players.' Imagination is the starting line of art. About the adaptation, he explained that half of Yohangza's productions are creative works. But I don't mind producing adapted works, if I can create a work with my own unique style. I think that is also a creative work. In spite of some of the harsh criticism on his production of A Midsummer Night's Dream, it can not be denied that it was the first remarkable achievement by a Korean director at the Barbican Theatre and on the world stage.

Even though Yang's production achieved a great deal in terms of the Koreanization of Shakespearean drama, the Barbican performance of Yang's A Midsummer Night's Dream brought its limitation to the foreground. In the case of subtitles, the problem of inelegant text was pointed out by Sam Marlowe in The Times review of the play on July 3, 2006. Sam Marlowe mentioned Roo(Demetrius)'s line to the besotted Ick(Helena) as an example:

Nor does Yang's inelegant text, translated by Winny Yoon, offer much lyricism or psychological complexity. Oh my, you drive me really crazy, whinges Roo/Demetrius to the infatuated Ick/Helena.

The English subtitles were designated as having a lack of lyricism and psychological complexity. In the original Shakespeare texts, the line is Tempt not too much the hatred of my spirit(2.1.211). The process of making early modern English into modern and prosaic English expressions might have caused the problem. The problem with subtitles is an enormous undertaking for all Korean Shakespeare productions. As Hyon-u Lee stated in his article, British Responses to Oh Tae-suk's *Romeo and Juliet* at the Barbican Centre, that many of the English subtitles, which were retranslated from Korean translations or adaptations of the original Shakespeare texts, have caused the side effect of distancing the work further and further from the original play. In order not to make the uncomfortable disparity between the Korean dialogue and Shakespeare's poetry, as referenced in Sam Marlowe's criticism of Oh's *Romeo and Juliet*, the English subtitles should have been translated as close to the original lines as much as possible.

The problem concerning the lack of poetry was also mentioned by Sam Marlowe in his review of the play. He took an example of Ajumi/Bottom, who is wearing not an ass's head but that of a pig, its ears flapping like half-cooked rashers of bacon. His analysis was that this does not greatly enhance the understanding of Shakespeare, thereby serving to diminish the play's metaphorical richness. This judgment may be caused by cultural differences in the symbolic representation of the animals. In Western culture, an ass means a stupid person, or buttock, whereas in Korean culture a pig stands for that quality. In Korea, a pig is synonymous with stupidity and fortune. Therefore in

Korean culture, if you dream of a pig or see a pig in your dreams, rush next morning to buy a lottery ticket as you are bound to win. Yang's Korean folkloric spin of the original Shakespeare's play could be understood as a fresh cultural perspective if one is provided with plausible explanations. As I mentioned earlier, Yang discussed criticism concerning the lack of poetry in an interview, saying it is nonsense to talk about philosophical depth. The original play is a romantic comedy. I tried to focus on the aspects of love and life which are fading and evanescent in a humorous and Koreanized way. Yang emphasized he tried to focus on the cheerful aspect of love, and I think the Korean style of jocularity is the strong point of his production. However, to achieve the globalization of a Koreanized Shakespeare production, it is necessary to objectify Yang's production and open our ears to foreign audience's criticism as well as praise.

Works Cited

Butler, Judith. *Bodies That Matter: On the Discursive Limits of Sex.* London and New York: Routledge, 1993.

Kim, Jong-Hwan. The Nature of Love in *A Midsummer Night's Dream. Shakespeare Review* 45.1 (2009): 5-25.

Kim, Yongtae. I have had a most rare vision: Gender inversions in *A*

Midsummmer Night's Dream in *Shakespeare Review* 40.3 (2004): 541-63.

Cho, Chung un. Korean musicals: a homegrown success story. 16 Aug. 2007. *The Korea Herald*.

http://news.naver.com/main/tool/print.nhn?oid=044&aid=0000066704

Choi, Minwoo. Yang Jung Ung's *A Midsummer Night's Dream* got harsh reviews from England. 11 Aug. 2006. *Joongang Daily Newspaper*.

http://article.joins.com/article/print.asp?ctg=15&AID=2416154

Chung, Ah-young. Growing Interest in Korean Theater. 11 Dec. 2006. The Korea Times.

http://news.naver.com/main/tool/print.nhn?oid=040&aid=0000037401

Couzens, Mary. Interview with Jung-Ung Yang, Director of Yohangza Theatre Company. *Extra! Extra!*

http://blog.daum.net/_hdn/blank_article.html

Hwang, Hyosik. Love and Marriage in *A Midsummer Night's Dream* and the socio-historical context in *Shakespreare Review* 38.1 (2002): 277-97.

Jacobson, Rivka. Jung-Ung Yang- Dream from the East. *The British Theatre Guide.* http://blog.daum.net/_hdn/blank_article.html

Jung, Sang Young. Shakespeare dressed in Hanbok. 2 Dec. 2008. *The Hankyoreh Daily Newspaper*.

http://www.hani.co.kr/arti/culture/music/325255.html

Lee, Hwan Tae. Solving problems by Cancellation: The Multiplex plots of *A Midsummer Night's Dream in Shakespeare Review* 39.1 (2003): 221-49.

Lee, Hyon-u. British Responses to Oh Tae-suk's *Romeo and Juliet* at the Barbican Centre. *Classical and Renaissance English Literature* 18.1 (2009): 139-69.

Marlowe, Sam. *A Midsummer Night's Dream.* 3 July. 2006. *The Times.*

http://entertainment.timesonline.co.uk/tol/sitesearch.do?query=Sam +Marlowe%2C+A+Midsummer+Night%27s+Dream&turnOffGoogleAds=

false&submitStatus=searchFormSubmitted&mode=simple&sectionId= 974&x=7&y=13

Montrose, Louis. *A Midsummer Night's Dream* and the shaping fantasies of Elizabethan culture: Gender, Power, Form in *New Historicism and Renaissance Drama*. Ed. Richard Wilson and Richard Dutton. London and New York: Longman, 1992. 109-30.

Patterson, Annabel. *Shakespeare and the Popular Voice*. Oxford: Blackwell, 1989.

Tennenhouse, Leonard. Strategies of State and political plays: *A Midsummer Night's Dream, Herny IV, Henry V, Henry VIII* in *Political Shakespeare: New essays in cultural materialism*. Ed. Jonathan Dollimore and Alan Sinfield. Manchester: Manchester UP, 1985. 109-29.

5
장

The Witch's Transgressive Body and Transvestism: *1, 2, 3 Henry VI*

The demonisation of women as witches in Renaissance drama makes it clear that 'witch' is a category flexible enough to cover any sort of female deviance and rebellion. The best example of a dramatic fusion of witchcraft is, of course, in Shakespeare's *Macbeth*. The pervasive disorder in the play is expressed in a series of multiple inversions of witches, and the witches' presence in the play embodies and provokes misrule and topsy-turvydom. The projection of political issues onto supposedly supernatural dimensions is deployed to justify the demonisation of women in the Renaissance period. This infinite variety of patriarchal discourse can be observed through the damnation of disorderly or rebellious women as witches and through the containment of them in patriarchal gender relations. Certainly, it is not esoteric to claim that witches are the projection of exaggerated patriarchal fears, and female punishment by familial, judicial, and religious aruthorities has its ideological effect.

As C. L. Barber has suggested, "the threatening mother survived as an immediate, physical, supernatural presence in Protestant countries after the benign Holy Mother had been drastically reduced in scope and presence - for the terrible mother was still conjured up and pursued with terrible persecution in the witch manias well into the seventeenth century. Thus, the abolition of the cult of the Virgin Mary can be related to the problematical role of women in Elizabethan drama. According to Keith Thomas, the belief in witches survived in England after many Catholic resources of exorcism had been dispensed with. In fact, as Catherine Belsey notes, "witchcraft was first made a statutory offense in 1542 and the last statute against witchcraft was repealed in 1736··· Within this period there were peaks in the 1580s and 1590s, during which the divorce debate was also reaching a climax, and in 1645-7, when women were claiming an unprecedented voice in the affairs of church and state." In this case, the political allusions were not esoteric. It is clear that the meaning of witchcraft is anchord to the containment of women's power. According to Malcolm Gaskill, historical studies of witchcraft in early modern England have expained the rise and fall of prosecutions between about 1560 and 1680 through reference to the deterioration of social cohesion in communities which raised fears in innocent villagers and made them use witchcraft against those who denied them traditional charity. He explains:

> In later 16th and 17th century England, opportunities to live According to individual preference were rare, and for most People the pattern of life was determined by adverse economic Conditions over which they had little or nor control: population Increase, land hunger, inflation, dearth, and, as a result, competition for power, space and resources. Under such harsh conditions, it is easy to imagine that an atmosphere of fear and insecurity might form the backdrop to the daily life of many communities, and that charity and good neighbourliness existed as unrealized Christian ideals as much as they faithfully mirrored social relations in the period. In many instances of conflict, often between close neighbours, and especially where disputants were too poor to engage in protracted litigation, impotence prevailed and a tense state of deadlock emerged.

It is true that social disorder can be found in an acute instability wrought by inflation, social mobility, sectarian violence and warfare. Moreover, 16th and 17th century witchcraft beliefs were a coherent, meaningful and indeed necessary component of a larger intellectual system based upon principles of hierarchy, opposition and inversion. This system linked together demonism, political sedition and rebellion, and female misrule as inversions of the divinely sanctioned order in the cosmos, state and family. For Stuart Clark, "each detailed manifestation of demonism presupposed the orderliness and legitimacy of its direct opposite, just as, conversely, the effectiveness of exorcism, judicial process and even a royal presence in actually nullifying magical powers confirmed the grounds of authority of the priest, judge or prince as well as the felicity of his ritual performance. Undeniably, the projection of political issues onto supernatural dimensions attributes inversion and misrule to the witches' presence. And demonology imposed images of disorder onto the voluble and unwomanly female. Social disorder and instability are attributed to diabolic women who were seen as possessed of an unauthorized power. Of the witches executed in England, 93 per cent were women. Thus, the projection of specific historical crises onto demonized women is coterminous with psychological processes and the politics of the unconscious. Psychological process and the collective unconscious can be confirmed through the fact that "witchcraze" was reaching a climax when there was a crisis in the definition of women and the meaning of the family. As I have mentioned above, the peaks of the persecution were during 1580s and 1590s, when women's subversive and disruptive power was foregrounded through the divorce debate and their participation in politics.

The texts in which witches are represented allow us to glimpse the cultural contours of the Elizabethan psyche. Sixteenth-century travel narratives often recreate the ancient Amazons of Scythia in North Asia or in Africa whose kingdom is inherited by the daughters. For example, William Painter's "Novel of the Amazons" which opens the second book of *The Palace of Pleasure,* describes the Amazons as "most excellent warriors" and as females having an "extreme penchant for male infanticide".[1] In Painter's text, the attitude toward the Amazons is ambivalent and contradictory, because it is a mixture of attraction and repulsion. Montrose writes, "Amazonian mythology seems symbolically to embody and to control a collective anxiety about the power of the female not only to dominate or reject the male but to create and destroy him. It is an ironic acknowledgment by an androcentric culture of the degree to which men are in fact dependent upon women: upon mothers and nurses, for their birth and nurture; upon mistresses and wives, for the validation of their manhood.[2] Descriptions of witches are ubiquitous in Elizabethan texts. A significant example is in Shakespeare's *Macbeth.* The pervasive

---

[1] William Painter, *The Palace of Pleasure Vol. II.* London: David Nutt in the Strand. 1968. pp. 159-65. This book was originally imprinted at London by Thomas Marshe in 1575.

[2] Louis Montrose, "Shaping Fantasies-Figurations of Gender and Power in Elizabethan Culture" in *New Historicism and Renaissance Drama*, edited and introduced by Richard Wilson and Richard Dutton, London and New York: Longman, 1992. p. 115

disorder in the play is expressed in a series of multiple inversions of contraries in the personal, political and natural planes. The inversions are articulated and foregrounded not only by the famous ritual utterance, "Fair is foul and foul is fair," but also by the suggestion of misrule and topsy-turvydom. Terry Eagleton, discussing the witches in *Macbeth,* remarks:

> The withes are the heroines of the piece, however little the play itself recognizes the fact, and however much the critics may have set out to defame them. It is they who, by releasing ambitious thoughts in Macbeth, expose a reverence for hierarchical social order for what it is, as the pious self-deception of a society based on routine oppression and incessant warfare. The witches are exiles from that violent order, inhabiting their own sisterly community on its shadowy borderlands, refusing all truck with its tribal bickering and military honours. . . . Their teasing word play infiltrates and undermines Macbeth from within, revealing in him a lack which hollows his being into desire. . . . ; and their words to Macbeth catalyze this region of otherness and desire within himself, so that by the end of the play it has flooded up from within him to shatter and engulf his previously assured identity. In this sense the witches figure as the 'unconscious' of the drama, that which must be exiled and repressed as dangerous but which is always likely to return with a vengeance. That unconscious is a discourse in which meaning falters and slides, in which firm definitions are dissolved and binary oppositions eroded, fair is foul and foul is fair, nothing is but what is not.[3]

Eagleton voices a concern with the subordinate, the marginal and the displaced. According to Dollimore, "the witches are fascinatingly deviant," "but they also problematise and interrogate "the social order which demonises them."[4] This rereading of transgression provides a positive meaning to the trespasses of the witches who were strategically positioned as the marginalized voices. In this context, some of the recent criticism convincingly asserts that witchcraft foregrounded women as a powerful agent in the drama of history, rather than as a feeble victim of the history.[5] This interpretation posits witchcraft as "channels of female force. female power, and female female action," and suggests that women were not the victims of patriarchal legal systems but the "historical actors" of legal processes. Jim Sharpe points out that "the high level of participation of women witnesses in witchcraft cases, and the ready participation of women in searching for the witch's mark, were areas in which women could enter the male dominated milieu of legal process, and in which women, perhaps within parameters dictated and maintained by

---

3 Terry Eagleton, *William Shakespeare.* Oxford: Blackwell, 1986. p. 2

4 Jonathan Dollimore, *Radical Tragedy.* N. Y. & London: Harvester. 1984. p. xxvi

5 Refer to Jim Sharpe, "Women, witchcraft, and the Legal Process" in *Women, Crime & The courts: In Early Modern England.* Eds. Jenny Kermode & Garthine Walker. London: UCL Press, 1994. pp. 106-24: Malcolm Gaskill, "Witchcraft and power in early modern England: the case of Margaret Moore in Women, Crime & the Courts. pp. 125-145: Jim Sharpe. "Witchcraft and women in 17C England; Some Northern Evidence" in *Continuity & Change* 6 (1991) pp. 179-99

men, could carve out some role for themselves in the public sphere.[6] These women were active participants in the legal system that enforced restrictions upon them. These disorderly women, or the images of the disorderly women, even when contained and demonized, provided behavioural options for women. Accordingly, we must suppose that women were not passive victims or dupes of patriarchy but that they were, albeit within the limits set for them by a male-dominated culture, social actors with concerns and goals of their own.

In Edward Jorden's *Brief Discourse* from 1603, hysteria manifests itself in symptoms that are often ascribed to witchcraft: "Suffocation in the throate, croaking of frogges, hissing of snakes, frenzies, convulsions, hick-cockes, laughing, singing, weeping, crying, & c.[7] As a medical doctor, Jorden wrote a treatise to diagnose hysteria correctly rather than to attribute the symptoms to witchcraft. But, as Elizabeth Harvey suggests, "hysterical symptoms··· had the effect of transposing maleficent agency from supernatural causes to the body of woman, converting religious and social disorder into a more localized somatic disruption.[8] In witchcraft, the female body is vehicular, a receptive conduit for the voices of demons, and her own voice is silenced and

---

[6] Jim Sharpe. "Women, Witchcraft and the Legal Process" p. 120

[7] Edward Jorden, *A Brief Discourse of a Disease Called the Suffocation of the Mother*, London, 1603, Sig. B2

[8] Elizabeth D. Harvey, *Ventriloquized Voices: Feminist Theory and English Renaissance Texts*, London & New York: Routledge, 1992. p. 66

repressed. However, it should not be ignored that witchcraft was perceived as a means of attaining power by ordinary people and the style and content of the witch's confessions concerned these imagined powers and implications for the ordinary people. With regard to this point, Malcolm Gaskill writes:

> To ordinary people, given that many relied on magic in their daily lives, witchcraft could be both evil and beneficial; therefore, its deviant or criminal aspects were largely restricted to its destructive manifestations. Indeed, one could say that the only characteristic shared by cunning magic and maleficent witchcraft in the popular mind was the exercise, or the imagined exercise, of supernatural power by persons who were otherwise relatively powerless in terms of wealth and social status – particularly women. As J. A. Sharpe reminds us, witchcraft was "an explanation for misfortune, but also a means by which the powerless could wield power."[9]

Indeed, witchcraft was a classical resort of vulnerable subordinate groups to challenge a form of domination that constrained them. And it provided an extension of power or a potential source of power to them. Thus, the causes of witchcraft accusations can be found not only in social tensions but also in the participation of the witch in a shared culture of popular beliefs. Witchcraft is not

---

[9] Malcolm Gaskill, "Witchcraft and power in early modern England: the case of Margaret Moore" in Jenny Kermode and Garthine Walker eds. *Women, Crime and the Courts*, London: UCL Press, 1994, pp. 128-9

only a paranoid and oppressive dogma existing solely in the mind of the accuser, but also a belief in the mind of the accused. The style and content of witches' confessions concerned imagined power, and therefore held implications for her active role in the world. Even if her imagined power remains an illusion, her active participation in a shared belief functions as an important event historically, because it foregrounds the concrete form of the vision and the manner in which she interpreted and described the world.

Based on this background, in section II, I will examine the representation of Joan of Arc in *I Henry VI*. Her representation as witch is closely related with her transvestism, which signals a transgression of her class and gender. It does not just pervert biology, it upsets the social hierarchy. Recently, academic studies have shown a marked fascination with crossdressing on the ground that the rise of new interdisciplinary studies have found an ideal site for the study of cultural discourses about gender and sexuality in the topic of transvestism. This can be better understood by the emergence of feminist criticism which challenged the authority of Western male thought and its legitimacy. This criticism created a cultural climate of uncertainty where old forms of power, identities, histories, and legitimacy have been called into question, what has been termed the complex, destructuring, disintegration of the founding structures in the West.[10] This crisis has thrown into question the naturalized status of the sexual divisions of patriarchal society, and a number of feminist texts have since proposed that such a crisis resulted in a re-imagining and re-conceptualization of both masculinity and femininity. It can be also pointed out that the historical representation of women is primarily based on the prejudiced knowledge of past dominant values, actions and behaviours. The narrowing of those systems of difference was feared during the Renaissance. This resulted in the mass-scale burning and torture of women who were branded as witches and the persecution of crossdressed women who were thought to disrupt the social hierarchy and cultural binaries.

In section III, I will deal with the representations of Queen Margaret and Lady Grey respectively in *2 Henry VI* and *3 Henry VI*. It is quite important that their fatal marriages are represented as strong factors which aggravated the civil dissension. This is one of the many patriarchal discourses which inscribed disorderly or rebellious women as witches and contained them. In section IV, I will discuss the transformation of the witches into the heroines of history. According to Foucault, the technique of confession on the scaffold is closely related with the knowledge of a subject which causes him to be ignorant of himself. The great machinery of repression attempts to inscribe its ideology through the technique of confession and the subsequent establishment of a

---

10 Craig Owens, "The Discourse of Others: Feminists and Postmodernism" in Hal Foster ed. *Postmodern Culture*. London: Pluto Press. 1985. pp. 57-82

system of legitimate knowledge. However, this patriarchal deployment of witchcraft provided ordinary people with a means of perceiving power, and resulted in the transformation of a witch into a heroine of history paradoxically. This transformation can be observed in the historical figure of Joan who became an object of adoration by her admirers such as Friedrich Schiller, Bernard Shaw, and Mark Twain. As can be witnessed in Joan's case, witches and transvestism held a subversive and transgressive potential against a normative social order and the strict principles of hierarchy and subordination. According to Natalie Davis, the subversive potential of transvestism can be found in other cultural contexts such as carnival and food riots in which crossdressed figures were predominant, so that gender and class boundaries were simultaneously tested and confirmed.[11] The subversive potential of transvestism and the transformation of a witch into a heroine of history will show the dialectical view of history which may foreground not only the success of dominant groups in regulating the discourse but also their failures in which subaltern and marginal groups contest hegemonic impositions.

---

[11] Natalie Davis, "Women on Top: Symbolic Sexual Inversion and Political Disorder in Early Modern Europe" in *The Reversible World: Symbolic Inversion in Art and Society*. Ed. Barbara Babcock. Ithaca and New York: Cornell UP, 1978. pp. 154-5 and 176-83.

1. Witch and Transvestism: Beyond the Cultural Boundaries of Class and Gender

It is worth noting that intimations and denials of witchcraft and demonism form a persistent undercurrent in Shakespeare's *Henry VI* plays. In their metamorphoses, descriptions of elemental disorder, action and language, the plays evoke intimations of witches. As exemplars of the demonic and explicitly sexual power of women, these witches logically share a place with the Amazons in the man-made sex/gender system of *Henry VI*. The first scene of *1Henry VI* opens on the funeral of king henry V who was too famous to live long. It predicts the coming 'change of times and states' and offers a theme from which the latent 'intestine divisions' of the English nobles can at once break out. Now that the powerful reign of Henry V, the conqueror of France, is removed, his conquests immediately begin to crumble. Exeter's mourning phrases, "Or shall we think the subtle-witted French/ Conjurers and sorcerers, that afraid of him,/ By magic verses have contriv'd his end?" (I. i. 25-7), impute Henry's death to the malicious tricks of French sorcerers, and anticipate the role assigned to Joan of Arc. The representation of the witch as the nation's enemy is closely related with the Elizabethan political situation. According to Diane Purkiss, there was the sudden panic about witches in the regime of queen Elizabeth, because there were many attempts on the queen's life by witchcraft: "The witch-alarm began with the discovery of three female wax figures in August of 1578, found buried in a London dunghill, with bristles stuck through the heart. The Spanish ambassador reported the widespread dismay thus caused; it was assumed that the poppets were an attempt on the queen's life by withcraft. The queen excluded witchcraft and sorcery from a general pardon given the same year."[12] *1 Henry VI* comes after Amada year and after many plots against the queen's life using sorcery which involved an alliance between foreign foes and traitors at home. The malicious plots caused pressing political anxieties, and these worries were deepened by the unclear succession, the regime by a female ruler, and the threat from Spain and France. Considering the political context which was preoccupied with the witch-alarm, it is not surprising that Joan is represented as a witch and nation's enemy. As many critics have pointed out, the portrait of Joan is considerably distorted by sheer nationalism; out of patriotism Talbot is idealized to a hero and consequently Joan's triumphs are compelled to diminish and all her successes assigned to witchery and sorcery. Joan took Rouen in the play — which was never taken, but opened its gates 17 years after her death — by a trick and Talbot acquired the glory of retaking it by sheer English courage. Furthermore, a scene is absolutely invented in which she denies her shepherd father and asserts that

---

[12] Diane Purkiss, *The Witch in History: Early Modern and Twentieth-century Representations*. London and New York Routledge, 1996. p. 185.

she is "nobly born" for no reason, or rather in defiance of reason, for she has already in the first act avowed her parentage to the Dauphin: "Dauphin, I am by birth a shepherd's daughter." (I. ii. 72) To our wonder, she says to her father, "Decrepit miser, bare ignoble wretch!/ I am descended of a gentler blood:/ Thou art no father nor no friend of mine." (V. iv. 7-9) This invented scene might be inserted in the play, because her transvestism was interpreted as an attempt to transgress cultural hierarchies of class and gender. The continuing alignment of the French with magic, the British with God and righteousness, could be written off as understandable patriotism or chauvinism. The magical, diabolical means used by the French are also continually associated with women and with femininity, while England represents masculinity and male principle. Fiedler notes, "In the very first scene of *Part I,* the keening wail has gone up: 'Our isle be made a nourish of salt tears,/ And none but women left to wail the dead.' (I. i. 50-1) 'None but women left': it is the threat which hangs over a realm ruled by a boy king obviously destined never to become a real man. In all England, so far as the play will permit us to see, there is only a single claimant to the role of male champion, one warrior capable of resisting the incursion of the female from without and creeping feminization from within. And this is Talbot" [13] In particular, the father-son relation is

---

[13] Leslie A. Fiedler, *The Stranger in Shakespeare.* St. Albans: Paladin, 1974, p. 46

central in *1 Henry VI*. With regard to this, Marilyn French argues: "the scenes from IV. v. 16 through to IV. vii. 32 are written in rhymed couplets. The verse form sets off this section and raises it to a different level from the surrounding material, indeed from the rest of the play. Its formality turns the scenes into ritual."[14] Actually, as Shakespeare knew very well from his sources, John Talbot did not die with his son, but survived both him and Joan, outliving her in fact by twenty years. Fiedler writes, "Talbot does not exit from the scene until he has tried to rape Joan in prison. It is a particularly ignominious encounter, in which the English captain, who has been made Joan's official guard after her recantation before the ecclesiastical court, only dares to assault her with the aid of an accomplice as drunk as himself – and fails. But for Shakespeare, Talbot's dignity must be preserved to the last."[15] The myth of Talbot can be understood in the context that he is represented as the veritable apotheosis of national identity. This is explicitly stated in the scene with the countess of Auvergne: "No, no. I am but shadow of myself/ You are deceived, my substance is not here;/ . . . These are his substance, sinews, and strength." (II. iii. 49-50, 62). This scene emphasizes that he is not an individual but a representative of English heroism,

---

[14] Marilyn French, *Shakespeare's Division of Experience*. London: Jonathan Cape. 1982. p. 50

[15] Leslie A. Fiedler, *The Stranger in Shakespeare*, St. Albans: Paladin. 1974. p. 48.

masculine honour and power. Talbot's "substance" is England.

Sharply contrasted is the characterization and representation of Joan of Arc. It is not mere chance that St. Joan became, in Shakespeare's first tetralogy and in popular British imagination, not only a witch but a whore. In the first scene in which she appears, the relationship with Charles Dauphin takes on an amatory meaning: "Charles. Then come. o'God's name / I fear no woman" "Puc. And while I live / I'll ne'er fly from a man" (I. ii. 111-4). Talbot is permitted to abuse her, calling her "witch" and "high-minded strumpet" (I. v. 6; 12) Above all, her bewitchment of Burgundy reveals her demonic power and exploitation of English males in her pursuit of French triumph. As Deborah Willis points out, she turns the Englishmen from fierce dogs into "whelps", and the language of "turning" and "whirling" is used to describe her effects of bewitchment. [16] She enchanted and turned Burgundy into a loyal Frenchman by her appeal to his attachment to his native land: "See, see the pining malady od France, / Behold the wounds, the most unnatural wounds / Which thou thyself hast given her woeful breast / O, turn thy edged sword another way" (III. Iii. 49-52). After Joan's appeal, Burgundy confesses; relent." (III. Iii. 58-9) Her invoking of the breast and bosom in this appeal reminds us of maternal body and witches' teats; "Where I was

---

[16] Deborah Willis, "Shakespeare and the English witch-hunts" in *Enclosure Acts: Sexuality, Property, and Culture in Early Modern England.* Ed. Richard Burt and John Michael Archer. Ithaca and London: Cornell UP. 1994. p. 101.

wont to feed you with my blood," (V. iii. 14) As we can observe in Burgundy's change, Joan is represented as a witch whose supernatural power manifests itself in her clever manipulation of English males. She has a malevolent power to turn the Englishmen and she shows exceptional physical strength and skill in combat. Moreover, she enacts her conjuration (V. iii) and the stage display of the witch's practices provokes political anxiety about witches as a threat to the nation. Her conjuring signifies real threats to the queen, Elizabeth which were posed by the alliance of secret and foreign powers. The conversion of the strong other from a foreign virago into a witch can be explained by this political context and English nationalism. The representation of Joan in the play foregrounds and, at the same time, interrogates this sheer nationalism which transforms a capable warrior to a diabolic sorcerer. The witch's presence in the play embodies topsy-turvydom, and problematises the projection of political issues onto supernatural dimensions.

In addition, Joan is represented as a veritable harlot in the text. As Marilyn French points out, "promiscuous sexuality is one of the major characteristics of Shakespeare's Joan, whose portrait goes far beyond anything found in Hall or Holinshed or in the Burgundian chronicler Monstrelet."[17] There is also some sarcasm in both Hall and Holinshed's description of Joan as a virgin.

---

17 Marilyn French, *Shakespeare's Division of Experience*. London: Jonathan Cape. 1982. pp. 46-7

Holinshed writes, "Of favour was she counted likesome, of person stronglie made and manlie, of courage great, hardie, and stout withal, an understander of counsels though she were not at them, great semblance of chastitie both of bodie and behavior, the name of Jesus in hir mouth about all hir businesses, humble, obedient, and fasting diverse daies in the weeke. A person (as their books make hir) raised up by power divine, onelie for succour to the French estate then deeplie in distresse."[18] This promiscuous sexuality is inextricably related with her masculine dress, the sign of sexual ambiguity. Joan's act which seems most to have outraged her English captors and her chronicler is her wearing of men's clothing. Holinshed writes, "shamefullie rejecting hir sex abominablie in acts and apparel, . . . she should cast off hir unnaturall wearing of mans abilliments and keepe hir to garments of hir owne kind."[19] Joan, a peasant girl from Domremy, dressed throughout her brief period of public action as a man - and not just as a man, but as a noble man.

> The said Jeanne put off and entirely abandoned woman's clothes, with her hair cropped short and round in the fashion of young men, she wore shirt, breeches, doublet, with hose joined together, long and fastened to the said doublet by twenty points, long

[18] Geoffrey Bullough ed. *Narrative and Dramatic Sources of Shakespeare*, Vol. III, London: Routledge and Kegan Paul, 1960. p. 75

[19] Geoffrey Bullough, *Narrative and Dramatic Sources of Shakespeare*. Vol. III. London: Routledge and Kegan Paul. 1960. pp. 76-7

leggings laced on the outside, a short mantle reaching to the knee, or thereabouts, a close-cut cap, tight-fitting boots or buskins, long spurs, sword, dagger, breastplate, lance and other arms in the style of a man-at-arms . . . not only did she wear short tunics, but she dressed herself in tabards and garments open at the sides, besides the matter is notorious since when she was captured she was wearing a furcoat cloak of cloth of gold, open on all sides, a cap on her head, and her hair cropped round in man's style. And in general, having cast aside all womanly decency, not only to the scorn of feminine modesty, but also of well instructed men, she had worn the apparel and garments of most dissolute men, and in addition, had some weapons of defense.[20]

The description makes clear Joan's sumptuary 'presumptuousness'. This feature of her dress was not simply that she had adopted male dress, but that it had been well above her rank, and implied a transgression of order and hierarchy. By adopting male dress of a lavishness which signaled superior class and authority, Joan took upon herself a kind of visual authority which overrode her womanhood and her inferior class origins. As the charges against her show, both these functions of her dress were seen as a blatant and unforgivable challenge to social and political order. As Marina Warner puts it, "That a woman

---

[20] Marina Warner. *Joan of Arc: The Image of Female Heroism.* London: Weidenfeld & Nicolson, 1981. p. 143

contravened the destined subordination of her sex when she wore men's clothing underlies many of the prohibitions against it. Transvestism does not just pervert biology: it upsets the social hierarchy."[21] We can see that Joan was aware of this desirable effect, or at least that she was alert to the difficulties raised by discarding it, in the account of her conditions for reverting to female dress during her imprisonment (Warner p. 144). To bear arms was a privilege of rank, to wear cloth of gold was equally a privilege. To adopt both when not entitled to them by birth was to usurp rank. For a woman to adopt male dress was correspondingly to shift position in the social hierarchy; to move from subordination into equality with men. Joan of Arc did both. In anti-women tracts of the 16th and 17th centuries, both in England and in France, the adopting of male fashions by women figures was remarkably prominent. What is reiterated again and again is a sense of breakdown of order between class and sex. Phyllis Rackin, discussing Joan's transvestism, remarks:

> Joan's masculine dress, like the beards of the witches in *Macbeth*, is the sign of the uncanny. It associates sexual ambiguity with the dangers that lurk at the boundaries of the known, rationalized world of sexual difference, and exclusion constructed by patriarchal discourse, the inconceivable realities of female power and authority that threatened the idealized world

---

[21] Ibid. 147

of masculine longing constructed by Shakespeare's historical myths.[22]

Indeed, Joan's transvestism is the sign of 'the uncanny', which disrupts the social hierarchy and cultural boundaries. Interestingly, we have an example of the way in Owhich such anxieties about dress and degree occur, when Cleopatra reminisces about dressing. Antony in her tires and mantles.

> That time? O times!
> I laugh'd him out of patience; and that night
> I laugh'd him into patience; and next morn,
> Ere the ninth hour, I drunk him to his bed;
> Then put my tires and mantles on him, whilst
> I wore his sword Philippan. (*Antony and Cleopatra*, II. v. 18-23)

This passage explicitly foregrounds Cleopatra's transvestism as the core of her effeminizing power. Dressing the passive drunken Antony in her female clothing is represented as effeminizing Antony. Cleopatra insists that she will go to the wars not only in person, but will more specifically "appear there for a man" (III. Vii. 18). As Laura Levine has suggested, "the decision to allow Cleopatra to come to battle is dangerous not only because of Cleopatra's capacity to stimulate sexual appetite and appetite's

---

22 Phyllis Rackin, *Stages of history*, Ithaca & New York: Cornell UP, 1990. p. 200.

capacity to demilitarize [If we should serve with horse and mares together,/ The horse were merely lost; the mares would bear/ A soldier and his horse" (III. Vii. 7-9)], but also because of a more serious kind of transvestism it implies: a transvestism not of costumes but of roles, a transvestism based on adopting the behavior of the opposite sex." [23] Another example of anxiety about dress and degree can be found in *Henry VI part II*, when Queen Margaret characterizes the presumptuousness of the Duchess of Gloucester by means of the Duchess's dress and retinue.

Not all these lords do vex me half so much
As that proud dame, the Lord Pretector's wife
She sweeps it through the court with troops of ladies,
More like an empress than Duke Humphrey's wife
Strangers in court do take her for the queen:
She bears a duke's revenues on her back,
And in her heart she scorns our poverty.
Shall I not live to be aveng'd on her?
Contemptuous base-born callet as she is.
She vaunted 'amongst her minions o'other day,
The very train of her worst wearing gown
Was better worth than all my father's lands,

---

23   Laura Levine, *Men in Women's Clothing: Anti-theatricality and Effeminization, 1579-1642*, Cambridge: Cambridge UP. 1994, pp. 51-2. In this book, Laura Levine suggests that "the gendered body has no ontological status apart from the acts that create it, and male and female bodies are lacking an ontological status apart from the performances that create them."

Till Suffolk gave two dukedoms for his daughter.

(2 Henry VI, I. iii. 75-87)

In this passage, Queen Margaret complains bitterly that the Duchess of Gloucester is wearing dress above her rank. The Queen is conscious of the extreme social sensitivity about dress and feels threatened by the presumptuousness of the Duchess' dress. In this case, the Lord Protector's wife, Eleanor, is represented not as a gender crossdresser but as a class crossdresser. Yet her violations of status hierarchies, embodied in her sartorial splendor not befitting her station, are paralleled by her gender insubordination. Jean Howard remarks, "Refusing to obey her husband's commands that she be content with her status as his wife, she defies him and calls in Margery Jourdain, the witch, and Roger Bolingbrook, the conjurer, to give her the information about the king and other prominent members of the court that might further her ambitious plans." [24] The Duchess of Gloucester is represented as a virago by her language: "Were I a man, a duke, and next of blood/ I would remove these tedious stumbling-block/ And smooth my way upon their headless necks." (2 Henry VI. I. ii. 63-5). Her conjuration with Margery Jourdain and prophesying of the future might have been considered as the threat to the nation, considering the

---

[24] Jean E. Howrd, *The Stage and Social Struggle in Early Modern England*, London & New York: Routledge, 1994. p. 135.

Elizabethan political context in which it was widely believed that there were nation's enemies who threatened to do Elizabeth's horoscope to determine her date of death.[25] The Duchess of Gloucester's attempt to get prophecy can be interpreted as politically dangerous because it is likely to incite rebellion. Like Joan's case, the Duchess' connection with the witch signifies a dramatic occasion which reveals the witch as a threat to the state. As we can witness in the cases of Joan and the Duchess of Gloucester, the effort to reach beyond the cultural boundaries of class and gender through witchcraft and cross-dressing is represented as extremely diabolic and destructive. Furthermore, it is quite intriguing to note that the theatre took up the role to discover domestic enemies and foreign foes, and to expose them.

According to Jardine, "Dress, in the early modern period, was regulated by rank, not by income," but "at the same time, the wealthy but 'base-born' could flout the regulations and exploit the extreme social sensitivity about dress to score political points" The Duchess of Gloucester's lack of respect for the queen is demonstrated by her crossdressing, and the power of her own husband is foregrounded by the lavishness of her own dress. Elenor's sartorial presumptuousness foregrounds her political ambitions and represents her as a theatrical overreacher. She recounts a dream to her husband: "Methought I sate in seat of

25 Diane Purkiss, *The Witch in History: Early Modern and Twentieth-century Representations*, London and New York: Routledge, 1996, p. 191.

majesty/ In the cathedral church of Westminster,/ And in that chair where kings and queens were crown'd,/ Where Henry and Dame Margaret kneel'd to me,/ And on my head did set the diadem." (*2 Henry VI*. I. ii. 36-40). Her political ambition is reflected in her clothes and she exploits sartorial sensitivity to display the power of her own husband. It is intriguing to note that the conflict between the old, outgoing feudal order and the new mercantile order is mapped out in the Elizabethan preoccupation with dress and status. The historical background for this preoccupation can be explained through "the greater shifts in landownership (and hence in the composition of the peers of the realm) than any previous period in English history since the Norman Conquest" during the reign of Henry VIII and through "the new peers who set their faces most firmly against any further social mobility during the reign of Elizabeth."[26] In this political context, Elizabethan sumptuary legislation can be regarded as a significant control of real social power and influence. Jean Howard, discussing the cross-dressing and the gender struggle, remarks:

> Social mobility was a fact, its effects strikingly clear in an urban center such as London, and economic and cultural changes were creating tensions between a social order based on hierarchy and deference and one increasingly based on entrepreneurship and

---

[26] Ibid. p. 142

the social relationships attendant upon the emergence of early capitalism. In general, official social ideologies did not acknowledge such changes. Rather, enormous energy was devoted to revealing the "monstrous" nature of those who moved out of their places.[27]

In this context, control of dress for individuals and their households was seen as a significant control of real social power and influence. According to Baldwin's research, the earliest English sumptuary laws of which any record has been found were enacted by Parliament during the reign of Edward III, who came to the throne in the year 1327; the reign of Elizabeth marked the zenith of sumptuary legislation in England; a multitude of penal laws to restrain excess in apparel were repealed by James I.[28] Baldwin notes, "the 1597 sumptuary legislation stipulated that gold, silver and purple should be used only by the hereditary peerage, velvet as the mark of luxury for those who could only claim the rank of gentleman, and only knights and those above that rank were entitled to wear ornate arms or spurs.[29] If the

---

[27] Jean Howard, "Crossdressing, the Theatre, and Gender Struggle in Early Modern England" in *Shakespeare Quarterly* 39 (1988) p. 422. Refer also to Francis Barker. The Tremulous Private Body: Essays on Subjection, London: Methuen. 1984. pp. 31-3.

[28] Frances Elizabeth Baldwin, *Sumptuary Legislation and Personal Regulation in England.* In Johns Hopkins University Studies in *Historical and Political Science under the direction of the dept. of History, Political Economy, and Political Science,* volume XLIV. Baltimore: The Johns Hopkins University Press, 1926.

[29] Ibid. pp, 228-9

apparel is not appropriate to the status of the wearer, it is automatically perceived as grotesque and as a flouting of natural order and rank. Dress denotes difference in degrees for the Elizabethan. Thus, 'a woman clad in armour' must have been considered a whore during the time when there was an increase in the power of the husband and father over his wife and children through the support of both church and state for a reinforcement of the despotic authority of the husband and father.[30] The Renaissance defined women as male property, and required them to keep a closed mouth (silence), a closed body (chastity), and an enclosed life in the home.

According to Bakhtin, the differentiated habits of the Renaissance body can be classified into "grotesque body" and "classical body."[31] With regard to this idea of the body, Peter Stallybrass has noted that the grotesque body is "unfinished, outgrows itself, transgresses its own limits," while the classical body is, on the contrary, an image of something "finished, completed"[32] This conception of the body was transformed as a

---

[30] Lawrence Stone, *The Family, Sex and Marriage in England 1500-1800*. London: Penguin, 1977, pp. 109-146. Refer also to Jonathan Goldberg, "Family Authority" in Rewriting the Renaissance, M. Ferguson et al. Chicago & London: Chicago UP, 1986. pp. 3-32.

[31] Bakhtin, *Rabelais and His World*, Bloomingtin: Indiana UP, 1984. pp. 303-67.

[32] Peter Stallybrass, "Patriarchal Territories: The Body Enclosed" in *Rewriting the Renaissance: The Discourses of Sexual Difference in Early Modern Europe*, Chicago and London: Chicago UP, 1986, p, 124.

locus of gender struggle in connection with cross-dressing in Renaissance England. As Jardine points out, "the individual who adopts dress too elevated for his or her station in life is automatically to be perceived as grotesque — or so the committed supporter of the status quo would have it.[33] For Jean Howard, "crossdressing as fact and as idea threatened a normative social order based upon strict principles of hierarchy and subordination," and therefore "the subversive or transgressive potential of this practice was recuperated in a number of ways." [34] In the early modern period the regulation of dress was part of this apparatus for producing and marking gender difference. At the same time, the worries about the unruly crossdressed woman going beyond her sex and class are signs that early modern England was not only permeated by social mobility and unsettling economic change, but by considerable instability in the gender system as well.

The relationship between cross-dressing and theatricality, and the ways in which clothing constructs and deconstructs gender and gender differences are not esoteric in modern culture. For Garber, "the binarism of male/female, one apparent ground of distinction between this and that, him and me, is itself put in question or under erasure in transvestism, and a transvestite

---

[33] Lisa Jardine, p. 146.

[34] Jean E. Howard. "Crossdressing, The Theatre, and Gender Struggle in Early Modern England" in *Shakespeare Quarterly* 39 (1988). p. 418.

figure, or a transvestite mode, will always function as a sign of overdetermination and a mechanism of displacement from one blurred boundary to another." Hence, one of the most significant characteristics of cross-dressing is the way in which it disrupts the easy notions of binarity. Transvestism problematizes the categories of "female" and "male", whether they are essential or constructed, biological or cultural. This category crisis, according to Lacan, is the crisis of the symbolic order which is the register of language, hierarchy, law, and power—the world out there to which the human subject must come to relate not only through one-to-one or face-to-face dyads but through immersion in the codes and constraints of culture. Fredric Jameson writes, "The Symbolic order restructures the Imaginary by introducing a third term into the hitherto infinite regression of the duality of the latter's mirror images." With regard to identity crisis, the spectre of transvestism and the uncanny intervention of the transvestite, and cone to mark and indeed to overdetermine the space of anxiety about fixed and changing identities.

Transvestism has been located at the juncture of "class" and "gender" and increasingly through its agency gender and class are revealed to be commutable, if not equivalent. Stephen Greenblatt has suggested that the transvestite is the space of anxiety and desire in which "an improvisational self-fashioning that longs for self-effacement and reabsorption in the community" can take place. He writes:

We should add that the unique qualities of Roasalind's identity —those that give Rosalind her independence, her sharply etched individuality—will not, as Shakespeare conceives the play, endure: they are bound up with exile, disguise, and freedom from ordinary constraint, and they will vanish, along with the playful chaffing, when the play is done. What begins as a physiological necessity is reimagined as an improvisational self-fashioning that longs for self-effacement and reabsorption in the community. This longing is the sign of a social system that marks out singularity, particularly in women, as prodigious, though the disciplining of singularity is most often represented in Shakespearean comedy as romantic choice, an act of free will, an expression of love.

It is remarkable that his notion of culural anxiety foregrounds and articulates the social system that marks out singularity particularly in women as prodigious, and revaluates the space which is denied by ordinary constraint and oppression. However, he underestimates this singularity in women by asserting that Rosalind's unique qualities—her capacity for becoming or constrcting Ganymede—will not endure, will vanish when the pla is done. With regard to Greenblatt's contention, Majorie Garber has noted that "the vanishing will happen to Rosalind and Orlando and all the rest of the dramatis personae whoa re part of how "Shakespeare conceives the play"" and pointed out that "What lingers—like the smile of the Cheshire Cat—is precisely that residue, that supplement: Ganymede." When discussing

Rosalind's cross-dressing, she remarks:

In returning dress as a woman, she allows for the possibility of a recuperative interpretation (of which Greenblatt's is a very subtle and powerful version) that suggests a transformed woman now "reabsorbed" into the community and thus capable of "vanishing." Rosalind, according to this repuperative fantasy, has finished her job of education and self-instruction (Greenblatt calls if "improvisation", but it it is clearly very temporary indeed), and can now take up her wifely role. . . . Here, then, is the paradox. Only by looking at the transvestite on the stage, in the literary text, can we see clearly that he or she is not there. Only by regarding Ganymede not as other version of Rosalind but as constructs that have a subjectivity and an agency, can we understand something of his relation to narcissism, desire, and possibility.

Crossdressing is a phenomenon that throws into crsis the binary opposition cultures set up between men and women, and the cultural imperative to be either one or the other. Indeed, when we look at transvestism, what we perceive is a breach of convention that throws into relief the conventionality not merely of male and female dress but of masculinity and femininity themselves.

Transvestism has subversive and transgressive potential against a normative social order and gender binary in modern culture as well as in Elizabethan society. Readings of the past are motivated by present concerns and involve taking a position within present critical debates. The way we reproduce tha past in the present is influenced by different investments, perspecties and positions, hence we construct our own past and present by asserting our relation to the society. Intriguingly, "it is virtually impossible today to pick up a newspaper or turn on the television or go to the movies without encountering the question of sartorial gender bending." The question of transvestism in modern culture. I think, consist in subverting the oppressive institutionalized binarity such as class, gender, sexuality, and erotic style. By transgressing dress codes which are precise indicators of gender and degree, it is possible to foreground and problematize culture boundaries and hierarchical strategies of gender and class. In *The Postmodern Condition,* Lyotard discusses in detail "the question of knowledge" and "the problem of its legitimation" in so-called advanced societies by what he sees as "a collaspe of the Great Narratives." For Craig Owens, not only is the status of narrative in question but also that of "representation," specifically man's androcentric representation of the world in which he has constructed himself as subject. Thus, "the increasing emphasis on the androgynous figure in popular culture (Madonna, Michael Jackson, Boy George) and the woman/man in the cinema (*Victor/Victoria, Tootsie, Yentl, The Crying Game*)" can be explained through "the post-modern fascination with the androgyne, the 'neuter' subject", and "breaking down boundaries"

This is not just a postmodern phenomenon, for cults of the androgyne have occurred throughout history.

In 16C England, the authorities became so concerned with the fashion in women's clothing and hairstyle that they passed law forbidding gender confusion of this kind. For example, Elizabeth's sumptuary proclamation of August 3, 1597 blamed the inordinate excess in apparel for a falling off in hospitality, for an increase in crime, and for the confusion of degree. In this case, cultural fear about the general social change is related to the anxiety the change of women's dregs, which reflects the social pursuit for order and stability. With regard to this, Elizabeth Harvey suggests that "what the society most fears, especially a culture rent asunder by epistemological, religious, and economic shifts that undermine its foundational certainties, is displaced onto the female body, where it its contained as the stable locus of unknowability." There is nothing ingerently subversive about transvestite ventriloquism, but it has the radical potential to expose the contingency of gender, opening cultural discourse to the voices it otherwise marginalizes and silences.

In the *Hic Mulier Haec-Vir* dispute (1620), transvestism is so well articulated and foregrounded that we can grasp the representation of crossdressing in Elizabethan and Jocobean culture. The title page of the anonymous *Hic Mulier: or The Man-Woman* shows one woman being itted with a man's plumed hat, which she admires in a mirror: another woman awaits, in a baber's chair, the shearing of her lock. In *Hic Mulier*, the speaker's derision specifically targets ornamentation, cosmetics, particular items of dress, and hair styles, and the carrying of weapons:

From the first you got the false armoury of yellow Starch (for to weare yellow on white, or white vpon yellow, is by the rules of Heraldry) basenesse, bastardie, and indignitie; the folly of imitation, the deceitfulnesse of flatterie, and the grosest basenesse of all basenesse, to do whatsoeuer a greater power will command you. From the other, you haue taken the monstrousnesse of your deformitie in apparell, exchanging the modest attire of the comely Hood, Cawle, Coyfe, handsome Dress or Kerchiefe, to the cloudy Ruffianly broad-brim'd Hat, and wanton Feather, the modest vpper parts of a concealing straight gowne to the loose, lasciuious open embracement of a French dublet, being all vnbutton'd to entyce, all of one shape to hide deformitie, and extreme short wasted to giue a most to hide deformitie, and extreme short wasted to giue a most easie way to euery luxurious action: the glory of a faire large hayre, to the shame of most ruffianly short lockes; the side. thicke-gather'd, and close guarding Sauegards, to the short, weake, thinne loose, and euery hand-entertaining short basses; for Needles, Swords; for Prayer bookes, bawdy ligs; for modest gestures, gyant-like behauiours, and for womens modestie, all Mimicke and apish inciuilitie: These are your founders, from these you tooke your copies, and (without amendment) with these you will come to pertition.

The terms of abuse contrast the immutable essence of woman with the historical and cultural vicissitude of fashion, thus linking fashion with the dangers of change. The problematic mature of the transvestism both pictorial and discusive, is that it it "hermaphroditic," for it depicts a female body beneath male attire, and it figures women "partaking of male privilege and engaging in male pursuits." Harvey argues that " the fear that is voiced in *Hic Mulier* is that costume will become essence, that women will really turn into men, but the threat registered in the disturbing representations of gender hybridism is a more fundamental threat of ambiguity, of sexual indeterminacy." However, in *Haec-Vir*, or *The Womanish Man* which answered *Hic Mulier* one week later by another anonymous writer, the Man-Woman proclaims that:

He is much iniurious that so baptiz'd vs: we are as free-borne as Men, haue as free election, and as free spirits, we are compounded of like parts, and may with like liberty make benefit of our Creations: my countenance shall smile on the worthy, and frowne on the ignoble, I will heare the Wise, and bee deafe to Ideots, guie counsell to my friend, but bee dumbe to flatteres, I haue hands that shall be liberall to reward desert, feete that shall moue switly to do good offices, and thoughts that shall euer accompany freedome and seuerity. If this bee barbarous let me leaue the Citie, and liue with creature of like simplicity.

The difficulty, the challenge and the interest of transvestism lie in combating the oppressive effects of institutionalized binarity, manifested in such loci as class, gender, sexuality, and erotic style. Transvestism represents a transgressvie effort to disrupt the institutionalized binarity. By transgressing dress codes, which ar e precise indicators of status and degree, it is possible to disrupt entrenched cultural boundaries and social hierarchical strategies of gender and class. It is a transgression which may open a greater space for woman's speech and action.

2. Witches and Assertive Women: Queen Margaret and Lady Grey

As soon as Joan disappeared from the stage, or more accurately as soon as she lost her power and fell prey ot the Duke of York, her true successor, the 'scourage of England,' Margaret of Anjou turned up. (1 Henry VI, V. iii.) It is no accident that as one captured French 'enchantress' is led off as a prisoner, another, her direct successor, is led on as a 'prisoner'. Margaret, future wife of Henry VI, is described as an ideal woman for the king by Suffolk. (V. v. 68-72) The quality of courage and undaunted spirit exceeding women is represented as a positive aspect for the issue of a king, but it is not long before we realize that the positive interpretation can be made only by the man who became instantly mesmerized by her (V iii). A strong opposition against thet marriage of Henry VI and Margaret is raised frome the Duke of Gloucester and Exeter in terms of land and money which is the most important factor in the marriage of nobles and kings. In spite of that, "the breaking of Henry's betrothal" to the daughter of the Earl of Armagnac "is justified ironically in terms of disparagement," that is , "marrying the ward downwards in the social class structure." Suffolk prevailed with the king by his logic that "A poor Earl's daughter' is not a fit match for Henry: Margaret's father is 'King of Naples and Jerusalem,' is meaningless, and her father an impoverished nobody." To the king who is much more feudal-minded that mercantile-minded, this logic of Suffolk might have been more convincing than the dowry itself. But this royal marriage is an investment in a lineal future for England, and thus has a public identity from the start and a place in the power structure. Within this matrix, Henry's decision can be considered indiscreet as Exeter puts it cynically, "Beside, his[the Earl of Armagnac's] wealth doth warrant a liberal dower/ where Reignier sooner will receive that give." To make matters worse, King Henry commanded to gather up a tenth from the people for the expenses of the marriage which will be the blight and seed of resentment for the commoner.

2 *Henry VI* opens on the intimate meeting of Margaret of Anjou Henry. Henry is ravished by her sight and her speech of wisdom. But Gloucester is grieved and angry from the fact that this marriage should entail the surrender of Anjou and Maine, 'the key of Normandy,'for which the nobles had fought so long. Also by the

fact that his own arrangement of a marriage between Henry and the daughter of the Earl of Armagnac has been set aside. Thus, the marriage which was arranged as the public symbol of truce between France and England cause England to lose a substantial amount of land and aroused the domestic feud which will be deepened by the Civil War. Even though Margaret is the object of truce, she does not respond in a passive way as Katherine did in *Henry V.* Instead of that, she shows more political mind that Henry and after she has had enough time to become aware of Henry's character and of the factious sate of the nobility, she takes the initiative to perform the function of the strong leader of a nation. in act I scene iii, when a suitor begins his supplication with the phrase 'under the wings of our protector's grace' she violenty tears the supplication and commands to begin his suits anew and sue to the king. That is the commencement of the representation of her domineering character which is sharply contrasted with her husband who typically weeps, prays, or entreats rather than commands. She is the woman who broke silence and found a voice, but she should pray a high price for the privilege of being heard. It is inevitably clear that she was condemned because her political sence overrode the principles of female reticence and obedience. She is condemned simply by a metaphor that she has a "tiger's heart wrapped in a woman's hide," or by a phrase that women are soft, mild, pitiful, and flexible/Thou stern, obdurate, flinty, rough, remorseless." In the above accusation, gender difference is presupposed and it its taken for granted that women should be tender, nurturing, and compassionate, while men should be aggressive, cruel, and tyrannical. It is unquestionably thought in terms of men and women, male and female, not as similar members of a single species, but as very different creatures, subject to different needs and desires, capable of different kinds of action and judged by different standards. Thus, any female who attempts to exercise authority and to show physical prowess is branded as 'unnatural' and 'subversive,' because she threatens the system of differences which gives meaning to patriarchy. The techniques of patriarchal discourse and subversive potentiality of women can be foregrounded through the conflict between the Renaissance fear and condemnation of strong women and the transgressive power of those eloquent women against that condemnation.

Another case of an audacious woman in *Henry VI* is that of Lady Grey. Lady Grey's faal marriage' with king Edward IV involves, like Henry's (1 Henry IV, V.v., 2 Henry VI, I.i), a breach of faith besides the aggravation of civil dissension resulting from the disgrace of Warwick and the alienation of France. In spite of this civil dissension, it is clear that Edward IV is immediately mesmerized by the looks and words of the widow, Lady Grey, at their fist meeting (3 Henry VI, III, ii). He ridiculously and abruptly asks how many children she has while her suit is being considered which is about the repossessing of those lands lost during the civil war. She is a widow and she has three children but she has no financial capability because her husband's land has been seized by the conqueror after her husband was slain at St. Albans field. Thus, there is no alternative other than to make a suit to the king, and it that context, the king imposes his will that unless she marries him she shall not have her husband's land. The only way to live is to remarry. This anecdote can be historically endorsed by the fact that in the 16-17C, "in spite of the church's emphasis on the chastity of widows" and the teaching that they "should remain true to the loving memory of the man they married with God's blessing, the widows of wealthy men were married off again with quite undignified haste where those responsible for them considered it financially advantageous to the line to do so." In Lawrence Stone's book. An *Elizabethan: Sir Horatio Palavicino,* we can see that kind of pressed remarriage in Lady Anne who was one the wife of Sir Horatio Palavicino and after his death was obliged to remarry Oliver Cromwell, which was inextricably relate with succession and administration of lands and money. As this anecdote makes clear, 'family', particularly for the nobly born, came first and foremost in the 16th and 17th centuries, and within it the individual played an extremely small part. Intriguingly and naturally, after Lady Grey's remarriage with Edward IV, her family, particularly her brother and her sons, could take much advantage of their marriage.

In both cases, the two pairs' 'fatal marriages' are represented as strong factors which aggravate the civil dissension and are considered as unfit matches because of the women's inferior rantk and inferior financial state. It is feasible that through the representation of these marriages, male anxiety imputes the historical crisis to the fatal female whom they regard as devastating to the mand and society. The society represented throughout the *Henry VI* plays is one in which that paternal inheritance becomes a license to kill. In young Clifford's vow to avenge his father, which justifies and sets the tone for the rigidly schematic series of father-son murders to follow, lineal succession becomes identified with vengeance and slaughter. Thus reverence for the father now sanctions not order but anarchy. In these plays, the shadow of the male and of masculine identity is so string that it is to become the dominant motif. Arguably, these relationships of father-son bonds are represented as ideal, and they are elevated through fictive stories such as the death of Talbot and his son John. On the contrary, those unfit marries are represented as extremely fatal to the future of England. The prejudices are presumably deeply linked with male anxieties about their own political performance and with the Renaissance imagination which inflicts humiliation upon strong women. It is clear that those systems of difference were believed in and the narrowing of the difference was feared during the Renaissance period. Thus, male anxieties about the disruption of difference brought in the mass-scale burning and torture of women who were branded as witches and the persecution of crossdressed women who they thought disrupted social hierarchy and erased cultural binaries. Indeed, the infinite variety of patriarchal discourse inscribed disorderly or rebellious women as witches and contained those viragos through the projection of exaggerated patriarchal fears and the punishment of those rebellious women. However, the repercussion of the subversive female was not completed, because the witches and the devilish crossdressed women were transformed into the heroines of history.

3. Witch and Transformation

Perhaps he recent revival of interest in the *Henry VI trilogy*, particularly part I, owes something to the growing concern with witches. Historical definitions of the witch agree in finding her essentially a woman in some way challenges the role attributed to her by nature, that is, what males perceive to be nature. In *Henry VI part I*, Joan of Arc is condemned as fiend, witch and whore, and the mose usual term applied to her is 'unnatural.' Female who attempt to incorporate the masculine principle, to exercise authority, to show physical prowess, to kill, inevitably fall into whore or witch identification. And La Pucelle is exactly the case of someone who is placed outside and beyond the system of differences which defines and delimits men and women. Catherine

Belsey's suggestion that witches were usually voluble can be endorsed through the characteristics of Scottish witches who were described in terms of volubility in Christina Larner's eminent book *Enemies of God*. Larner remarks: "the essential individual personality trait does seem to have been that of a ready, sharp, and angry tongue. . . . The richness of language attributed to witches is considerable." These women show themselves to be discursively active and mobile. Allotted a subject-position in a familiar discourse, they seize it eagerly and sometimes eloquently. Indeed, enjoined to silence, women have no position from which to define their own being. Catherine Belsey remarks:

The supreme opportunity to speak was the moment of execution. The requirement for confession from the scaffold, so that the people could see ho church and state combined to protect them from the enemies of God and society, paradoxically also offer women a place from which to speak in public with a hitherto unimagined authority which was not diminished by the fact that it was demonic.

It is not impossible to observe that kind of paradox in Joan's case. Joan begins her confession on the scaffold and English soldiers attempt to blacken her reputation by concentrating on the charge of sexual aggressiveness(*1 Henry VI. V. iv*). She confesses; "I am with child, ye bloody homicides./Murder not then the fruit within my womb," and she concludes by crying "Oh, give me leave, I hate deluded you./'Twas neither Charles nor yet the

Duke I named/ But Reignier, King of Naples, that prevailed." She attempts to save herself from execution by a last desperate appeal to pregnancy. Her confession legitimately and instantly offers the persecutor the authority to burn her, stigmatizing her as an incorrigible strumpet and liar. Through the techniques of confession and the subsequent establishment of a system of legitimate knowledge, the great machinery of repression is inscribed on the concrete female body. According to Foucault, "the singular ritual of obligatory and exhaustive confession" "was the first technique for producing the truth of sex" "in the Christian West" It is clear that this technique is closely connected with the long history of the Christian and juridical confession and with the shifts and transformations of knowledge-power. But the knowledge of a subject is a knowledge not so much of his form, but of that which divides him, determines him perhaps, but above all causes him to be ignorant of himself. Thus, the proliferation of these devices is capable not only of stimulating and provoking the discourse but also of producing formidable pleasure of analysis.

Despite all of the blackmails, Joan of Arc attains her fame as an object of adoration and a saint in history. As Fiedler notes, the historical figure of "Joan remains an object of adoration, however heterodox; the honourable ist of her admirers comes immediately to mind: Friedrich Schiller, Bernard Shaw, Jean Anouih, Eugene Sue, and Mark Twain, dissenters in a Protestant or post-Protestant culture" The transformation of Joan can be endorsed through Foucault's discourse on 'thee spectacle of the scaffold.' in which he proes that a convicted criminal could become a sort of saint after his death. He writes of the case of Tanguy, executed in Brittany about 1740.

The criminal has been almost entirely tramsformed into a positive hero. There were those for whom glory and abomination were not dissociated, but coexisted in a reversible figure. Perhaps we should see this literature of crime, which proliferated around a few exemplary figures, neither as a spontaneous form of 'popular expression' nor as a concerted programme of propaganda and moralization, it was a locus in which two investments of penal practice met—a sort of battleground the crime, its punishment and its memory.

In the same way, as patriarchy seeks to deny women's power, their demonization of women endows the strong women with a supernatural prowess. The patriarchal deployment of witchcraft paradoxically provided ordinary people and vulnerable subordinate groups with a meas of perceiving power. Also the style and content of witches' confessions articulated and foregrounded the discourse of hegemony, which was made possible by the transformation of the dominated group into the heroines of history. It is intriguing to observe the way in which the witches' ransgressive body and transvestism are closely intersected with each other, and finally with the project of nation-building. As we examined through the *Henry VI* plays, the representation of the witch as a national threat was a reflection off political anxiety which was prevalent in the Elizabethan regime, and the theatre functioned as a secret agency which discovered and exposed inside and outside enemies. The damnation and punishment of Joan and the Duchess of Gloucester as witches in the theatre may have relieved the queen's regime which was seriously in crisis and also given the audience dramatic relief. In Joan's case, her demonisation was certainly a scapegoating that pandered to the anti-French prejudices of English audiences, of Shakespeare's contemporaries. Her burnig in act 5 is a climax to turn audiences into a mob with a propensity for collective violence. It is not harsh to say that Joan's crime lies with English prejudices and the theatre has collaborated with the audience in rewriting Joan's history.

6
장
—

The Female Body and the Political Economy of Sex: *Richard III, Henry V,* and *Richard II*

1. The Political Economy of Sex

The parallel construction of the female body and the political economy of sex is represented in which characters are negotiating and struggling for power. The female body and sexuality can be deployed by various power strategies which manoeuvre and inscribe their ideological positions. The relation between erotic desire and the construction of male and female subjectively in the power relations. The masculine perspective of desire toward female bodies is so inextricably intertwined with the questions of subjectivity and power that the issues of sexuality cannot be separated from cultural and political power. For Valerie Traub, "sexuality . . . embodies . . . a power relation, not only for those members of erotic minorities who are positioned so as to feel most overtly the effects o institutionalised oppression, but for all sexual subjects (perhaps most insidiously for those who do not recognize the extent to which they are ideologically incited to act/ think/ fantasise erotically in prescribed ways)." Sexuality exists in all cultures and its significance lies in reproduction, ritual, instrument for pleasure, locus of self-discipline, mode of symbolic of political exchange, and key to identity. Considering sexuality in the mode of political exchange would be intriguing particularly because the female body is inscribed as territory and property in the political exchanges of women between men. Considered in its social and anthropological aspect, the traffic in women and the political economy of sex can be an illuminating example of the trope of sexuality and power. Francis Barker suggests that "Whether positive representation or symptomatic clue, sexuality is a cultural and political force in the text, and one associated both with what is allowed as challenging the master-discourse and with what is figured as the popular underside of the erstwhile sovereign rule of the king." Sexuality is an empty construct, a kind of power vacuum which is formulated and influenced by class, gender, and racial location. Erotic desire is, in itself, "an ideological vacuum that is also a domain of power," and "the erotic body is a material site for inscriptions of ideology and power" The parallel construction of the female body and the political economy of sex has been observed specifically by Claude Levi-Strauss, Gayle Rubin, and Luce Irigaray. By these critics, the exchange of women is articulated and interrogated in a social and anthropological aspect as an instrument for security and alliances. The exchange can also be foregrounded by an idiosyncratic and exegetical reading of the traffic in women.

Levi-Strauss remarks: "the prohibition of incest is only the group's assertion that where relationships between the sexes are concerned, a person cannot do just what he pleases. The positive aspect of the prohibition is the initiation of organisation." In the exchange of women, the prohibition of incest is based upon a rule of reciprocity in which prohibition is instituted only in order to guarantee and establish an exchange. For Levi-Strauss, "This skillful game of exchange consists in a complex totality of conscious or unconscious manoeuvres in order to gain security and to guard oneself against risks brought about by alliances and by rivalries." In this context, the female body is merely the conclusion to an uninterrupted process of reciprocal gift which transforms hostility to alliance, anxiety to confidence, fear to friendship. Thus, it is not difficult to articulate that women are functioning only as the object in the exchange. Levi-Strauss points out in the discussion of marriage that:

The total relationship of exchange which constitutes marriage is not established between a man and a woman, where each owes and receives something, but between two groups of men, and the woman figures only as one of the objects on the exchange, not as one of the partners between whom that exchange takes place. This remains true even when the girl's feelings are taken into consideration, as, moreover, is usually the case. In acquiescing to the proposed union, she participates or allows the exchange to take place; she cannot alter its nature. This view must be kept in all strictness, even with regard to our own society, where marriage appears to be a contract between persons.

The structural exchange of women which constitutes marriage is accomplished between two groups of men, and women are positioned structurally, whether they are conscious of it or not, as the objects of exchange. For Gayle Rubin, the gift-giving of primitive society is a means of trust, solidarity, and mutual aid. She takes the example of the Trobriand Islands' exchange of women: "In the Trobriand Islands, each household maintains a garden of yams and each household eats yams. But the yams a household grows and the yams it eats are not the same. At harvest time, a man sends the yams he has cultivated to the household of his sister, the household in which he lives is provisioned by his wife's brother." This example shows that patriarchal heterosexuality deploys the traffic in women, which is the use of women as exchangeable, perhaps symbolic, property for the primary purpose of cementing the bonds of men with men. Kinship systems are made up of, and reproduce, concrete forms of socially organized sexuality. Rubin agrees with Levi-Strauss on the respect that Levi-Strauss interprets incest taboo as an ideology imposed upon the biological events of sex and procreation by the social aim of exogamy and alliance. It is women who are transacted as a conduit of a relationship between men, and it is men who give and take them as gifts for reciprocity. In the exchange of women, the ultimate locus of women's oppression is located within the traffic in women and within social systems rather than within the traffic in merchandise and within biology. It is certainly not difficult to define that "the political economy of sex has implied the conversion of female lives into marriage alliances, the conversion of female labour into male wealth, the contribution of marriage to political power, and the transformations which all of these varied aspect of society have undergone." Under this structure, women exist only as the possibility of mediation, transaction, and transference between man and his fellow-creatures.

Luce Irigaray, in her feminist rewriting of Levi-Strauss, argues that Western patriarchal culture is organized and subtended by the exchange of women, who function as commodities to be passed between men. Within the social context, women have value only as they facilitate among men. She writes:

> For woman is traditionally a use-value for man, an exchange value among men; in other words, a commodity. As such, she

remains the guardian of material substance, whose price will b established, in terms of the standard of their work and of their need/desire, by "subjects": workers, merchants, consumers. Women are marked phallically by their father, husbands, procurers. And this branding determines their value in sexual commerce. Woman is never anything but the locus of a more or less competitive exchange between two men.

She focuses on a nature of society which is based upon the exchange of women, and argues that without the exchange of women society would all back into the anarchy of that natural world and the randomness of the animal kingdom. Men's socio-cultural endogamy requires and exploits the participation of women, but it excludes women from the benefits of trade. Hence, as Irigaray suggests, "women's role as fetish-objects in exchanges is the manifestation and the circulation of a power of the Phallus, and it established the relationships of men with each other." The power of the Phallus can be endorsed through the assignment of roles in the economy, that some are given the role of producing and exchanging subjects, while others are assigned the role of productive earth and goods. Irigaray asserts that "women, signs, goods, currency, all pass from one man to another or suffer the penalty of relapsing into the incestuous and exclusively endogamous ties that would paralyse all commerce." Just as goods can only enter into relations under the surveillance of their guardians, women can go to the market only under the guardianship of the exchanging subject. Thus, it would be out of the question for women to profit from their own value, to talk to each other, without the manoeuvring of the subjects.

Through the discourse of Levi-Strauss, Rubin, and Irigaray, it can be seen that sexuality is not an ahistorical form but a sensitive register for delineating relationships of power and meaning. It offers tools for making graphically intelligible the play of desire and identification by which individual negotiate with their societies for empowerment. It is certainly not difficult to find ethnographic and historical examples of trafficking in women. Women are objective in marriage, taken in battle, exchanged for favours, sent as tribute, traded, bought, and sold. Furthermore, far from being limited to the primitive world, these practices seem only to become more sophisticated and commercialized in more civilized societies.

Based on these theoretical assertions, I will deal with specific representation of the exchange of women in Shakespeare's plays. In particular, the wooing scenes of *Richard III* and *Henry V* will be focused on in section II, because they delineate quite dramatic and significant relationship between power and sexuality. Sexuality functions as a conduit for the consolidation of alliance and friendship, and women's body as a locus of negotiation. In the wooing scenes, I will foreground and interrogate the political economy of sex and the homosocial exchange of women between men. In addition to that, the cult of the Virgin Queen will be investigated as an actual political representation of the exchange of women. Queen Elizabeth's physical body is inscribed as territory and deployed as an image and an embodiment of golden time of the Tudor period. This religious cult suggests a mystical identification of the inviolate female body of the monarch with the unbreached body of her land. At the same time, it affirms the exchange of women through the inscription of women's body as territory.

Through an analysis of images of the maternal body in *Richard II,* section III contrasts the articulation of feminine value with the exchange of feminine imagery which is inscribed for the validation of national glory and unification. Feminine imagery of fertility and procreation is deployed to glorify England, in its state of unity by Richard and Gaunt. However, the whole exchange of metaphor is interrogated and problematised by the disparity between metaphor and the reality, that is, the contradiction between the affluent images of femininity and the real emptiness and sterility of female existence in its substance. Besides, as a counter-discourse to male-dominated misogynistic discourse, the positive and active maternal voice embodied in Queen Isabel and the Duchess of York will be examined to reveal particular feminine experience and values.

2. The Female Erotic Body in *Richard III*, *Henry V*, and Virgin Queen Cult

[1] *Richard III*

The instrumentation of sexuality is particularly represented through the demonisation of female characters and inscription of the resources of misogyny. Whether it is anthropological or historical, the traffic in women is the locus in which male desire and anxiety for empowerment are inscribed and the female body is inextricably transformed into property and territory. For example, Richard's wooing of Lady Anne (*Richard* III.I.ii.) is a representative case for discursive proof of the exchange of woman and inscription of male ideology on the concrete female body. It is one of the most strange scenes in *Richard III,* and it is strange not only because it takes place across the coffin of her murdered father-in-law, but also because she changes so quickly without any convincing reason. Because of her abrupt transition from the curse against the horrible Richard III to the falling in love with him, the actress, Ellen Terry remarked that Anne is a study in female weakness: "in her one short scene with Richard, she sees him, rails at him, spits on him, then falls into his arms like a ripe plum"[1] But in this strange scene, Anne's weakness should be considered in connection with Richard's calculatedly powerful

---

[1] Judith Cook, *Women in Shakespeare*, London: Harrap, 1980. p. 74.

language and his sadistic pleasantry. His demonic skill in manoeuvring Anne is manifest; she serves as an object lesson of Richard's power to dominate even those implacably his enemies. However, Marguerite Waller suggests that "the speaking, writing, knowing subject of the discourse of knowledge does not itself escape its violent rhetorical origins and its own status as a linguistic artifact precludes the possibility of its serving as the ground of meaning and being."[2] The violence of language underwrites all moral and aesthetic judgement and the illusoriness of language evades what literariness suggests or seems to promise. By foregrounding a certain violence implicit in Richard's rhetoric, Waller argues that "Richard is seduced by the dream of a commom language in which the radical potential of heteronomy is suppressed."[3] Indeed, this scene does not simply display Richard's brilliance and his rhetorical power, but foregrounds and interrogates the insatiable need of such a sovereign subject to set up for itself an exchange of women.

The ideological character of Richard's wooing is dramatically revealed in his contemptuous misogynistic remarks on Queen Elizabeth and Mistress Shore (I. I. 62-5, 76-83): "Why, this it is, when men are rul'd by women: / 'Tis not the King that sends you

---

[2] Marguerite Waller, "Usurpation, Seduction, and the Problemarics of the Proper: A "Deconstructive," "Feminist" Rereading of the Seduction Richard and Anne in Shakespeare's *Richard III*." in *Rewriting the Renaissance*, Margaret W. Ferguson et al., Chicago and London: Chicago UP, 1986. pp. 159-60.

[3] Ibid. p. 161.

to the Tower;/ My Lady Grey,[4] his wife, Clarence, 'tis she/ That tempers him to this extremity" (62-5); "Humbly complaining to her deity/ Got my Lord Chamberlain his liberty./ I'll tell you what: I think it is our way,/ If we will keep in favour with the King,/ To be her men, and wear her liverty./ The jealous o'er-worn widow and herself,/ Since that our brother dubb'd them gentlewomen,/ Are mighty gossips in our monarchy" (76-83). His idiosyncratic and exegetical explanation is that since he cannot prove a lover he is determined to prove a villain, and hate the idle pleasures of those days. Considering his strong abomination of women, his sudden change of attitude toward women in the case of Anne can be inevitably interpreted as a politically ambitious plan, which is represented in his soliloquy: "For then I'll marry Warwick's youngest daughter/. . . . The which will I, not all so much for love/ As for another secret close intent,/ By marrying her which I must reach unto." (I. I. 153; 157-59). Richard's motive here is obscure, and one of the most plausible reasons is that the Earl of Warwick is the 'king-maker' and Anne is the younger of his two daughters (3 *Henry VI.* V. ii.). We cannot chase the most deep secret of his heart, but a certain sign of political ambition is implied in his wooing of Anne. An exchange of woman is quite apparent in this scene in the sense that Richard chose Anne because she is Warwick's daughter and he wanted a political

---

[4] His naming of her shows that he refuses to acknowledge her as queen.

alliance through this marriage. Marriage renders woman as a gift for seeking solidarity, friendship, and alliance. In this context, Anne is merely an object of a political discourse and an ideological vacuum which is doomed with an inscription of Richard's powerful ideology.

However, moral accusation and judgement are likely to be put on Lady Anne because she so easily succumbed to Richard who is implacably her enemy. Moreover, it happened in front of her father-in-law's and her husband's coffins. But I think we have to consider that this is the moment when her existential crisis is extremely climaxed, on the ground that her life is totally uprooted not only on the political level but also on the personal level. Her dispossessed condition is revealed when she defines herself as "Poor Anne,/ Wife to thy Edward, to thy slaughtered son" (I. ii. 9-10). When she is articulating this, the realities are not figural or allegorial indicators but the literal embodiments of authority. Waller notes that implicit in Anne's account is "a kind of double focus in which woman's position and identity are thought of as derivative, and therefore in some sense representative, of a male position, while a woman is also supposed to possess a kind of autonomous subjectivity."[5] Woman's position as derivative from and representative of a male position can be well-observed when Anne extended the harm she wished to Richard to his wife, if he

---

[5] Marguerite Waller, "Usurpation, Seduction, and the Problematics of the Proper," in *Rewriting the Renaissance*, p. 171

should ever have one: "If ever he have wife, let her be made/ More miserable by the life of him/ Than I am made by my young lord and thee[Henry VI]" (I. ii. 26-8). Anne manages to serve as a testimonial to Richard's manipulative talents and is still represented as a powerful, power-giving figure by Richard. Anne's sense of her own power over herself is increased by Richard's encouragement, which reaches its apotheosis when Richard offers her his sword and encourages her to kill him. Anne is encouraged to think of herself as author and director of the situation, even though she is dependent upon Richard's sense of authorship. She accepted an illusory autonomy and reasserted her autonomy that is doomed to be seized upon by Richard as an abjective, external indicator of his power. Richard's misogynistic ideology and the instrumentality of sexuality are implicitly predicated in the language he employs and the image he provokes during the wooing of Anne. Richard deploys and foregrounds sensual images through pure cliche of love poetry of the period to win her mind: "Your bed-chamber./. . . till I lie with you. . . .(114,116)/ Your beauty was the cause of that effect:/ Your beauty, that did haunt me in my sleep/ To undertake the death of all the world,/ So I might live one hour in your sweet bosom. (125-8)/ Thine eyes, sweet lady, have infected mine. (153)/ For now they kill me with a living death. (156)/Teach not thy lip such scorn; for it was made/ For kissing, lady, not for such contempt" (175-6). When it is impossible to move her with those sweet words, he uses violence with his sword; "Lo here I lend thee this sharp-pointed sword,/ Which if thou please to hide in this true breast,/ And let the soul forth that adoreth thee,/ I lay it naked to the deadly stroke,/ And humbly beg the death upon my knee." (178-82) He penetrates that she is not so courageous as to stab him with the sword, thus he exploits her by giving his sword to her. Sensual images and the strategies of violence are employed to attain a certain political purpose, and during the process sexuality serves as a point of support and as a linchpin for the strategy. This wooing sense functions as a display of power and as a confirmation of the power. There is indeed a sexual charging in this discourse, and while male subjectivity is dominant, object-woman, female corporeality, is exchanged very overtly for the purpose of seeking solidarity, alliance, and political power.

Indeed, sharply contrasted to the representation of Lady Anne is that of the strong female characters who are demonized by the charge of female voicing. Even through those strong female characters are also under the structure of the exchange of women, they seek to project their own subjectivity and identity through aggressive and active self-assertion. The demonization of strong women characters can be construed as another expression of male anxiety, the feeling of fear on the rupture of central assumptions about ethical action, hierarchical order, and gender role. By this ideology, Queen Margret is represented as an extremely demonized character and monstrous lunatic throughout

1, 2, 3 Henry VI and *Richard III*. Particularly in *Richard III*, she is on stage, even though in actual history she went back to France by the time of Edward's reign.[6] The ideological representation of a demonized character is embodied in the ghost-like figure of Margaret and her prophetic but powerless harangue. Her violence and brutality are referred to by Richard:

> Rich. The curse my noble father laid on thee
> When thou didst crown his warlike brows with paper,
> And with thy scorns drew'st rivers from his eyes,
> And then to dry them, gav'st the Duke a clout
> Steep'd in the faultless blood of pretty Rutland —
> His curses then, from bitterness of soul
> Denounc'd against thee, are all fall'n upon thee,
> And God, not we, hath plagu'd thy bloody deed.
>
> (*Richard III*. I. iii. 174-181)

Margaret dominates act 1, scene 3 with her appalling litany of revenge, but as a crazed figure of impotence brought back from the past. She is a woman who exerted herself to seize the time, rather than subordinately inhabiting the ever-established order. She was willing to unsex herself and become such man to murder the Duke of York and his son Rutland so ruthlessly for one fixed purpose. The reversed gender roles between the weakling Henry VI

---

6 About her unexpected reappearance as a ritual, and the lack of reality, see 'introduction' of *the Arden Shakespeare: King Richard III*, p. 109-10

and the Lioness Queen Margaret are strongly paralleled by those of Macbeth and Lady Macbeth. In both cases, these subversive reversals of gender roles are represented as unacceptable. Margaret's active struggle in the political power game is rendered as extremely monstrous and subversive to the established social order. Jardine suggests, "'the woman of fluent speech is never chaste'" was a patriarchal strategy to vilify learned women such as female scholars and intellectuals as "'monstrous,' 'unnatural,' and (inevitably) sexually rapacious", "any activity" and articulateness "in woman" which was "inconsistent with her traditional domestic role" and overcame "woman's essential nature" was "to become other than woman," and "that otherness was readily translated into the otherness of sexual deviancy."[7] This negative representation of female activity, and voicing is remarkably prevalent in the representation of Queen Margaret. Monstrous activism in the female is represented as 'demonic' by a certain set of ideological resources. Julia Kristeva's *Powers of Horror* provides us with a preliminary hypothesis for an analysis of the representation of woman as socially monstrous. Her study has suggested a way of situating the monstrous-feminine in a society in relation to the "maternal figure" and "abjection," which "does not respect borders, positions, rules," and which "disturbs identity, system, order."[8] Kristeva's theory of abjection has

---

[7] Lisa Jardine, *Still Harping on Daughters*, London and New York: Harvester, 1983, pp. 56-7.

provided a significant theoretical framework for analysing the representation of the monstrous-feminie. It is certainly apparent that the monstrous is produced at the border which separates those who take up their proper gender roles from those who do net. The border is constructed between the clean and proper body and the abject body which has lost its form and integrity. Margret is certainly represented as an abject body which disturbed established social order and political behaviour. Women were traditionally understood as having noting to do with politics in the early modern period, thus when Margaret took the place of King Henry VI who was impotent in solving domestic feuds, she was rendered as monstrous feminine. However, she was not subservient to the social structure of the exchange of women which projects its ideology of homosocial bond between men. Instead, she audaciously pursued her own political power without regard to the demonization of female activity and voicing.

[2] Henry V

The ideological relation of sexuality and power can be found dramatically from the beginning of *Henry V*. As is well-known, *Henry V* deals mainly with England's glorious victory over France, which is based on the historical transition from feudalism to

---

8 Julia Kristeva, *Powers of Horror: An Essay on Abjection*, trans. Leon S. Roudiez, New York: Columbia UP, 1982. p. 4.

absolute monarchism. The righteousness of the war being the crucial point in the historical context, the Salic law is ingeniously deployed to justify the cause of war by the leaders of church and Henry himself. The Archbishop of Canterbury explains in detail the falsity of the Salic law which bars claims from the female line, enumerating the long line of succession (*Henry V*, I. I. 33-95). The arbitrary deployment of Salic law can be witnessed by the fact that Henry requested the religious leaders who were in financial difficulties to provide a plausible reason for the righteousness of the war(I. I. 1-5). Thus the uncanny conspiracy between king and religious leaders cannot be denied, the king offering financial support to religious leaders and religious leaders the legitimate cause for the war. Furthermore, the arbitrary exploitation of Salic law is strongly foregrounded when the king has to face the conspiracy of the Earl of Cambridge. In Act 2, Scene 2, the dramatic revelation of the conspiracy, and the execution of the conspirators, are treated as a relief before the important war. But on the other hand, the fact that this conspiracy is not 'for a few light crowns' but for the purpose of making Mortimer a legitimate king of England following the female line, engenders an ironical dilemma for Henry V. Edmund Mortimer was the person Richard II appointed as "heir-apparent" before he started for the Irish expedition.[9] Because Mortimer had no heir, his sister Anne, with

---

[9] Geoffrey Bullough ed. *Narrative and Dramatic Sources of Shakespeare*, vol. VI. London: Routledge, 1962. p. 184.

her husband the Earl of Cambridge, is the appropriate successor after Richard II. Thus, Henry has to agree to the claim from the Earl of Cambridge, which follows the female lime, because he has earlier protested against the Salic law which bars claims from the female line. But he distorted the claim from Cambridge as a dishonourable conspiracy with the enemy France. In this Salic law case, the female line and body is an instrument in the conspiratorial action by power, the object of that masculine discourse which seeks to justify the cause of war.

In *Henry V.* male subjectivity and sexuality have been thoroughly permeated by the violence of war. Henry's explicitly charismatic deployment of language demonstrates how deeply the phallus and military aggressiveness are mutually intertwined and constitutive. The phallic violence with which Henry V menaces the citizens of Harfleur endorses the ideology of identification between territory and female body: "What is it to me/ If your pure maidens fall into the hand/ Of hot and forcing violation?" (III. iii. 19-21). The image of rape is used to articulate the invading of the city and a city is figured as a territory "all girdled with maiden walls that war hath never ent'red." (V. ii. 321-2) This territorialized female body is well-embodied in the exchange of Katharine between the French king and Henry V in which Katharine is figured by her father as virginal property, In this interchangeable terminology, the military metaphors portray sexuality as a form of conquest and victory, and the concrete female body of Katharine is correspondingly identified with the territory of France. After the conquest of France, the most "unseemly" but formally organised scene is represented by Henry's wooing of Katharine. In this abrupt scene, Henry persistently uses the same military metaphors to persuade Katharine's mind, and her himself confesses that he is aware of his inadequacies as a lover. He deploys military language to win Katharine's mind; "If I could win a lady at leap-frog, or by vaulting into my saddle with my armour on my back... I should quickly leap into a wife." (V. ii. 138-42). He demonstrates his sexuality as a form of military aggression and conquest.

When Katharine asks him "Is it possible dat I should love de enemy of France?" (147-5), he replies that "No; it is not possible you should love the enemy of France, Kate; but, in loving me, you should lobe the friend of France, for I love France so well that I will not part with a village of it; I will have it all mine: and Kate, when France is mine and I am yours, then yours is France and you are mine." (176-182). According to Claire McEachern. "Henry's verbal confusion—of pronouns, of political and sexual desires, indeed, of territorial boundaries—forges an accommodation between power and affect, political possession and sexual possession, which accommodates the body to hegemony and vice versa."[10] Imperial domain may have been

---

[10] Claire McEachern. "*Henry V* and the paradox of the Body Politic" in *Shakespeare Quarterly* 45 (Spring 1994). p. 56.

produced at this point by taking the conquered France as Other and as the concrete female body, and eventually power excludes all traces of that Other. We can assume that in no discourse is identity established in the total absence of the Other. As David Baker notes, "identity is necessarily relational, a matter of differences, and this is especially so under colonialism, with its elaborate and precarious schemes of racial classification."[11] A voicing of imperial authority is powerful in *Henry V*, and the exalted integrity of English power and its splendid wholeness are dependent upon partial traces of a presence of a threatening Other. This Other is represented as France and as the concrete female body of Katharine in *Henry V*. Katharine must be absorbed and converted into the tropes of English colonial power which were incipient at that time, in the sense that the threatening difference Katharine represents—her language and nationality—is finally repudiated.

The recording of alien voices—the voices of those who have no power to leave literate traces of their own existence—is foregrounded and articulated in this wooing scene, with no chance of the Other ever emerging into recognition. Stephen Greenblatt has remarked on the coherence and impermeability of English power and its linguistic colonialism in his essay "Learning to Curse."[12] He declares that "Europeans in the sixteenth

---

[11] David J. Baker. ""Wildehirissheman": colonialist representation in Shakespeare's *Henry V*" in *English Literary Renaissance* (winter 1992). p. 42

century, like ourselves, find it difficult to credit another language with opacity. In other words, they render Indian language transparent, either by limiting or denying its existence or by dismissing its significance as an obstacle to communication between peoples."[13] Even though he confined his definition of linguistic colonialism to the relationship between European coloniser and Indian colonised, linguistic colonialism can certainly be applied to Henry's linguistic domination of Katherine in the wooing scene. The military dimension of Henry's sexuality is paralleled by his linguistic domination of Katherine. Katherine's linguistic status positions woman as a foreign language, that is to say, the other. Henry deploys linguistic penetration rather then the acquisition of a new language, and it is she that must give up her native tongue and that must learn the language and nationality of England. Thus, insofar as Katherine is the object of Henry's discourse, Henry's subjectivity and sexuality are predicated by Henry's linguistic power and it can be understood under the rubrics of 'identity' and 'power'. Compared to the vigorous self-presentation of Henry V (166 lines), her maidenly embarrassment and deference (27 lines) is represented as containable and repressible. However, as Traub points out, "Katherine's predicament is structural; whatever her individual

---

[12] Stephen J. Greenblatt, "Learning to Curse: Aspects of Linguistic Colonialism in the Sexteenth Century" in *Learning To Curse: Essays in Early Modern Culture*, N.Y. & London: Routledge, 1990. pp. 16-39

[13] Ibid. p. 32.

power, it is subsumed by her ideological, political, and economic function in the systematic exchange of women between men."[14] The ineradicable structure of the exchange can also be observed in Levi-Strauss's account that "the woman figures only as one of the objects in the exchange, not as one of the partners between whom the exchange takes place. This remains true even when the girl's feelings are taken into consideration, as, moreover, is usually the case. In acquiescing to the proposed union, she participates or allows the exchange to take place; she cannot alter its nature." (*The Elementary Structures of Kinship*, p. 115). The exchange of women in society is ineradicably deep-rooted and can be found in our own society in a more sophisticated and commercialised form. Katherine is structured in the exchange of woman between France and England, and the political economy of sex renders her as a conduit of political alliance, friendship, and solidarity. The power relationship is well expressed in her answer to Henry when he asks if she will have him, "Dat is as it sall please de roi mon pere."(V. ii. 261)

Women's bodies are figured as territory and the territory is figured as women's body in *Henry V*, and the territory is the object of the war and of military violence. When Henry describes Katharine as "our capital demand, compris'd/ Within the fore-rank of our articles" (V. ii. 96-7), not only does the giving of her body symbolise the capitulation of French territory, her body

---

14 Valerie Traub, *Desire and Anxiety*, p. 63.

becomes that territory. Once married to the masculine kingdom of England, Katharine who embodied the subservient state of France will be tamed and appropriated through its transfiguration into a more manageable state. Thus, Katharine's virginal body is an entity in which male subjectivity and sexuality project their ideology and power. Katharine's body provides a context within which the development of Henry's subjectivity occurs, and subjection, dependency, power, control occur within the particular social relations of *Henry V*. In *Henry V*, subjectivity, power, and sexuality are inextricably interwoven. For Henry, subjectivity can be maintained only in gendered terms, because for him to be a person is to be his father's son and heir, which is to be a soldier and a king. His subjectivity becomes meaningful by means of sexuality and power, for to be masculine in Henry's world is to be the active subject of a sexualised violence and a violent sexuality. The circuitous interdependency of subjectivity, sexuality, and power is one of the most powerful tropes in this drama. In the projection of Henry's subjectivity, Katharine's virginal body is transformed into a locus where Henry's masculine power is foregrounded and articulated through the projection of its manipulative and exploitative ideology. The exchange of woman is a powerful strategy of political alliance in this drama, and it appropriates the concrete female body as a territory to be possessed and exploited, whether the female body is aware of it or not.

The classical body of Katharine is implicated upon male upon male fantasies of maternal omnipotence, nurturance, and fecundity. The "classical body" is "elevated, static, and monumental"[15] The gendered "classical body" is a masculine projection and a defensive idealisation of the physical body of women. Henry embodies this masculine projection and idealisation, when he urges the combination of pleasure with power and gives Katharine's body a utility for the state; "If ever thou beest mine, Kate, as I have a saving faith within me tells me thou shalt, I get thee with scambling, and thou must therefore needs prove a good solder-breeder. Shall not thou and I, between Saint Denis and Saint George, compound a boy, half English, that shall go to Constantinople and take the Turk by the beard?" (211-8).[16] The brute exercise of a sovereign will is rehabilitated into an ideologically useful corporeality, the biological reproduction of dynastic pover. It offers "an image of the alliance of an international aristocracy secured through the exogamous exchange of a women."[17] The image represents a mutual alliance between the two different cultures which are collaborative rather than coercive. The alliance is embodied in the wooing scene of *Henry V* which reveals a fantasy of social union which employs

[15] Peter Stallybrass & Allon White, *The Politics and Poetics of Transgression*, Ithaca and New York: Cornell UP, 1986. pp. 22-3.

[16] Ironically, Henry V's hoy proves to be a weakling Henry VI.

[17] Claire McEachern, "Henry V and the paradox of the body politic." in *Shakespeare Quarterly* 45 (Spring 1994) p. 56.

the tropes of sexuality as a means of its realisation.

[3] The Cult of Elizabeth

The inscription of woman's bodies as territory was given a more serious precedent in the Virgin Queen Cult in the Elizabethan period. Interestingly, women's bodies figure territory not only in Shakespeare's plays but alco in the actual political world. For examply, Queen Elizabeth, a women, a secular virgin Mary married to the kingdom of England, was believed to have allowed herself to "invest her maternity in her political rather than her natural body, and perpetuate her maidenhood in a cult of virginity transferring her wifely duties from the household to the state."[18] As can be noted by this Elizabethan self-fashioning, the images of the Queen represented in the portraits and the poetry are closely connected with the enigmatic legind of the Queen herself, a myth deliberately created and sustained over four decades by public spectacle and by private sonnet and official oration. Roy Strong's remarkable book, *The Cult of Elizabeth* demonstrates the meaning of the most famous and potent of all Elizabethan pictures and pageantry such as Nicholas Hilliard's "Young Man amongst Roses," the famous "Blackfriars Procession," and "The Ermine and Rainbow Portraits of the

---

[18] L. Montrose, "The Elizabethan Subject and the Spenserian Text" in *Literary Theory/Renaissance Texts* ed. Patricia and David Quint, Boltimore: Johns Hoplins UP.1986. p. 310.

Queen."[19] The phantasmagoria of obscure and often extremely bizarre images are used to celebrate the Queen's glorious presence. As Strong argues, "Certainly they establish a way of thinking about a monarch totally foreign to us, a structure of the psyche in which images are not merely fanciful flattering labels but embody attributes of the person concerned—a comprehensiveness in multiplicity matched only in religious cults"[20] These visions are created to a level of secular mythology, making Elizabeth an object of worship and a heroine of the period. Enigmatically enough, in this mythology the body of Elizabeth becomes a territory, a context within which the 'ideology of nationalism' projects itself and the power of a female monarch displays itself. I used the term, nationalism, because calculated spectacular presentations of the Queen to ger adoring subjects might have provoked patriotic feelings in the spectators, and the cult of Elizabeth was skillfully created to buttress public order and deliberately to replace the rituals of Christianity with the English Monarch's Virgin Queen Cult. This English patriotism represents the needs of the nation-state which was forming specifically at

---

[19] Roy Strong, *The Cult of Elizabeth: Elizabethan Portraiture and Pageantry*, London: Thames and Hudson, 1977. This book brings together six studies in Elizabethan portraiture and pageantry, and in particular chapter 1, "The Queen: *Eliza Triumphans*" (pp. 17-55) is primarily concerned with images of the Queen represented in many portraits such as "The Rainbow Portrait," and "The Sieve Portrait."

[20] Ibid. p. 16.

that time.[21] Elizabeth functioned as emblem of national integrity and the portraits of the Queen are intensely charged with significance of nationalistic ideology. In particular, we can grasp nationalism in "The Armada Portrait" which celebrates the mighty monarch whose imperial hand extends to defeat foreign enemies. In this secular mythology, the body of the Queen symbolises the glorious and peaceful golden time of the Tudor period. For example, "The Rainbow Portrait" represents this ideology in a very subtle way. The springtime theme is embodied in the spring flowers; eyes and ears, pillars and rocks, and crescent moon are all the metaphor and visual statement of the Elizabethan state on order, the order of the body politic which she animates.

Stallybrass remarks: "the normative "Woman" could become the emblem of the perfect and impermeable container, and hence a map of the integrity of the state. The state, like the virgin, was a *hortus conclusus*, an enclosed garden walled of from enemies.[22] For instance, the Ditchely portrait demonstrates Elizabeth as the imperial virgin, symbolising and symbolised by, the enclosed garden of the state which is walled off from enemies. It conjunctures imperial virgin and cartographic images by portraying Elizabeth I standing upon a map of England, which constitutes the terrain of Elizabethan rule. This symbolic

---

[21] Refer to Peter Stallybrass, "Patriarchal Territories" in *Rewriting the Renaissance*, Margaret W. Ferguson et al. Chicago: Chicago UP. 1986 p. 130.

[22] Ibid. p. 129.

conjuncture represents the needs of the nation-state which was developing gradually at that time, and the specific female body was refashioned according to the forming of the nation-state and for the purpose of national integrity.[23] Projected onto a religious plane, her body was the garden of the state, and the body of the virgin which was walled off from enemies. For Montrose, this erotic channelling of a powerful female who is at once lover, mother, and Queen is "enhanced by the promotion of her maidenhood into a cult of virginity" and "the displacement of her wifely duties from a household to a nation."[24] Indeed, the Queen's two bodies—political and natural—provided a cognitive map for Elizabethan culture and a veritable matrix for the Elizabethan forms of desire. The body of Queen Elizabeth is inscribed as territory and deployed as an image of the spring time theme of the Tudor period. This religious cult implies a mystical identification of the inviolate female body of the monarch with the unbreached body of her land, and the powerful myth of the virgin Queen convincingly affirms the exchange of women through the inscription of women's body as territory.

---

[23] Ibid. p. 130

[24] Louis Montrose, "*A Midsummer Night's Dream* and the Shaping Fantasies of Elizabethan Culture: Gender, Power, Form" in *New Historicism and Renaissance Drama*, Richard Wilson and Richard Dutton eds., London and New York: Longman, 1992. p. 124

3. Images of the Maternal Body and the Articulation of Feminine Value in *Richard II*

In *Richard II*, exchange of feminine imagery is so skillfully deployed that it would be difficult to detect the spuriousness of the political use of the metaphor. We can retrieve from *Richard II* much of the vestigial traces of femininity. It is not difficult to witness unification in *Richard II*. The prevailing imagery of the final prophecy of Gaunt is closely related to the feminine imagery with its insistence upon jewels as symbols of value and upon the association of royalty and beneficent fertility. His references to England as a "nurse" and as a "teeming womb of royal kings" draw attention to the specifically female capacities of parturition and nurturing.

> Gaunt: This blessed plot, this earth, this realm, this England,
> This nurse, this teeming womb of royal kings,
> Feared by their breed and famous by their birth,
> Renowned for their deeds as far from home
> For Christian service and true chivalry
> As is the sepulchre in stubborn Jewry
> Of the world's ransom, blessed Mary's son;
>
> (*Richard II*, II. I. 50-6)

As Holderness remarks, "the allusion to the Virgin Mary is perhaps a characteristic feature of Gaunt's view of women" in the sense that "her primary significance is the fact that she gave birth to a remarkable man, Jesus."[25] In his view, women are the passive conduits by means of which the patriarchy is reproduced. Holderness points out that even though "the femininity of his metaphorical 'England' is ultimately spurious, since that maternal symbol is so completely a construction of the kings and warriors who have served their country in loyalty," "a feminine dimension of meaning"—"nurses, and wombs, and birth, and breeding"—is important "once that meaning occupies a space inside the imaginative universe of the play."[26] England, in its state of unity, is as it were, an anticipation of perfection—this other Eden, demi-paradise—and the substance of its blessed state is conveyed through a sublimation of the chivalry which survives, as a shadow blemished with strife and egoism, in Richard's own court. The reference to the Holy Sepulchre will be taken up repeatedly in the later action as Bolingbroke will see in gis projected crusade a symbol of the dedicated unity which political realities will never allow him to establish under his own rule. The whole exchange is elaborate, artificial and beneath its elaboration a means to convey the state of contradiction is poised between the form and the meaning. Richard II's attempts to assume a maternal sovereignty

---

[25] Graham Holderness, "A Woman's War: A Feminist Reading of *Richard II*" in *Shakespeare Left and Right*, ed. Ivo Kamps, New York and London: Routledge, 1991. p. 174.

[26] Ibid. p. 174.

over his kingdom in his speech at Act 3, Scene 2, also reveals the masculine deployment of feminine imagery which inscribes the validation of national glory and unification.

> Richard. As a long-parted mother with her child
> Plays fondly with her tears and smiles in meeting
> So weeping, smiling, greet I thee, my earth
> And do thee favours with my royal hands
>
> (III. ii. 8-11)

This passage makes it explicit that there is an adroit political use of metaphor and an arbitrary association of royalty and beneficent female capacities of affection. The disparity between the metaphor and the reality is apparently embodied in this paradoxical passage of Richard's as well as the metaphor of Gaunt's final prophecy of England. The metaphors of Richard and Gaunt contain the affluent image of femininity which is contradictory to the real emptiness and sterility of female existence in its substance. The whole exchange of metaphor deployed by Gaunt and Richard foregrounds and interrogates contradiction and paradox which are predicated upon the disparity between the metaphor and the reality. The whole exchange conveys the state of contradiction in an elaborate and artificial way, and complexity of interpretation. Feminine imagery is typically matrixed in the plurality and complexity of interpretation. Feminine imagery is deployed by masculine ideology to strengthen their positions, nevertheless, as we will examine, female characters themselves participate in the contest for meaning and the struggle for their own honour and identity through their sexual difference and their own feminine experience which prove exclusive and positive feminine value.

With regard to sexual difference between men and women, as well as exclusive and positive feminine value, Luce Irigaray has provided a theory of sexual difference as a crucial issue. As Margaret Whitford suggests, "Irigaray may be thought eccentric for insisting on difference (also partly in the name of nature) at a moment when it is being loudly and persuasively said that difference has been used to oppress women and not to liberate them, and that liberty lies in other directions—equality, or undecidability, or beyond sexual difference."[27] Irigaray has remarked, discussing Simone de Beauvoir's *The Second Sex*, that:

> Women's exploitation is based upon sexual difference; its solution will come only through sexual difference. . . . What is important, on the other hand, is to define the values of belonging to a gender, valid for each of the two genders. It is vital that a culture of the sexual, as yet nonexistent, be elaborated, with each sex being respected. . . . Equality between men and women cannot be achieved without *a theory of gender as sexed* and a rewriting of the rights and obligations of each sex, *qua different*, in social

---

27 Margaret Whitford, *Luce Irigaray: Philosophy in the Feminine*, London & New York: Routledge, 1991. p. 191.

rights and obligations.[28]

For Irigaray, "an ethics of sexual difference" is "an ethics which recognizes the subjectivity of each sex," and locates "the symbolic division which allocates the material, corporeal, sensible, 'natural' to the feminine, and the spiritual, ideal, intelligible, transcendental to the masculine."[29] The problem is that of fertility and the symbolic distribution of roles, in which women are only allowed to be fertile in the body, while men are fertile intellectually and spiritually. Both sexes need to be fertile according to the sprit, and while men need to take back and own their body, women need to accede to a symbolic representation of their own. Irigaray's new vision of sexual difference and positive theory of feminity will crystallize feminist political thought and women will collectively be able to find in her work some of the materials for the creation of their future. This sexual difference as a critical issue problematizes the destructive patriarchal culture, and suggests new values corresponding to women's creative capacities. She remarks:

> Women have to constitute a social entity if love and cultural
> fecundity are to take place. This does not mean that it is entirely
> as men that women come into today's systems of power, but

---

[28] Luce Irigaray, *Je, tu, nous: Toward a Culture of Difference*, trans. Alison Martin, New York and London: Routledge, 1993. pp. 12-3.

[29] Margaret Whitford, *Luce Irigaray: Philosophy in the Feminie*, p. 149.

rather that women need to establish new values that correspond to *their* creative capacities. Society, culture, discours would thereby be recognized as *sexuate* and not as the monopoly on universal value of a single sex—one that has no awareness of the way the body and its morphology are imprinted upon imaginary and symbolic creations.[30]

In the discussion of sexual difference, Irigaray firstly foregrounds 'paternal' and 'masculine' ariented discourse in the West which transforms nature into culture systematically excluding women; next, she emphasises that "women ought to rediscover herself, among other things, through the images of herself already deposited in history."[31] Feminine images are deposited and embedded in the West through Cartesian discourse. The "I" of the Cogito is self-engendered, constituted through a radical denial both of the other and of man's corporeal origins. The "I" thinks, "therefore this thing, this body that is also nature, that is still the *mother*, becomes an extension at the "I"'s disposal for the regulated exercise of the imaginary and the utilitarian practice of technique.[32] In the context, Irigaray suggests the idealistic

---

[30] Luce Irigaray, *An Ethics of Sexual Difference*, trans. Carolyn Burke and Cillian C. Gill, London: The Athlone Press, 1993. pp. 67-8.

[31] Luce Irigaray, 'Sexual Difference' in Toril Moi ed., *French Feminist Thought*, Oxford: Basil Blackwell, 1987. pp. 119 & 121.

[32] Naomi Schor, "This Essentialism Which Is Not One: Coming to Grips with Irigaray" in *Engaging With Irigaray: Feminist Philosophy and Modern European Thought*, ed. Carolyn Burke et al., New York: Columbia UP, 1994. p. 70.

alliance of the physical and the metaphysical, the material and the transcendental.

In *Richard II.* there are three primary female characters who denote the positive feminine value and sexual difference which we examined through the theory of Irigaray. They are all, primarily and even exclusively, wives and mothers; the Duchess of Gloucester is there to lament and preserve the memory of her murdered husband; Queen Isabel has literally nothing to do in the play except to feel sadness and pity for her husband; the Duchess of York is there to plead, successfully, for th life of Aumerle her son. Even though all three are present in the play in terms of their relationship with men, they are all repersentatives of the potentiality of female assertiveness and power. The Duchess of Gloucester's very strength and courage dismisses Christian patience as the natural subjection of the common, the "mean" men, and she seeks to persuade Gaunt to take revenge against Richard.

> Duch. Call it not patience, Gaunt, it is despair,
>   In suff'ring thus thy brother to be slaught'red,
>   Thou showest the naked pathway to thy life,
>   Teaching stern murder how to butcher thee.
>   That which in mean men we intitle patience
>   Is pale cold cowardice in noble breasts. (I. ii. 29-34)

During the accusation she appeals strongly to brotherhood and blood by using the word 'blood' up to 5 times (9-22). Her militant violence of language proves the Duchess' capability of that hot-blooded martial vigor defined by Mowbray as a peculiarprerogative of the male sex. "O, sit my husband's wrongs on Hereford's spear,/ That it may enter butcher Mowbray's breast!/ Orif misfortune miss the first career/ Be Mowbray's sins so heavy in his bosom/ That they may break his foaming courser's back/ And throw the rider headlong in the lists/ A caitiff recreant to my cousin Hereford!" (I. ii. 47-53). Her strong feelings and forceful expression negate her role in the activities she deems essential to her personal honour and her familial bond.

The faithfulness to familial bond is strongly prevalent even in a character like Queen Isabel who seems to be so silent, self-effacing and passive. The adjectives attributed to her are historically appropriate because she was a child of ten when the deposition of king Richard II happened. Her self-effacing character can be endorsed decisively through a scene (II. I,) in which Isabel is present but strangely absent amongst the men who were so preoccupied with the "specifically "masculine" preserves: politics, war, economics, law, property."[33] Thus, it seems natural that critics have trivialized the Queen's role in spite of her unhistorical mature passions and her powerful prophetic forebodings. Some

---

[33] Graham Holderness. "A Woman's War: A Feminist Reading of Richard II." p. 173.

critics have usually commented on her character in a way such as the following; "her forebodings and her formal and conceited expressions of grief at his downfall are not so much imprtant in revealing anything of herself as they in impressing upon the spectators the essentially personal side of Richard's tragedy, as opposed to the kingly side of it"; "she is introduced in fictitious scenes in order to get some women into the cast and to provide occasional pathos. A vast increase in pathos is one of Shakespeare's main devices for gaining sympathy for his hero."[34] According to the above interpretations, the Queen has little purpose other than to be decorative and to suggest a side of Richard's character not otherwise touched on in the play, and the Queen's true function seems to be to excite sympathy for Richard for she is no more than one facet of a many-sided character. However, all of these criticisms smoothly gloss over the Queens own feminine experience located in her powerful metaphoric language. Her premonition of imminent calamity is conveyed through the imagery of pregnancy and parturition, envisaging the suffering of her own body attached to the exclusive feminine experience.

> Isabel. Some unborn sorrow ripe in Fortune's womb
> Is coming towards me, and my inward soul

---

[34] Geoffrey Bullough ed., *Narrative and Dramatic Sources of Shahespeare* vol. III. London: Routledge and Kegan Paul. 1960. p. 357.

With nothing trembles, at something it grieves
More than with parting from my lord the king

(II. ii. 10-13)

The image of engendering (unborn, womb) embodies the particular historical and cultural circumstances through the association of the origin of the voice with pregnancy and childbirth. After she heard the tiding of the arrival of banished Bolingbroke, she tragically discovered that her "child" was the "Prodigy" of Blingbroke's usurpation.

Isabel. So, Greene, thou art the midwife to my woe,
And Bolingbroke my sorrow's dismal heir,
Now hath my soul brought forth her prodigy
And I, a gasping new-deliver'd mother,
Have woe to woe, sorrow to sorrow join'd (II. ii. 62-6)

The image continues the "engendering"—midwife, heir, bring forth, prodigy, gasping new delivered mother—and it proves that woman's putatively unlimited capacity for pregnancy and childbirth associates her with the power of voice. According to Elizabeth D. Harvey, "woman's ability to be a receptacle or mouthpiece for discourse other than her own is closely tied to cultural constructions of gender and, specifically, to female physiology. . . . Ventriloquism, literally the act of appearing to speak from the abdomen or belly, is . . . closely linked to prophecy, for in both casses the voice proceeds from a locus other than the organs of speech, since the ventriloquized voice originates in another place (the stomach) or being (a deity or evil spirit)."[35] Thus, woman's putatively unlimited capacity for speech associates her with the power of specific female physiology, and voice or language appears to emerge from her body in a process analogous to birth. Woman is impregnated or filled with voice, as in Christian tradition Mary becomes the receptacle of the Word. From the historical viewpoint, the Queen's metaphoric language of pregnancy and parturition is paradoxical, since she was a child of ten and her relationship with Richard II was blemished by flatterers like Bushy, Bagot and Greene. It seems that conjugal faithfulness did not exist between king and queen as is well mentioned in Bolingbroke's accusation that Bushy and Green have misled the king and made a divorce between him and his queen.

> Bolingbroke. You have in manner, with your sinful hours,
> Made a divorce betwixt his queen and him,
> Broke the possession of a royal bed,
> And stain'd the beauty of a fair queen's cheeks
> With tears, drawn from her eyes by your foul wrong,
> (III. i. I 1-15)

---

[35] Elizabeth D. Harvey, *Ventriloquised Voice: Feminist Theory and English Renaissance Texts*, London and New York: Routledge. 1992. pp. 94-4.

Thus, her metaphoric language of pregnancy and parturition strangely and explosively conveys the tragedy of personal impotence as well as that of political crisis. However, unlike another Isabella, in *Edward II*, who loves Edward but turns to Mortimer after suffering neglect, and so becomes his deadly enemy, Richard's Isabel remains faithful to the last. In the last scene, she encourages her husband with language of power and audacity and reproaches Richard for his weakness with the considerable dignity of her soul, "The lion dying thrusteth forth his paw/ And wounds the earth, if nothing else, with rage/ To be o'erpow'r'd, and wilt thou, pupil-like./ Take the correction mildly, kiss the rod,/ And fawn on rage with base humility,/ Which art a lion and the king of beasts?" (V. i. 29-34). She articulates powerful metaphoric language and it reveals her capacity for speech which is associated with the power of specific female physiology and the faithfulness to her blood bond.

The trope of maternal power in *Richard II* is embodied in the figure of a particular mother, Duchess of York, even though her audacity is fragmented and occluded by the masculine ideology represented by Bolingbroke and the Duke of York. She is mother to Aumerle, the close companion and supporter of Richard who joins the Abbot of Westminster's conspiracy against the life of Henry. She is a mother now past the age of child-bearing, the prospect of losing her son would rob her of her very existence, abolish her only hope; "Is not my teeming date drunk up with time?/ And with thou pluck my fair son from mine age?/ And rob me of a happy mother's name?"(V. ii. 91-3). The principle and economy of contiguity and association rather than that of sacrifice and substitution figure prominently for maternity, and they are distinctively prevalent in the mother figure of the Duchess of York. As Irigaray points out, "contiguity" is a figure for the vertical and horizontal relationships between women, the maternal genealogy and the relation of sisterhood.[36] Correspondingly, Margaret Whitford suggests that the father-son relationship that organises the oedipal complex is based on renunciation and "metaphoric substitution," whereas the mother-daughter bond is founded on "metonymic identification," what is contiguous, associative, or combinatory.[37] What is crucial now is not the mother-daughter relationship which is very difficult to find out in the history plays. Instead, it is the mother-son relationship contrasted to the father-son bond which is representatively revealed in the relationship between the Duke of York and his son, Aumerle.

For example, the Duke of York's response to the Duchess's desperate appeal for her son's life can be defined as "the techniques of the subject" and "the construction of the self."[38] He

---

[36] Luce Irigaray, *This Sex Which Is Not One*, trans. Catherine Porter with Carolyn Burke, Ithaca: Cornell UP. 1985. pp. 24 & 29.

[37] Margaret Whitford, *Luce Irigaray: Philosophy in the Feminine*. p. 180.

[38] Michel Foucault, *The History of Sexuality Vol. III: The Care of the Self*, trans. Robert Hurley, London: Penguin. 1986. pp. 43-5.

encounters with the other—the Duchess of York—through the gaze or visual spectacle, as well as through more institutionalised cultural interventions, establishing a pattern of dominance and marginalisation that is available for exploitation. Estrangement as a strategy, the identification of an other against which the self may be not only measured but defined and demarcated can be found in the Duke of York's condemnation pf the Duchess, and this is practised by his labeling her as "a foolish, frantic, unruly, and mad woman." (V. ii. 89-93) The Duke of York is ready to impeach his son for treason against his new master, sweeping aside his wife's plea, and apparently unmoved by the prospect of being left heirless. He is ready to sacrifice his own blood for a usurper who has only used him as an instrument and who will from now no distrust him as a possible rival. This cruel attitude is not understandable to the Duchess who experienced suffering in her childbirth to deliver Aumerle which predisposes her to a pity her husband cannot feel, "Hadst thou groaned for him/ As I have done, thou wouldst be more pitiful." (103-4) Her accusation reminds as that femininity has its own peculiar experiences and values, in some ways quite separate from the world of masculine ideology. This potential affirmation of femininity is fragmented and interrogated when Bolingbroke mocks her by commenting that "our scene is alt'red from a serious thing/ And now changed to *The Beggar and the King*." Bolingbroke's facetiousness represents the general idea of masculine ideology that woman is not appropriate for the domain of politics and history. Linda Woodbridge has suggested "the traditional effect of jest" in her research into Renaissance texts.[39] According to her, almost all formal misogynistic attacks of the Renaissance represent themselves as jest. Wit and humor loom very large in Western misogyny and literary jest has had its effect on real women. Thus, if women are not taken seriously it is partly because they have been viewed far so many centuries through the eyes of jesters. What is worse is that women have internalised all the old jokes fatal to their own subjectivity. This has resulted in the same comtempt for herself that the jester feels for her. However, in spite of the attempt to marginalise and mock woman by masculine ideology, the Duchess of York successfully attained her goal by her aggressive and affirmative feminine audacity. The contest for meaning and the contest for power between the Duke and the Duchess of York evoke the feeling of sexual difference which responds differently to the crises of momentous historical events. The Duchess is much more faithful to the natural bond of blood than the Duke of York who is obsessed with political success and filled with fear under the regime of a new king.

Arguably, "women's place" has been "yet more problematic in the group of texts which are prominent participants in the new

---

[39] Linda Woodbridge, *Women and the English Renaissance: Literature and the Nature of Womankind*, 1540-1620, Sussex: The Harvester Press Ltd., 1984. pp. 30-2.

intertextuality... the master texts of theory (Freud, Lacan, Derrida, Foucault, Marx, Althusser, Levi-Strauss), or of social history Lawrence Stone, Keith Wrightson, Keith Thomas, Peter Laslett)."[40] In these texts, women remain nothing other than the other itself. Besides, "feminist criticism . . . is restricted to exposing its own exclusion from the text. It has no point of entry into it, for the dilemmas of the narrative and the sexuality under discussion are constructed in completely male terms . . . and the women's role as the objects of exchange within that system of sexuality is not at issue."[41] Thus, female signifier metamorphoses into the male signified. Against this transformation, it seems necessary "to read to excess, the possibility of human (especially female) gendered subjectivity, identity and agency, the possibility of women's resistance or even subversion."[42] It does not mean to erase the historicity of the text by exclusively emphasising and focusing on the gender politics. It means to foreground and problematise masculine ideology and patriarchal power, unfixing traditional stereotypes and social roles, replacing and re-evaluating it with the history of women, by the betrayal of women's unruliness.

---

[40] Carol Thomas Neely, "Constructing the Subject: Feminist Practice and the New Renaissance Discoursse," in *English Literary Renaissance* (Winter 1988) p. 9.

[41] Kathleen McLuskie, "The Patriarchal Bard: Feminist Criticism and Shakespeare" in *Political Shakespeare*, eds. J.Dollimore & Alan Sinfield, Manchester: Manchester UP, 1985. p. 97.

[42] Carol Thomas Neely, "Constructing the Subject: Feminist Practice and the New Renaissance Discoursse," in *ELR* (Winter 1988) p. 15.

According to Belsey, "modes of resistance to what was dominant are ignored if they could not be formulated in so many words, were not allowed a voice, were not experienced as resistance or can be defined as deviant.[43] The vacillating possibility of new interpretations of past and future should be discovered by the contest for meaning and power. If 16th century patriarchy was an unstable ideological system, a site of contest and struggle, then it would be possible to re-engender the Renaissance texts in which historical contradictions were entailed in the construction of gender. If the past can be visible as past, intelligible as difference rather than continuity, the possibility would arise of projecting the routine marginalisation of women and of formulating the sexual difference to an extent that reveals particular feminine experience and values. Feminist interpretation of Renaissance drama can therefore claim that even though masculine ideology and exploitation, embodied in the exchange of women and in the deployment of feminine imaginary, are prevalent and powerful in Renaissance texts, it is not difficult to find a counter-discourse which evaluates a particular feminine experience and its own values.

---

[43] Catherine Belsey, "Literature, History, Politics" in *New Historicism and Renaissance Drama*, eds. R. Wilson and R. Dutton, London and New York: Longman, 1992. p. 39.

The Eroticized Male Body and
the Policing of Sexuality: *1, 2 Henry IV*

1. Heterotopology and Homoeroticism

The expertise of sexuality is manoeuvred and inscribed by the strategies of institutions such as religious belief, educational system, and political power. At the same time, sexuality is challenging the master-discourse as a cultural and political force. In this context, considering sexuality in the mode of power relations would be intriguing particularly because the disciplining of sexuality by institutional power is being interrogated and problematized by individual sexuality. For example, homoerotic relationship and the eroticized male body have been considered as perverse and deviant. However, gay culture is becoming a powerful counter-discourse in modern culture. Since the nineteenth century, "social controls" in the area of homoeroticism produced "the formation of a "reverse" discourse," and "homosexuality began to speak in its own behalf, to demand that its legitimacy or "naturality" be acknowledged."[1] It is apparent that the new approach to sexuality succeeded in circumventing conventional belief which deployed with its different strategies the notion of sexuality. Foucault remarks, "Homosexuality appeared as one of the forms of sexuality when it was transposed from the practice of sodomy onto a kind of interior androgyny, a hermaphrodism of the soul. The sodomite had been a temporary aberration; the homosexual was now a species.[2] However, there still exists a multiple implantation of perversions and the endeavour to expel from reality the forms of sexuality that are not amenable to the strict economy of reproduction. Nowadays, the interpretation of homoeroticism is explicitly linked to public fears generated by the media representations of AIDS. Our generation is experiencing the public redefinition of sexuality in the wake of AIDS. As Ed Cohen suggests, "the interpretation ascribed to sexual activities between men is mediating new forms of medical, legal, religious, political and moral authority designed to delimit

---

[1] Michel Foucault, *The History of Sexuality*, vol. 1, translated from the French by Robert Hurley, London: Penguin Books, 1978. p. 101

[2] Ibid. p. 43

the range of various and legitimate sexual practices."[3] Indeed, "the insertion of minority erotic practice into cultural discussion often results in its annexation, the automatic response of many is "oh, that refers to them, not me.""[4] Yet, the possibility to resist such authority is predicated upon our refusing the ideology that naturalizes the power to name homosexual experience as unnatural. In addition to this, it is crucial to comprehend the historical consequences that this power has in and for our everyday lives. Michel Foucault mentioned heterogenous spaces in which utopias and heterotopias that can be found within the culture are simultaneously represented.

> First there are the utopias. Utopias are sites with no real place. They are sites that have a general relation of direct or inverted analogy with the real space of Society. They present society itself in a perfected form, or else society turned upside down, but in any case these utopias are fundamentally unreal spaces. There are also, probably in every culture, in every civilization, real places — places that do exist and that are formed in the very founding of society — which are something like counter-sites, a kind of effectively enacted utopia in which the real sites, all the other real sites that can be found within the culture, are simultaneously represented, contested, and inverted.[5]

---

3 Ed Cohen, 'Legislating the Norm: From Sodomy to Gross Indecency' in *South Atlantic Quarterly* 88 (1989), p. 211.

4 Valerie Traub, 'Desire and the Difference it Makes' in *The Matter of Difference*, ed. by Valerie Wayne, London and New York: Harvester, 1991. p. 91.

As a description of the space in which we live, this could be called heterotopology. By heterotopology. Foucault means the coexistence of a large number of fragmentary possible worlds in an impossible space, or more simply incommensurable spaces that are juxtaposed or superimposed upon each other. Every single culture in the world constitutes heterotopias. Foucault suggests that "heterotopia can be found in the privileged or scared or forbidden places, reserved for individuals who are, in relation to society and to the human environment in which they live, deviant to the required mean or norm."[6] For instance, that kind of heterotopia can be found in grammar schools or in the military service, in which the first manifestations of sexual virility took place. Alan Bray notes that there is evidence of "institutionalized homosexuality" in grammar schools in the 16C, and Lawrence Stone also suggests homosexual influences on students at school or university in the 17C.[7] The heterotopia is capable of "juxtaposing in a single real place several spaces, several sites that are in themselves incompatible" and take the form of "contradictory sites."[8] In addition to this, heterotopias

---

[5] Michel Foucault, 'Of Other Spaces', *Diacritics*, Spring (1986). p. 24.

[6] Ibid. pp. 24-5.

[7] Alan Bray, *Homosexuality in Renaissance England*, Boston: Gay Men's Press, 1982, p. 71, and Lawrence Stone, *The Family, Sex and Marriage in England 1500-1800*, Harmondsworth: Pelican, 1979. p. 493.

[8] Interestingly, we can trace the same preoccupation with the concept of heterotopia in the postmodernist discourse. About the postmodernist techniques of superimposition of ontologically different worlds in an impossible single space,

have a function that unfolds between two extreme poles; "either their role is to create a space of illusion or else, on the contrary, their role is to create a space that is other, another real space, as perfect, as meticulous, as well arranged as ours is messy, ill-constructed, and jumbled."[9] The Former can be called heterotopia of illusion and the latter, of compensation.

Sexual transgressiveness and the symbolism of borders in relation to ideas of pollution, taboo, is a kind of heterotopical tradition in which sex is already moralized or systematized in such a way that the dominant discourse excludes the multiplicity of discursive elements that exist in the dominated one. Consider, for example, the history of homosexuality. Foucault suggests: "the moral dilemma of homosexuality was implanted by an economic socialization via all the incitements and restrictions, the "social" and fiscal measures brought to bear on the fertility of couples; a political socialization achieved through the "responsibilization" of couples with regard to the social body as a whole."[10] The irreducible human body is indeed located as a site at which all forms of repression are ultimately registered and inscribed. "Being unwarranted" and contrary to the political socialization of

---

refer to David Harvey, *The Condition of Postmodernity*, Oxford: Blackwell, 1989. p. 48. Harvey appropriately took an example of the two films, *Blue Velvet* and *Citizen Kane*.

[9] M. Foucault, 'Of Other Spaces,' p. 27

[10] M. Foucault, *The History of Sexuality*, vol. 1. translated from the French by Robert Hurley, London: Penguin Books, 1978. pp. 104-5

procreative behaviour, "homosexual activity posed physical and moral, individual and collective dangers." (Foucault, p. 104) "Deployment of sexuality," according to the terminology of Foucault, was formed "on the basis of the Christian notion of the flesh, and its development through the four great strategies that were deployed in the nineteenth century: the sexualisation of children, the hysterisation of women, the specification of the perverted, and the regulation of population."[11] With regard to the Christian notion of sexuality, the book of Genesis chapters 18-19, provides the most striking example in the cautionary tale of Sodom and Gomorrah, with its awesome culmination of divine punishment. In addition to Genesis. Leviticus and Romans and also take examples of the castigation of sodomy as the most abominable sin against God. The intensification of the male body and the specification of homoeroticism must be rejected and frustrated by a powerful agency of prohibition. In this way, the exploitation of the sexual body is practised by the demand of violent and physical constraints. And the politics of the body requires the elision of sex or its restriction solely to the reproductive function. It recuperates the perverted male body into the controlled circuits of the economy, that is, hyper-repressive desublimation. But contrary to the techniques of the socialization of procreative behaviour, homoeroticism brings a production of

---

[11] Ibid. p. 114

virile sexuality of nonprocreation.

The field of problematisation, the constitution of homoeroticism as a domain of moral concern, has to investigate the system of power that regulates the practice of sexuality. Within the system of power, individuals are obliged to recognize themselves as subjects of their sexuality. But Foucault argues that discourses are not once and for all subservient to power or raised up against it any more than silences are.

> There has been a two-fold operation in the history of sexuality: on the one hand, there was an severity—punishment by fire was meted out well into the 18C without there being any substantial protest expressed before the middle of the century—and on the other hand, a tolerance that must have been widespread, which one can dedude indirectly from the infrequency of judicial sentences, and which one glimpses more directly through certain statements concerning societies of men that were thought to exist in the army or in the court.[12]

The history of sexuality has long been linked to a modality of power with the techniques of subjugation, a procedure that is the manipulation of the sexual human being. As Foucault notes, It will be granted no doubt that relations of sex gave rise, in every society, to a *deployment of alliance*: a system of marriage, of

---

[12] Ibid. p. 101. About the ambivalent and contradictory attitude yoward homosexuality particularly in the 17C, see Section II.

fixation and development of kinship ties, of transmission of names and possessions.[13] With the mechanisms of constraint, the society created and deployed the politics of the body and the quality of pleasures. The economy of the body, the body that produces and consumes, has the function of maintaining and reproduction which are considered as the most important phase for marriage. The field of problematisation, the constitution of male friendship and homoeroticism as a domain of moral concern, has to yield to the type of subjection that the practice of self had to undergo in order to be morally valorized. The systems of power regulate the practice of sexuality and the forms within which individuals are obliged to recognize themselves as subjects of their sexuality. Their experience of sexuality is distorted through "the politics of morality" which seems to be inherited from a long Christian tradition which is based on the negative notion of the principle of "desiring man."[14] The formidable codification of the moral experience and ethics-oriented moralities have been very important in Christianity. Thus, homoeroticism is inscribed as a practice which is rebellious against the principle of morality. And the eroticised male body is considered as the domain in which the principle of desiring man subverts that of ethics.

---

[13] Ibid. p. 106.

[14] Michel Foucault, *The History of Sexuality: The Use of Pleasure*, Vol. 2, translated from the French by Robert Hurley, London: Penguin Books, 1985, p. 5 & p. 13.

2. Homoeroticism in the 17C

[1] 17C Attitudes Toward Homoeroticism

It is not so difficult to detect the contradictory ambivalence in seventeenth century attitudes toward homoeroticism which has been pointed out by many critics.[15] Caroline Bingham provided an example of the execution of the Earl of Castlehaven who was castigated for the rape of his wife and also indicted for sodomy.[16] Because Charles I held religiously orthodox views contrary to his father James I who was an unequivocal homosexual, he could not forgive the abominable impieties of Lord Castlehaven, who was executed in 1631. But considering Castlehaven's sister Eleanor's madness, her particular belief that she was a reincarnation of the prophet Daniel, his morbid obsession with sexuality and his hedonist tendency could have been regarded as one of the familial experiences of madness. But Lord Castlehaven's case was not considered as such and it must have resulted from the social

---

[15] About this, see C. Bingham, '17C Attitudes toward deviant sex' in *Journal of Interdisciplinary History* I (1971) pp. 447-68; Jean Howard, *The Stage and Social Struggle in Early Modern England* London and New York: Routledge, 1994; Stephen Orgel, 'Nobody's Perfect: Or Why Did the English Stage Take Boys for Women?' in *South Atlantic Quarterly* 88(1989), pp. 7-29; Ed Cohen, 'Legislating the Norm: From Somody to Gross Indecency' in *South Atlantic Quarterly* 88(1989) pp. 181-217; Alan Bray, *Homosexuality in Renaissance England*, Boston: Gay Men's Press, 1982.

[16] Caroline Bingham, 'Seventeenth Century Attitudes Toward Deviant Sex' in *Journal of Interdisciplinary History* I (1971) pp. 447-68.

context in which his sins were considered by his contemporaries not as sexual but as religious. Sodomy was seen as pestiferous and pestilential, as defiling the land, as a plague. How about the case of his sister Eleanor? Undoubtedly she was permitted to preach, though she was mad, in front of the public without any detention. As Foucault point out appropriately, before the major shift in man's attitude toward madness in 1656-1657, the pivotal date of the construction of the 'General Hospital', madness is seen as another from of "reason" with a language of its own; afterward, it is a mental illness.[17] The creation of the 'General Hospital' in 1656-1657, for example, leads to the great confinement of the mad along with the poor whereas before they were kept at a sacred distance, since their derangement could lead to salvation. Therefore the social context in which the sacredness of madness was seen as an experience of man rather than as an illness, must have provided Eleanor with a safe space for her preaching, whereas fanatically religious-oriented Charles I and his contemporaries could not forgive Castlehaven's unequivocal felony.

In the Renaissance, the boundary between the sexes was not demarcated. Medical and anatomical treatises cited homologies in the genital structure of the sexes to show that male and female were versions of the same unitary species.[18] Ian Maclean writes

---

[17] Michel Foucault, *Madness and Civilisation*, transled by Richard Howard, London:Routledge, 1967.

that "Many doctors at the end of the sixteenth and the beginning of the seventeenth centuries write eloquently against the wrong done to the honour of woman by Aristotle, and it is possible to argue that there is a feminist movement in medical spheres, where in theology there is little evidence of one.... One sex is no longer thought to be an imperfect and incomplete version of the other. Indeed, far from being described as an inferior organ, the uterus now evokes admiration and eulogy for its remarkable role in procreation."[19] Moreover, Elizabeth children of both sexes were dressed in skirts until the age of seven or so. The breeching of boys was considered as the formal ceremony foregrounding "the transition from the common gender of childhood, which was both female in appearance and in mentality largely controlled by women, into the world of men."[20] This event was traditionally regarded as a significant family ceremony. English Renaissance culture, to judge from the surviving historical evidence, does not show a morbid fear of homosexuality. Anxiety about the fidelity of women and "the threat of female sexuality," on the other hand, seem to have been strikingly prevalent, compared to the liberal and permissive attitude toward homosexuality.[21] Heterosexual

---

[18] This is summarized in the work of Ian Maclean, *The Renaissance Notion of Women*, Cambridge: Cambridge UP, 1980, pp. 28-46.

[19] Ibid. p. 29 & p. 33.

[20] Stephen Orgel, 'Nobody's perfect: or Why Did the English Stage Take Boys for Women?' in *South Atlantic Quarterly* 88 (1989), p. 11.

[21] Lisa Jardine, *Still Harping on Daughters*, London and New York: Harvester,

fornication was much more energetically prosecuted than the crime of sodomy. And this has a very practical reason. Magistrates took an interest in heterosexual crimes because they resulted in illegitimate births, which increased the poor rolls. However, there was rarely anything in homosexuality worth bothering about unless the activity involved coercion or malfeasance.

One of the noticeable things in the charges of sodomy is that they always occur in relation to other kinds of subversion. The activity has no independent existence in the Renaissance mind, just as there is no separate category of the homosexual. It becomes problematized in Elizabethan society only when it intersects with some other behaviour that is recognized as dangerous and antisocial. Thus, "it is invariably an aspect of atheism, papistry, sedition and witchcraft."[22] King James' public and overtly physical displays of affection for young men are frequently remarked in the period. For example, his excessive homoerotic feeling towards Buckingham can be witnessed in his letter.

1983. pp. 127-8. Jardine illustrates the masculine anxiety about cuckoldry and about the threat of promiscuousness of female sexuality, and takes as examples Chaucer's wife of Bath, the Duchess in *The Duchess of Malfi*, and Gertrude in *Hamlet*.

  22 Stephen Orgel, 'Nobody's perfect: or Why Did the English Stage Take Boys for Women?' in *South Atlantic Quarterly* 88 (1989), pp. 20-1.

I cannot content myself without sending you this present, praying God that I may have a joyful and comfortable meeting with you and that we may make at this Christmas a new marriage over to be kept hereafter, for, God so love me, as I desire only to live in the world for your sake, and that I had rather live banished in any part of the earth with you than live a sorrowful widow's life without you. And so God bless you, my sweet child and wife, and grant that ye may ever be a comfort to your fear dad and husband James R.23

They are considered to be in bad taste by the puritan mind, but not even the most rabid puritan connects them with the abominable crime against nature. In *Homosexuality in Renaissance England,* Alan Bray extrapolates the implications of the overlapping meanings and indicates that sodomy played a complex role in the religious, political and literary texts of the period.24 While sodomy in theory was a heinous offense, there were relatively few sodomy prosecutions during the period. The crime in daily life seems seldom to have been associated with what we would now term ordinary homosexual activity, for which there is quite a bit of evidence in the period, especially between men of unequal status, such as master and servant, schoolmen

---

23 *Letters of King James VI and I,* ed. G.P.V.Akrigg. Berkeley: Berkeley UP, 1984, p. 431.

24 Alan Bray, *Homosexuality in Renaissance England,* Boston: Gay Men's Press, 1982.

and students. Bray notes that "so long as homosexuality was expressed through established social institutions—such as the household, the educational system, homosexual prostitution and the like—the courts were not concerned with it."[25] For the 66 year period 1559-1625, for the whole of the countries of Kent, Sussex, Hertfordshire and Essex there are only four indictments for sodomy.[26] The evidence of the courts, Assizes and Quarter Sessions alike, tends to the same conclusion Prosecutions for homosexuality were very rare occurrences, and the concern of the courts with the regulation of homosexual behaviour was only marginal. As Bray suggests, "prosecutions for homosexuality between masters and servants are noticeably absent unless undue violence was involved, and the homosexual component in the educational system was largely unrecognized by the courts in the same way."[27] There is evidence that homosexuality was institutionalized not only at the universities but also in grammar schools and even in the village schools. Emmison writes that: "Mr. Cooke, schoolmaster of Great Tey, was presented on a serious charge, presumably paederasty. 'He is a man,' the wardens reported, 'of beastly behaviour amongst his scholars, and teacheth them all manner of bawdry' (1594). Cited to attend the next

---

[25] Ibid. p. 74.

[26] James Swanston Cockburn, ed., *Calendar of Assize Records: Home Circuit Indictments, Elizabeth I and James I*, London: Her Majesty's Stationery Office, 1985.

[27] *Homosexuality in Renaissance England*, pp. 52-3.

session, he failed to appear, and there is no further entry of this case."[28] Lawrence Stone demonstrates the singular lack of anxiety shown by parents to the end of the 17C about the homosexual influences their sons might be subject to at school or university.[29] So long as homosexuality did not disturb the peace or the social order and in particular so long as it was consistent with patriarchal mores, it was largely ignored in practice. The prosecution of homosexuality usually occurred in times of social upheaval which means that a sodomite was a likely candidate for the role of a scapegoat in the mentality of 17C England. It was exactly at such times that fear crystallized around those customary figures of evil which in more normal times were kept at a distance from everyday life. The case study of prosecutions for homosexuality illustrates in microcosm the discrepancy between the society's extreme hostility to homosexuality and its reluctance to recognize it in most concrete situations.

During its brief session in 1533, the English parliament took time to pass the first civil injunction against sodomy in British history. Prior to this secularization, sodomy had been defined in strictly ecclesiastical terms as one of the gravest sins against divine law, When Henry VIII's parliament made sodomy a felony

---

[28] F. G. Emmison, *Elizabeth Life: Morals and the Church Courts, Mainly from Essex Archidiaconal Records*, Chelmsford: Essex Country Council, 1973, p. 47.

[29] Lawrence Stone, *The Family, Sex and Marriage in England 1500-1800*, Harmondsworth: Pelican, 1979, p. 493.

in 1533, it transformed the broader implications of the religious offense into a specific legal injunction against a set of nonprocreative sexual practices.[30] The transformations of sodomy from an ecclesiastical to a secular crime must also be seen as part of a large-scale renegotiation in the boundaries between the Catholic church and the British state for Cohen, "sodomy had became an important element in the reproduction of the British government's sovereignty by the early 17C."[31] Sodomy reinforced the state's right to adjudicate personal, social and even spiritual limitations on the human body. It is because those convicted of sodomy were liable to public execution, which produced a spectacle that confirmed the crown's absolute power to seize upon the bodies of its subjects. At the moment of publishment, the sodomite becomes the text upon which ideological power of the state's authority is inscribed. In other words, "the punishment of the sodomite provided an occasion for the state to inscribe the offender's body with a hieroglyph signifying its power to use death in order to regulate the very basis of life."[32] It seems that sodomy was located in the universal potential for disorder and a sodomite was a scapegoat in times of social upheaval.

---

[30] H. Montgomery Hyde, *The Other Love: An Historical and Contemporary Survey of Homosexuality in Britain*, London: Heinemann Ltd., 1970. pp. 38-39.

[31] Ed Cohen, 'Legislating the Norm: From Sodomy to Gross Indecency', *South Atlantic Quarterly*, 88 (1989) p. 188.

[32] Ibid. p. 202.

[2] Representation of Homoeroticism in 17C Texts

Homoeroticism might have been recognized by a Renaissance audience of Shakespeare's work frequently in the form of warrior camaraderie, in which an all-male environment might have affected the relationship in an exclusive and enormous way. Noticeably, the male bonding of warrior camaraderie is as sexual as marriage, both sexual and violent, and certainly singular. We can find a good example of this in Aufidius when he confesses his powerful sexual feeling toward Coriolanus.

> Auf. Know thou first,
>   I love the maid I married, never man
>   Sigh'd truer breath; but that I see thee here,
>   Thou noble thing, more dances my rapt heart
>   Than when I first my wedded mistress saw
>   Bestride my threshold. (*Coriolanus*, IV.v. 114-19)

The homoerotic inflections of the metaphors used here are considered to be provided by the substitution of sexual and familial metaphors for those of national and military solidarity. The male bonding shown in the military camp becomes much more strong, sexual, and violent through these metaphors. But this warrior camaraderie is indicted for its individual and threat to national interest, which can be witnessed in the betrayal of the country by Coriolanus and the killing of Coriolanus by Aufidius.

An all-male institution fosters this military camaraderie. According to Freud, all men are bisexual, and that latent homosexuality can be perceived by many people as very threatening, especially in a hard, masculine, puritanical society.[33] A good example can be found in Arthur Gilbert's essay on buggery in the British Navy, 1700-1861.[34] According to Gilbert, harsh punishments were meted out to convicted buggers in the navy, and military attitudes reflected what the navy saw as their own unique problems of order and discipline. He writes:

> Between May 1, 1705 and June 29, 1708, for example, twelve men were sentenced to death in the Royal Navy. Of the 12, 6 were deserters, one was convicted of murder, and the remaining ive were found guilty of buggery. . . . It is clearly shown that buggery was as serious as murder and mutiny when we use capital convictions measured against total number of cases tried and those convicted of buggery were far more likely to receive death sentences than men charged with mutiny or murder. . . . In capital cases, the king could exercise this royal prerogative and pardon capitally convicted sailors and mariners. Courts martial records show, however, that the king would not pardon convicted buggers. Further, courts martial boards rarely recommended

[33] Sigmund Freud, "Leonardo da Vinci and a Memory of His Childhood" in *Standard Edition of the Complete Psychological Works of Sigmund Freud*, Vol. 11. London: The Hogarth Press, 1955, pp. 59-106.

[34] Arthur Gilbert, "Buggery and the British Navy, 1700-1861" in *Journal of Social History* 10 (1976) pp. 72-91.

mercy for homosexuals. . . . Thus, in spite of the supposed legal difficulty of proving buggery in the courts, a high percentage of purported sodomites were convicted and executed. . . . It is possible that homosexuals were singled out for punishment in wartime as part of the usual upsurge of patriotism and lack of tolerance for dissenters of all kinds that is often a concomitant of war.[35]

The navy was an all-male environment with very limited access to women. As a result, human relationships were governed by an extremely strict code of conduct. Particularly, the Royal Navy was close to a total institution. Total institutions have some characteristics: "control by one authority, the regulation and regimentation of all phases of daily activity, and a rigid body of rules imposed by officials and administrators."[36] The line between public and private behaviour can not be sustained in these circumstances. The individual can not maintain a private life in total institutions. However, in civil society, he can keep his private life even though it is not acceptable to the mores of the society. This total institution had not fully emerged in Shakespeare's time, but the all-male institution of military society in the Renaissance period can be understood as an incipient form of this total institution. Soldiers were controlled by one authority and the

---

[35] Ibid. p. 79, p. 81 & p. 86.

[36] Irving Goffman, *Asylums: Essays on the Social Situation of Mental Patients and Other Inmates*, Harmondsworth: Penguin, 1961. p. 17.

regulations were imposed on the concrete body of subjects. This all-male environment might have affected the male friendship and the eroticization of the male body in the military camp.

In addition to this warrior camaraderie, another frequent form of Renaissance homosexuality can be noted in the ruler's favorite. The bonding between king and favourite has naturally been recognized by their contemporaries as wasteful and decadent. "The myth of absolutism" and "the display of the power of the absolute monarch" in the matter of his favourite, were challenged by "the power of the wealth-generating gentry" when they had developed their power to confront the authority of the absolute monarch.[37] For example, in Shakespeare's *Richard II*, Bushy and Greene are represented as the most well known favourite type obviously located in the figure of the Renaissance homosexual. We can see the homosexual as analogous to the most dangerous national threat in Bolingbroke's accusation and indictment of Bushy and Greene.

> Bol. I will unfold some causes of your deaths:
> You have misled a prince, a royal king,
> A happy gentleman I blood and lineaments,
> By you unhappied and disfigured clean;
> You have in manner, with your sinful hours,

---

[37] Simon Shepherd, "Shakespeare's Private Drawer: Shakespeare and Homosexuality" in *The Shakespeare Myth*, ed. by G. Holerness, Manchester, 11988, p. 102.

> Made a divorce betwixt his queen and him,
>
> Broke the possession of a royal bed,
>
> And stain'd the beauty of a fair queen's cheeks
>
> With tears, drawn from her eyes by your foul wrongs;
>
> (*Richard II*, III. I. 7-15)

The dramatic instance of a homosexual relationship is presented as anti-social, seditious, ultimately disastrous. It is more explicit in Christopher Marlowe's *Edward II*.

> King. What Gaveston! welcome! — kiss not my hand,
>
> Embrace me, Gaveston, as I do thee.
>
> Why shouldst thou kneel? Knowest thou not who I am?
>
> Thy friend, thyself, another Gaveston!
>
> Not Hylas was more mourned of Hercules,
>
> Than thou has been of me since thy exile.
>
> (*Edward II*, I.i. 140-5)

Sexual imagery (kiss, embrace) is prevalent in the linguistic deployment of Edward II's affection, and the King-Gaveston relationship is something more than just friendship. Both politically and morally, Edward's relationship with Gaveston is represented as the most destabilizing factor in the play, even though, in reality, the power-hungry nobles and the queen's adultery with Mortimer are more destabilizing than Edward's homosexuality. Gaveston's sexuality is not the only reason for the complaint of the nobles against Gaveston, but it is related to the fact that he is being given preferments over other powerful and ambitious courtiers. With regard to this, we can find evidence in the generous titles given to Gaveston: "King, I here create thee Lord High Chamberlain, / Chief Secretary to the state and me, / Earl of Cornwall, King and Lord of Man." (I. I. 154-6). About the representation of homosexuality in *Edward II*, Stephen Orgel suggests that Edward's sexuality is 'a way of protecting the play, a way of keeping what it says about power intact.'

> For Marlowe to translate the whole range of power politics into sodomy certainly says something about his tastes and that of Elizabethan audiences, but it also has to be added that it was probably safer to represent the power structure in that way than it would have been to play it, so to speak, straight. Had Richard IIbeen presented as a sodomite would the authorities have found it necessary to censor the deposition scene? Maybe Edward's sexuality is a way of protecting the play, a way of keeping what it says about power intact. This is the work of Marlowe, the government spy, at once an agent of the establishment and deeply subversive.[38]

Obviously in Renaissance texts, male-male bonding, denoted in the relationships of warrior camaraderie and of the ruler's favourite, has been considered a disaster and a threat to the

---

[38] Stephen Orgel, "Nobody's Perfect," p. 25.

national interest. We can witness male homoerotic relationships finally destroyed in all the three cases of *Coriolanus*, *Richard II* and *Edward II*. The picture of homosexual conspiracy is analogous with the so-called communist threat that produced the MacCarthyite witch-hunts of communists.

In addition to warrior camaraderie and the ruler's favourite, there also existed a high aristocratic attitude toward male friendship and the sacred bond between them. We can trace it in Michel de Montaigne's "essay on friendship." In this essay. Montaigne describes the singularity of his relationship with his loving older friend Etrienne de la Boetie. He writes in his essay "If I were pressed to say why I love him, my only reply could be: "Because it was he. because it was I." . . . At our first meeting, we found ourselves so captivated, so familiar, so bound to one another, that from that time nothing was closer to either than each was to the other"[39] La Boetie, a judge at Bordeaux and a Hellenist, undoubtedly fostered Montaigne's taste for speculative writing and his influence lasted with his younger friend to the end of his life. Interestingly and questionably, Montaigne compared friendship with sexual love as follows:

Affection for women (sexual love) is a reckless and fickle flame, wavering and changeable, a feverish fire prone to flare up and die

---

[39] Michel de Montaigne, "On Friendship" in *Essays*, translated with an introduction by J.M. Cohen, London: Penguin Books, 1958, p. 97.

down, which only catches us in one corner. In friendship there is a general and universal warmth, temperate, moreover, and uniform, a constant and settled warmth, all gentleness and smoothness, with no roughness or sting about it. . . . It such a free and voluntary relationship could be established in which not only the soul had its perfect enjoyment, but the body took its share in the alliance also, and the while man was engaged, then certainly it would be a fuller and more complete friendship.[40]

The highest of all relationships is in his eyes a spiritual communion that could not coincide with the tie of kinship or heterosexual sex. He suggests that the idealistic relationship should involve both the soul and the body. However, he admits simultaneously that the sexual relationship between men which was permitted by the Greeks, is abhorred by contemporary morality. It represents the cultural context in which homoerotic relationship is considered a deviation. But as he insists, if female sex has no capability of this free and voluntary soul relationship, what he implies in this sentence is, ironically, male homoerotic bonding. Even though the physical was fortuitous and secondary to Montaigne, it was a requisite for the perfect friendship in his theory. Thus, his theory resulted in an inexplicable moral dilemma and discursive contradiction. Montaigne's idea demonstrates a locus in which profound ambivalence and

---

[40] Ibid. pp. 94-95.

contradiction toward homoerotic bonding are revealed not only on the personal level but also on the social and political level.

3. Male Friendship and the Eroticized Male Body in 1, 2 Henry Ⅳ

Prince Hal's subjectivity is deeply constituted in his relation to Falstaff, whose somatic iconography metonymically evokes a homoerotic charging between them. It is apparent that homoerotic desire infuses the relationship of Falstaff and Hal, signaled by both men's predominant lack of interest in women. Explicitly there is no woman who is represented to have a relationship with Hal. As we can judge from Henry IV's accusation against his son, little would suggest that Hal is spending himself in the company of women.

> Bol. Can no man tell me of my unthrifty son?
>   'Tis full three months since I did see him last.
>   If any plague hang over is 'tis he.
>   I would to God, my lords, he might be found.
>   Inquire at London, 'mongst the taverns there,
>   For there, they say, he daily both frequent
>   With unrestrained loose companions,
>   Even such, they say, as stand in narrow lanes
>   And beat our watch and rob our passengers,
>   While he, young wanton, and effeminate boy,

> Takes on the point of honour to support
> So dissolute a crew. (*Richard II*. V. iii. 1-12)

Hal's loose friends are highway robbers and tavern companions. It appears that they are exclusively male like the public world of court and battlefield. As for Falstaff, even though "he portrays himself as a womanizer, his relations with neither Mistress Quickly nor Doll Tearsheet carry the erotic impress and tenderness of his bond to Hal."[41] Their bond is explicitly expressed in terms of love as Falstaff insists.

> Host. So he doth you, my lord, and said this other day you
>   ought him a thousand pound.
> Prince. Sirrah, do I owe you a thousand pound?
> Fal. A thousand pound, Hal? A million, thy love is worth a
>   million, Thou owest me thy love. (*1 Henry IV*, III.iii.132-6)

Falstaff's declaration of love is protected from being read at face value, because the more serious his expression of love becomes, the more comic it is. In this scene, Falstaff is being shamed, lying to the Hostess and defrauding her. Thus, his declaration of love is not taken seriously at all. Falstaff is said to be fond of hot wenches and leaping houses but he is no Dun Juan even in Part

---

[41] Valerie Traub, "Prince Hal's Falstaff: Positioning Psychoanalysis and the Female Reproductive Body" in *Desire and Anxiety*, London and New York: Routledge, 1992, p. 59.

2 when his sexual relations with Doll Tearsheet and Mistress Quickly are made more explicit. Falstaff's indifference to women is represented dramatically in the argument of Mistress Quickly's protest that Falstaff's promised to marry her but he did not keep his promise.

> Host .... thou
> didst swear to me then, as I was washing why wound,
> to marry me, and make me my lady thy wife. Canst
> thou deny it? Did not goodwife Keech the butcher's
> wife come in then and call me gossip Quickly? –

The Hostess plays a part here. Falstaff's declaration of love is shielded by putting a woman between the two men. Placed between men, "she is nonetheless outside their circuit of relations. She functions to protect the dangerous homoerotic bond between Hal and Falstaff; and she becomes the site for the production of male anxiety. However, it would not be appropriate to conclude that she is totally excluded from the relationship with Falstaff; because it was she who conferred sublime weight on his death through her account of it (*Henry V*, 2.3. 9-27). Nonetheless, the structure of desire between Hal and Falstaff promulgates a homoerotic bond which is unavailable to women.

Elizabethan society lacked the idea of a distinct homosexual minority. The image of male friendship and the figure of the sodomite paralleled each other in an uncanny way. Male friendship was universally admired, while the sodomite was execrated and feared. However, there was a surprising affinity between these two categories. The term "bedfellow" blurs the distinction between the idea of friendship and the practices it involved. It shows that ordinary transactions between men in the period sometimes took place sexually. King Henry V blames his companion, Scroop, when he turns out to be a traitor.

> K. Hen. What shall I say to thee, Lord Scroop? thou cruel,
> Ingrateful, savage and inhuman creature!
> Thou that didst bear the key of all my counsels,
> That knew'st the very bottom of my soul,
> That almost might'st have coin'd me into gold
> Would'st thou have practis'd on me for thy use,
> May it be possible that foreign hire
> Could out of thee extract one spark of evil
> That might annoy my finger?
>
> (*Henry V*, 2. 2. 94-102)

Their intimacy is suggested by Henry's long accusation. His powerful and intense emotion, the passionate language, and the signs of a homoerotic friendship suggest sexual ambiguity. Who can know the key of all the counsels and the very bottom of his soul? To be someone's 'bedfellow' means that he can have influence and make fortune out of the relationship. Goldberg analyses that Scroop has been Hal's bedfellow and their physical intimacy is apparently implied in Hal's passionate emotion (Goldberg, *Sodometries*, p. 162-3). We can infer from the network of subtle male bonds that ordinary transactions between men in the period include in some cases sexual relationship and a potential ambiguity about sexual intimacy.

Obviously, Falstaff is associated with metaphors of carnality and corpulence. His being is exceedingly corporeal and his corpulence is referred to constantly, invoked in the emphasis on a swollen and distended body. Hal calls Falstaff 'fat rogue', 'damn'd brawn', 'embossd rascal' and 'my sweet beef'. Such a focus on the bulging and protuberant, the openings, permeabilities, and effusions of Falstaff's body situates him as a "grotesque body". According to Bakhtin's paradigm, early modern somatic concepts were classified into the grotesque and the classical body. The grotesque body is unfinished, outgrows itself, transgresses its own limits and it is not isolated from the world by exclusively defined boundaries. On the contrary, the classical body is an image of finished, completed man (Bakhtin, *Rabelais and His World*, 49).

Bakhtin's carnival tradition can be applied to the paradigm of *Henry IV* in the sense that market place and festive language can be found in the Boar's Head tavern and in Falstaff's language of festive obscenity. Falstaff's favoured space is the Eastcheap tavern. Jean Howard remarks, "Unexpectedly, in the *Henry IV* plays, the tavern is both the place where the pressure of modernity is most felt, and where possible solutions to this question of effective kingship are worked out. Significantly, the Boar's Head tavern seems not to be congruent, historically, with the world of early fifteenth-century England in which it is anachronistically inserted. As many commentators have noted, there is little doubt that it very much resembles taverns in late 16C London. It is here that the prince drinks the beer and sees the peach-colored stockings that would respectively have been consumed and worn in Shakespeare's own London. It is from the tavern that one gets a sense of the urban commercial world in which the London theater had its own existence and a sense of the range of people who might have paid to see history plays, the theater's representation of England's national past." (Jean Howard, *The stage and social struggle in early modern England*, 141-2) In the Eastcheap scenes, prose dialogue, colloquial diction, and abundance of imagery are drawn from daily life, and suggest an ordinary conversation recorded in a familiar location. In particular, the use of imagery displays the abundance and the exuberance of the carnival tradition. For example, Falstaff's melancholy is compared to a series of animals and objects with gloomy associations.

> Fal. Sblood, I am as melancholy as a gib cat, or a lugged bear.
> Prince. Or an old lion, or a lover's lute.
> Fal. Yea, or the drone of a Lincolnshire bagpipe.

Prince. What sayst thou to a hare, or the melancholy of
Moor-ditch?

Fal. Thou hast the most unsavoury similes, and art indeed the
most comparative rascalliest sweet young prince.

(*1 Henry IV*, 1.2.71-9)

Prince Hal's father, Henry IV, usurped the legitimate king, Richard II, and is undergoing serious domestic feuds and struggles. At the opening of *Henry IV, part 1*, the king is presented with problems of internal strife, "civil butchery". And the struggle between monarchy and aristocracy is revealed in the great structural conflict of post-feudal society. Hal needs a close male bonding in this historical crisis, which can be secured in times of war and militaristic hard times. In the all-male institution, both political alliances and homoerotic idylls are nurtured. Their homoerotic desire is transformed into the liminal spaces of romance and of popular carnival. Figures of carnival, forms of inversion and misrule, play an important role in these structures, since authority needs to define itself as order against oppositional energies that can be designated as disorder. Henry V's misspent youth as the unruly Prince Hal bestows on him the oppositional character of a contender, a power of challenge to legitimacy. However, they are forced to submit to the constituted authority and the state. Carnival vitality is transformed to serve the power of the state and violently reinscribed to the established social order. Thus, the uneasiness between masculine friendship and marriage is resolved, and the last scene of *Henry V*—Henry V's wooing of Katherine—represents an ideological and institutional investment. Katherine is not simply used as a locus of political negotiation but as a mediator to strengthen male bond and alliance. The patriarchal exchange of women is deployed as a virtual cover for male/male relations. Katherine is rendered a site of strengthening homosocial exchange. Desiring Hal negotiates with a French representative on the exchange through the traffic in women. This homosocial exchange is disguised and justified by the name of love and marriage, a domain of sexuality and power. The irreducible desire of the individual human being is irrevocably interrelated with a power struggle to achieve his own goal. Admitting that "Katherine is not being excluded entirely from male/male relations at the end of the play because she is allowed into the charmed circle of sovereignty", the fact remains that her erotic body is a significant locus for ideological and institutional investment in the political power game.

As can be seen in the erotic relationship of Falstaff and Hal, the erotic body is a material site for the inscriptions of ideology and power. Historically observed, Falstaff and Hal's relation is quite different from typical male homoerotic relations of the early modern period, in the sense that their relationship does not assume "a powerful older man who protects and mentors his young lover"; instead, "the Falstaff/ Hal relation concerns an older, less attractive, socially marginalized man who is emotionally and financially dependent on a younger, more attractive, increasingly independent and powerful prince" (Valerie Traub, *Desire and Anxiety*, p. 59). I have already mentioned that ordinary transactions between men in the period include sexual relationship in some cases and a potential ambiguity about physical intimacy. With regard to this, Jonathan Goldberg remarks, "In what situation, after all, does Falstaff ask his first question — now, Hal, what time of day is it, lad ?—If he is just waking up, what is Hal doing? . . . Is this attraction to his sleeping companion what the critics claim, a sign of infantilism? What is Hal talking about when he charges Falstaff with being an exorbitant "bed-presser" (2. 4. 238)" (Jonathan Goldberg, *Sodometries*, p. 163)

We do not know whether Hal sleeps with Falstaff and has sexual relations with him or not. There is no absolute answer to this question. However, we can say that a boundary could not be drawn clearly between male friendship and homosexual relations in Renaissance England. Hal has a bedfellow, Scroop, and their intimacy is revealed to the public in *Henry V*, act 2, scene 2. Scroop's crime is not what he did in bed but what he did as a traitor to the king. What is significant here is the way in which the plays police and discipline male/male sexual behaviour. It appears that Hal's loose tavern companions are almost exclusively male, and they are apparently the source of the king's accusation (*Richard II*. 5.3.1-12). Hal's misdeeds are enacted in his relations with Falstaff, and his 'shame' is placed on that unspeakable terrain. Falstaff, as we know, is far from being subject to social hierarchies and distinctions. The fact that Hal is allied to Falstaff, and that their relation implies physical intimacy, is almost tantamount to rebellion, in the historical context that there is a serious historical crisis in the usurped power of Bolingbroke. In contrast to this 'effeminate' Hal, Henry IV's ideal sonship is embodied in a masculine warrior, Hotspur.

> King. Yea, there thou mak'st me sad, and mak'st me sin
> In envy that my Lord Northumberland
> Should be the father to so blest a son;
> A son who is the theme of honour's tongue,
> Amongst a grove the very straightest plant,
> Who is sweet Fortune's minion and her pride;
> Whilst I by looking on the praise of him
> See riot and dishonour stain the brow
> Of my young Harry. O that it could be prov'd
> That some night-tripping fairy had exchang'd
> In cradle-clothes our children where they lay,
> And call'd mine Percy, his Plantagenet!
> Then would I have his Harry, and he mine.
> But let him from my thought. (*1 Henry IV*, 1. 1. 77-90)

Hotspur is the symbol of proper masculinity and the locus of the repudiation of femininity, while prince Hal is considered an effeminate boy by his father (*Richard II*, 5. 3. 10). His militarism and male camaraderie is emblematized by his devotion to rebellion, and he is willing to sacrifice his love for wife for the solidarity of male bonding: "When I am a-horseback, I will swear/ I love thee infinitely" (*1 Henry IV*, 2. 3. 102-3). It is from Hotspur that Hal seeks a proper masculinity, a sexuality that will permit relations with men not tainted with effeminacy. For Michel Foucault, dominant social formations not only manipulate but produce erotic desire through ideological and institutional means (Michel Foucault, *The History of Sexuality*, Vol. 1. 3-13). As Traub suggests, "sexuality thus embodies a power relation, not only for those members of erotic minorities who are positioned so as to feel most overtly the effects of institutionalized oppression, but for all sexual subjects, perhaps most insidiously for those who do not recognize (Valerie Traub. *The Matter of Difference: Materiality Feminist Criticism of Shakespeare*, p. 91). Sexuality becomes a locus of the manifestation of power and of the ideological and institutional investments. The contradictions between subjective internal need and material, institutional pressures are all foregrounded and interrogated in the exchange of the dominant discourses and the subversive practices of sexuality. Sexuality in the mode of power relations exposes the ways individuals negotiate within ideological matrices to satisfy their complex needs and desires. This foregrounding and interrogation emphasize "the social and ideological character of the process of subjectification by which various modalities of desire are manipulated and disciplined." (Traub, p. 101)

The rejection of Falstaff has been a locus of incessant debate for critics, providing a crucial focus for interpretation. Roughly speaking, there have been two recent perspectives in its interpretation: the first represented by the New Historicist emphasis on reinforcement of authority by containment, and the second by Cultural Materialist and Marxist criticism of carnival as liberation (Stephen Greenblatt, *New Historicism and Renaissance Drama,* pp. 83-108). The banishment of Falstaff performed in the public streets before a crowd of onlookers, rather than in private, is one of the first signs of Henry V's histrionic skills in action. In this episode, Hal performs kingship as an embodiment of justice. He speaks to Falstaff impersonally and formally:

> King. I know thee not, old man, fall to thy prayers.
> How ill white hairs becomes fool and jester!
> I have long dreamt of such a kind of man,
> So surfeit-swell'd, so old, and so profane:
> But being awak'd I do despise my dream.
> Make less thy body hence, and more thy grace;
>
> (*2 Henry IV*, 5. 5. 47-52)

These are not the teasing and colloquial terms in which previous exchanges between the two of them have been couched. When Hal replaces his father and discards his companion, he sees Falstaff as the blot on his wanton youth. He chose the Lord Chief Justice as father now in place of both the king and Falstaff. In his first soliloquy, Hal composes the image of himself as the king's true son by taking upon himself the form of Hotspur's honour. Hal's promised redemption can be achieved only by casting the northern youth as the locus of his glory and by casting off the contagious, gross body of Falstaff. Goldberg remarks, "Hal has designs on Falstaff and Hotspur; only by engrossing them can he be unspotted. What criticism has called Hal's maturity is this process of economization: the life and honour that he takes from Falstaff and Hotspur make him an ego ideal" Hal's retroactive rewriting of himself depends on betrayal and merciless calculation. The scheme of Hal's moral redemption is carefully laid out in his soliloquy at the close of the first tavern scene:

> Prince. I know you all, and will awhile uphold
> The unyok'd humour of your idleness.
> Yet herein will I imitate the sun.
> Who doth permit the base contagious clouds
> To smother up his beauty from the world,
> That, when he please again to be himself,
> Being wanted he may be more wonder'd at
> By breaking through the foul and ugly mists
> Of vapours that did seem to strangle him.
>
> (*1 Henry IV*, 1.2. 190-8)

Game theory is used to suggest that prince Hal's career as an agent provocateur in the London underworld is typical of the theatricality with which the modern state incites subversion, the better to contain it. (Greenblatt, pp. 83-108) I think Early Modern is a transitional period in which individualism is being transformed into the state governed by total administration, because the conflict between the liberating power through tradition like carnival and the reinforcement of authority was contested in the period. In particular, the conflict between total administration and individualistic dynamism is foregrounded in *1, 2 Henry IV* through the binary opposition between Falstaff's carnivalesque figure and the state's containing power.

This total transformation of carnivalesque figures can be considered as a function to clarify rather than to interrogate the distinction between legitimate and illegitimate powers. It firmly draws "the distinction between aristocracy and populace even as they overturn this primary categorical distinction". In other words, carnival figures as the constituent elements of a cultural formation which is the locus in which state power is producing the images of its own legitimacy, and provoking the oppositional energies against which it can define its own licit authority. But the play can be evaluated politically as much more committed to "oppositional exposure of such strategies, rather than the political manoeuvring of containment" (Holderness, *Shakespeare: The play of History.* p. 61). Male bonding between Falstaff and Prince Hal takes the form of a heterogeneous space which is incompatible with dominant social formations and institutionalized sexuality. The intensification of the male body and the specification of homoeroticism are ultimately rejected and frustrated by a powerful agency of prohibition. However, individual sexuality interrogates and problematises the mechanic hand of institution against the plurality of human experience. This interrogation underlines the social and ideological process of transformation by which the various modalities of desire are manipulated and disciplined. In this sense, it is instructive to analyze male friendship and the eroticised male body in relation to other modes of power.

2

1
장

초기 식민주의 담론에 나타난 기독교적 팽창주의와 여성의 몸: 콜럼부스의 『일기』와 셰익스피어의 『폭풍』을 중심으로

1. 서론

이 글에서는 콜럼부스(Christopher Columbus)의 『일기』(*Diario*)와 윌리엄 셰익스피어의 『폭풍』(*The Tempest*)을 살펴봄으로써 초기 서구 식민주의 담론에 나타난 기독교적 팽창주의와 여성의 재현에 대하여 연구한다. 위의 글들에서 우리는 식민개척자들의 처녀지를 착취하고자 하는 열망을 찾아볼 수 있으며, 이러한 열망은 남성화된 서구와 여성화된 식민지라는 이분법에 의하여 나타나고 있음을 알 수 있다. 정복과 성의 은유적 관계는 신세계를 여성의 몸으로 묘사하는 콜럼부스의 글에서 찾아볼 수 있다. 위의 담론에서 여성의 몸은 서구의 우월성과 주체성을 돋보이게 하는 매개체로서 기능하고 있으며, 차별화의 과정과 밀접하게 연관되어 있다.

셰익스피어의 작품 『폭풍』에서 클라리벨의 아프리카 왕과의 결혼은 전혀 반갑지 않은 매매로 그려져 있으며, 미란다의 순결성과 시코락스의 악마성과의 대조는 식민주의자와 피식민주의자의 도덕성을 대표하는 전형적인 재현으로 분석될 수 있겠다. 그런 의미에서 시코락스의 형상화는 피식민주의자의 입장에서 새로 쓰기를 요하는 중요한 대목이라고 본다. 성적으로 타락한 시코락스의 상태는 프로스페로의 정복을 합리화하는 방편으로 이용되고 있으며, 프로스페로가 미란다의 처녀성에 전전긍긍하며 훈시하는 것은 아버지로서의 당연한 의무감이기도 하지만 자신의 딸의 순결성이 자신의 정치적 재기에 있어 얼마나 중요한가라는 문제와 맞물려 있기 때문이다. 시코락스와 미란다의 재현은 성(sexuality)과 식민주의 담론의 연관성에 대해 시사하는 바가 크다. 흥미로운 사실은 위의 두 글에서 사회적 결집과 국가적 운명의 이름으로 행해진 식민개척이 기독교적 팽창주의와 여성의 재현과의 밀접한 관계 속에서 행해졌다는 사실이다.

2. 콜럼부스의 『일기』

콜럼부스의 『일기』는 허구라는 테두리 안에 갇혀 있는 문학작품과는 상당한 차이를 보일 수 있는 가능성을 다분히 지니고 있다. 그러나 흄(Peter Hulme)의 논의에서 볼 수 있듯이 식민주의 담론에서 진실과 허구의 구분은 다소 경계를 명확히 하기에는 어려운 점이 노출된다(Hulme 7-8). 콜럼부스의 『일기』가 여행기라는 형식을 취하고 있고 좀 더 사실에 기초하고 있다는 점을 감안한다면 사실에 기초한 담론인가, 아니면 허구에 좀 더 기초를 두고 있는 문학작품인가의 논의는 사실은 좀 더 지면을 요구하는 문제이다. 그러나 이 글에서는 장르의 문제보다는 그의 글에 나타난 신세계의 형상화 문제에 좀 더 초점을 두고 있기 때문에 장르의 문제는 여기서 더 이상 다루지 않기로 한다. 여성을 물화하고 차별화 하는 과정을 콜럼부스의 원문을 직접 인용함으로써 살펴보기로 한다.

이제, 제가 이미 말씀드렸던 것처럼, 저는 대단한 불규칙성을 보았습니다. 그래서 그 결과 지구에 대하여 저는 다음과 같은 견해를 가지게 되었습니다. 제가 발견한 바로는 다른 사람들이 지구에 대하여 묘사하는 것처럼 지구가 그렇게 둥글지 않다는 것입니다. 지구는 배의 모양을 하고 있고, 꼭지 부분이 있는 매우 눈에 뜨이는 여자의 유두부분과도 같은 일부분을 제외하고는 거의가 매우 둥글다는 것입니다. 그리고 이 부분은 가장 높고 천상에 가장 가까운 부분입니다.

Now, as I have already said, I have seen so great irregularity, that, as a result, I have been led to hold this concerning the world, and I find that it is not round as they describe it, but that it is *the shape of a pear* which is everywhere very round except where the stalk is, for there it is very prominent, or that *it is like a very round ball*, and *on one part of it is placed something like a women's nipple*, and that *this is the highest and nearest to the sky*…. (Italics are mine) (Columbus 30)

신대륙의 위치를 여성의 몸에 비유하고 그것을 하늘에 가장 가까운 곳이라고 묘사하는 것은 흥미롭다. 콜럼부스의 관점에서 보면 신대륙은 여성의 몸에 비유되면서 설득력을 얻고 그리고 그곳은 천국에 의해 비유됨으로써 많은 예비 서구 식민개척자들의 구미를 자극한다. 영토의 여성화를 통하여 권력의 위계질서가 확립되어지는 것이다. 즉 식민개척자는 권력을 지닌 남성, 그리고 신대륙은 그 권력에 의해 착취되어질 수 있는 여성이라는 이분법이 성립되어지는 것이다. 그러므로 성별의 정치학이 민족의 정치학과 맞물려 식민지 여성은 이중억압의 객체로서 기능하고 있는 것이다. 이를 통해 재현의 정치성, 특히 여성의 타자화와 관련한 정치성의 문제가 야기된다. 신대륙과 에로틱하게 재현된 여성의 몸의 강한 은유는 성별화된 문화적 가치를 초기 식민주의 담론에서 차용하고 있는 방식으로 작용하고 있는 것이다. 즉 성별의 정치학이 가치, 권력, 그리고 지배의 문제와 관련된 문화적 경제의 문제로 환원되어 나타난다.

콜럼부스의 식민지 개척에 있어서 기독교의 전파는 중요한 목표로서 기능한다. 콜럼부스의 『일기』의 편집자인 카사스(Las Casas)는 콜럼부스의 기독교 전파의 의지를 표명하는 엄숙한 어조를 다음과 같이 직접 인용하고 있다.

> 그 해군제독은 다음과 같이 말했다. 폐하, 제가 생각하기에는 그들이 경건한 종교적 인품을 소유하고 있고 그들의 언어가 있으므로 즉시 기독교인이 될 것입니다. 그리고 주님 안에서 제가 바라는 것은 폐하께서 이러한 위대한 민족들을 교회로 인도하고 개종시키도록 조속한 조처를 취해주셨으면 하는 것입니다. 폐하께서 성부와 성자와 성령을 고백하지 않으려는 자들을 멸망시켰던 것처럼 말입니다. 폐하의 생애가 다한 후에, 우리는 모두 유한하므로, 폐하께서는 가장 평온하고 이단과 사악함이 없는 상태에서 당신의 왕국을 떠나게 될 것입니다. 그리고 당신은 영원한 창조주 앞에서 잘 영접받을 것이고 그분은 영생과 많은 왕국의 증가와 주권, 그리고 당신이 지금까지 해왔던 것처럼 숭고한 기독교를 전파하려는 의지와 생각을 당신에게 기꺼이 주실 것입니다. 아멘. 오늘 저는 배를 이초 시키고 하나님의 이름으로 목요일에 배를 출발시킬 준비를 하고 있습니다. 그리고 금과 향료, 신대륙을 찾기 위해 동남방향으로 갈 것입니다.

'I hold, most Serene Princes,' the admiral says here, 'that having devout religious persons, knowing their language, they would all at once become Christians, and so I hope in our Lord that Your Highnesses will take action in this matter with great diligence, in order to turn to the Church such great peoples and to convert them, as you have destroyed those who would not confess the Father and the Son and the Holy Ghost, and after your days, for we are all mortal, you will leave your realms in a most tranquil state and free from heresy and wickedness, and you will be well received before the eternal Creator, Whom may it please to give you long life and great increase of many kingdoms and lordships, and the will and inclination to spread the holy Christian religion, as you have done up to this time. Amen. Today I refloated the ship and I am preparing to set out on Thursday in the name of God, and to go to the south-east to seek for gold and spices and to discover land.' (Columbus 57)

콜럼부스가 쓴 글에서 그가 가진 종교적 열망, 즉 신대륙의 원주민들에게 기독교를 전파하겠다는 열망을 잘 엿볼 수 있다. 그의 말에 의하면 그가 찾고자하는 금과 향료, 그리고 신대륙도 궁극적으로는 기독교의 전파라는 목표를 이루기 위한 수단으로 기능하고 있을 뿐이다. 콜럼부스의 경우에서 볼 수 있듯이 초기 신대륙의 발견 열풍 이면에는 기독교적 팽창주의가 내재하고 있었던 것이다. 그런데 이러한 콜럼부스의 종교적 열의에 대하여 냉소적인 비판을 가하는 비평가도 있다. 토도로프(Todorov)는 콜럼부스에게 복음전파자의 모습과 식민주의자의 모습이 양존하고 있다고 지적한다. 신대륙의 원주민들이 모두 고분고분하게 기독교에 귀의했던 것은 아니었다. 11월 12일자 일기에는 "원주민들이 우리가 가르쳐주는 기도문을 기꺼이 따라하며 십자가의 모양을 만들어 보이기도 한다."라고 적고 있지만 원주민들 모두가 기독교의 신상에 경의를 표했던 것은 아니었다. "교회를 떠나자마자 이들은 신상을 땅에 내던졌다. 그리고 흙으로 그것을 덮어버리고 그 위에 소변을 누었다." 그 장면을 보고서 콜럼버스의 형제인 바돌로메는 '매우 기독교적인' 방식으로 그들을 처벌하게 된다. 즉 군중들 앞에서 기독교를 모독한 이들을 불태워 죽여 버린 것이다(44). 이 이야기는 당시 식민주의자들의 이중적인 면모를 단적으로 보여주고 있다. 복음주의에 입각하여 하나님의 사랑과 자비를 전파하려 했던 이들은 원주민들의 반발에 부딪히게 되고 이를 호된 처벌로써 다스리려함으로써 식민주의자들의 이중성을 드러내게 된다.

복음전파자의 모습 속에 감추어진 식민주의자적 면모는 기독교의 영적 팽창을 위해 물질적 정복을 서슴지 않았던 이들의 모습에서 또한 드러나고 있다. 콜럼버스에게 있어 영적인 팽창과 물질적 이익은 불가분의 관계로서 인식되고 있다. "폐하께서는 우리의 성스러운 믿음이 전파되어서 많은 부를 취할 수 있는 또 다른 세계를 이곳에서 보시게 될 것입니다"(Your Highnesses have here another world in which our Holy Faith may be so propagated and whence may be taken so much wealth) ("Letter to the Sovereigns" 31/8/1498)라는 말에서 볼 수 있듯이 콜럼버스는 스페인 국왕에게 신세계 탐험의 유익에 대하여 두 가지를 지적하고 있는데 그것이 바로 기독교의 전파와 물질적 이득이다. 그리고 물질적 이득은 기독교의 영적인 전파보다도 더욱 설득력 있는 사안으로 부각된다. 그의 "신의 뜻에 따라서 저는 국왕과 여왕의 권위 하에 다른 세계를 복종시켰고 가난했던 스페인은 가장 부유한 국가가 되었습니다"(By the Divine will, I have thus placed another world under the authority of the King and of the Queen, our Sovereigns, and thereby Spain, which was reckoned poor, has become the richest realm of all) ("Letter to Dona Juana de Torres" November 1500)라는 말은 신세계의 정복으로 콜럼부스가 의도하고 있는 것이 물질적 이득임을 확인해 주는 부분이다. 콜럼부스는 마치 일정한 평등관계가 스페인과 신세계 사이에 성립되는 것처럼 기술한다. 스페인은 원주민에게 종교를 주고 대신 신세계로부터 금을 취한다. 그러나 이러한 교환이 다소 불평등하고 반드시 원주민에게 이득을 주는 것은 아니다라는 점을 별도로 하더라도, 이러한 두 가지 행위가 암시하는 바는 서로 상충적이다. 기독교의 전파는 인디언들이 신 앞에서 자신들과 평등한 존재라는 점을 전제하고 이루어진다. 그러나 만약 인디언들이 자신의 부를 주기를 꺼려한다면 어떻게 할 것인가? 그렇다면 인디언들은 군사적이고 정치적인 방법으로 강제적으로 정복되어져야 한다. 다시 말하면, 원주민들은 이번에는 인간적인 관점에서 자신들보다 열등한 위치에 처해져야 된다. 콜럼부스는 "50명의 병사로 폐하께서는 그들을 복종시킬 수 있고 원하시는 대로 무엇이든 하실 수 있습니다"(With fifty men Your Highnesses would hold them all in subjection and do with them all that you could wish)라고 말함으로써 어떠한 주저함도 없이 원주민들을 굴복시키는 것의 필요성에 대하여 논하고 있다. 이 시점에서 느껴지는 아이러니는 콜럼부스가 자신이 말한 기독교의 전파라는 신성한 사명과 물질의 착취라는 인간적인 사명 사이에 불연속적이고 모순적인 면을 함축하고 있다는 사실을 인식하지 못한 채 자신의 논의를 전개시키고 있다는 점이다. 이것이 기독교인의 목소리인가? 여전히 평등한 관계인가? 그는 신대륙으로의 3차 탐험을 떠나면서 스페인 국왕에게 자신과 함께 죄수들을 보내줄 것과 신대륙 개척과정을 통해 죄수들을 사면해 줄 것을 요청하게 된다. 죄수들을 통한 원주민의 복음화, 이것이 진정 복음주의자의 참된 모습인가?

콜럼부스의 의식에 나타난 원주민은 철저하게 타자화의 과정 속에 위치한 사람들이다. 콜럼부스가 원래 의도했던 동화주의(assimilationism)는 점차 노예화의 이데올로기로 변해가고 있었던 것이다. 동화주의에 함축되어 있던 원칙적인 평등주의는 노예화의 논리 속에서 인디언들의 열등한 존재를 강조하여 부각시키는 타자화의 과정으로 변화한다. 콜럼부스가 원주민들에 대하여 "그들은 착하고 성실한 하인들이 될 것입니다."(They would make good and industrious servants 11/10/1492)라고 묘사하는 것과 "그들을 복종시키는 것이 적합한 일입니다"(They are fit to be ruled 16/12/1492)라고 단언하는 것을 볼 때 그에게 있어 기독교에 귀의하지 않는 인디언들은 오직 노예로써 그들의 물질적 효용성을 발휘할 수밖에 없었던 것이다. 그렇다면 식민주의자의 의식에 비친 인디언 여성의 모습은 어떠한가? 사보나의 귀족으로서 콜럼부스의 항해에 참여하였던쿠니오(Michele de Cuneo)는 자신이 경험한 일화를 친구에게 보낸 편지에서 자랑스럽게 떠벌린다. 내용인즉 자신이 매우 예쁜 카립 여자를 범했는데 처음에는 매우 거칠게 반항하다가 채찍을 몇 대 때려줬더니 창녀보다 더욱 순종적으로 자신의 욕망을 채우도록 해주었다는 것이다(Todorov 48-9). 주목할 만한 점은 그가 원주민 여성을 창녀에 비유했다는 점이다. 그리고 그 동일시의 과정에서 주체의 욕구의 부도덕성은 무마되고 그러한 욕구를 불러일으키도록 만든 타자에게 책임을 전가시키고 있다는 점이다. 그 타자화의 과정에서 인디언 여성은 열등하고 비난받아 마땅한 존재로서 창녀에 비유되고 있고 식민주의자는 자신의 행위를 합리화시키는 노련함을 보인다. 권력의 역학관계 속에서 인디언 여성은 이중강간의 객체로서 기능하게 되는 것이다. 콜럼부스의 글에서 신세계가 천상의 희열을 줄 수 있는 매력적인 여성의 몸으로 묘사되었던 것처럼 원주민 여성은 식민주의자의 욕구를 채워줄 수 있는 객체로서 존재하는 것이다. 여기서 남성화된 서구와 여성화된 식민지라는 이분법이 뚜렷하게 부각된다. 남성과 공격성, 여성과 수동성, 서구와 남성성, 식민지와 여성성의 동일시를 통해 남성과 여성 사이에 존재하는 차별성이 서구와 식민지사이에 존재하는 차별성을 합리화시키고 공고화시키는 방식으로 나타나게 된다. "아메리카"라는 제목의 그림은 당대 식민개척의 열풍이 유럽을－특히 스페인, 영국, 포르투갈 등의 국가를－휩쓸던 시기에 사람들의 관념에 고정화된 서구와 신대륙의 이미지를 남성과 여성의 만남으로 형상화하고 있다(Peter Hulme의 *Colonial Encounters*의 figure 1 참조). 서구 식민주의자는 십자가 모양의 장식을 한 지팡이와 제대로 갖춘 복장을 하고 위엄 있는 자세로 신세계로 다가간다. 원주민인 여자는 벌거벗은 상태에서 무기력한 자세로 도움을 요청하듯 오른손을 내밀어 식민주의자를 맞이한다. 이 그림에서 식민개척자들의 처녀지를 착취하고자 하는 열망은 남성화된 서구와 여성화된 식민지라는 이분법에 의하여 나타나고 있다. 위의 담론에서 여성의 몸은 서구의 우월성과 주체성을 돋보이게 하는 매개체로서 기능하고 있으며, 차별화의 과정과 밀접하게 연관되어 있다. 위에서 언급한 그림에서 나타나듯 서구 식민주의자의 모습은 십자가와 완전히 갖춘 복장, 그리고 남성의 권위적인 모습으로, 그리고 신대륙의 이미지는 원시적인 벌거벗음과 무력함, 그리고 여성화된 식민지라는 이분법에 의하여 형상화되고 있다. 이러한 시각화된 이미지는 또한 셰익스피어의『폭풍』에서도 반복적으로 형상화되고 있고 차별화 된 점은 셰익스피어의 극에서는 성적으로 타락한 여성의 몸으로 형상화되고 있다는 점이다. 이는 콜럼부스의 글과 셰익스피어의 글 사이에 이미 100년 이상의 시간이 흘러서 식민지에 대한 서구 지식인들의 인식이 바뀌었기 때문이라는 점도 간과할 수 없겠다. 신세계 원주민들의 식민주의자들에 대한 태도가 변화되어가기 시작하는 상황에서 식민주의자들에게는 신세계가 단지 낭만적 상상을 불러일으키는 매력적인 여성의 몸

정도로 이상화되어 인식되기보다는 반란을 일으킬 수 있는, 그리고 통제할 수 없는 시코락스와 같은 여성의 몸으로 인식되고 있다고 볼 수 있겠다.

3. 셰익스피어의 『폭풍』

셰익스피어의 『폭풍』의 공간적 배경은 지중해의 한 섬이다. 폭풍에 의해 표류한 배가 지중해의 한 외딴 섬에 상륙하면서 이야기가 전개된다. 그런데 이 섬의 공간적 배경이 지중해일 뿐만 아니라 신대륙이라는 견해가 학계에서 지배적으로 인정되고 있다(Fiedler 167-212 Hulme 89-134). 이러한 관점의 주요한 근거는 칼리반(Caliban)의 형상화에 초점을 두고 있는데, 『폭풍』에서 칼리반은 당대 영국 사람들의 상상력 속에 강하게 자리 잡았던 신대륙의 원주민의 모습과 너무나 흡사하게 형상화되어 있다. 작품에서 칼리반은 원래 그 섬의 주인이었던 시코락스(Sycorax)의 아들로서, 시코락스가 등장인물들의 기억 속에서만 회상되어지고 실제로 무대에 나타나지 않는 반면 칼리반은 자신이 그 섬의 주인임을 내세우며 프로스페로(Prospero)의 통치에 대적해 반란을 꾀하는 인물이다. 서구 식민개척자와 신세계 원주민과의 대립이라고 보면 되겠다. 그런데 칼리반의 형상화와 관련하여 주지할 점은 당대 17세기 영국에서 실제로 런던거리에서 원주민을 전시하며 돈을 받던 관행이 있었다는 점이다. 그는 미개인의 전형으로서 존재하며, 셰익스피어의 작품 『폭풍』에서 다음과 같이 묘사된다.

이상한 생선이군! 만일 내가 지금 전에 가본 적이 있는 영국에 있다면 이 물고기에 색칠을 해서 구경거리로 내세워 한몫 잡을텐데. 구경온 사람들이 은전 한 닢쯤은 선선히 내겠지. 영국에서는 이 괴물로 한 밑천 잡을 수 있을 거야. 어떤 괴상하게 생긴 짐승도 영국에서는 돈을 벌어들일 수 있지.

그곳에선 절름발이 거지에겐 한푼도 인심을 쓰지 않으면서 죽은 인디언을 구경하기 위해서라면 은전 열 닢도 아끼지 않거든.

A strange fish! Were I in England now, as once I was, and had but this fish painted, not a holiday-fool there but would give a piece of silver. There would this monster make a man─any strange beast there makes a man. When they will not give a doit to relieve a lame beggar, they will lay out ten to see a dead Indian. (2.2.27-34)

칼리반이 이상한 냄새가 풍기는 생선, 내지는 괴물로 묘사되고 있는 대목이다. 칼리반은 당대 영국 식민 개척자들이 신대륙에서 마주쳤음직한 원주민의 모습을 갖추고 있다. 이러한 신대륙으로의 식민개척 열풍이 유럽을 휩쓸고 있었던 당대에 서구 유럽인들의 머릿속에 상상되어지던 신대륙 원주민들의 모습은 동등한 인간으로서가 아니라 반야수의 모습을 취하는 열등한 존재로서 자리 매김 되는 것이다.

Gaberdine(망토)에 대한 논의에서 볼 수 있듯이 반쯤 벌거벗은 칼리반의 모습은 자유로움보다는 문화적 열등으로서 묘사된다. 2막 2장에서 트린큘로(Trinculo)의 대사를 보면 "이런! 또 태풍이 몰려오는군. 이 녀석의 옷 밑으로 기어들어 가는 게 상책이야. 이 부근에는 몸을 감출 만한 곳도 없지 않은가. 진퇴양난일 때는 낯선 친구와도 동침하게 되는군."(Alas, the storm is come again! My best way is to creep under his gaberdine ─there is no other shelter hereabout. Misery acquaints a man with strange bed-fellows)(2.2.36-39)에서 'Gaberdine'이라는 단어가 나온다. 이 말은 오글(Stephen Orgel)의 주석에 의하면 조야한 망토(Cloak of coarse cloth)이다. 즉 소매가 없고 몸통만 가리게 되어있는 망토 같은 옷이다. 옷으로 보기에는 조야하고 격식이 갖추어지지 않은 셈인데 이 옷을 묘사하기에 적당한 단어를 찾기가 힘들었던 트링큘로는 영국적 옷에나 사용되던 이 단어로 칼리반의 이상한 옷차림을 묘사한다. 그런데 길리스(John Gillies)의 논의에서도 나타나듯이 칼리반의 이러한 조야한 옷차림은 리어왕에서 에드가(Edgar)가 'poor Tom'으로 몸에 걸쳤던 옷(blanket)과 같은 맥락에서 이해될 수 있다. 리어는 알몸의 에드가를 보며 "너는 알몸으로 이 극심한 날씨를 견디느니보다는 아예 무덤 속에 있는 게 낫다. 사람이란 이렇게 밖에 될 수 없는 것이냐? 이 사람을 잘 보아라. 너는 누에한테서 비단도 짐승한테서 가죽도 양한테서 털도 사향고양이한테서 사향도 빌지 않았구나. 그래! 여기 있는 우리 셋은(리어, 광대, 켄트) 인위적인 옷을 입었다. 너는 物 그 자체구나. 옷을 입지 않은 사람은 너처럼 불쌍하고 알몸뚱이인 두발짐승에 불과하다"(Thou wert better in a grave than to answer with thy uncovered body this extremity of the skies. Is man no more than this? Consider him well. Thou owest the worm no silk, the beast no hide, the sheep no wool, the cat no perfume. Ha, here's three on's are sophisticated; thou art the thing itself. unaccommodated man is no more but such a poor, bare, forked animal as thou art)(*King Lear* 3.4.99-106)라고 묘사하고 있는데 그의 대사에서 나타나듯이 이 망토 같은 옷은 '벌거벗음'에 대한 무대 관례였던 것이다(Gillies 96-7). 벌거벗은 칼리반은 앞에서 언급한 'America'라는 그림에 등장하는 벌거벗은 여성으로 묘사되었던 신세계의 모습을 강하게 상기시킨다. 벌거벗은 여성은 문명의 힘을 갖추지 못한 원주민이며 힘없이 손을 내밀어 위엄 있는 복장과 기독교의 장식을 갖춘 서구 식민주의자에게 도움을 요청한다. 이렇듯 문명 대 비문명의 만남, 서구와 신세계의 만남, 그리고 남성과 여성의 만남은 의복이라는 가시적인 매개체를 통하여 형상화되고 있다. 그러므로 칼리반의 벌거벗음은 신세계의 문명적 상태를 가시적으로 보여주는 중요한 모티프가 되고 있는 것이다.

또한 칼리반은 성별화된 민족적 위계질서의 논리에서 벌거벗은 여성의 위치를 차지하게 된다. 실제적으로 칼리반은 작품 속에서 여성적인 면모를 다분히 내포하고 있는 인물로 묘사된다. 그는 자신이 느끼는 섬의 아름다움에 대하여 여성적인 감수성을 가지고 묘사한다.

> 겁낼 거 없습니다. 이 섬에서는 늘 별별 소리가 다 나고 아름다운 곡조도 들려오지만 기분이 좋을 뿐, 아무 해도 없어요. 때로는 별 오만가지 악기소리가 들려 오지요. 어떤 땐 늘어지게 자고 난 후에도 다시 잠을 청하는 노랫소리가 들려오기도 합니다. 꿈을 꾸면 하늘 문이 활짝 열리는 것 같고, 보물들이 온통 나한테 떨어질 것 같아요. 그래서 다음에 눈을 떴을 때에는 다시 한번 꿈을 꾸고 싶어 안달이죠.

> Be not afeard, the isle is full of noises,
> Sounds, and sweet airs, that give delight and hurt not.
> Sometimes a thousand twangling instruments
> Will hum about mine ears; and sometime voices,
> That if I then had waked after long sleep,
> Will make me sleep again, and then in dreaming
> The clouds methought would open and show riches
> Ready to drop upon me, that when I waked
> I cried to dream again. (3.2.133-41)

그의 시각과 청각은 섬의 작은 소리와 풍부한 자연의 아름다움까지도 아주 미세한 부분까지 감지하여 향유할 수 있는 능력을 지니고 있다. 그리고 이 능력은 여성성의 긍정적인 능력으로 페미니즘 비평가들에게 예찬되었던 자질이기도하다(Irigaray 116-129; Whitford 53-74). 그는 여성의 긍정적인 자질로 인식되어온 상상력의 풍부한 능력을 이 부분에서 유감없이 보여주고 있다. 그의 양성적인 면에 대하여 존슨(Lemuel Johnson)은 다음과 같이 말한다. "칼리반은 마녀와 악마의 불만족을 모두 지니고 있다. 따라서 부계와 모계의 혈통에 걸맞는 인성과 언어 그리고 성격을 갖추고 있다. 그의 많은 선언들은 선한 것이든 난폭한 것이든 남성적이며 동시에 여성적인 것으로 이해 될 수 있다"(Caliban has all the discontents of a witch and of a devil and has accordingly been most judiciously furnished with a person, a language, and a character which will suit him both by father's and mother's side. . . . His various manifestations, virtuous or violent, may thus be proposed as male and female) (242). 존슨이 지적하듯이 칼리반이 가지고 있는 마녀적이고 악마적인 요소들은 그의 어머니 시코락스를 통하여 그에게 전해진 자질들일 것이며 그래서 작품 속에서 그의 형상화는 그의 어머니와의 불가분의 관계 속에서 이루어진다. 칼리반은 "시코락스의 모든 마력이(두꺼비, 딱정벌레, 박쥐) 너한테 떨어져라"(All the charms of Sycorax-toads, beetles, bats, light on you)라고 말함으로써 어머니의 주술의 힘이 프로스페로와 자신의 권력 투쟁에서 자신을 지원하는 힘이 되어주길 기원한다.

이와 관련하여 프로스페로는 식민주의자의 면모를 강하게 보여주고 있다. 육체적인 노동을 원주민에게 전가시키고 칼리반의 교육과 교화에 대한 절실함을 반복적으로 강조하고 있는데 이는 초기 식민주의자의 담론에서 기독교적인 팽창주의와 물질적 착취에 대한 갈망의 욕망구조가 반복적으로 강조되던 것과 흡사하다. 프로스페로의 모습에서 콜럼부스의 모습이 나타난다. 또한 신세계를 여성으로 묘사하고 인디언들의 긴 머리와 바디 페인팅을 여성적인 면모로 인식했던 콜럼부스처럼 프로스페로에게 이 섬은 시코락스와 불가분의 관계에 있고 그녀의 후손인 칼리반과의 관계속에서 자리매김 되는 공간이다. 프랭크 커모드(Frank Kermode)의 해석에 의하면 프로스페로는 작가의 의식과 동일시될 수 있으며 더 나아가 신과 셰익스피어, 그리고 프로스페로의 삼자의 동일시까지 가능하다. 그는 또한 작품의 근저에 신의 계시가 가장 중요한 특성으로서 자리 잡고 있으며 이 작품이 기독교의 서술방식을 차용하고 있다고 주장한다(Kermode 47-51). 이 관점에 의하면 셰익스피어의 마지막 작품에서 작가의 완벽한 예술성이 발휘되고 있으며 이는 기독교의 신이 완벽한 우주에 내재하는 것에 비유될 수 있겠다. 프로스페로가 눈에 보이지 않게 그리고 궁극적으로는 선하게 섬을 통치하는 것은 신의 내재와 통치를 상기시킨다(Hulme 105-6).이러한 신의 내재하심은 기독교의 역사관에서 'felix culpa'라고 불리는데 이는 현재에 지독한 재난으로 보이는 것이 신의 전체 계획에서는 궁극적으로 합당하고 필요한 과정임을 의미한다. 미란다의 질문 "그런데 무슨 불행한 일로 여기 오게 됐어요? 혹시 이리 온 게 잘된 일은 아닐까요?"(What foul play had we, that we came from thence?/ Or blessed was't we did?)(1.2.60-1)에 대하여 프로스페로는 "행복과 불행이 겸한 거야." (Both, both, my girl)(1.2.61)라고 대답하는데 이는 처음에는 나쁘게 보이는 것들이 궁극적인 신의 계시에 있어서는 그렇지 않다는 것을 의미한다. 비록 알론소(Alonso)가 그걸 깨닫게 되는 데는 5막이라는 긴 시간이 필요하지만 말이다. 이러한 관점은 셰익스피어의 작품 『폭풍』을 이해하는 데 있어 중요한 점을 제시해 주고 있다. 즉 프로스페로의 형상화가 기독교의 팽창주의와 불가분의 관계 속에서 이루어졌다는 점이다. 프로스페로는 전지전능하신 기독교의 신의 모습을 취하고 주술의 힘으로 자연 세계를 통제하려는 인물이며, 또한 서구의 우월한 기독교 문명으로 원주민인 칼리반을 교화시키려는 '숭고한' 의도를 가졌으나 그 의도가 관철되지 않자 모든 잘못을 칼리반의 야수성에 돌린다. 이러한 그의 모습은 초기 식민주의자가 기독교를 전파하겠다는 영적 목적과 물질적 이득을 추구하는 현실적 목적을 가지고서 원주민들에게 접근했을 때 영적인 목적에 부합되지 않는 인디언들을 나쁜 인디언들(bad indians)로 규정하고 가차 없이 처형하던, 혹은 노예로 팔아넘기던 아이러니컬한 모습을 연상시킨다.

그런데 그의 완벽해 보이는 통치는 결코 완벽할 수 없다는 사실이, 그리고 기독교적 팽창주의와 식민주의 담론이 제시하는 현실 읽기가 원주민의 현실 읽기가 될 수 없다는 사실이 칼리반의 반란에서 증명된다. 칼리반의 주장, "이 섬은 저의 것이었죠, 어머니인 시코락스의 권리로. 그런데 당신이 저한테서 빼앗아 간 거죠"(This island's mine, by Sycorax my mother,/ Which thou tak'st from me)(1.2.333-4)은 원래 섬의 통치권이 자신에게 있었음을 강조하며 프로스페로에게 정면 도전한다. 그의 주장은 일관되게 나타난다. 그는 프로스페로를 폭군이자 마술사 그리고 교활한 사람이며 사기꾼이라고 규정한다(I am subject to a tyrant, a sorcerer, that by his cunning hath cheated me of the island)(3.2.40-2). 프로스페로는 그의 힘과 주술을 이용하여 칼리반의 권리를 찬탈하였던 것이다. 프로스페로의 히스테리컬한 반응은 간접적인 부인, "이 거짓말쟁이 노예놈"(Thou most lying slave)(1.2.346)이나, 혹은 칼리반이 자신의 딸을 겁탈하려 했다는 사실에 대한 강조, "네 놈은 나의 딸의 정조를 강탈하려 했다"(thou didst seek to violate/ The honour of my child)(1.2.349-50)로 나타난다. 이는 원주민과 식민주의자 사이의 교환의 가능성을 전면부인 하는 것이며 자신이 이 섬에 초기에 정착했을 때에 대해서 그가 내세울 수 있는 전부이다. 실제로 그는 정착초기에 칼리반의 도움이 절대적으로 필요했다. "그가 없어서는 안 돼"(We cannot miss him)(1.2.313)라는 말에서 나타나듯 그에게 칼리반은 필수 불가결한 존재이다.

그렇다면 그는 왜 칼리반과 같은 천한 노예에게 자신을 의존해야 했을까? 만약 그가 주장한대로 자신이 주술의 힘으로 나무를 뽑고 죽은 사람을 살리고 할 수 있다면(5.1.33-57) 굳이 칼리반에게 도움을 요청할 필요가 있었을까? 피터 흄이 제시하듯이 그것은 프로스페로가 무능력하거나 아니면 게을렀거나 둘 중의 하나일 것이다. 모든 일을 할 수 있는데 나무를 한다든지 물고기를 잡는다든지 하는 생존에 가장 필수적인 일에는 무능력 했던 것이다. 이는 초기 식민주의자들이 총과 같은 최신식 무기를 통해 원주민들에게 자신의 힘을 과시할 수 있었지만 자신들의 생존을 위해 원주민들에게 의존할 수밖에 없었던 역사를 상기시킨다(Hulme 128). 자발적으로든 강제적으로든 원주민들은 식민주의자의 생존에 필요한 식품을 제공하는 역할을 담당했던 것이다. 이러한 작품의 요소들이 이 작품을 신대륙의 역사로 보게 하는 중요한 요소들이다.

칼리반이 시각화되어 무대 위에 등장하는 원주민의 모습의 전형으로서 존재하는 반면, 그의 어머니 시코락스는 프로스페로와 에어리얼, 그리고 칼리반의 기억 속에서만 존재하는 인물이다. 시코락스의 재현은 그의 정적인 프로스페로에 의해서 왜곡되어 나타나는데 이는 프로스페로가 계속해서 에어리얼에게 시코락스의 사악함을 반복적으로 진술하도록 강요함으로써 나타난다.

프로스페로   그럼 시코락스가 어디서 났는지 말해 봐.
에어리얼   예. 알지에르에서요.
프로스페로   음, 그래? 너 같은 놈에겐 한 달에 한 번쯤 지난 얘기를 들려줘야지 그렇지 않으면 잊어버린단 말야. 그 못된 년 시코락스는 고약한 짓은 혼자서 맡아 하는데다가 끔찍한 마술을 쓴 죄로, 너도 알다시피 알지에르 에서 쫓겨난 거다. 그

	렇지만 한 가지 공로를 봐서 목숨만은 살려줬지. 안 그래?
에어리얼	예. 그렇습니다.
프로스페로	파란 눈을 한 임신 중인 요귀를 선원들이 이 섬에 호송해

프로스페로 파란 눈을 한 임신 중인 요귀를 선원들이 이 섬에 호송해
다가 버렸는데, 그때 너는 네 말대로 시코락스의 종이었지
만 워낙 가냘픈 정령이라 그녀의 가증한 명령에 질겁을 하
여 따르지 않았단 말야. 그래 마녀는 노발대발하여 힘깨나
쓰는 부하의 도움으로 소나무를 쪼개어 그 틈바구니에 너
를 끼워 놓았어. 넌 그 틈바구니에 끼어 12년 동안이나 고
통을 받지 않았느냐? 그 동안에 마녀는 죽고 넌 살아 남아
서 네 신음소리는 물방아소리처럼 줄곧 새어 나왔지. 그 무
렵 이 섬에는 오직 그 마녀가 낳은 얼룩진 괴물 한 놈이 있
었을 뿐, 사람이 살고 있지 않았다.

Prospero	Where was she born? Speak; tell me.
Ariel	Sir, in Algiers.
Prospero	O, was she so—I must
	Once in a month recount what thou hast been,
	Which thou forget'st. This damned witch Sycorax,
	For mischiefs manifold and sorceries terrible
	To enter human hearing, from Algiers
	Thou know'st was banished-for one thing she did
	They would not take her life. Is not this true?
Ariel	Ay, sir.
Prospero	This blue-eyed hag was hither brought with child,
	And here was left by th' sailors. Thou, my slave,
	As thou report'st thyself, was then her servant,
	And for thou wast a spirit too delicate
	To act her earthy and abhorred commands,

Refusing her grand hests, she did confine thee,

By help of her more potent ministers

And in her most unmitigable rage,

Into a cloven pine, within which rift

Imprisoned thou didst painfully remain

A dozen years; within which space she died

And left thee there, where thou didst vent thy groans

As fast as mill-wheels strike. Then was this island —

Save for the son that she did litter here,

A freckled whelp, hag-born — not honoured with

A human shape. (1.2.260-84)

프로스페로의 관점에서 쓰인 시코락스는 사악한 악마이며, 성적으로 타락한 여자이고 마녀의 모습을 취한다. 이러한 경멸받을 만한 그녀의 성적타락은 프로스페로가 섬에서의 지배자의 권력을 합리화하는 한 방편으로 기능 하게 된다. 시코락스는 성적으로 타락한 그래서 아비가 누구인지도 모르는 아이를 임신하고서 북아프리카의 알제리라는 자기의 조국에서 추방당한 여자인 것이다. 그런데 이 사실은 프로스페로가 에어리얼을 통해서 알게 된 사실이고 에어리얼은 시코락스에 의해 처벌을 받았던 적이 있었던 인물로 결코 시코락스에 대해 공정하게 평가할 수 있는 증인이 되지 못한다. 프로스페로는 자신이 보지도 못했던 시코락스에 대해 원망할 명분이 있는데 그것은 칼리반의 존재이다. 칼리반은 자신의 딸인 미란다를 겁탈하려 했던 인물이다. 그래서 칼리반을 "악마의 자식"(got by the devil himself)(1.2.321), "타고난 악마, 천성적으로 교양이 결코 교육될 수 없는 놈"(a born devil, on whose nature/ Nurture can never stick)(4.1.188-9)이라고 묘사함으로써 사탄적이고 야수적인 면모를 강조한다.

"그 당시에는 이 섬에 시코락스가 낳아놓은 얼룩진 괴물 한 놈이 있었을 뿐 사람이 살고 있지 않았다"(Then was this island－/ Save for the son that she did litter here,/ A freckled whelp hag-born－not honour'd with/ A human shape)(1.2.281-4)라는 프로스페로의 말은 칼리반이 인간적 면모를 결핍하고 있다는 사실에 대한 반복적 강조이다. 그런데 스티븐 오글의 글에서도 볼 수 있듯이 칼리반이 미란다를 겁탈하려 했다는 점에 대해서는 재고가 필요한 부분이다. 오글이 제시하듯이 이는 원주민의 관점에서 이해한다면 자유연애(free love)의 차원에서 이해될 수 있는 부분이다(Orgel 42). 즉 서구의 관점으로는 섣불리 재단할 수 없는 원주민의 사랑의 방식과 언어가 있었던 셈이다. 그러므로 프로스페로는 원주민의 관행에 대해선 무지하면서 자신만의 관점을 반복적으로 주장하고 있는 셈이다.

4. 결론

위에서 살펴본 콜럼부스의 『일기』와 셰익스피어의 『폭풍』에서 우리는 식민개척자들의 처녀지를 착취하고자 하는 열망을 찾아볼 수 있으며, 이러한 열망은 남성화된 서구와 여성화된 식민지라는 이분법에 의하여 나타나고 있음을 알 수 있다. 정복과 성의 은유적 관계는 신세계를 여성의 몸으로 묘사하는 콜럼부스의 글에서 찾아볼 수 있다. 위의 담론에서 여성의 몸은 서구의 우월성과 주체성을 돋보이게 하는 매개체로서 기능하고 있으며, 차별화의 과정과 밀접하게 연관되어 있다. 또한 『폭풍』에서 시코락스의 형상화는 신세계에 대한 서구 기독교 전파자의 모습을 취한 프로스페로의 반복적 지시를 통하여 에어리얼의 기억 속에서 회상되는 형식을 취하고 있는

데 그들 삼자의－프로스페로, 에어리얼, 시코락스－이해관계를 분석해 볼 때 객관적인 진술이라고 보기 어렵다. 그러므로 피식민주의자의 입장에서 새로 쓰기를 요하는 중요한 대목이라고 본다. 성적으로 타락한 시코락스의 상태는 프로스페로의 정복을 합리화하는 방편으로 이용되고 있으며, 시코락스의 성적 타락은 성(sexuality)과 식민주의 담론의 연관성에 대해 시사하는 바가 크다. 본론에서 한 식민주의자의 일화를 통해 언급했듯이 그는 카리브(Carib) 여성을 창녀로서 묘사하는 과정에서 자신의 행동을 합리화 시키고 정당화 시키는 모습을 보여 주었다. 위의 두 담론을 종합해 볼 때 흥미로운 사실은 위의 두 글에서 사회적 결집과 국가적 운명의 이름으로 행해진 식민개척이 기독교적 팽창주의와 여성의 몸과의 밀접한 관계 속에서 행해졌다는 사실이다. 서구 기독교 전파의 사명이라는 허울 하에서 신세계 식민지는 착취할 수 있는 여성의 몸이라는 범주 안에서 형상화 되었고 그 과정에서 여성의 몸으로 묘사된 신세계는 서구의 우월성과 주체성을 부각시키는 이분법적 차별화의 과정을 겪는다.

그런데 시코락스의 재현의 문제와 관련하여 서구 식민주의자의 관점에서 본 신대륙의 모습이 성적으로 타락한 여성의 몸과 연관되어 나타났다는 점이 흥미롭다. 위에서 살펴본 콜럼부스의『일기』에서는 신대륙의 이미지가 단지 천상의 희열을 줄 수 있는 매력적인 여성의 몸, 그리고 강탈하고 싶은 욕망을 불러일으키는 처녀지로서 재현되었던 반면, 셰익스피어의『폭풍』에서는 비록 자신의 목소리로 자신의 입장을 진술할 수 있는 위치는 아니지만 상당히 위협적이고 공격적인 모습을 취하고 있다는 점이다. 실제로 시코락스가 없었다면 이 섬의 역사는 쓰여 질 수 없었을 것이다. 그녀는 이 섬에 정착하고 칼리반을 생산한 중요한 인물이다. 칼리반도 자신의 섬에 대한 소유권에 대하여 자신의 어머니를 내세우고 있고(This island's mine, by Sycorax my mother), 실제로 시코락스가 없었다면 그의 소유권에 대한 주장은 무의미했을 것이다. 시코락스는 또한 자신의 주술의 힘과 마술을 통하여 에어리얼에게 권력을 행사했던 인물로서 무기력하고 나약한 모습으로서가 아니라 공격적이고 적극적인 모습으로 재현되어 있다. 두 작품에서 신세계의 재현이 여성의 몸과 밀접하게 연관되어 있는데 차별화된 점은 콜럼부스의 글에서는 식민지가 매력적인 처녀지로 재현된 반면 셰익스피어의 극에서는 성적으로 타락한 여성의 몸으로 형상화되고 있다는 점이다. 이는 앞에서 언급했듯이 콜럼부스의 글과 셰익스피어의 글 사이에 이미 100년 이상의 시간이 흘러서 식민지에 대한 서구 지식인들의 인식이 바뀌었기 때문이라는 점과 밀접한 연관이 있다. 신세계 원주민들의 식민주의자들에 대한 태도가 변화되어가기 시작하는 상황에서 식민주의자들에게는 신세계가 단지 낭만적 상상을 불러일으키는 매력적인 여성의 몸 정도로 이상화되어 인식되기보다는 반란을 일으킬 수 있는, 그리고 통제할 수 없는 시코락스와 같은 여성의 몸으로 인식되고 있다고 볼 수 있겠다. 초기 서구 식민주의자의 담론에서 그들은 식민지를 묘사하기 위하여 여성의 몸과 직결된 성적 용어들을 은유로 선택했고, 성적 위계질서는 민족적 위계질서에 정당성을 부여하는 방식으로 기능 했다. 그런데 흥미로운 점은 아니러니컬하게도 그들의 의도와 상관없이 여성의 몸에 가해진 치명적인 언어폭력을 행하려는 그들의 시도는 시코락스와 같은 위협적이고 강력한 이미지를 가진 원주민의 재현을 통해 해체되어 나타난다는 점이다.

Works Cited

Columbus, Christopher. *Select Document Illustrating the Four Voyages of Columbus, Vol. II.* Trans. and Ed. with additional material, an introduction and notes by Cecil Jane. Oxford: Oxford UP, 1932.

Fiedler. L. *The Stranger in Shakespeare.* St. Albans: Paladin, 1974.

Gillies, John. *Shakespeare and the Geography of Difference.* Cambridge: Cambridge UP, 1994.

Hulme, Peter. *Colonial Encounters: Europe and the Native Caribbean, 1492-1797.* London: Methuen, 1986.

Irigaray, Luce. "An Ethics of Sexual Difference" in *An Ethics of Sexual Difference.* translated from the French by Carolyn Burke and Gillian C. Gill. London: The Athlone Press, 1993. 116-29.

Johnson, L. A. "Shoeing the Mule: 'Caliban' as Genderized Response," in *Latin America and the Carribbean: Geopolitics, Development and Culture.* ed. by Arch R. M. Ritter, Ottawa: CALACS, 1984. 241-54.

Kermode, Frank, ed. 'Introduction' of *The Tempest*, The Arden Shakespeare, London: Methuen, 1954, 47-51.

Orgel, Stephen. "Shakespeare and the Cannibals" in *Cannibals, Witches, and Divorce: Estranging the Renaissance*, ed. Margorie Garber, Baltimore and London: The Johns Hopkins UP, 1987. 40-66.

Shakespeare, William. *The Tempest.* Ed. Stephen Orgel. Oxford and New York: Oxford UP, 1987.

Todorov, Tzvetan. *The Conquest of America: The Question of the Other.* Translated from the French by Richard Howard. New York: Harper Colophon Books, 1985.

Whitford, Margaret. "Rationality and the imaginary" in *Luce Irigaray: Philosophy in the feminine.* London: Routledge, 1991. 53-74.

2
장
—

여성의 주체성 추구와 복장전도:
톰 스토파드의 〈사랑에 빠진 셰익스피어〉

1

　셰익스피어가 활동하던 시기에 강력한 왕권을 행사하였던 엘리자베스 여왕은 평생을 독신으로 살았고 결혼을 거부함으로써 가부장제에 편입되기를 거부하였다. 적자계승의 문제와 관련하여 늘 반란의 위험 속에서 통치하였던 그녀로서는 강력한 왕권의 창조가 늘 숙제인 셈이었다. 그런데 로이 스트롱(Roy Strong)에 의하면 엘리자베스는 자신의 처녀성을 영국 국민들의 애국심을 자극하는 기제로서 적극적으로 사용하였다고 한다. 그는 그의 저서 『엘리자베스 숭배』(*The Cult of Elizabeth*)에서 엘리자베스 당대의 유명한 그림과 시들을 분석하고 있는데 특히 1장에서는 많은 초상화에 형상화되어 나타난 여왕의 이미지에 초점을 두고 있다. 여왕의 초상화들은 군주에 대한 국민들의 정신구조를 형성시키는데 핵심적인 역할을 하고 있다. 즉 여왕의 몸을 영국의 영토로 환원시키고 그 과정에서 민족주의를 고무함으로써 여왕에 대한 절대적인 숭배사상을 고취하고 있는데 이는 거의 종교적인 수준에서 찾아볼 수 있는 그런 정도의 포괄적이고 복합적인 것이었다. 이러한 예를 단적으로 보여주고 있는 초상화가 바로 '무지개 초상화'(The Rainbow Portrait)이다. 이 초상화는 안정과 평화를 구가하던 엘리자베스 통치시기의 황금시대를 여왕의 복장에 나타난 그림들을 통해 형상화함으로서 이 초상화가 내포한 이데올로기를 보여주고 있다. 황금시대의 재현은 구체적으로 봄꽃들—pansies, gillyflowers, cowslips and honeysuckle—과 지성을 상징하는 눈(eyes)들, 그리고 귀(ears)들, 영속성을 상징하는 기둥들(pillars), 바위들(rocks), 그리고 엘리자베스 여왕이 바다와 육지의 여왕 신시아(Cynthia)라는 것을 암시하는 초승달(crescent moon)의 메타포를 통해, 그리고 시각화를 통해 그 구체성을 획득하고 있다. 여왕이 오른손에 쥐고 있는 무지개는 폭풍 후에 다가올 평화에 대한 전망을 제시하며, 왼쪽 소매에 그려진 하트모양을 입에 물고 있는 뱀은 여왕이 지혜로써 열정을 다스려야 함을 암시하고 있다. 엘리자베스의 몸은 개인의 몸이 아니라 국가의 정체성을 공고히 하는, 그녀가 구현하고 있는 몸의 정치에 대한 하나의 보기였다(Stallybrass 129-30). 또한 여왕의 초상화가 형상화하고 있는 황금시대의 이미지는 그녀의 복장에 그려진 각각의 사물들의 메타포를 통해 그 구체성을 획득하고 있으며, 민족주의는 여왕의 복장을 통해 전달되고 있는 것이다. 이처럼 복장은 단순한 의복의 의미를 넘어 그 복장의 착용자가 구현하고 있는 이데올로기를 표현하는 수단으로서 기능하고 있다.

르네상스시기에 몸의 이미지의 정치성이 가장 확연하게 구현되었고 요즘 셰익스피어 연구자들에게 흥미를 불러일으키고 있는 분야가 바로 복장전도 현상이다. 르네상스시기 영국에서는 의복이 단순한 옷의 의미만이 아니라 신분이나 계급의 척도였다. 그래서 옷에 대한 엄격한 규제가 존재했고 실제적으로 어느 계급 이상이어야만 어느 색깔의 옷을 입을 수 있고 여성은 남성의 복장을 모방하면 처벌을 받는다는 법이 존재했다(Stallybrass 125-6). 이 법을 어긴 사람들은 공개처형을 당했고 역사기록을 보면 상당수의 여성들이 처벌을 받았다. 의복에 대해 이렇게 민감해진 데는 사회적, 역사적인 배경이 있었다. 당시는 인구증가, 상업 활동의 증가, 교육 확대 등으로 사회 계급간의 변동이 전례 없이 활발하게 이루어지던 시기였고 이러한 대 격변의 시기에 사회 질서의 붕괴에 대한 공포를 느끼는 것은 어쩌면 당연한 일이었다. 이러한 맥락에서 돈을 많이 번 상인 계층의 사치스런 옷차림은 사회의 위계질서를 흐리는 행위로써 배척되었고 특히 남녀의 차별화를 흐리는 남장은 반사회적이고 반윤리적인 행위로 낙인 되었다. 셰익스피어의 희극들에는 남성의 복장을 착용한 여성들이 많이 등장한다. 예를 들면 『당신 좋으실 대로』(As You Like It)의 여자주인공 로잘린드(Rosalind)가 그렇고 『십이야』(Twelfth Night)에 나오는 바이올라(Viola), 그리고 『베니스의 상인』(The Merchant of Venice)에 나오는 포샤(Portia)가 그렇다. 『당신 좋으실 대로』에 나오는 여자 주인공 로잘린드는 추방당한 아버지를 찾으러 먼 길을 떠나는 과정에서 자신을 보호해야 되는 현실적 필요에 의해 남자 옷을 입고 남자로 행세하게 된다. 사랑하는 연인을 발견했을 때에도 수동적이고 수줍어해야 하는 여자로서가 아니라 적극적인 남자로서 행동하고 사랑을 쟁취한다. 이 극에서 여성의 복장전도는 여성의 주체성 추구를 위한 하나의 매개체로서 역할을 하고 있다. 또한 『십이야』에 나오는 바이올라는 새로운 땅에서 여성으로서 새롭게 적응해야 하는 이중부담을 복장전도를 취함으로써 극복해 나간다. 『베니스의 상인』의 포샤는 자신의 연인을 구하기 위해 불가피하게 남장을 하고 법정에 선다.

이들은 모두 적극적인 사회적 역할이 사회적으로 여성에게 봉쇄된 상태에서 불가피하게 복장전도를 함으로써 주체성을 추구하는 동일한 모습을 보여준다. 이는 복장이 지니는 단순한 의미를 넘어서 복장전도를 통해 불평등한 성 역할에 반항하고 여성에게 사회적으로 주어진 한계를 극복하려는 주체적인 추구로서 이해될 수 있다. 복장전도에 대한 찬반 논쟁이 치열하게 전개되었던 1620년에 런던에서 출판되었던 『힉 뮐리에: 남자 같은 여자』(Hic Mulier: or, The Man-Woman)라는 팸플릿의 표지를 보면 머리를 짧게 자르기 위해 이발소에 앉아 있는 여자와 깃털장식이 된 남자의 모자를 쓰고 자신의 모습을 거울로 바라보고 있는 두 여자의 모습이 등장한다. 이 두 여자는 '타고 났다고 세뇌된' 성별의 차이에 반항하고 도전하는 당시 소수 급진 여성들의 목소리를 대변하고 있다. 이 글에서는 당대 사회적으로 중요한 이슈가 되었던 남장의 모티브가 최근의 영화 <사랑에 빠진 셰익스피어>(Shakespeare in Love, 1998)에서 어떤 방식으로 차용되어 나타나는지 살펴보고자 한다. 그리고 바이올라에게 남장은 르네상스시기에 여성에게 가해진 문화적, 사회적 제약을 전복적으로 해체시키고 주체성을 추구하도록 작용한 적극적인 기제였음을 밝히고자 한다.

2

스토파드의 영화 <사랑에 빠진 셰익스피어>에 대한 기존 연구를 분석해 보면 영화에 대한 평가는 대조적으로 나타난다. 영화에 대한 긍정적인 평가를 견지하는 입장은 영화가 할리우드적 요소들도 다분히 내포하고 있지만 스토파드의 대본을 꼼꼼히 분석해 보면 이 영화가 흥행위주의 가벼운 영화라기보다는 셰익스피어의 원전에 충실하게 임하면서 새로운 의미생산에 주력했다는 평가이다(이교선, 「바이올라 인 러브, 셰익스피어 인 러브」, 최영주, 「거슬러간 시간, 그 상상의 즐거움 -<사랑에 빠진 셰익스피어>」). 영화에 대한 부정적인 평가는 이 영화가 셰익스피어의 미국화 전략을 동원하고 있으며 할리우드 영화의 상업주의적 속성과 자본주의 메커니즘을 여실히 보여주고 있다고 평가한다(이현우, 「셰익스피어와 할리우드 이데올로기」). 이교선은 이 영화가 <로미오와 줄리엣>의 제작을 둘러싼 셰익스피어의 실제 삶과 그의 작품세계에 대한 얘기에 그치는 게 아니라, 바이올라라는 한 여성이 단지 『로미오와 줄리엣』의 재료나 셰익스피어의 뮤즈로서가 아닌 그녀 자신의 삶을, 『십이야』의 삶을 사는 얘기라는 것에 대하여 주목하고 바이올라의 남장의 중요성에 대하여 언급한다. 최영주는 영화에 나타난 예술 예찬적 요소의 재현을 높이 평가하고 이 영화가 텍스트의 풍요로움과 재미를 영상으로 배가하며 그 중심에 작가성이나 페미니즘 문제를 떠올려 보다 다원적인 관점의 가능성을 보여주는 데 성공하고 있다고 평가한다. 위의 세 연구와 비교해 볼 때 필자의 연구는 기본적으로 이 영화가 할리우드의 상업주의적 속성을 보여주고 셰익스피어의 연극 텍스트를 영상 텍스트화 하는 과정에서 셰익스피어의 원전에 충실하게 임하면서 새로운 의미생산에 주력했다는 이교선과 최영주의 견해에 동의하는 입장을 취한다. 한편 최영주의 연구는 셰익스피어 원전의 영상화의 과정에 주목하고 진지한 논의가 영상에서도 가능한가? 라는 보편적인 질문으로 시작해서 윌과 바이올라의 운명적인 사랑과 예술 예찬적 요소의 재현에 초점을 맞추고 있다. 또한 이교선의 연구는 바이올라의 남장의 중요성에 대하여 언급하고는 있으나 구체적인 텍스트의 분석 없이 개괄적인 영화소개와 바이올라의 주체적인 삶의 재현의 중요성에 대하여 언급하고 있다. 필자의 연구는 위의 두 연구에서는 구체적으로 분석되지 않았던 주제인 바이올라의 복장전도에 나타난 주체성 추구의 문제와 그 전복성에 대하여 주목한다. 필자는 이 영화가 셰익스피어의 16세기 말 연극 텍스트를 20세기 말 영상 텍스트로 차용하는 과정에서 새로운 시대적 요구와 재현수단의 변화에 따라 바이올라의 남장을 통한 자기추구라는 측면을 강하게 부각해서 재현하고 있음에 주목하고 이 영화에서 복장전도가 바이올라의 주체성 추구의 중요한 기제로서 기능하고 있음을 밝히고자 한다.

90년대의 가장 매력적이고 지적인 낭만희극 중의 하나이며 오스카상을 수상한 <사랑에 빠진 셰익스피어>는 명랑한 로맨스, 생동감 있는 재담으로 가득 차 있어서 완전히 압도적이다. 아름다운 바이올라(Viola)는 남자들만이 참가할 수 있는 오디션에서 무사히 통과하기 위해서 자신을 남자로 분장해서 로미오의 배역을 맡게 되고, 그리고 많은 오해 후에 극작가의 마음도 얻게 된다. 곧 윌(Will)의 해적 희극은 아름답고 비극적인 『로미오와 줄리엣』(Romeo and Juliet)이 된다. 그리고 이 비극은 윌과 바이올라의 낭만이 가진 고통과 환희를 보여준다. 그는 결혼했고 그녀는 가까운 미래에 웨섹스와 결혼하기로 되어 있었던 것이다. 오스카 시상식에서 대본 작가상을 수상한 마크 노먼(Marc Norman)과 톰 스토파드(Tom Stoppard)가 『로미오와 줄리엣』의 이야기 내에서, 그리고 『십이야』의 이야기 내에서 그들의 이야기를 전개시키는 방식은 거의 환상적이다. 무수히 많은 비유들과, 자주 인용되는 대사, 줄거리 전개 그리고 주제의 차용 등을 분석하기 위해서는 셰익스피어를 연구하는 학자를 필요로 할 정도이다. 그러나 이 영화의 성공을 가져온 중요한 요소는 두 배우의 유백색 어깨이다. 오스카 시상식에서 설명할 수 없게도 외면당했지만 핀즈(Fiennes)는 저돌적이고 진실한 윌의 역을 연기했다. 그리고 여우주연상을 받은 팰트로우(Paltrow)는 이전에 그녀의 연기를 보아왔던 관객들도 예상하지 못할 만큼 놀라운 연기를 보여주었다. 숨막힐 정도로 아름답고, 맹렬하게 지적이며, 강한 의지를 가진, 그리고 사랑에 빠진 바이올라의 연기는 여러 가지 면에서 셰익스피어의 가치에 값하는 연기이다. <사랑에 빠진 셰익스피어>는 연극을 사랑하는 바이올라의 이야기를 복장전도와 성 역할의 전도라는 개념과 연결시키고 크게는 『로미오와 줄리엣』의 이야기 구조를 차용함으로써 셰익스피어에 대해 문외한인 사람들에게도 사랑을 받았던 작품이다. 바이올라는 연극을 너무나 사랑하기 때문에 연기를 하기 위해서 남자로 분장한다. 이러한 성 역할이 전도되는 줄거리는 과거의 영화에서 몇 번 시도된 적이 있었다. <투씨>(*Tootsie*)와 <엔틀>(*Yentl*)은 비슷한 줄거리를 가진 뛰어난 작품들이다. 그런데 우리는 이 영화에서 윌이라는 극작가와 사랑에 빠지는 바이올라를 보게 된다. 그녀의 윌과의 사랑이 또한 그녀가 연극의 세계를 추구하며 차용한 복장전도와 성 역할 전도의 문제와 어떻게 연결되어 있는가가 이 영화에서 가장 독창적인 요소이다. 역사적으로 사실적이지는 않지만 독창적이다.

바이올라는 여성이 무대에 서는 것을 근본적으로 허용하지 않는 당대 영국의 법으로 인해서 연극에서 진실한 사랑이 표현될 수 없다고 생각한다. 궁정에서 공연된 연극 <베로나의 두 신사>를 보고서 실비아의 배역에 대하여 바이올라는 다음과 같이 평가한다. 실비아의 역은 맘에 들지 않았어. 그의 손가락들은 주먹질로 인해 빨개져있었고 마치 수업을 듣는 학생처럼 대사를 말했어. 이 나라의 법이 속치마를 입은 하찮은 소년들에게 여주인공을 맡기는 동안 무대 위의 사랑은 결코 진실된 사랑이 될 수 없어 (But Silvia I did not care for much. His fingers were red from fighting jand he spoke like a schoolboy at lessons. Stage love will never be true love while the law of the land has our heroines played by pipsqueak boys in petticoats)(*Shakespeare in Love*, 20)! 남녀 간의 사랑을 주제로 한 연극에서 여자의 배역을 변성기 이전의 소년이 맡는 관행을 비판하는 근거가 바이올라의 관점에서 보면 사랑이 진실되게 표현되지 못한다는 점이다. 실비아의 역을 맡은 소년의 손이 십대 소년들이 으레 그렇듯이 주먹질로 인해 빨갛게 된 상황에서 관객들은 결코 사랑의 표현을 자연스럽게 느낄 수가 없다는 것이다. 이러한 부자연스런 상황을 법으로 규제하고 있는 현실에서 바이올라는 자신이 추구하는 연극의 세계를 체험하기 위하여 과감하게 복장전도의 기제를 취하게 된다. 로즈 극장에서 <로미오와 에델>(*Romeo and Ethel*)이라는 연극에 필요한 배우들을 위한 오디션이 열리게 되는데 바이올라는 토마스 켄트(Thomas kent)라는 가명을 쓰고 남자배우로서 자신의 실력을 발휘하게 된다. 말더듬이들과 허풍장이들의 연기에 질려버린 셰익스피어에게 켄트의 생생한 연기는 깊은 인상을 주었고 결국 주연배우 로미오의 역을 맡기게 된다. 가슴을 묶고 남자아이의 가발을 구해달라고 유모에게 부탁을 한(you will bind my breast and buy me a boy's wig) 바이올라는 자신이 꿈꾸던 삶을 토마스 켄트라는 소년으로서 남장을 함으로써 성취하게 된다.

바이올라는 자신이 원하는 연극에의 꿈을 실현시키기 위하여 남성의 복장을 취하고 무대에 서게 된다. 주지하다시피, 16세기 영국에서는 여성이 무대에서 연기를 하는 것이 철저하게 금지된 상황이었다. 이러한 역사적, 사회적 맥락 속에서 그녀의 복장전도는 단순히 여성이 남성의 복장을 취했다는 외면적인 의미 외에도 여성의 성 역할에 대한 근본적인 도전으로서 기능하고 있다. 복장과 성별에 대한 의미 있는 고찰을 한 마조리 가버(Marjorie Garber)는 자신의 책 *Vested Interests: Cross-dressing and Cultural Anxiety*의 서문에서 우리가 성별과 색깔에서 당연시하고 있는 남자아이는 파랑색, 여자아이는 핑크색이라는 이분법적 구조가 사실은 2차 대전 이후 생겨난 개념이라는 사실을 언급한다. 그녀는 뉴욕 타임즈 기사를 인용하며 20세기 초반에는 남자아이들이 그 당시 좀 더 강렬하고 명확한 색으로 인식되었던 핑크색 옷을 착용했다고 한다. 우리가 성별과 복장에 대하여 고착된 사실로서 이해하는 것들이 사실은 특정한 문화적, 사회적 구조 속에서 생성되고 유포되는 것임을 알 수 있게 해주는 단적인 사실이라고 볼 수 있다. 그러므로 옷의 차이로 성별의 차이를 고착화시키고 남성의 여성에 대한 우위를 그리고 고위층의 하위층에 대한 우위를 고착화시키려는 의도는 복장전도라는 전복적 행위를 통하여 해체되어 나타나는 것이다. 복장전도가 가지는 도전성을 복장이 차이를 만들어낸다는 사회적 관행에 대하여 그러한 정치적 목적이 의도하는 바가 얼마나 부자연스럽고 연극적인가를 드러내 보여줌으로써 효력을 발휘한다. 복장전도는 고정된 그리고 변화하는 정체성, 변환할 수 있는 혹은 부재하는 자아에 대한 갈망의 장소로서 자리매김 된다. 계급과 성별의 접합지점에 위치한 복장전도는 계급과 성별이 동등하지는 않다고 하더라도 변환할 수 있는 것임을 입증하였다. 계급과 성별의 범주와 사회적 규범이 침해될 수 없는 고정된 것이라는 전제에 대해 의문을 제기하고 그러한 범주 정하기가 계획되고 유포되는 것임을 해체적으로 보여주고 있다.

연극에 심취해 있는 바이올라는 셰익스피어 선생님의 극에 나오는 대사를 외우고 있을 정도로 연극작품을 사랑하며 또한 극작가인 윌리엄 셰익스피어에게 연모의 정을 느낀다. 한편 바이올라 집에서 열린 파티에서 바이올라를 보게 된 윌은 즉시 그녀를 사랑하게 되고 토마스 켄트를 통해 (그가 바로 바이올라라는 사실을 까맣게 모른 채로) 바이올라에게 자신의 연애편지를 전달하게 한다. 가면(mask)을 쓴 남자의 상태에서 바이올라는 윌이 자신을 얼마나 사랑하는지를 묻는다. 윌의 대답을 통해 바이올라는 윌이 사랑에 심취한 사람이 느낄 수 있는 그런 상대에 대한 깊은 몰입과 마취의 상태에 있음을 알 수 있다. 윌에게 있어 바이올라의 눈은 자신을 성찰할 수 있게 해 주는 힘이 있으며, 그녀의 입술은 이른 아침 장미도 질투하여 시들 정도로 아름다우며, 그녀의 음성은 종달새의 지저귐보다 더

깊고 은은하다(65-6). 물론 이러한 묘사가 당대 연애시에 자주 등장하는 상투적인 표현이라는 점을 감안한다 하더라도 바이올라에 대한 윌의 묘사는 그가 바이올라를 깊이 사랑하고 있으며 그녀에게 매료되어 있음을 충분히 알 수 있게 할 정도로 극찬과 이상화로 가득 차 있다. 윌의 답변으로 그의 자신에 대한 사랑을 검증한 바이올라는 자신의 가면을 벗고 본인의 정체를 드러낸다. 적극적으로 먼저 자신의 사랑을 표현하고 그리고 사랑 받기를 갈망한다. 두 사람의 서로에 대한 애정은 연극에 대한 공통된 열정에서 시작된다. 바이올라가 엘리자베스 여왕과의 면담장면에서 표명하는 자신의 연극에 대한 애정은 확신에 차 있으며 확고하다.

> 여왕. 너를 본적이 있다. 너는 화이트 홀과 리티몬드에서 공연하는 모든 연극에 왔었지.
> 바이올라. 여왕폐하.
> 여왕. 무엇을 그렇게 좋아하느냐?
> 바이올라. 여왕폐하.
> 여왕. 솔직히 말해 보거라. 나는 내가 누구인지 안다. 왕과 여왕의 이야기를 좋아하느냐? 아니면 무훈담이냐? 그렇지 않으면 궁정 연애담이냐?
> 바이올라. 저는 연극을 좋아합니다. 극단의 단원들이 저를 위해 연기하는 것을 보는 것은 정말로. . . .
> 여왕. 그러나 극작가들은 사랑에 대해 아무것도 가르쳐 주지 않아. 사랑을 아름답거나, 희극적이거나 욕정적으로 그릴 뿐 진실되게 표현하지는 못하지.
> 바이올라. 그렇지만 그들은 할 수 있어요! 제 말은 . . . 폐하. . . . 극작가들이 사랑을 진실되게 표현 못하고 여태껏 표현한 적이 없지만 한 사람만은 할 수 있다고 믿어요.
> 웨섹스. 바이올라 양은 세상물정을 잘 모릅니다. 여왕폐하는 그것을 잘 아시죠. 본질과 진실은 연극의 매우 큰 적이죠. 저의 재산을 걸고 내기

를 하겠습니다.

여왕. 나는 자네가 재산이 없어서 여기 온 걸로 알고 있는데. 자, 아무도
　　　자네의 내기를 받아들이지 않는 것 같군.

윌. 50파운드요.

여왕. 50파운드. 매우 가치 있는 질문에 대한 가치 있는 액수로군. 연극이
　　　사랑의 진실과 본질을 보여줄 수 있을까? 내가 그 내기에 증인이 되
　　　고 그러한 상황이 발생하면 심판관이 되겠네.

Queen. I have seen you. You are the one who comes to all the
　　　plays—at Whitehall, at Richmond.

Viola. Your Majesty.

Queen. What do you love so much?

Viola. Your Majesty.

Queen. Speak out! I know who I am. Do you love stories of kings
　　　and queens? Feats of arms? Or is it courtly love?

Viola. I love theatre. To have stories acted for me by a company
　　　of fellows is indeed—

　　　　　　　. . . . .

Queen. But playwrights teach nothing about love, they make it
　　　pretty, they make it comical, or they make it lust.　They
　　　cannot make it true.

Viola. Oh, but they can! I mean. . . . Your Majesty, they do not,
　　　they have not, but I believe there is one who can. . . .

Wessex. Lady Viola is . . . young in the world. Your Majesty is
　　　wise in it. Nature and truth are the very enemies of
　　　playacting. I'll wager my fortune.

Queen. I thought you were here because you had none. Well, no
　　　one will take your wager, it seems.

Will. Fifty pounds!

Queen. Fifty pounds! A very worthy sum on a very worthy
question. Can a play show us the very truth and nature of
love? I bear witness to the wager, and will be the judge of it
as occasion arises. (*Shakespeare in Love*, 93-5)

권력의 정점에 있는 엘리자베스 여왕은 연극이 사랑의 진실을 표현할
수 없다고 단언하고 이에 대하여 바이올라는 과감하게 자신의 연극에 대한
신념을 표현하고 여왕의 의견에 대하여 반박한다. 세상물정을 아직 잘 모
르는 언동이라고 웨섹스경이 끼어들지만(Lady Viola is . . . yound in
the world), 바이올라의 이러한 단언은 그만큼 자신이 추구하는 연극의 세
계가 한낱 허구에 불과한 것이 아니라 사랑의 진실과 본질을 현실적으로
표현할 수 있다는 확신에 차 있기 때문에 가능한 행동이라고 볼 수 있다.
바이올라의 연극에 대한 열정과 확신은 구체적으로 연극의 세계에 동참하
는 행동을 통해 나타나고 그녀의 노력은 <로미오와 줄리엣>이 성황리에
공연되고 연극을 비판하던 청교도들마저 박수갈채를 아끼지 않는 장면에
서 결실을 맺는다. 그런데 연극이 성공리에 공연된 후 바이올라는 위기를
맞이하게 되는데 이는 연회 사무국장인 틸니(Tilney)가 줄리엣 역할을 맡
았던 배우가 진짜 여자임을 폭로함으로써 드러난다. 법적으로 여성이 무대
에서 연극배우로서 활동하는 것을 금지했던 당대의 상황을 고려해 보면 바
이올라의 공연이 폭로되는 순간 그녀의 위법 행위는 가볍지 않은 법적 제
재를 받을 것임이 분명한 상황이 연출된다. 이때 등장한 여왕은 본인이 직
접 줄리엣 역할을 맡았던 토마스 켄트를 면밀히 살펴보고 다음과 같이 결
론을 내린다.

여왕. 그래, 분장이 뛰어나군, 그리고 틸니 자네의 실수는 쉽게 용서가 되 겠군. 그러나 나는 남성의 직업을 가진 여성에 대하여 아는 바가 있 네. 신께 맹세코 나는 그것에 대해 아네. 그만하면 됐네. 켄트군.

Queen. Yes, the illusion is remarkable and your error, Mr. Tilney, is easily forgiven, but I know something of a woman in a man's profession, yes, by God, I do know about that. That is enough from you, Master Kent.

(Shakespeare in Love, 148)

여왕은 켄트를 면밀히 관찰한 후 바이올라가 켄트로 변장했다는 사실을 눈치챈다. 그러나 '남성의 직업을 가진 여성에 대하여 아는 바가 있다'라는 대사에서 알 수 있듯이 여왕은 당대 여성에게 금지되었던 연극의 세계에 과감하게 참여하였던 바이올라를 이해하고 그녀의 위법행위를 눈감아 준다. 이는 여왕 자신이 남성의 전유물로 치부되고 여성에게는 철저하게 차단되었던 정치의 세계에서 많은 남자 귀족들의 반란을 제압하며 강력한 왕권을 행사하였던 당대의 역사적 맥락을 고려한다면 좀 더 이해가 쉬워지는 부분이기도 하다. 엘리자베스 여왕은 자신이 여성으로서 겪었던 권력투쟁에서의 어려움을 기초로 바이올라가 자신이 추구하는 연극세계에의 동참과정에서 불가피하게 발생되는 어려움을 공감하고 있는 것이다. 그런 과정에서 여왕은 바이올라에게 '남성의 직업을 가진 여성'으로서 유대감을 느끼고 있다고 볼 수 있다. 즉 누구보다도 바이올라의 일에 대한 추구와 복장전도를 통한 주체성 추구를 이해하며 공감하는 인물이 바로 여왕인 것이다. 영화상에서 바이올라의 연극세계에의 추구에 대하여 강력한 지지세력으로 재현된 인물이 바로 여왕과 유모이다. 그리고 이것은 셰익스피어의 원전을 발전적으로 전유한 일례이기도 하다. 바이올라의 유모 또한 시종일

관 바이올라의 남장을 도와주고 걱정 반 격려 반의 시선으로 그녀의 일에 동조하며 그녀의 지지 세력이 된다. 엘리자베스 여왕은 비록 영화상에서 직접 남장을 하고 전장을 지휘하여 남성적 제왕의 풍모를 과시하는 장면은 등장하지 않지만 마커스가 지적하듯 역사적 기록을 보면 자신이 여성의 약한 육체를 지니고 있으나 자신의 정신은 어느 군주보다 강하고 위엄이 있다고 공언하고 공식행사에 남장을 하고 군주의 위용을 드러내 보였다. 이러한 관행은 복장의 젠더규정을 통해 자신의 강한 군주로서의 이미지를 부각시키고자 하는 정치적 의도가 명백한 관행이었다(Marcus 145). 군주의 육체적 몸과 정치적 몸의 이중적 수행 속에서 여왕은 자신의 남장을 통해, 그리고 자신의 양성성의 정치적 공언을 통해 수많은 반란의 위협을 제압하고 강력한 왕권을 행사한 군주로서의 면모를 보여주고 있는 것이다. 이러한 맥락에서 영화에 나타난 여왕과 바이올라의 동지애에 가까운 공감대 형성을 이해할 수 있다. 틸니의 체포령을 무마시킨 후 여왕은 이전에 바이올라와의 면담 장면에서 바이올라와 열띤 논쟁을 일으켰던 '연극이 사랑의 진실과 본질을 보여줄 수 있는가?'라는 논제에 대하여 결론을 내린다. 웨섹스 경에게 '내가 기억하기로 내기를 했었지. 연극이 사랑의 진실과 본질을 보여줄 수 있는 지에 대해서. 오는 자네가 진 것 같군(148)'이라고 말함으로써 연극이 사랑의 진실과 본질을 표현할 수 있다는 바이올라와 윌의 신념이 옳았음을 인정하고 연극의 위대성에 대하여 시인한다. 연극이 사랑의 진실과 본질을 표현할 수 없다고 확언했던 여왕이 윌과 바이올라가 주연한 "로미와와 줄리엣"을 보고서 자신이 판관이 되겠다고 약조했던 웨섹스와 윌의 내기에서 윌의 편에 손을 들어 주는 것은 연극의 힘에 대하여 다시 한번 상기시키는 계기가 된다. 자신의 연극에 대한 애정을 실현시키는 과정에서 바이올라가 취한 복장전도는 그녀가 16세기 영국이라는 시간적, 공간적인 상황 속에서 여성으로서 당면한 사회적, 문화적 제약을 극복하려는 적극적인 기제로서 이해될 수 있다. 여성에게 가해진 복장과 사회참여에 대한 문화적 제한을 주체적이고 능동적으로 극복하려는 시도에서 복장전도를 하게 되고 자신의 연극에 대한 열정을 구체적으로 검증하는 작업을 거치게 되는 것이다. 복장에 대한 관례나 법률은 차별화의 과정에서 연극적으로 가해진 임의적 강제성이라고 볼 수 있으며 성별의 차별화에 대한 복장전도는 이러한 사회적 규약에 대한 해체적이고 전복적인 행위로써, 바이올라의 경우 자신의 연극에 대한 열정을 구체적으로 실현시키기 위한 적극적인 기제였다.

바이올라는 연극에 대한 자신의 꿈을 실현시키기 위하여 남장을 하고 법을 위반하며 성의 정체성과 성 역할에 대한 고정관념의 근본적 전복을 시도하였다. 이러한 그녀의 주체성 추구와 전복적 행위는 결혼이라는 당면한 과제에 대응하는 그녀의 자세에서 현실타협적 태도를 드러내게 된다. 바이올라는 아버지와 남편이라는 두 '주인님'이 만들어 주는 삶, 그리고 결혼이라는 제도속에서 교환의 대상으로 존재하는 여성의 삶이라는 틀 안에서 크게 벗어나지 못하는 한계를 노출한다. 여성의 가치가 첫째, 지참금이 얼마냐, 둘째, 아이를 잘 낳을 수 있느냐, 라는 기준으로만 정해지던 삶의 시대적 한계 속에서 바이올라는 여왕과 아버지의 명령에 순순히 굴복하게 된다. 여성의 가치가 지참금과 다산성에 의하여 정해지던 16세기의 사회적 맥락 속에서 바이올라의 내면의 욕구, 연극에 대한 열정, 윌과의 사랑은 한 치의 고려의 가치도 없는 것으로 치부된다. 그녀의 웨섹스 경과의 결혼은 그녀의 아버지와 웨섹스 경의 협상 과정에 의해 결정되고 그녀는 선택권을 원천적으로 박탈당한 상태이다. 이러한 맥락에서 바이올라의 아버지 로버트 경과 웨섹스 경의 대화는 결혼의 매매성에 대하여 시사하는 바가 크다.

로버트 경. 제 딸은 아주 작은 지참금만으로도 왕과 결혼할 수 있을 정도로 미인이죠.

웨섹스 경. 버지니아에 있는 저의 농장은 작은 지참금으로는 대출받을 수 없죠.

나는 당신의 손자가 웨섹스 가문의 사람이 될 때 당신에게 신분의 상승을 가 져다줄 전통 있는 이름을 가지고 있소. 그녀가 아이는 잘 낳을 것 같소?

로버트 경. 아이는 잘 낳을 것이오. 만약 낳지 못하면 돌려보내시오.

웨섹스. 고분고분한가요?

로버트. 기독교 국가의 어떤 노새만큼이나 순종적이죠. 그러나 만약 자네 가 내 딸아이와 결혼할 거라면 많은 지참금을 가지고 갈 걸세.

웨섹스. 그녀가 맘에 듭니다.

Sir Robert. She is a beauty, my lord, as would take a king to church for a dowry of a nutmeg

Wessex. My plantation in Virginia are not mortgaged for a nutmeg. I have an ancient name that will bring you preferment when your grandson is a Wessex. Is she fertile

Sir Robert. She will breed. If she do not, send her back.

Wessex. Is she obedient?

Sir Robert. As any mule in Christendom. But if you are the man to ride her, there are rubies in the saddleback.

Wessex. I like her. (*Shakespeare in Love*, 42)

상품화된 예비신부의 가치기준은 오로지 지참금의 액수에 의해 결정되 며 예비신랑 웨섹스의 관심사도 오로지 돈이라는 사실이 명백하게 나타나 있는 대화이다. 'dowry' 'mortgage' 'rubies' 등과 같은 단어는 이러한 사 실을 뒷받침해주는 증거들이며 현실적으로 빈털터리 귀족가문 출신인 웨섹스가 경제적인 문제에 촉각을 곤두세우는 것이 그리 이상할 것은 없는 상황이라고 볼 수 있다. 첫 번째 관심사인 결혼의 경제적인 가치에 대하여 지참금 문제를 넌지시 언급하면서 장인이 될 로버트 경에게 자신의 의도를 확인시킨 웨섹스는 자신이 결혼에서 신부에게 요구하는 덕목으로서 다산성(fertility)과 순종적인 성격(obedience)을 언급한다. 세 가지 요구조건에 대하여 분명하게 전달한 웨섹스에게 로버트 경은 자신의 딸을 통해 신분 상승하려는 욕구를 또한 분명하게 전하고 있다. 자손을 생산하지 못하면 다시 친정으로 돌려보내라는 말과 지참금을 두둑이 들려 보낼 것이라는 암시를 하면서 이 결혼이 가문과 경제력의 결합이 될 것임에 대하여 추호의 여지가 없음을 확인시켜 준다. 이 대화는 레비 스트라우스가 지적했듯이 결혼에서 주체는 당사자인 남성과 여성이 아니라 두 그룹의 남성들이며 이 과정에서 여성은 교환의 대상으로서만 존재한다는 것을 단적으로 보여준다. 당대 사회적 구조 속에서 결혼에 당면한 여성은 구조적으로, 그들이 그 사실을 인식하든 인식하지 못하든, 교환의 대상으로서 존재한다. 그런데 결혼의 당사자인 바이올라가 꿈꾸고 있는 것은 당대의 구조상 상대를 선택할 수 있는 권리가 박탈된 상태에서 여성의 주체성이 완전히 차단된 결혼이 아니라 자신의 자아를 온전히 발휘할 수 있는 사랑이다. 그녀는 결혼 문제를 언급하며 웨섹스 경을 들먹이는 유모에게 자신이 원하는 것이 시와 사랑임을 분명히 한다. 유모와 바이올라가 나누는 대화를 살펴보자.

유모. 웨섹스 경이 오늘 밤 아가씨를 보고 계셨어요.
바이올라. 궁정에 있는 남자들은 시를 몰라. 만약 그들이 나를 본다면 그들은 나의 아버지의 재산을 보는 거야. 나는 평생 시와 함께 할 거야. 그리고 모험 사랑도. 무엇보다도 사랑을 할 거야.
유모. 발렌타인과 실비아처럼요

바이올라. 아니요 기교적인 사랑말고요. 삶을 뒤 엎을 수 있는 그런 사랑. 명령할 수 없고 통제할 수 없고 마음속에 일어나는 폭동 같은 사랑. 파멸이 오든 환희가 오든 어떻게 할 수 없는 그런 사랑. 연극에서 결코 나온적이 없는 그런 사랑. 저는 사랑을 할 거예요. 그렇지 않다면 평생을. . . .

유모. 유모로 보내신다구요?

Nurse. Lord Wesse was looking at you tonight.

Viola. All the men at court are without poetry. If they look at me, they see my father's fortune. I will have poetry in my life. And adventure. And love. Love above all.

Nurse. Like Valentine and Silvia?

Viola. No. . . . Not the artful postures of love, but love that overthrows life, unbiddable, ungovernable, like riot in the heart, and nothing to be done, come ruin or rapture. Love like there has never been in a play. I will have love or I will end my days as a. . . .

Nurse. As a nurse? (*Shakespeare in Love*. 21)

위 대사에서 알 수 있듯이 바이올라의 꿈은 시를 아는 사람을 만나 지극히 열정적인 사랑을 하는 것이다. 사회적 제도로서 정해진 결혼이라는 의식에서 상품화되고 수동적인 위치에 처해있는 바이올라가 과감하고 적극적으로 자신이 이상적으로 여기는 상대에 대한 주체적인 관심을 제시하는 것으로 볼 수 있다. 그녀가 제시한 이상적인 사랑의 대상자는 시와 문학을 아는 사람이다. 이것은 그녀가 인생에서 추구하는 것이 연극에 대한 열정이라는 점과 밀접한 관련을 지니고 있다(I would stay asleep my whole life if I could dream myself into a company of players. p.

21). 그녀는 궁정에서 공연되고 있는 연극을 보며 대사를 따라할 정도로 연극작품에 대한 각별한 애정과 열정을 가지고 있다. 그러므로 자신이 진정으로 사랑할 수 있는 대상도 자신이 추구하는 세계를 이해하고 공유할 수 있는 인물이어야 한다고 믿는 것이다. 한편, 웨섹스와의 결혼식은 2주 후로 다가오고 바이올라는 자신이 웨섹스경을 사랑하지 않는다는 사실을 분명하게 전달한다(I do not love you, my lord). 결혼의 문제에서 중요한 이슈가 되는 것이 사랑이라고 굳게 믿는 바이올라에게 웨섹스의 대답은 냉담하다.

> 웨섹스. 당신의 마음은 변덕스럽군요! 당신의 아버지는 상인이었고 당신의
> 자녀들은 귀족 가문의 문장을 지니게 될 것이오. 그리고 나는 재산을
> 회복하게 될 것이오. 그것이 오늘 우리가 토론할 유일한 문제요. 당신
> 도 버지니아가 마음에 들 거요.
> 바이올라. 버지니아라뇨?
> 웨섹스. 물론이요. 나의 재산은 나의 농장의 성패에 달려 있소. 담배사업말
> 이요. 배를 의장시키고 투자를 착수하는데 4000파운드가 필요하요. 담
> 배사업은 전망이 좋소. 오래 머무르진 않을 거요. 3,4년쯤. . . .
> 바이올라. 그런데 왜 저죠?
> 웨섹스. 당신의 눈 때문이요. 아니 입술 때문이요.

Wessex. How your mind hopes about! Your father was a shopkeeper, your children will bear arms and I will recover my fortune. That is the only matter under discussion today. You will like Virginia.

Viola. Virginia?

Wessex. Why, yes! My fortune lies in my plantations, the tobacco weed. I need 4000 pounds to fit out our ship and put my

investment to work—I fancy tobacco has a future. We will not
stay there long, 3 or 4 years. . . .

Viola. But why me?

Wessex. It was your eyes. No your lips. (*Shakespeare in Love* 60)

결혼에서 중요한 쟁점이 되는 것이 사랑이라고 믿는 바이올라와는 대조적으로 웨섹스는 그것이 가문과 재력의 결합임을 다시 한 번 상기시킨다. 두 사람의 결혼으로 몰락한 귀족가문의 후예인 웨섹스는 재력을 회복하게 되는 것이고 한편 부유한 상인인 바이올라 집안은 귀족이라는 계급의 상승을 획득하게 되는 것이다. 결혼을 통한 자신의 목표 추구가 명확한 상태에서 사랑이라는 추상적인 개념은 웨섹스에게 아무런 가치가 없는 것이다. 경제적인 가치가 최우선인 웨섹스의 가치관과 시와 사랑, 연극의 세계를 추구하려는 바이올라의 가치관은 절대적으로 상이한 것이며 웨섹스는 결코 바이올라의 사랑의 대상이 될 수 없다. 그러나 아버지와 여왕이 승인하고 결정지은 결혼의 문제에 대하여 바이올라는 순순히 순종할 것임을 밝힌다. 바이올라는 결국 사랑에 대한 자신의 신념을 관철시키지 못하고 결혼이라는 사회적 제도 안에서 자신이 비록 사랑하지는 않지만 결혼의 대상으로서 웨섹스를 받아들이게 되는 것이다. 이러한 그녀의 현실 타협적 순응은 시대적으로 결혼에 대해 주체적 선택을 할 수 없었던 당대 여성들의 현실적 제약과 그 구조적 한계성을 전형적으로 재현하고 있다. 결혼과 사회참여에 대한 제약 속에서 연극에 대한 그녀의 꿈은 마치 기적처럼, 신기루처럼, 아주 제한적으로 밖에 이루어질 수 없었다. 그러나 이교선이 지적하듯 그녀가 여성에게 가해진 사회적 제약을 연극을 통해 전복시킨 그 순간의 광채는 웨섹스와 함께 해야 할 나머지의 삶에 대하여 희망을 주는지도 모른다. 또한 영화가 바이올라의 결혼과 그 후의 삶에 대하여 보여주는 결말은 그리 어둡지만은 않다. 남편과 함께 버지니아로 가던 바이올라는 폭풍을 만나 바다에 빠지고 깊은 바다 속에서 기적처럼 살아난 유일한 인물이 된다. 서양 문학에서 물에 빠진다는 것은 정화와 재생을 의미하며 이 장면은 바이올라가 자신이 얻은 주체적인 삶에 대한 자각을 간직한 채 새로운 사람으로 거듭난다는 의미를 암시하고 있다. 이 장면은 그녀가 연극에 대한 자신의 열정을 실현시키는 과정에서 복장전도를 통해 과감하게 사회의 불합리한 법적 규제에 대하여 위반적 주체성을 실천했듯이 새로운 삶에서도 용기를 잃지 않고 주체적 삶을 살아갈 것임을 강하게 암시한다. 이 장면은 오늘날을 살아가는 바이올라의 후예들에게, 그리고 수많은 사회적 제약과 규제 속에서 꿋꿋하게 자신의 주체적 삶을 위하여 한 걸음씩 나아가는 여성들에게 보내는 찬사의 메시지를 전달한다. 이 영화의 마지막 장면은 엘리자베스 여왕의 말대로 "남성의 일을 하는 여성들에게" 그리고 스토파드의 말대로 "바다보다 더 큰, 바다가 덮치기에는 너무나 강인한" 여성들에게 바치는 찬사인 것이다.

3

<사랑에 빠진 셰익스피어> 작품을 분석하면서 바이올라가 어떤 맥락에서 남장을 취하게 되는지 사회적, 역사적 맥락에 대하여 고찰하여 보았다. 바이올라는 자신이 원하는 연극에의 꿈을 실현시키기 위하여 남성의 복장을 취하고 무대에 서게 된다. 여성의 연극 활동이 근본적으로 금지된 16세기 영국의 상황 속에서 바이올라의 선택은 그녀의 복장전도가 단순히 여성이 남성의 복장을 취했다는 외면적인 의미 외에도 여성의 성 역할에 대한 근본적인 도전을 함축하고 있다. 가버가 지적했듯이 우리가 성별과 복장에

대하여 고착된 사실로서 이해하는 것들이 사실은 특정한 문화적, 사회적 구조 속에서 생성되고 유포되는 것임을 감안할 때 옷의 차이로 성별의 차이를 고착화시키고 남성의 여성에 대한 우위를 고착화시키려는 의도는 복장전도라는 전복적 행위를 통하여 해체되어 나타나는 것을 볼 수 있다. 복장전도가 가지는 도전성은 복장이 차이를 만들어낸다는 사회적 관행에 대하여 그러한 정치적 목적이 의도하는 바가 얼마나 부자연스럽고 연극적인가를 드러내 보여줌으로써 효력을 발휘한다. 바이올라는 변성기 이전의 소년 배우가 여성의 역할을 수행하는 당대 연극에서의 사회적 관행이 남녀 간의 사랑이라는 주제를 표현하는데 있어 얼마나 부자연스럽고 사실적이지 못한 효과를 만들어내는 지에 대하여 주목하고 그러한 관행을 주체적으로 전복시키기 위하여 남장을 취하게 된다. 바이올라의 복장전도는 고정된 성 역할, 그리고 여성에게 가해진 사회적 제약에 대한 극복의 한 기제로서 자리매김 된다. 그러므로 그녀의 남장은 성별의 범주와 사회적 규범이 침해될 수 없는 고정된 것이라는 전제에 대해 의문을 제기하고 그러한 범주 정하기가 계획되고 유포되는 것임을 해체적으로 보여주고 있다. 이러한 그녀의 선택과 결단은 양성적 가능성에 대하여 시사하는 바가 크다. 영화 <사랑에 빠진 셰익스피어>의 바이올라의 모델이 되었던 셰익스피어의 연극 <십이야>에서의 바이올라는 밸지가 지적하였듯이 세자리오라는 역할의 수행 속에서 양성적 가능성을 보여준 전형적인 인물이다. <십이야>에서의 바이올라는 세자리오라는 남성으로서 자신의 역할을 수행하는 동안 남성과 여성의 긍정적 자질을 고루 갖춘 양성적 자질을 드러냄으로써 자신의 꿈을 적극적으로 이루어내는 인물로 그려진다. 이러한 관점에서 캐더린 벨지(Catherine Belsey)는 올리비아와 오시노에게 동시에 매력을 느끼게 하는 주요한 요인으로서 그녀의 양성적 가능성을 분석한다(Belsey 187). 영화 중에서 바이올라는 토마스 켄트로서의 남성 역할 수행하기와 바이올라로서의 여성 역할 수행하기의 이중적 수행성을 숨 가쁘게 잘 소화해 내고 있는 인물이다. 자신의 연극에 대한 열정을 실천하는 과정에서 바이올라는 불가피하게 사회적 규약과 법적 제재를 극복하기 위하여 과감하게 여성의 옷을 벗어 던지고 남성인 켄트로서 자신의 역할을 당차게 수행하고 그 연극세계에서 유감없이 실력을 인정받게 된다. 그리고 연극 무대에서 그녀는 켄트로서의 자신의 정체성을 획득한다. 이러한 그녀의 이중적 성역할의 수행은 성이 고정 불변하는 범주로서가 아닌 수행성에 의하여 정의되는 것임을 보여준다. 주디스 버틀러가 지적했듯이 성(sex)에 대한 범주 정하기는 사회의 주요 담론 속에서 생성되고 인식되며 이러한 범주 정하기는 수행성(performativity)의 개념에 의해서 해체되고 전복된다(Butler 12-16). 바이올라는 남성 역할 수행하기의 기제로서 남장이라는 적극적인 방법을 시도하였고 그녀의 복장전도는 성 역할이 고정된 불변하는 것이라는 지배담론에 대하여 그러한 범주 정하기가 계획되고 유포되는 것임을 해체적으로 보여주고 있다. 이 영화는 윌과 바이올라의 사랑이라는 축을 중심으로 전개되고 있지만 이 영화에서 간과해서는 안 되는 중요한 주제가 바로 문학의 힘에 대한 물음이다. 문학은 혹은 연극은 무엇이고 연극은 무엇을 할수 있고 연극은 어떻게 우리의 삶에 기능하는가? 필자는 스토파드의 영상텍스트를 분석하는 과정에서 연극의 힘에 대한 신념을 실현시키는 주체적인 여성 바이올라에 주목하였다. 그리고 <사랑에 빠진 셰익스피어>에서의 바이올라의 남장은 자신이 추구하는 연극의 세계에 참여하기 위하여 당대의 사회적 제약을 벗어나는 과정에서 취해진 방법이었으며 르네상스시기에 여성에게 가해진 문화적 사회적 제약을 전복적으로 해체시키고 여성에게 가능성을 열어준 적극적인 기제로서 작용했다는 점을 강조하였다. 바이올라는 적극적인 사회적 역할이 근본적으로 여성에게 봉쇄된 상태에서 불가피하게 복장전도를 함으로써 주체성을 추구하는 모습을 보여준다. 이러한 남장의 방식은 또한 현실 세계에서 엘리자베스 여왕의 정치적 재현에서 그 효력을 발휘한다. 비록 영화상에서 여왕이 남장을 하고 전장을 지휘하는 남성적 제왕의 풍모를 과시하는 장면은 등장하지 않았지만 마커스가 지적하듯 역사적 기록을 보면 엘리자베스 여왕은 자신이 여성의 약한 육체를 지니고 있으나 자신의 정신은 어느 군주보다 강하고 위엄이 있다고 공언하고 공식 행사에 남장을 하고 군주의 위용을 드러내 보였다. 이러한 관행은 당대 승계자가 정해지지 않은 불안정한 정치 상황 속에서 자신의 강한 군주로서의 이미지를 부각시키고자 하는 정치적 의도가 명백한 관행이었다 (Marcus 145). 군주의 육체적 몸과 정치적 몸의 이중적 수행 속에서 여왕은 자신의 남장을 통해, 그리고 자신의 양성의 정치적 공언을 통해 수많은 반란의 위협을 제압하고 강력한 왕권을 행사한 군주로서의 면모를 보여주고 있는 것이다. 이러한 맥락에서 영화에 나타난 여왕과 바이올라의 동지애에 가까운 공감대 형성을 이해할 수 있다. 켄트가 여자임이 폭로되고 바이올라가 법적 제재를 받게 되는 위기에 처한 상황에서 여왕은 남성의 일을 하는 여성의 고충을 이해한다고 공언하고 바이올라를 위기 상황으로부터 구해준다. 이렇듯이 주체적인 자기 삶의 추구를 실현하는 여성들의 몫이 영화에서는 극적으로 강조되어 재현되어 있으며 이러한 주체성 추구에 있어 남장은 중요한 역할을 수행한다. 영화 <사랑에 빠진 셰익스피어>에서 바이올라는 남장을 통해 연극 세계에서 주체적으로 참여하고, 현실 세계에서 엘리자베스 여왕은 남장을 통해 군주로서의 위용을 드러낸다. 그러므로 남장은 복장이 지니는 단순한 의미를 넘어서 복장전도를 통해 불평등한 성 역할에 반항하고 여성에게 사회적으로 주어진 한계를 극복하려는 주체적인 추구로서 이해될 수 있다.

Works Cited

이교선. 「바이올라 인 러브, 셰익스피어 인 러브」. 『안과 밖』 6 (1999): 153-67.

이현우. 「셰익스피어와 할리우드 이데올로기」. *Shakespeare Review* 40 (2000): 537-69.

최영주. 「거슬러간 시간, 그 상상의 즐거움 ―<사랑에 빠진 셰익스피어>」. 『문학과 영상』 2001. 75-98.

Belsey, Catherine. "Disrupting sexual difference: meaning and gender in the comedies." *Alternative Shakespeare*. Ed. John Drakakis. London and New York: Routledge, 1985. 166-90.

Butler, Judith. *Bodies that Matter: On the Discursive Limits of Sex.* London: Routledge, 1993.

Garber, Marjorie. *Vested Interests: Cross-dressing and Cultural Anxiety.* London: Penguin Books, 1992.

Howard, Jean E. "Crossdressing, The Theatre, and Gender Struggle in Early Modern England" *SQ* 39 (1988): 418-40.

Jardine, Lisa. *Still Harping on Daughters: Women and Drama in the Age of Shakespeare.* London and New York: Harvester, 1983.

Levi-Strauss, Claude. *The Elementary Structures of Kinship.* Trans. James Bell and John Strumer. Ed. R. Needham. London: Eyre and Spottiswoode, 1969.

Marcus, Leah S. "Shakespeare's Comic Heroines, Elizabeth 1, and the Political Uses of Androgyny." *Women in the Middle Ages and the Renaissance: Literary and Historical Perspectives.* Ed. Mary Beth Rose. Syracuse: Syracuse University Press, 1986. 135-53.

Marotti, Arthur F. "Love is not Love': Elizabethan Sonnet Sequenes and the Social Order." *ELH* 49 (1982)

Norman, Marc and Stoppard, Tom. *Shakespeare in Love: A Screenplay.* New York: Miramax Film Corp and Universal Studios, 1998.

Shakespeare, William. *Twelfth Night*. London and New York: Routledge, 1988.

Stallybrass, Peter. "Patriarchal Territories: The Body Enclosed" *Rewriting the Renaissance*. Ed. Margaret W. Ferguson et al. Chicago and London: Chicago UP, 1986. 123-42.

Strong, Roy. *The Cult of Elizabeth: Elizabethan Portraiture and Pageantry*. London: Thames and Hudson, 1977.

Traub, Valerie. *Desire and Anxiety: Circulations of Sexuality in Shakespearean Drama*. London and New York: Routledge, 1992.

3
장
—

『오셀로』, 〈저녁 식사하러 누가 왔나 보세요〉, 〈정글 피버〉에 나타난 인종차별적 이분법과 백인남성의 집단불안심리

1. 서론

이 글은 『오셀로』를 분석하는데 있어 성과 권력의 문제에 집중한다. 또한 성과 권력의 문제의 중심에 인종의 문제가 자리 잡고 있음을 해부해 보고자 시도한다. 주지하다시피 흑백 결합이라는 측면에서 『오셀로』를 분석하는 경향은 이미 주류로 자리 잡고 있다. 박홍규는 『셰익스피어는 제국주의자다』에서 흑백 인종의 결혼에 대한 거부가 극의 초반부에서부터 표현되어 있고 혼혈에 대한 경멸, 공포, 흑인을 노예, 이교도, 동물로 보는 오리엔탈리즘적 본질주의가 극의 전체적인 시각이라고 분석한다. 또한 김종환은 『셰익스피어와 타자』에서 오셀로의 여성혐오담론과 남성의 소유의식을 분석하면서 아름답고 젊은 백인 아내에 대한 나이 많은 흑인남성으로서의 오셀로의 열등감을 오셀로 비극의 핵심으로 해부한다. 최영주는 『셰익스피어라는 극장 그리고 문화』에서 『오셀로』에 반영된 초기 근대사회의 계급, 인종, 성의 담론에 주목하고 영상매체를 통해 재생산, 강화, 유포되는 계급, 인종, 성의 문제를 분석한다.

위의 논문들은 주로 성과 인종의 문제에 중심을 두고 『오셀로』를 분석한 논문들이고 이외에도 다른 관점에서 『오셀로』를 분석하는 경향의 논문들도 있다. 예를 들면 김미예의 「오셀로와 이야고: 추리작가 아가서 크리스티의 눈을 통하여」는 아가서 크리스티의 *Curtain*과의 비교분석을 통하여 이야고의 행동양식을 분석하고 있다. 닐리(C.T. Neely)는 이 극의 주된 갈등이 남성과 여성의 갈등이라고 생각하면서 남성 중심 비평에서 무시되어 왔던 여성인물의 긍정적 면모를 부각시킨다(212). 본 논문에서는 『오셀로』에서 제시되었던 흑인남성과 백인여성의 이종족 결합이 최근 영화에서 어떻게 반영되어 나타나는가를 분석하고자 한다. 이러한 시도는 위에서 언급하였던 논문들이 주로 작품 자체의 분석에 주력하였던 것에 비해 최근의 영상 매체에서 이종족 결합의 주제가 어떻게 반영되어 재현되는지에 초점을 맞추고 있다. 『오셀로』에서 제시되었던 흑백결합의 주제가 최근 영상매체에서는 어떻게 반영되고 수용되는 지를 두 편의 영화 <저녁 식사하러 누가 왔나 보세요>(*Guess Who's Coming to Dinner*, 1967)와 <정글 피버>(*Jungle Fever*, 1991)를 해부함으로써 알아보고자 한다.

흑백 결합을 다루고 있는 수많은 극작품이나 영화 중에서 이 두 편의 영화를 선택한 이유는 무엇보다도 이 두 영화의 대중성과 예술성 때문이다. <저녁 식사하러 누가 왔나 보세요>는 1967년 아카데미상 10개 부문에 후보로 지명되었을 뿐만 아니라 여우주연상(Katharine Hepburn)과 각본상을 거머쥔 작품이다. 또한 <정글 피버>는 흑백문제에 천착하였던 스파이크 리(Spike Lee) 감독이 직접 출연하기도 한 작품으로서 스티비 원

더(Stevie Wonder)의 배경음악과 안소니 퀸(Anthony Quinn)의 조연이 빛나는 작품이다. 이 두 영화는 셰익스피어의 작품『오셀로』에서 재현되었던 성과 인종, 권력의 문제가 시대의 변화에 따라 어떻게 역동적으로 상호 작용하고 있는지를 극명하게 보여주는 영화이다. 또한 필자는 17세기 초 셰익스피어의 연극 텍스트를 20세기 말 영상 텍스트로 차용하는 과정에서 새로운 시대적 요구와 재현수단의 변화에 따라 흑인의 성 파워의 측면이 강하게 부각되어 재현되어 있음에 주목하고 흑인의 성 파워가 성과 인종의 패러다임 안에서 중요한 기제로서 기능하고 있음을 밝히고자 한다. 이 글에서는 시대적, 장르적으로 서로 다른 작품들을 다루면서 시대적, 문화적 차이 또한 분석할 것이다.

2. 『오셀로』에 나타난 흑백 결합 해부

엘리자베스 1세 시대에 스페인과 포르투갈에서 추방된 흑인 난민이 증가하자 2차에 걸쳐 흑인 추방령이 내려졌다. 당시 흑인은 그 피부색으로 천대받음과 동시에 관능의 상징으로 백인의 갈망의 대상이 되기도 했다. 이는 당시의 시, 이야기, 연극 등에 흑인은 언제나 성적 에너지의 화신으로 등장하는 것에서 알 수 있다. 흑인에 대한 이러한 이중적 관점은 사회적 담론을 통하여 형성되고 유포되어 왔다. 1571년 베니스는 스페인, 로마교황과 신성동맹을 체결하고 그 연합 함대가 레판토 해협에서 오스만 함대를 격파했다.『오셀로』1막 3장에 나오는 오스만 함대의 침략과 2막 1장에 나오는 오스만의 패배가 바로 그것이다. 그러나 실제 역사에서는 1573년 베니스와 오스만 제국이 강화조약을 맺는다. 베니스는 사이프러스를 포기하고 오스만 제국에 대한 공납을 약속한다. 즉 1604년『오셀로』저술 시점 당시 사이프러스는 투르크의 식민지였다(박홍규 184). 투르크에 대한 경멸적인 어투는 이러한 상황을 잘 반증한다. 2막 3장에 나오는 베니스 병사들 간의 싸움에 대해 오셀로가 다음과 같이 말한다.

우리는 모두 투르크 놈으로 타락했는가? 하느님이 오스만 놈들에게 금한 것을 스스로 범한다는 말이냐? 기독교도라면 창피한 줄 알고 야만인과 같은 싸움은 그만둬.

Are we turned Turks, and to ourselves do that Which Heaven hath forbid the Ottomites? For Christian shame, put by this barbarous brawl. (163-6)

이슬람세력에 대한 공포와 배척, 경멸은 실제 당대 이슬람의 공격적 제국주의로 고전하던 유럽 국가들에서 공통으로 나타난다. 박홍규가 지적하듯 셰익스피어를 비롯한 유럽인들은 그들 모두의 공동의 적인 오스만에 이겨 환호했던 1571년만을 기억하고 싶었을 것이다(박홍규 195). 셰익스피어는 그러한 대중심리를 정확하게 파악하고 그 승리를 배경으로 『오셀로』의 내용을 저술했을 것이다. 또한 베니스의 오스만 제국과의 세력경쟁 시점은 런던이 엘리자베스 당대 안고 있던 이민족과의 공존, 세력의 충돌, 흑인추방 등의 시대적 배경과 정확하게 맞아 떨어지고 있다. 그러므로 『오셀로』의 시대적 장소적 배경인 1571년 베니스는 초기 공격적 제국주의로 열병을 앓고 있던 1604년 런던의 시대적 상황을 잘 반영하고 있다고 할 수 있다.

『오셀로』의 전반부에는 흑백 인종의 결혼에 대한 강한 거부가 표출되어 있다. 이는 베니스의 원로원 의원인 데스데모나의 아버지 브라반시오에게 승진에 탈락한 이아고와 데스데모나에게 퇴짜 맞은 로더리고가 데스데모나와 오셀로의 결합을 묘사하는 장면에서 극명하게 나타난다. 오셀로는 장군으로서의 상류층 신분을 유지하고 있으나 흑인이라는 이유로 경멸과 배척의 대상이 된다. 이아고와 로더리고는 자신들의 장군을 '그 작자', '그 무어', '그 입술 두터운 놈', '시커먼 늙은 숫양', '바아바리(북아프리카) 산양' 등으로 묘사하고 있다. 또한 브라반시오에게 '시커먼 늙은 숫양이 당신의 흰 양을 올라타고 있는 중'(1.3.64)이라고 고자질한다. 브라반시오는 이에 대하여 "만약 이러한 상황이 자유롭게 진행된다면 노예나 이교도가 우리의 통치자가 될 것이다."(For if such actions may have passage free, Bond-slaves and pagans shall our statesmen be)라고 대답하는데 이는 그가 흑백간의 결합을 노예나 이교도가 통치자가 되는 무질서한 상황으로 인식하고 있다는 것을 증명한다. 이는 당대 만연해 있던 이종족 결합에 대한 경멸, 공포가 흑인을 노예, 이교도, 동물로 보는 오리엔탈리즘적 본질주의와 결합되어 나타난 것이다. 오셀로는 인종적으로는 이슬람교 흑인이지만 베니스의 기독교 사회에 속한 인물이다. 신분으로는 장군이지만 원로원 의원인 장인과의 관계에서도 드러나듯 고생 끝에 장군의 신분을 성취하게 된 그는 백인 사회에서는 이방인에 불과할 뿐이다.

브라반시오가 오셀로와 데스데모나의 결합을 무질서한 현실로 인식하고 이종족 결합에 대한 경멸을 표출하듯 흑백 결합은 백인 사회에서 부적절한 결합으로 인식되어 왔다. 또한 브라반시오의 태도에서 여성이 남성들 간의 교환대상이고, 딸에 대한 아버지의 소유권이 남편의 손으로 이전되던 당대의 관행을 살펴볼 수 있다(Stone 38). 베니스 사회에서 이방인에 불과한 오셀로는 데스데모나와의 결혼을 통해 백인 주류에 합류한 듯이 보이나 이아고가 주입한 여성혐오담론과 오셀로 자신의 남성으로서의 소유의식에 의해 파멸의 길을 걷게 된다. 이아고의 여성혐오사상은 2막 1장 108-11에 잘 나타나 있다.

여자들이란 밖에 나오면 그림 속의 요조숙녀요, 거실에선 깨진 종소리요, 부엌에선 살쾡이지. 나쁜 짓을 하면서도 성자 같은 얼굴을 하고, 성이 나면 악마가 되고, 살림살이에는 게으르면서, 이불 속에선 바지런을 떠는 여편네가 되지.

You are pictures out of doors,
Bells in your parlors, wild-cats in your kitchens,
Saints in your injuries, devils being offended,
Players in your housewifery, and housewives' in your beds.

(2. 1. 108-11)

이아고에게는 어떤 여성도 부정적으로 비칠 뿐이고, 아름다운 여자이든 추한 여자이든, 현명한 여자든 바보 같은 여자든 모두 음탕한 존재들이고 창녀이다. 이아고의 여성 혐오는 근본적으로 자신의 성격으로부터 기인한 것이다. 모든 것을 부정적으로 보고 모든 인간을 천하게 보는 이아고는 자신의 계략을 좀 더 편한 마음으로 실천하기 위해 베니스의 모든 여성을 비하하고 혐오한다고 할 수 있다. 그에게 있어 여성이 할 수 있는 최상의 일은 육아와 가사이다. 이아고가 열거하는 칭찬 받을 수 있는 여성의 목록에는 6개의 '하지 말아야 할 것'(never)이 명시되어 있는데, 이는 여성의 미덕이 주로 제한된 범위에서 행동할 때 드러나고 있음을 시사한다(Wayne 164). 그러나 오셀로의 여성혐오는 이와 다르다. 그의 여성 혐오는 데스데모나에 대한 그의 소유욕과 불가분의 관계에 있다. 오셀로의 경우 강한 애착을 가진 대상을 소유할 수 없음으로 인해 자신의 자존심이 상처받지 않기 위해 대상을 더욱 혐오하는 형태로 나타난 경우이다. 그에게 여성의 순결은 하나의 강박 관념이고, 남성으로서의 명예가 있는 중요한 기표이다. 아내의 순결에 대한 집착은 자연스럽게 소유의식과 연결되고 남편의 명예가 아내의 순결에 달려 있는 것처럼 반응하는 오셀로는 여성의 정조 파기에 대한 르네상스 시대 남성들의 불안을 반영하고 있다(Khan 121-22). 오셀로는 이아고가 꾸며낸 아내의 가상적 부정을 마치 실제로 목격한 사실인양 기정사실로 받아들이고 데스데모나도 베니스의 다른 음탕한 여자와 다를 바 없다고 생각하게 된다. 그러나 데스데모나는 실제로 아무런 부정도 저지르지 않았다. 오셀로에게서 "갈보"와 "매춘부"라는 비난이 주어질 때 데스데모나는 강하게 저항하지 않고 오델로가 옳을지도 모른다고 생각한다.

내가 이런 취급을 받게 되는 것도 당연한 일이지. 도대체 내가 어떻게 처신을 했기에 장군께서 저토록 꼬치꼬치 따지고 꾸짖는 것일까?

'Tis meet I should be used so, very meet.
How have I been behaved, that he might stick
The small'st opinion on my least misuse? (4.2.106-8).

데스데모나는 후반부에 이르자 초반부에서 아버지에게 자신의 입장을 분명하게 전달하던 단호함과 당당함을 상실하고 남편의 추궁에 대해 자신을 적극적으로 방어하는데 실패한다. 스탈리브라스(Stallybrass)는 그녀의 이런 태도가 가부장제라는 렌즈를 통해서 굴절되어 있기 때문이라고 주장한다(141). 롤프 브라이텐슈타인은 『강한 여성을 위한 셰익스피어 다시 읽기』에서 데스데모나가 당당하고 능숙하게 할 말을 했더라면 극의 전개가 달라졌을 것이라는 재미있는 가설을 제시한다. 브라이텐슈타인은 3막 4장에서 자신이 정표로 준 손수건을 찾는 오셀로와 카시오의 복직을 간청하는 데스데모나 사이에 벌어지는 의사소통의 단절에 주목하고 이 단절이 인형극의 끈을 잡고 있는 이아고에 의해 전개되고 있다는 사실을 직시한다(브라이텐슈타인 29). 또한 데스데모나가 자기 방어를 위해 했어야 할 멋진 연설을 제시하고 있는데 이는 현대적인 관점에서 데스데모나의 실수가 그녀의 경험미숙과 상황대처 능력부족에 기인한 것으로 분석되었기 때문이다. 데스데모나가 남편이 제시한 여성혐오 담론에 대해 이를 르네상스시기 여성의 정조 파기에 대한 남성들의 두려움의 투사로서 이해하고 그의 소유의식에 현명하게 대응했더라면이라는 가설을 필자는 제시한다.

그러나 비극의 최종적 책임은 오셀로 자신에게 있다. 그리고 그것은 개인적이라기보다는 인종적, 사회적 차별의 문제와 밀접하게 연관되어 있다. 그는 나이 많은 흑인남성으로서의 열등감과 아름답고 젊은 백인 아내에 대한 불안을 극복할 수 없었다. 오셀로는 데스데모나를 자신만의 소유로 하고 싶지만 그녀의 가상적 성욕과 불륜은 끊임없이 오셀로를 괴롭히고 불안하게 한다. 더욱이 그녀는 젊고 아름다운 백인 귀족 여성이며 오셀로는 늙고 검은 피부를 가진 베니스 사회의 이방인이다. 그러므로 오셀로의 불안은 개인적인 것이라기보다는 시작부터 잉태되어 있었던 자신의 정체성에서 기인한 흑인으로서의 근원적 열등감과 당대 베니스 사회에서 오셀로가처한 사회적 신분이라는 제약 속에 잠재해 있었다. 잠재된 틈이 이아고라는 인물에 의해 벌어지게 되고 이는 이아고의 승진탈락과 카시오에 대한 질투, 오셀로에 대한 원망과 맞물려 발생된다. 여성혐오와 냉소의 화신인 이아고라는 인물에 의해 오셀로, 데스데모나의 잘 믿고 너그러운 천성이 조종당하고 파멸의 틈으로 벌어지게 된 것이다. 성적 열등의 화신 이아고는 "눈에 뜨이지 않는", "무기력한" 인물로서 아름다움이나 미덕을 조롱하면서 자신의 우월성을 확인하고자 하는 습관을 지니고 있으며 이는 그의 결여를 더욱 확인시켜 준다. 오셀로의 무어인으로서의 이방성과 기독교 사회와의 관계 속에서 모호함은 내재화된 인종적 자기 증오를 생산시키고 극에서 무어의 성욕을 음탕한 것으로 그리고 심지어는 괴물 같은 것으로서 재현하게 하는 논리적 귀결을 보인다(Traub 35). 오셀로의 주체를 이해하는데 있어 결정적인 것은 바로 인종적 역동성이다. 비록 인종차별 이데올로기의 대표적 대변인은 이아고, 로더리고, 그리고 브라반시오이지만 이 극의 비극의 하나는 오셀로가 자신의 종족에 대한 부정적 재현을 얼마나 내재화 하느냐에 달려있다. 첫 세 장면에서 이아고, 로더리고, 브라반시오의 대화는 다음 이분법을 설정한다. 흑인, 어둠, 악, 동물, 과도하게 성적인 vs. 백인, 밝음, 선, 인간, 정조라는 이분법은 백인남성들의 담론에서 설득력을 지니며 이러한 담론은 위의 주류인물들에 의해 생산되고 유포된다. 이러한 인종차별적 이분법은 오셀로 자신이 3막 3장에 표현함으로써 좀 더 강력하게 각인된다. 데스데모나의 불륜에 대한 이아고의 암시에 대해 그의 결론은 "그녀의 이름은 신선했으나 이제 나의 얼굴처럼 검고 더럽혀졌다"이다. 그 순간 오셀로는 피부색을 미덕의 존재와 부재로 연결시키는 인종차별주의의 인식을 받아들이고 있다. 즉 그가 데스데모나에 대한 신뢰를 지속할 수 없었던 것은 그가 자신의 인종적 정체성과 자아존중을 신뢰할 수 없었던 것과 직접적으로 연결되어 있다.

그러나 이러한 흑인의 자기 부정적 인식과 백인의 흑인의 성 파워에 대한 부정적 재현 이면에는 이아고가 오셀로의 성적 에너지를 갈망하고 질투하는 욕망을 은폐하고 있음을 알 수 있다. 이아고는 자신의 성적 열등감을 극복하기 위하여 무어의 성욕을 부정적이고 음탕한 것으로 재현하고 백인남성의 집단 심리를 조종하는 것이다. 실제로 작품에서 보면 그는 아무런 근거 없이 자신의 아내인 에밀리아와 오셀로의 관계를 의심하는 발언을 한다.

나도 그 여자가 좋아. 음탕한 생각에서만 그런 건 아니지. 복수를 위한 거야. 저 음탕한 무어 놈이 내 이부자리에 뛰어 들어간 모양이니까. 그 생각만 해도 독약으로 오장육부가 찢기는 것 같아. 마누라를 서로 바꾸어서 저 놈하고 피장파장이 되지 않고서는 도저히 참을 수가 없어. 그게 안 되면 온통 미치게 할 정도로 무서운 질투를 저 무어 놈한테 불러일으키겠어.

Now I do love her too,/ Not out of absolute lust,…/ But partly led to diet my revenge,/ For that I do suspect the lustful Moor/ Hath leap'd into my seat, the thought whereof / Doth like a poisonous mineral gnaw my inwards,/ And nothing can, nor shall content my soul,/ Till I am even with him, wife, for wife:/ Or failing so, yet that I put the Moor,/ At least, into a jealousy so strong,/ That judgment cannot cure; (2.1.286-297)

위의 대사에서 나타나듯 이아고는 자신의 계략을 편한 마음으로 실천하기 위해 자신의 아내와 오셀로의 불륜을 의심하는 발언을 서슴지 않는다. 또한 아내의 불륜 사실을 제보 받고 증거를 요구하는 오셀로 에게 카시오와 같이 잠자리를 하던 순간을 묘사하며 위증하는 장면에서는 성적으로 노골적인 묘사를 한다. 3막 3장 419-432에서 그는 카시오와 같이 잠자리를 하던 밤을 묘사하게 되는데 이 대사에서 gripe and wring my hand, kiss me hard, pluck'd up, roots, my lips, his leg, my thigh 등의 표현은 동성애를 연상시킬 정도로 육체적인 표현이 노골적이다. 오셀로가 아름다운 백인 귀족여성과 열정적인 사랑을 성취하고 자신의 아내와 불륜 관계에 있다고 의심하는 상황이 되자 그는 백인남성들 특히 로더리고 안에 내재된 백인으로서의 좌절된 성적 욕망을 상기시키고 백인남성의 집단 심리를 조종하여 성 욕망의 좌절을 인종이라는 권력 패러다임 안에서 회복시키고자 한다. 즉 성적 열등감을 해소시키는 기제로서 인종적 우위를 역설하는 것이다. 그리고 그 과정에서 우리를 형성시키고 백인남성 우월 담론으로 오셀로를 철저하게 타자화한다. 이방인으로서의 오셀로의 정체성을 부각시키는 담론을 생산하고 유포하는 논리적 과정을 거치게 되는 것이다.

이러한 분석에서 드러나듯 흑인의 성 파워에 대한 백인의 불안과 집단 심리 조종은 개인적인 문제라기보다는 인종적 사회적 차별의 문제와 밀접한 연관을 갖고 있다.

3. 〈저녁 식사하러 누가 왔나 보세요〉(1967)

『오셀로』에서 살펴보았듯이 백인남성의 이종족 결혼에 대한 반감은 백인남성 우월 담론에 기초한 것으로서 흑인남성을 철저하게 타자화하는 과정을 통해 강화된다. 이러한 사회심리학적 쟁점을 추적하는데 있어 현대 미국의 영화 두 편에서 어떤 식의 변용과 현재성을 확보하고 있는지 밝히고자 한다. 이 장에서는 우선 스탠리 크래이머(Stanley Kramer) 감독의 <저녁 식사하러 누가 왔나 보세요>에 대한 분석을 시도해 보고자 한다. "이 영화는 이종족 결혼을 충격적으로 받아들이던 1960년대의 미국사회를 배경으로 하고 있으며 이 영화가 제작된 이후로 수많은 영화들이 이종족 연인에 대한 주제를 다루었다"는 매그넘(Thomas Magnum)의 말처럼 이 영화는 이종족 결혼에 대한 사회적 논쟁을 영상화한 기념비적인 영화이다. 신문사 경영자인 Matt의 진보주의적 성향은 자신의 딸인 Joey가 국제적인 명성을 가진 흑인의사 John과의 결혼의사를 밝히면서 시험대에 오른다. 조이의 엄마인 Christina는 조이의 결정을 순수하게 받아들이지만 맽은 자신의 동의를 유보한다. 또한 조이 집의 흑인식모인 Tillie는 조이가 실망할 정도로 첫 대면부터 존의 출현을 달갑지 않게 여긴다. 이러한 틸리의 태도에 조이는 "당신이 이러한 어리석은 태도로 존을 대할 거라는 걸 전혀 예상하지 못했다(You're the last person that I expect to take such a silly attitude)"라고 당혹해 한다. 엄마인 크리스티나는 남편과의 대화에서 "우리는 백인이 흑인보다 우월하다고 믿는 것은 잘못된 일이라고 조이에게 가르쳤다(We told her it was wrong to believe that white people were superior to black people)"라고 회상하면서 인종차별주의에 대한 반대관점이 자신들의 교육관이었다고 말한다. 그리고 남편의 유보적인 태도에 대해 농담을 던지듯 그러나 절대로 유색인종과 사랑에 빠져서는 안 된다고 주의를 줬어야 했다고 언급한다. 테라스에서 행복하게 대화를 주고받는 조이와 존의 모습을 보며 크리스티나는 딸의 결정을 받아들인다. 한편 틸리는 "인권과 이 문제는 별개이다(Civil right is one thing and this is another)"라고 여전히 본인이 흑인임에도 불구하고 인종차별주의 발언을 반복한다. 맽 또한 자신이 신문사를 소유하고 있고 당시 인종차별주의에 반대하여 싸운 자신의 공적 영역에 대해 언급하면서 그러나 사적 영역은 다르다고 말한다. 사회 전반에 만연해 있는 인종차별적 편견과 편협한 생각을 극복해나가는 것은 개인적인 문제라기보다 사회적 문제이기 때문에 쉽게 딸의 결정을 받아들이지 못하는 것이다. 10%의 흑인이 살고 있는 미국에서 소수의 입장을 다수의 백인이 호의적으로 받아들이기란 쉽지 않음을 직시하는 것이다. 그럼에도 불구하고 마지막 결론은 감동적이다. 이 영화의 결론은 그들의 편견은 그들의 이성적 사고에서 기인한 것이지만 당사자 본인이 서로에게 확신하고 있고 느끼고 있는 현재의 감정을 전복시킬 수 없다는 것이다. 존의 어머니는 맽에게 "남자들이 나이가 들면 도대체 무슨 일이 생기나요? 제가 믿기에는 이 두 젊은이는 숨 쉴 수 있는 공기를 필요로 하듯 서로를 필요로 하고 있다(What happens to men when they grow old? I believe these two young people need each other, like they need the air to breathe in)"이라고 언급하고 이 결혼을 반대하는 두 남자에게 공감할 수 없음을 분명히 한다. 맽은 자신의 마지막 결론에서 자신이 늙고 젊은 시절의 열정을 상실했지만 젊은 시절의 사랑의 환희의 기억이 명백하다고(memories are there clear, intact, indestructible) 회상한다. 또한 1억의 사람들이 이 두 사람의 결합을 편견의 시선으로 재단할 것이니 서로 친밀함을 잃지 말아야 할 것을 당부한다. 이는 제니(Jenny J.J.I.)가 맽의 마지막 대사인 "세상 사람들이 너의 사랑에 대해 생각하는 것을 비틀어 버려라(screw what the rest of the world thinks about your love)"를 인용하며 지적하듯 이 영화가 이종족 결혼에 대한 감동적인 결론을 제시하고 있음을 시사한다. 왜냐하면 사회의 편견에 확고부동하게 대처하고 다수의 편견에 대항해서 싸울 의지가 없다면 이 둘의 결혼이 곤경에 처할 것이 명명백백하기 때문이다.

이 영화에 나타난 존의 모습에서는 오셀로의 자신의 인종에 대한 부정적 내재화를 찾아볼 수 없다. 자기 확신에 가득 찬 전도유망한 젊은 의사, 자신의 아버지가 우체부라는 사회적 약자의 위치에 있으나 본인은 자신의 노력으로 최고의 위치에 오른 사람, 자신의 사랑하는 아내와 아들을 기차사고에서 잃은 후 개인적인 상실을 겪었으나 국제학회에서 조이를 만나 부모님의 허락을 받으러 온 한 흑인남자이다. 24세인 백인여성과 37세의 흑인남성, 신문사 사장의 외동딸과 국제적 명성을 얻은 의사, 둘의 결합은 인종적 편견에도 불구하고 다른 두 작품에 비해 양가부모님에게 거부감이 덜하며 미래가 희망적이다. 이것은 존의 사회적 신분이 확고하다는 점과 밀접하게 관련되어 있다. 맽은 처음 조이가 존을 소개했을 때 은밀하게 자신의 서재에서 비서에게 전화를 해서 존에 대한 신분조사를 의뢰한다. 존의 인종적 결함을 커버할 정도로 화려한 경력을 듣고서 그는 자신의 부정적 시선을 유보하게 되는데 이는 인종과 성의 문제가 권력의 문제와 맞물려 있음을 입증한다. 또한 앞서 언급했듯이 궁극적으로 성의 문제가 이 결혼을 결론짓는 열쇠가 되며 이 영화에서는 흑백의 인종의 문제가 핵심적인 쟁점이슈가 된다. 존은 자신의 인종적 정체성에 대한 부정적 내면화로 인한 자아존중의 상실의 모습을 보이지 않는다. 이는 오셀로가 자신의 인종적 정체성을 어둠, 악, 동물, 과도하게 성적인 등등의 수식어로 인식하는 것과 대조를 보인다. 흑인으로서 개인이 느끼는 열등감이나 자기비하 심리는 개인적이라기보다는 사회적 차별의 문제와 밀접하게 연관되어 있다. 오셀로가 나이 많은 흑인남성으로서의 열등감과 아름답고 젊은 백인 아내에 대한 불안을 극복할 수 없었던 것에 비해 존은 흑인남성으로서의 열등감보다는 확신에 찬 자기표현으로 조이에게 당당한 모습을 보인다. 조이 집에 첫 방문을 했을 때도 부모님의 허락이 없다면 이 결혼은 무효라고 선언함으로써 자신에 대한 자신감과 믿음을 표현한다. 즉, 오셀로의 불안이 개인적인 것이라기보다는 자신의 정체성에서 기인한 흑인으로서의 근원적 열등감과 당대 베니스 사회에서 오셀로가 처한 사회적 신분이라는 제약 속에 잠재해 있었던 것에 비해 존은 자신의 신분 자체가 인명 검색에서 화려한 경력을 가진 매우 중요한 인물로 열거될 정도이며 자신을 유색인종이라기보다는 한 남자로서 인식하는 인식의 틀에 있어서 차이를 보인다. 물론 『오셀로』에서는 오셀로와 데스데모나와의 결혼 후가 주요시점이고 이아고라는 악인에 의해 그들의 흑백 인종과 성, 권력의 문제가 파괴적인 양상으로 나타나는 반면 <저녁 식사하러 누가 왔나 보세요>는 존과 조이가 이제 막 사랑과 상대에 대한 신뢰를 시작한 시점이라서 결혼 후 그들이 직면하게 될 사회적, 인종적 차별의 장벽이 어떻게 전개될 지에 대해서는 미지수이다. 그러나 그러한 차이에도 불구하고 오셀로와 존의 형상화에서 보이는 두 사람의 흑인의 정체성에 대한 자기 인식에 있어서는 상당한 차이를 보이는 것이 사실이다. 존의 아버지가 조이와의 결혼을 반대하면서 사회적으로 보편화된 흑인에 대한 인식의 틀을 주장하자 존은 자신을 아버지와 차별화시키면서 아버지가 유색인종으로서 자신을 인식하면서 평생을 사셨다면 자신은 한 남성으로서 자신의 정체성을 확립하고 성공을 향해 노력했다고 회고한다. 흑인으로서 평생 우체부의 사회적 신분을 유지했던 아버지가 살았던 시대와 국제적인 명성을 얻은 존이 살고 있는 시대의 인종차별의 강도에 있어 차이 또한 고려해 볼 소지가 있다. 흑인에 대한 인종차별 폐지의 요구가 사회적으로 이슈화되고 있던 시기가 이 영화의 시대적 배경인 만큼 존이 살고 있는 1960년대 미국은 아버지가 흑인으로서 살았던 시대가 주는 인종차별의 편견을 덜 체감하는 시대인 것은 분명하다. 시대적 변화와 더불어 개인으로서 존이 확립하고 있는 흑인으로서 자신의 정체성에 대한 부정적인 자기인식을 하지 않는다는 점은 앞서 언급했듯이 오셀로와 비교할 때 현저한 차이를 보이는 부분이다. 그리고 이러한 인식의 기반 하에서 조이와의 결합은 긍정적이고 밝은 미래를 보장하고 있다.

성과 인종, 그리고 권력의 패러다임 안에서 두 작품을 비교, 분석해보면 오셀로와 존의 흑인으로서의 정체성은 개인적이라기보다는 인종적, 사회적 차별의 문제와 밀접하게 연관되어 있다. 앞서 언급했듯이 오셀로는 나이 많은 흑인남성으로서의 열등감과 아름답고 젊은 백인 아내에 대한 불안을 극복할 수 없었다. 오셀로는 데스데모나를 자신만의 소유로 하고 싶지만 그녀의 가상적 성욕과 불륜은 끊임없이 오셀로를 괴롭히고 불안하게 한다. 더욱이 그녀는 젊고 아름다운 백인 귀족 여성이며 오셀로는 늙고 검은 피부를 가진 베니스 사회의 이방인이다. 반면 존은 장래 장인이 될 맽으로부터 흑인이라는 점에서 부정적 평가와 명망 있는 의사라는 점에서 긍정적 평가를 동시에 받게 되는데 이는 인종과 성의 문제가 권력의 문제와 맞물려 있음을 입증한다. 또한 궁극적으로 성의 문제가 이 결혼을 결론짓는 열쇠가 되며 이 영화에서는 흑백의 인종의 문제와 맞물려 있다. 존의 어머니와의 대화 이후 맽은 자신이 인식하지 못하였던 성의 문제에 솔직하게 접근한다. 자신의 성적 욕망이 지금은 다 소진되었지만 그 기억만은 생생하다고 고백하며 조이가 존과 함께 행복할 것을 기원해 준다. 여기서 성과 인종의 문제가 핵심적인 이슈로 부각되며 흑인의 성은 부정적 측면보다는 긍정적 요소로 작용한다. 또한 존은 자신의 인종적 정체성에 대한 부정적 내면화로 인한 자아존중의 상실의 모습을 보이지 않는다. 이는 오셀로가 자신의 인종적 정체성을 어둠, 악, 동물, 과도하게 성적인 등등의 수식어로 인식하는 것과 대조를 보인다. 또한 앞에서 필자는 흑인의 자기부정적 인식과 백인의 흑인의 성 파워에 대한 부정적 재현 이면에는 백인이 흑인의 성적 에너지를 갈망하고 질투하는 욕망을 은폐하고 있음을 언급하였다. 맬의 경우 존과의 대화 장면에서 은유적으로 흑인이 춤이나 야구 같은 육체적 에너지를 필요로 하는 분야에서 두각을 나타내는 경향이 있다고 하면서 인종적 편견을 표현하는데 이는 성적 에너지에 대한 부정적 함축 또한 포함하고 있다. 이는 백인남성의 집단 심리를 보여준다. 즉, 이아고는 오셀로가 아름다운 백인 귀족여성과 열정적인 사랑을 성취하자 백인남성들 특히 로더리고 안에 내재된 백인으로서의 좌절된 성적 욕망을 인종이라는 권력 패러다임 안에서 회복시키고자 성적 열등감을 해소시키는 기제로서 인종적 우위를 역설한다. 그리고 그 과정에서 우리를 형성시키고 백인남성 우월 담론으로 오셀로를 철저하게 타자화한다. 맬 또한 흑인으로서의 존의 정체성을 부각시키고 백인 우월 담론을 생산하고 유포하는 논리적 과정을 거치게 되는데 이는 흑인의 성 파워에 대한 백인의 불안과 집단 심리 조종이 인종적 사회적 차별의 문제와 밀접한 연관을 갖고 있음을 보여준다.

4. 〈정글 피버〉(1991)

『오셀로』에 나타난 흑백 결합에 대한 당대 사회적 편견은 현대적인 영화 <정글 피버>(Spike Lee, 1991)에도 극명하게 재현되어 있다. 영화에 묘사된 이종족 사이의 사랑에 대한 스파이크 리 감독의 태도가 지나치게 청교도적이라는 비판적인 시각도 있지만(Terrence Rafferty), 필자는 이 영화가 현대 미국의 흑백결합에 대한 편견을 사실적으로 묘사하고 있다고 본다. *Jungle fever*는 Flipper(Wesley Snipes 분)와 그의 여비서 Angie (Annabella Sciorra 분)의 애정행각을 다룬 영화이다. 플리퍼는 할렘출신의 건축가로 성공한 흑인으로서 유부남이다. 앤지는 이태리계 출신의 여비서이다. 둘은 자신이 속한 공동체에 대한 불안과 증오를 공유하고 이것이 계기가 되어 서로 관심을 가지게 된다. 즉, 서로에 대한 단순한 매력뿐만 아니라 사회적 장애물로서 인종, 전통, 남녀차별이라는 강요된 한계를 극복하려는 공통된 좌절 때문에 서로 끌리게 된다. 오셀로의 심리와 플리퍼의 심리 사이에는 공통점이 있다. 사회적으로 성공한 위치에 있으나 백인사회에서 둘 다 흑인으로서 이방인의 위치에 있다는 점이다. 그러므로 그들의 백인여성과의 결합은 일반적인 관례에서 벗어난 일탈로서 재현되고 가족과 주변으로부터 쉽게 공감을 도출시키기 어렵다. <정글 피버>를 해부해 보면 이 영화는 흑인 보스와 빈민 출신 백인 여비서와의 불륜을 다루면서 그 이면에 숨겨진 인종적 갈등을 노출시키고 있다. 또한『오셀로』에서 재현되었던 이종족 결합의 한계가 현대 미국사회라는 시대적 장소적 이동 속에서 재현되었고, 주인공들이 자신의 인종적, 사회적 신분의 한계를 극복하려는 개인적 심리가 성적 욕망으로 작용되었다는 점을 알 수 있다. 성공한 가장으로서 행복한 가정을 꾸리고 있는 플리퍼는 백인사회에서의 흑인으로서의 열등감과 인종적 한계를 극복하려는 욕망을 가진 인물이다. 그는 자신의 욕망과 집착에 공감하는 앤지와의 관계발전을 성취하고 이는 둘 사이의 성관계로 표출되고 있다. 그 과정에 성적 욕망은 중요한 위치를 차지한다. 두 사람의 관계에서 인종, 성별, 힘의 역학관계가 극명하게 표출되어 있는데 성과 인종의 이슈는 권력의 패러다임 안에서 역동적으로 상호작용하고 있다. 앤지의 성 파워는 여기서 그녀가 백인이라는 점과 육체적으로 매력적이라는 점에서 기인한다. 또한 플리퍼의 심리 이면에는 흑인으로서의 사회적 약점을 극복하려는 다층적 의도가 깔려있다. 둘의 결합은 둘이 결여하고 있는 것을 보충하려는 심리에서 기인되었으나 동거 후 현실인식에 도달하게 되고 다시 본래의 자리로 돌아오는 패턴을 보인다.

리틀(Arthur Little)은 그의 저서 *Shakespeare Jungle Fever*에서 흑인을 이방인 그리고 강간범으로 보는 문화적 현상을 셰익스피어의 세 작품들에서 분석하였다. 2장에서 『오셀로』를 다루면서 그는 데스데모나를 희생시키고 살해한 오셀로가 결국은 베니스 사회에서 이방인 이였고 마지막 장면에서 플로렌스 출신의 카시오가 오셀로의 권력을 이양하는 것이 자연스러운 백인 사회의 담론이라고 결론짓는다. 이는 이종족 결혼에 대한 사회심리학적 반감이 얼마나 강렬한지를 시사하는 분석이라고 볼 수 있다. 또한 델리더(Celia Daileader)는 *Racism, Misogyny, and The Othello Myth: Inter-racial Couples from Shakespeare to Spike Lee*에서 이종족 연인들이 등장하는 작품들을 셰익스피어에서 현대 영화까지 폭넓게 다루었다. 결론 부분에서 <정글 피버>의 한 이태리계 미국 남성이 한 대사 "My mother's not black! She's dark! There are dark Italians!"라는 대사를 인용하며 이태리계 백인의 흑인 경멸 사상을 단편적으로 보여주면서 또한 스파이크 리 감독의 이태리계 미국인의 카톨릭 보수주의에 대한 비판의식(satire)을 보여준다고 분석한다. 『오셀로』에 대한 분석에서는 데스데모나가 오셀로에게 충실하든 그렇지 않든 두 사람의 결합은 "불순한 (impure)" 그래서 은유적으로 불륜의 (metaphorically adulterous) 관계라고 규정하고, 이와 비교해 <정글 피버>에서의 플리퍼와 앤지의 결합은 실제적으로 불륜의 관계(literally adulterous)라고 분석한다(Daileader 209). 리틀과 델리더의 분석에서 제시되듯이 이종족 간의 결합은 전통적으로 셰익스피어의 작품에서뿐만 아니라 현대 영화에서도 부정적이고 불순한 관계로 재현되어 있음을 알 수 있다.

이 영화에서 보면 이종족 결합에 대한 경멸, 공포가 강렬한 언어를 통하여 구사되어 있다. 우선 플리퍼 자신의 흑인으로서의 열등감과 부정적 자아상부터 분석해 보자. 그는 야근하는 장면에서 앤지와 저녁식사를 같이 하게 되는데 자신의 흑인으로서의 정체성에 대하여 "당신의 피부색을 보세요. 얼마나 까만지. 난 당신의 피부색이 좋아요. 난 하얗고 창백하죠. 난 깜둥이, 얼룩이, 검댕이, 암흑, 더러움 등 당신이 생각할 수 있는 모든 흑인 경멸적 이름으로 불리어 왔죠(Wow, look at your skin color. How dark it is. I love your color complexion. I mean I'm so white I'm so pale. I've been called, black, dot, smut, midnight, spot, every black derogatory name you could ever think of)."라고 언급한다. 앤지의 시선에 대하여 부정적 함축을 예측하고 스스로 느끼는 모멸감을 냉소적으로 표현한 것이다. 흑인을 노예, 이교도, 악, 어둠, 동물로 보는 오리엔탈리즘적 본질주의를 본인 스스로 내재화 하고 있다. 백인여성과의 성적 접촉을 자신의 형제인 Cyrus 에게 실토한 후 사이러스의 반응은 함축적으로 간단 명료하게 "미쳤냐?(Are you on crack or something? Are you crazy?)" 이며 그에게 흑백의 성적 결합은 정신이상의 한 형태로 인식된다. 또한 엄격한 청교도 정신을 표명하는 목사인 플리퍼의 아버지에게 그들의 결합이 인정받지 못하는 것은 자명한 사실이다. 저녁식사에서 플리퍼의 아버지로부터 박대를 당하고 돌아오는 장면에서 주차한 후 벌어지는 플리퍼와 앤지의 차 위의 장난 장면은 이웃주민으로부터 강간장면으로 오해 받는다. 경찰은 주민이 Afro-American male이 Caucasian woman을 강간하려 한다는 제보로 출동했다고 설명하는데 상식적인 차원에서 두 연인간의 장난 장면은 강간장면으로 오해를 살 정도로 이웃들에게 비정상적이고 이례적이다. 앤지의 친구와 가족의 반응은 더욱 격렬하고 냉담하다. 그녀의 친구들은 그녀가 흑인과 데이트 중이라는 말에 대해 "개인적으로 역겹다(Personally, it's disgusting, it's gross)."라고 반응하며, 그녀의 아버지는 "깜둥이라고! 죽은 네 엄마가 무덤에서 벌떡 일어나겠다(A nigger! Your mother's turning over in her grave)."라고 격노하며 그녀를 구교 전통을 가진 이탈리아 사람들에게 수치스런 존재라며 그녀에게 폭력을 행사한 후 집에서 내쫓는다. 앤지의 남자친구였던 Paulie도 앤지와의 결별 이후 자신을 동정하는 백인친구들에게 또한 자신이 운영하는 가게의 단골손님들에게 흑인 경멸 발언들을 듣게 된다. 또한 지적이고 친절한 이웃주민인 흑인여성 Orin에게 데이트를 신청하다 백인남성들에게 뭇매를 맞는 봉변을 당한다. 영화에서 이종족 결합에 대한 경멸, 공포가 곳곳에 노출되고 있고 이러한 사회적 장벽은 플리퍼와 앤지, 폴리와 오린이 이종족에 대한 개인적인 호기심이나 관심으로 뛰어넘기에는 너무 높아 보인다.

『오셀로』와 <정글 피버>를 비교해 볼 때 흑인남성의 사회적 신분은 자신의 파트너인 여성과 비교해 볼 때 차이를 보인다. 오셀로에게는 데스데모나의 사회적 신분이 그의 흑인으로서의 열등감을 부채질 할 수 있었지만 이태리 출신의 여비서의 신분은 사회적으로 약자의 위치에 있다. 남성의 심리를 분석해보면 오셀로의 남성으로서의 성별우위, 인종적 신분적 하위, 플리퍼의 성별우위, 신분적 우위, 인종적 하위의 구조를 보인다. 즉 두 작품에서 두 남자 주인공의 백인여성과의 사랑은 서로 다른 역학관계 속에서 이루어진다. 공통점은 남자 주인공이 흑인이라는 점과 그들이 백인여성과 결혼 혹은 불륜을 맺게 되는 과정과 결말이 차이가 있다. 백인여성과의 성적 결합이면에 내재한 흑인남성과 백인남성의 집단 심리에 주목해 볼 필요가 있다. 그리고 흑인남성과 백인여성의 결합을 재현하는 데 있어 사회적으로 공유되는 부정적 시선에서 공통점을 찾아볼 수 있다. 『오셀로』의 경우 오셀로의 무어인으로서의 이방성과 기독교 사회와의 관계 속에서 모호함은 내재화된 인종적 자기 증오를 생산시키고 극에서 무어의 성욕을 음탕한 것으로 그리고 심지어는 괴물 같은 것으로서 재현하게 하는 논리적 귀결을 보인다. 그러나 앞서 언급했듯이 이러한 흑인의 성 파워의 부정적 재현 이면에는 이아고가 오셀로의 성적 에너지를 갈망하고 질투하는 욕망을 은폐하고 있다. 욕망과 불안의 순환고리 안에서 그러한 열등감을 극복하기 위하여 무어의 성욕을 부정적이고 음탕한 것으로 재현하고 백인남성의 집단 심리를 조종하는 것이다. 앤지의 아버지와 옛 남자친구 폴리의 반응도 비슷한 양상을 보인다. 그녀의 아버지와 남자 형제들은 그녀가 어머니의 부재를 보충해주는 현실적 역할로부터 이탈하게 된 시점에서 상대가 흑인이라는 사실에 분노한다. 상대의 사회적 지위나 성공은 중요하지 않으며 인종적 경멸만이 그들의 집단 심리를 조종한다. 흑인남성의 성 파워에 대한 질투나 선망의 은폐 또한 집단적이며 조직적이다.

한편 플리퍼의 백인여성과의 불륜의 심리이면에는 인종적 열등감을 백인여성과의 성적 결합을 통해 극복하려는 의도가 내재되어 있음을 알 수 있으며 이렇듯 권력의 패러다임 안에서 성과 인종의 문제는 복합적으로 작용하고 있음을 알 수 있다. 주지하듯이 플리퍼는 오셀로처럼 자신 안에 흑인에 대한 인종적 열등감과 증오를 내재화 시키고 있었다. 그리고 인종과 권력의 패러다임 안에서 그 한계를 극복하고자 하는 시도가 흑백결합으로 나타난다. 또한 백인남성은 흑인남성의 성적 에너지에 대한 질투와 선망을 은폐하고 역설적으로 그러한 성적 에너지를 부정적이고 타도되어야 할 악의 존재로서 재현하는 아이러니를 보인다. 지금까지의 분석에서 드러나듯 『오셀로』와 <정글 피버>를 이해하는데 있어 결정적인 것은 바로 인종적 역동성이다. 흑인, 어둠, 악, 동물, 과도하게 성적인 vs. 백인, 밝음, 선, 인간, 정조라는 인종차별적 이분법은 또한 백인남성의 집단 불안심리 속에서 생성되고 유포된 담론으로서 이는 역설적으로 흑인남성의 성 파워에 대한 불안과 그 성 파워를 전복시키고 수용하려는 백인남성의 성적 욕망과 직결되어 있다. 그리고 그 욕망은 교묘하게 은폐되고 흑인남성을 타자화시키는 과정을 통해 흑인남성의 성 파워를 전복시키고 수용하는 과정을 거치게 된다.

5. 결론

이 글은 『오셀로』를 분석하는데 있어 이종족 결합이라는 관점에서 시도하였고 최근의 영화 <저녁 식사하러 누가 왔나 보세요>와 <정글 피버>를 비교·분석하였다. 오셀로의 주체를 이해하는데 있어 결정적인 것은 바로 그의 성적 파워이다. 『오셀로』에서 살펴보았듯이 은폐된 백인남성의 성적 욕망은 이아고의 성적 열등감을 극복하는 기제로 사용된 인종차별주의와 백인남성의 집단 불안 심리에 의해 표출된다. 부정적이고 음탕한 것으로 재현된 흑인남성의 성 파워는 본질적으로 백인남성 이아고의 성적 열등감을 해소시키는 기제로서 기능한다. 그리고 그 과정에서 형성된 백인남성의 "우리" 의식은 흑인남성을 철저하게 타자화시키는 과정을 거치게 된다. 이방인으로서의 오셀로의 정체성을 부각시키는 담론을 생산하고 유포하는 논리적 과정을 거치게 되는 것이다. 앞에서 분석했듯이 <저녁 식사하러 누가 왔나 보세요>에서 조이의 아버지 맽은 인종차별 반대주의자로서의 자신의 공적 입장과 다른 사적 영역에서의 반응을 표출한다. 흑인 사위를 맞게 될 것이라는 사실에서 발생하는 불만으로 인해 흑인으로서의 존의 정체성을 부각시키고 백인 우월 담론을 생산하고 유포하는 논리적 과정을 거치게 된다. 이는 흑인의 성 파워에 대한 백인의 불안과 집단 심리 조종이 인종적 사회적 차별의 문제와 밀접한 연관을 갖고 있음을 보여준다. 또한 앤지의 아버지와 폴리가 경험하는 집단 심리는 인종차별주의 관점에 기반을 두고 있으며 흑인의 성 파워에 대한 질투나 선망을 은폐시키고 있다.

　이아고는 백인우월주의 담론으로 오셀로의 성 파워를 해체시킨다. 오셀로의 성 파워는 이아고의 백인 우월주의 담론의 틀 안에서 철저하게 해체되고 오셀로는 자신의 인종에 대한 부정적 내면화와 타자화를 통해 분열된다. 이아고는 성과 인종 그리고 권력의 패러다임 안에서 흑인으로서의 오셀로의 성 파워를 무력화시키고 인종적 우위의 틀 안에서 권력을 재편시킨다. 앞에서 분석한 세 작품은 백인남성의 집단불안심리의 측면에서 볼 때 연관성과 설득력을 지닌다. 흑인남성의 성 파워에 대한 부정적 재현은 백인남성의 집단 불안심리 속에서 생성되고 유포된 담론으로서 이는 역설적으로 흑인남성의 성 파워에 대한 불안과 그 성 파워를 전복시키고 수용하려는 백인남성의 성적 욕망과 직결되어 있다. 그리고 그 욕망은 교묘하게 은폐되고 흑인남성을 타자화시키는 과정을 통해 흑인남성의 성 파워를 전복시키고 수용하는 과정을 거치게 된다.

Works Cited

김미예. 「오셀로와 이야고: 추리작가 아가서 크리스티의 눈을 통하여」. 『셰익스피어/현대 영미극의 지평』. 서울: 동인, 2004.

김종환. 『셰익스피어와 타자』. 서울: 동인, 2006.

니콜라스 도일. 「눈을 멀게 하다: 오델로」. *How to Read Shakespeare*. 이다희 역. 서울: 웅진 지식 하우스, 2007.

롤프 브라이텐슈타인. 『강한 여성을 위한 셰익스피어 다시읽기』. 김소연 역. 서울:

좋은 책, 2004.

박홍규. 『셰익스피어는 제국주의자다』. 서울: 청어람미디어, 2005.

이혜경. 『셰익스피어 극의 해석 넓히기』. 서울: 동인, 2002.

최영주. 『셰익스피어라는 극장 그리고 문화』. 서울: 글누림, 2006.

Daileader, Celia R. *Racism, Misogyny, and The Othello Myth: Inter-racial Couples from Shakespeare to Spike Lee.* Cambridge: Cambridge UP, 2005.

Dusinberre, Juliet. *Shakespeare and the Nature of Women.* New York: Barnes & Noble, 1975.

J.J.I, Jenny. "Who says movies don't teach you anything?" 22 Aug, 2006. http://www.amazon.com/Guess-Whos-Coming-Dinner-Anniversary/dp/B000TXP56C/ref=sr_1_1?ie=UTF8&s=dvd&qid=1261045437&sr=8-1

Kahn, Coppelia. *Man's Estate: Masculine Identity in Shakespeare.* Berkeley: U of California P, 1981.

Kramer, Stanley. *Guess Who's Coming to Dinner*, 1967.

Little, Arthur. *Shakespeare Jungle Fever.* Stanford: Stanford UP, 2000.

Lee, Spike. *Jungle Fever.* CA: Universal City Studios, 1991.

Magnum, Th*omas*. "Powerful Drama." 28 Jan. 2003. http://www.amazon.com/Guess-Whos-Coming-Dinner-Anniversary/product-reviews/B000TXP56C/ref=dp_top_cm_cr_acr_txt?ie=UTF8&showViewpoints=1

Neely, Carol T. "Women and Men in Othello" *The Woman's Part: Feminist Criticism of Shakespeare.* Eds. C. R. Swift Lenz, Gayle Greene, and C. T. Neely. Chicago: U of Illinois P, 1980. 211-39.

Rafferty, Terrence. *The New Yorker.* 2006. http://www.amazon.com/Jungle-Fever-Michael-adalucco/dp/0783230389/ref=sr_1_1?ie=UTF8&s=dvd&qid=1261047329&sr=8-1

Shakespeare, William. *Othello.* Ed. Kenneth Muir. London: Penguin, 1968.

Stallybrass, Peter. "Patriarchal Territories: The Body Enclosed." *Rewriting the Renaissance: The Discourse of Sexual Difference in Early Modern Europe.* Eds. M. W. Ferguson et al. Chicago: U of Chicago P, 1986. 123-42.

Stone, Lawrence. *Family, Sex, and Marriage in England 1500-1800.* Abridged Edition. New York: Harper & Row, 1987.

Traub, Valerie. "Jewels, Statues, and Corpses: Containment of female erotic power." *Desire and Anxiety: Circulations of Sexuality in Shakespearean Drama.* London and New York: Routledge, 1992. 25-49.

Wayne, Valerie. "Historical Differences: Misogyny and Othello." *The Matter of Difference: Materialist Feminist Criticism of Shakespeare.* Ed. Valerie Wayne. Ithaca: Cornell UP, 1991. 153-80.

4
장
—

『안토니와 클레오파트라』에
나타난 과도함과 이국성

1. 들어가며

　『안토니와 클레오파트라』에 대한 연구는 지속적으로 한국 셰익스피어 학자들 사이에서 이루어져왔다. 최근 10년간 *Shakespeare Review* 지에 실린 이 작품의 연구 경향을 분석해본 결과 주로 주제적 분석과 형식적 분석, 그리고 뮤지컬이나 영화와의 비교 분석이 주류를 이루고 있었다. 예를 들면 이경옥, 김경혜, 이행수는 각각 작품에 나타난 에로스적 측면, 페미니즘 전략의 시도와 한계, 욕망의 추구에 대한 분석을 시도하였다. 형식에 대한 분석으로는 이용관, 윤희억의 논문을 예로 들 수 있는데 각각 이중파국의 설정의 특이성과 바흐친적 패러디 양식에 준거하여 작품을 분석하였다. 끝으로 조윤경은 두 편의 논문에서 각각 뮤지컬 <클레오파트라>(2008)와 영화 <클레오파트라>(1963)와의 비교·분석을 제시하였다. 2000년 이후의 해외 연구 동향을 살펴보면 Kluge는 도덕성과 비통함의 관점에서 이 작품을 분석하였고, Ryle은 영화화된 『안토니와 클레오파트라』에 대한 관점을 제시하였고, Havely와 Crane은 제국주의적 관점에서 이 작품을 분석하였다. 필자는 기존의 셰익스피어 학자들의 연구 주제로 다루어지지 않은 주제로서 안토니의 클레오파트라에 대한 과도한 사랑이 그녀의 이국성에 기초한 것임을 제시하고자 한다. 그동안 서구 비평에서 주류를 이루었던 엄격한 도덕주의적 비평과 낭만주의적 비평, 그리고 변증법적 비평 경향들을 기본으로 인식한 상황에서 필자의 글은 안토니와 클레오파트라의 관계에 대한 분석에 초점을 두고 있다. 그리고 그 관계의 핵심으로서 안토니의 과도함과 클레오파트라의 이국성에 주목하고자 한다.

　셰익스피어의 희곡 『안토니와 클레오파트라』에는 여행자로서의 안토니의 모습이 부각되어 재현되어 있고 "이국적임"과 "과도함"이라는 모티브가 주요하게 반복적으로 다루어지고 있다. 플루타크의 원전에서 방랑자의 신화는 중요하게 다루어지지 않는다. 반면 셰익스피어의 희곡에서는 알렉산더 신화와 헤라큘레스의 신화가 주요 모티브로 등장한다. 알렉산더 신화는 클레오파트라가 알렉산더의 후손이라는 점과 알렉산더가 페르시아의 공주 록사나와의 이종족 결합을 함으로써 이종족 결혼을 용인한 점에서 강화되어 나타난다. 또한 헤라큘레스의 신화는 영웅적 난잡함을 그 주요 내용으로 하고 있다. 덧붙여, 버질의 『이니아드』에서는 경건과 난잡함, 로마제국과 세계시민이라는 대립되는 모티브가 등장하고 타락한 알렉산더로서의 안토니가 재현되며, 안토니의 패배는 동양의 미개함에 대한 서양, 즉 로마의 승리로서 묘사되어 있다. 길리스가 정확하게 파악하고 있듯이 플루타크에서는 저자 자신이 그리스인이고 또한 알렉산더 숭배주의와 코스모폴리탄적인 관점을 유지하고 있었기 때문에 클레오파트라가 부정적으로 묘사될 시점에서 이는 인종적인 차원에서라기보다는 도덕적인 차원에서 부정적으로 묘사되어 있다. 본론에서는 셰익스피어가 원전인 플루타크나 버질과 차별화하는 과정에서 드러난, 그의『안토니와 클레오파트라』에 나타난 안토니의 과도함과 그 과도한 사랑의 기초로서 클레오파트라의 이국성에 대해 살펴보고자 한다.

2. 안토니의 과도함

플루타크 자신은 그리스인이었으며 알렉산더가 창시하고 안토니우스가 옹호했던 범세계주의적인 제국관의 열렬한 신봉자였다. 그러므로 우리는 플루타크에서 전형적으로 변절자 사령관이 현지인처럼 살려고 하고, 이국 여왕과 병력을 결합하고, 동양의 군대를 이끌고 로마를 침략하는 '과도함'의 로마 드라마를 거의 볼 수 없다. 또한 플루타크에서는 클레오파트라도 기본적으로 이국적인 여왕이 아니다. 앞서 언급했듯이 플루타크가 클레오파트라를 강력하게 반대하고 있기는 하지만 그것은 인종적인 이유에서라기보다는 도덕적인 차원에서이다. 안토니우스의 클레오파트라와의 관계는 이종족 결합이라기보다는 간음에 해당한다. '과도함'의 주제는『안토니와 클레오파트라』에 깊이 있게 스며들어 있다. 그러한 이미지는『줄리우스 시저』에서 시저가 콜로수스에 비유될 때 명백하게 나타나 있다: "그는 좁은 세계를 지배하죠, 마치 콜로수스처럼. 그리고 우리 하찮은 인간들은 그의 거대한 다리 밑에서 우리의 불명예스런 무덤을 찾아 기웃대죠. Why, man, he doth bestride the narrow world/ Like a Colossus, and we petty men/ Walk under his huge legs, and peep about/ To find ourselves dishonourable graves"(1.2.136-9). 이러한 종류의 이미지는 클레오파트라가 안토니를 콜로수스에 비유할 때 반복적으로 재현된다. "그의 다리는 대양을 지배하고 뒤쪽 팔은 세계의 정상에 이르렀죠 whose legs bestrid the ocean, rear'd arm crested the world"(*Shakespeare's Plutarch*, p. 180)라고 묘사하는 것은 참으로 흥미로운데 이는 셰익스피어가 안토니를 줄리우스 시저의 과도함의 전설을 통해서 형상화하고 있다는 점이다. 더욱 흥미로운 점은 셰익스피어가 시저보다는 안토니를 과도함의 전형으로서 더 선호하고 있는 것처럼 보인다는 사실이다.

안토니의 과도함은 제국주의적이라기보다는 에로틱하거나 존재론적인 과도함이다. 안토니는 로마 사령관으로서 주위 민족들을 정복하려는 제국주의자로서의 과도함을 보여주기보다는 클레오파트라에 대한 사랑이 보통의 수준을 넘어 과도함의 상태에 이른 것을 보여준다. 만약 '과도함'의 의미가 자신의 세계의 제한성에 대한 신에 유사할 정도의 만족성을 추구하는 것을 의미한다면 안토니는 사랑에 있어서 과도하다. 이 극의 첫 대사는 "우리 총사령관의 맹목적 애정이 도가 지나칠 정도로 넘쳐 흐른다 this dotage of our General's/ O'erflows the measure"(1.1.1-2)로서 우리에게 안토니의 클레오파트라에 대한 사랑이 얼마나 과도한가에 대한 정보를 제공한다. 필로(Philo)는 안토니가 앞에 앉아있는 황갈색의 피부를 가진 여인에게서 시선을 떼지 못하는 것에 놀라워한다. 안토니는 새로운 하늘과 땅에서가 아니라면 사랑에 한계를 두는 것을 거절한다. 그리고 여행자의 특성에 맞게 그의 새로운 세계는 그가 한때 소유했었던 세계의 소멸을 필연적으로 요구한다(Gillies. 116).

로마여, 티베르 강물 속에 빠져 없어져도 좋다. 튼튼한 아이치도 무너져 내려라. 여기가 나의 살 곳이다. 왕국도 한낱 흙덩이에 불과하다. 이 더러운 지구도 사람이나 짐승이나 다 같이 먹여 길러주는데 불과하다. 인생의 참된 고귀함은 바로 이런 데 있다.

Let Rome in Tiber melt, and the wide arch
Of the ranged empire fall. Here is my space.
Kingdoms are clay. Our dungy earth alike
Feeds beast as man. The nobleness of like
Is to do thus (1.1.35-39)

여기에서 안토니는 관습에 대한 과도한 남성의 경멸을 지닌 상태로 티버 강을 경계의 상징으로부터 소멸의 상징으로 바꾸어 놓는다. 그는 자신을 클레오파트라에게 굴복시키고 그로테스크한 나일 강을 자신의 대안으로 받아들인다. 만약 강이 안토니의 과도함에 대한 은유적인 장소를 대표한다면 바다는 또 다른 과도함의 장소로서 기능한다. 바다는 안토니의 과도함의 상징적인 요소이다. 바다는 자유로운 축제적 요소이며 이는 또한 치명적이다. 그래서 안토니는 두 번이나 해전을 치르지만 재앙에 가까운 결과를 초래한다. 안토니의 해전을 치르겠다는 첫 결정은 "우리는 육지전 에서 성공을 거두곤 했죠(3.7.64-65)"라고 그를 상기시키는 장군의 반대의견에 부딪힌다. 아이러니컬하게도 안토니는 자신의 다음번 전투인 육지전 에서 승리하지만 마지막 전투에서 다시 바다에 의존함으로써 패배한다. 그리고 이러한 바다의 이미지는 안토니의 클레오파트라에 대한 과도한 애정과 연관되어 과도함의 상징적 요소로 작용하고 있다.

안토니의 과도함은 갑작스러움과 연관되어 나타난다. 셰익스피어는 안토니를 갑작스럽게 자신의 모든 것을 클레오파트라에게 바치는 인물로 재현하고 있다. 클레오파트라를 만나기 전 안토니는 로마인의 전형으로서 간주되고 있다. 필로의 첫 대사는 안토니가 맹목적 애정으로 빠져드는 것의 갑작스러움과 완벽함에 대한 정신적 충격을 전달한다. 안토니의 대조적 모습은 시저의 대사에서 좀 더 강력하게 묘사된다.

안토니우스여, 그 쾌락의 술상을 거두어라. 모데나에서 패전했을 때 그대
는 집정관이던 히르티우스와 파느사를 살해했었지. 패전의 뒤를 이어 기아
가 휩쓸었지. 고생을 모르고 자란 그대가 야만인보다도 더 강인한 인내로
그 기아의 숲을 헤쳐 내지 않았던가. 말 오줌을 마시고, 짐승들도 마시면
구역질을 하는 누르무레한 웅덩이 물도 마셨고, 더러운 울타리에 열린 시
금털털한 열매도 꿀맛처럼 맛있게 먹지 않았던가? 아니, 초원이 눈으로 덮
였을 때는 수사슴처럼 나무껍질마저 먹었었지. 알프스 산 속에서는 그 누
군 보기만 하고도 죽었다는 이상한 날고기까지도 먹었다면서? 이와 같은
고난을-지금에 이런 말을 한다는 것은 그대의 명예가 손상되겠지만-용
사답게 잘 극복하여 얼굴조차 살이 안 빠졌었지.

Antony, / Leave thy lascivious wassails. When thou once/ Was
beaten from Modena, where thou slew'st/ Hirtius and Pansa,
consuls, at thy heel/ Did famine follow, whom thou fought'st
against-/ Though daintily brought up - with patience more/ Than
savages could suffer. Thou didst drink/ The stale of horses, and
the gilded puddle/ Which beasts would cough at. Thy palate then
did deign/ The roughest berry on the rudest hedge./ Yea, like the
stag, when snow the pasture sheets,/ The barks of trees thou
browsed. On the Alps/ It is reported thou didst eat strange
flesh,/ Which some did die to look on (1.4.55-67)

인용문에서 묘사하듯 클레오파트라를 만나기 전 안토니는 금욕적 인내의
전형이었다. 클레오파트라를 만난 후 그의 치명적으로 이상한 날고기를 인
내할 수 있는 능력은 좀 더 향연을 추구하는 적극적인 정욕이 되어 버렸다.

그의 과도함은 극의 전개상 1막 4장에서 서술된 그의 로마인의 전형으로서의 모습과 2막 이후 재현된 클레오파트라에 대한 맹목적 애정의 전개로 볼 때 매우 갑작스러우며 이러한 갑작스러움이 그의 과도함을 증폭시키는 역할을 하고 있다. 술과 향락의 늪에 빠져있는 현재의 안토니는 패전과 기근을 극복한 과거의 로마인의 전형으로서의 안토니가 더 이상 아닌 것이다.

안토니의 애정의 과도함에 대하여 테리 이글톤은 "실리주의자 로마인의 엄격한 균형이 격렬한 과도함과 연관된 꽤 다른 가치의 기준을 위해 거부되어 진다"(Eagleton, 87)라고 분석하고 있으며 그의 분석에서도 안토니의 에로틱한 과도함은 중요한 모티브로 등장한다. 이글톤이 언급한 꽤 다른 가치의 기준은 안토니와 클레오파트라의 애정에 있어서의 광신적인 격렬함을 가리키며 그는 이러한 격렬한 불균형으로부터 완고한 가치가 쟁취되어 진다고 분석했다. 모호하게 풍요롭고 치명적인 허구에서는 부분적이고 단편적인 것으로 여겨졌던 것이 궁극적인 것으로 바뀐다. 각각의 시간의 공허한 순간을 정신없는 기쁨으로 채우고 각각의 흘러가는 감각을 열정적인 예술작품으로 승화시키는 이러한 죽음을 향한 결연한 삶은 정치적 무책임의 결정판이다. 이글톤은 셰익스피어가 다른 극에서보다 귀족 계급의 안토니와 클레오파트라에 대해 좀 더 공감을 이끌어내는데 성공적이었다고 평가했다. 그는 안토니와 클레오파트라가 그들 자신의 독특한 규범이 되고 극적으로 방종하고 미완성의 상태인 것이 변증법적 과정을 통해 공감을 유도했다고 평가한다. 클레오파트라는 아름다움을 말로 표현할 수 없는 애인이며, 안토니가 머리가 둔한 레디푸스에게 악어를 무표정하게 묘사하는 장면은 그 자체 이외에는 어떤 것으로도 묘사될 수 없는 사물 자체의 본연의 모습을 상기시킨다(2막 7장). 안토니의 육지전보다 해전을 선택하는 성급한 결정은 존재주의론 자의 관점에서 본다면 그 자체를 위해서 무모하게 감행된 아무런 이유 없는 행위이다. 그것은 성공의 가능성이 반반의 확률인 상태에서 죽음을 재촉하는 선택이다. 한편, 셰익스피어는 안토니가 자살하려는 결심을 하는 것을 동정적으로 제시하고 있다. 자기 파괴의 선택은 결단, 용기, 자기주장, 그리고 변신의 행위이며 비열한 세상에서의 로마 장군의 최후의 명예로운 선택인 것이다(Miola, 147). 안토니의 자살은 독특하다. 로마인의 명예에 대한 사랑과, 불명예를 혐오하는 것을 입증하면서 그것은 또한 안토니의 로마와 로마적 가치들을 거부함을 보여준다. 자신의 목숨을 취하기 전에 안토니는 자신의 갑옷을 버린다(4.14.37-41). 갑옷의 제거는 상징적으로 모든 전투와 제국, 그리고 세계의 요구를 거부함을 보여준다. 7겹의 방패도 자신의 뛰는 심장을 견뎌내지 못할 것이라고 말하는 장면은 'The sevenfold shield of Ajax cannot keep/ The battery from my heart. (4.14.37-41)' 군사적 영웅주의의 한계를 시사한다. 안토니의 심장은 로마를 위해서가 아니라 클레오파트라를 위해서, 군사적 열정을 위해서가 아니라 사랑의 슬픔 때문에 터진다. 안토니의 죽음은 최소한 그의 마음속에서는 그를 클레오파트라에게 데려다 줄 것이다(4.14.50-4). 그의 조상들과는 다르게 안토니는 운명이 요구하는 대로 그리고 로마가 요구하는 대로 살기를 거절한다. 사랑과 의무의 원형적인 갈등 사이에서 사랑을 선택한다.

3. 클레오파트라의 이국성

필자는 안토니의 에로틱한 과도함의 기본으로서 클레오파트라의 이국성에 주목하고자 한다. 셰익스피어의 『안토니와 클레오파트라』에서 클레오파트라는 정치적, 성적으로 능동적인 여성인물로, 남성성으로 상징되는 로마의 제국적, 가부장적 권위에 도전하는 인물로 그려져 있다. 여왕은 나일 강의 악어나 뱀, 암말 등과 같은 동물적 은유로 자주 묘사되고 있고, 창녀, 집시, 마녀에 비유된다. 또한 그녀와 동일시되는 이집트 역시 정치적, 도덕적으로 로마와 상이하게 다른 세계로 재현되고 있다. 또한 흥미로운 점은 서론에서도 언급했듯이 셰익스피어의 원전이 되고 있는 플루타크나 버질에서는 기본적으로 클레오파트라가 그리스인으로 재현되어 있는 반면, 셰익스피어의 작품에서는 클레오파트라의 흑인성이나 능동적 섹슈엘러티가 부각되어 재현되어 있다. 즉 셰익스피어는 그녀의 이집트 여왕으로서의 신비로움과 이국성을 안토니를 매료시킨 치명적 요소로 재현하고 있으며, 그녀의 이국성이라는 모티브가 셰익스피어 작품에서 중요한 기제가 되고 있다는 것을 알 수 있다.

셰익스피어에게 있어 이집트와 이집트인들의 특성은 나일 강에 의해 전형적으로 보여 진다. 폼페이우스의 배에서 이루어지는 향연은 나일 강의 홍수에 대한 대화로 시작한다. "나일 강이 범람하면 할수록 풍년이 들 가망이 많습니다. 물이 빠진 뒤에 농부들은 끈적끈적한 진흙에다 씨를 뿌리지요. 그러면 얼마 안 돼서 수확기가 닥쳐옵니다. The higher Nilus swells,/ The more it promises; as it ebbs, the seedsman/ Upon the slime and ooze scatters his grain,/ And shortly comes to harvest" (2.7. 20-24). 그러나 곧이어 이 나일 강은 축제다운 면모를 띠게 된다. 레피두스는 술이 취한 상태로 "거기엔 이상한 뱀이 있다지요?" 라고 질문한다. 그리고 "당신의 이집트 뱀은 태양의 작용에 의해 진흙에서 자란다면서요? 악어도 그렇고요?"라고 논평한다. 이집트는 나일 강과 그것의 자연적 경이로움에 의하여 재현된다. 또한 자연현상에 있어서 기괴함은 인간영역에서의 축제와 병행한다. 그러므로 가장 이집트적인 민속적인 표현이 이 극의 가장 축제적인 장면에서 발견되어지는 것은 우연이 아니다. 셰익스피어의 나일 강에 대한 담론은 축제적일뿐만 아니라 몽상적이고, 신비롭다. 레피두스가 "악어란 놈은 어떻게 생겼소?"라고 묻자 안토니는 다음과 같이 대답한다.

> 모양은 제 모양 같고 넓이는 제 넓이만큼 넓으며 키는 제 키 만큼 크고 제 손과 발로 움직여 다니죠. 제가 먹은 자양분으로 살고 일단 그 몸에서 원소가 빠져 버리면 전생하죠.

> It is shap'd, sir, like itself, and it is as broad as it hath breadth. It is just so high as it is, and moves with it own organs. It lives by that which nourisheth it, and the elements once out of it, it transmigrates (2.7.41-44)

비유를 억제함으로써 안토니는 번역과 언어적 차용, 그리고 심지어 지식 그 자체의 가능성을 부인하고 있다. 그는 '다른 것'은 근본적으로 로마 부호로 번역될 수 없고 그러므로 '미지의 것'이라고 주장하고 있다. 사람들은 이국적인 것을 자신의 부호 밖으로 밀어냄으로써만 차용할 수 있다. 또한 이국적인 것은 진정으로 이국적인 것임을 지속할 때만 그 고유성과 가치를 지닌다(Gillies. 121). 안토니의 농담의 심오한 뜻은 악어가 클레오파트라를 상징하는 전령의 동물이라는 것을 깨닫게 될 때 더 잘 이해된다.

> 안토니우스는 지금 말씀을 하고 계실 거야. 어쩌면 나일 강의 내 정다운 뱀은 어디 있는가? 하고 중얼거리는 지도 몰라. 그분은 날 그렇게 부르셨지. 그런데 지금 나는 가장 맛있는 독을 마시고 있는 거나 다름없어. 태양에게 사랑스러움을 받아 살결이 까맣게 타고, 세월이 흘러 주름살이 많아진 나를 생각하고 계실까?

He's speaking now,
Or murmuring, 'Where's my serpent of old Nile?'-
For so he calls me. Now I feed myself
With most delicious poison. Think on me,
That am with Phoebus' amorous pinches black,
And wrinkled deep in time (1.5.24-29)

안토니의 악어처럼 클레오파트라는 자신의 '다름'에 있어 신비한 존재이다. 그녀는 고대인이고, 흑인이며, 태양에 그을렸고, 파충류와 같으며, 자신의 독에 취해 있다. 언어와 범주를 거부하는 기괴한 것과 경이로운 것의 혼합체이다. 그녀의 이미지는 시각적으로 이집트 여왕의 고유성을 대표하도록 설정되어 있다. 에노바부스가 비유적인 용어로 클레오파트라를 묘사하는 부분에서 그 역설적임이 나타난다.

나이가 들어도 시들지 않는 그 교태야말로 언제 봐도 싱싱한데 왜 버립니까. 다른 여자들은 한번 만족을 느끼고 나면 싫어지게 되지만 여왕에게선 가장 만족을 느끼고 난 그 순간부터 진짜 욕구를 느끼게 한답니다. 그도 그럴 것이 세상에서 가장 야비스런 짓도 여왕에게는 괜찮게 어울리거든요. 그러기에 거룩한 사제들도 여왕의 방종함만은 축복을 할 지경입니다.

Age cannot wither her, nor custom stale
Her infinite variety: other women cloy
The appetites they feed, but she makes hungry
Where most she satisfies. For vilest things
Become themselves in her, that the holy priests
Bless her when she is riggish (2.2.241-246)

클레오파트라의 다름의 번역할 수 없는 신비로움과 자율성은 반복적으로 전개되며 특히 2막과 5막에서 쟁점화 되어 재현된다. 에노바브스는 이집트의 매력에 대항하는 동시에 자신의 동료와 관객에게 클레오파트라의 독특한 매력을 말해주는 중심인물이다. "세월도 그녀를 시들게 할 수 없고 어떤 관습도 그녀의 무한한 다양성을 진부하게 만들 수는 없다 Age cannot wither her nor custom stale her intimate variety" (2.2.236-7). 그는 시드누스에서 안토니와 클레오파트라의 만남을 다음과 같이 묘사한다.

> 여왕이 탄 배는 번쩍번쩍 빛나게 닦아 놓은 황금 옥좌처럼 찬란했었죠. 배의 뒤쪽은 황금으로 얇게 깔려 있었고 돛은 자주색 비단인데 피워놓은 향내가 진동하여 바람조차 사랑에 애가 타는 듯 하느적 거렸죠. 그리고 당사자인 여왕은 표현이 따라가지 못할 정도로 아름다운 자태였죠. 금실을 섞어 짠 얇은 비단 차일 밑에 비스듬히 누웠는데 자연의 조화를 압도하는 어느 화가의 상상력보다 더 아름다운 그림속의 비너스 여신을 무색케 할 정도로 아름다웠소

> The barge she sat in, like a burnish'd throne
> Burn'd on the water: the poop was beaten gold;
> Purple the sails, and so perfumed that
> The winds were love-sick with them; the oars were silver, For her own person,
> It beggar'd all description: she did lie
> In her pavilion - cloth of gold, of tissue -
> O'er-picturing that Venus where we see
> The fancy outwork nature (2.2.191-201)

셰익스피어 작품의 매력은 이 유명한 로맨스의 양쪽 측면을 볼 수 있도록

하는 그 능력과 깊은 관계가 있다. 취한 안토니와 창녀 같은 클레오파트라라는 부정적인 시선을 재현함과 동시에, 그러한 존재 위에 사랑의 화신으로서의 존재로서 두 사람을 재현하고 있는 것이다. 그러므로 클레오파트라가로마의 거리에서 전시되며 즉석에서 희극배우의 역할을 하게 될 상황에 처한 것을 상상할 때 두려워하는 것은 진실인 것이다. 셰익스피어의 안토니와클레오파트라는 최고의 전성기를 지난 인물들이고 안토니는 자주 술에 취하고 우유부단한 인물이며 클레오파트라는 허영에 찬 변덕스런 인물이다. 그러나 동시에 그들은 이러한 한계를 뛰어넘는 자질들을 지니고 있다.

　스카루스(Scarus)는 클레오파트라의 도주에 대해 경멸스럽게 묘사한다(3.10.10-15). '그 이집트의 더러운 늙은 쓸모없는 말은 문둥병이나 걸렸으면 속시원 하겠네! 글쎄, 싸움이 무르익어갈 때 그것도 양편의 형세가분간하기 어려울 정도로 똑같은데, 아니지 어찌 보면 이쪽이 약간 우세해보이는 편인데—오뉴월 쇠파리에 물린 암소처럼 별안간 돛을 올리고 쏜살같이 달아납니다. Yon ribaudred nag of Egypt,/Whom leprosy o'ertake!—I' the midst o' the fight,/ When vantage like a pair of twins appear'd/ Both as the same, or rather ours the elder, -/ The breeze upon her, like a cow in June, / Hoists sails, and flies'. 클레오파트라를 늙어서 쓸모없어진 말(nag)에 견주어 묘사한 것은 많은 비평가의 관심을 끌었다. 자주 간과되어진 에노바부스의 당혹스러운 방백—전투 직전에 말해진 예언적인 음담패설—(3.7.6-9) '수말과 암말이 함께 전쟁터에 나가면 수말은 완전히 넋을 잃어버릴 거야. 암말이 군졸을 태운채로 수말을 낚아채 갈 테니 말이지 If we should serve with horse and mares together,/ The horse were merely lost; the mares would bear/ A soldier and his horse'에서 쓰인 말장난은 'merely lost'와 'bear'에서 연결되어진다. 그리고 이는 병사들과 그들의 수말이 여성과 암말이 함께하는 상태에서는 전쟁의 본연의 임무를 충실히 수행할 수 없다는 것을 암시한다. 암말들은 병사와 수말들이 임무를 수행하지 못하도록 할 것이며 그들을 등에 태움으로써 그들의 욕망을 드러낼 것이다. 암말은 공격적이고 파괴적인 여성의 성적 욕망을 상징한다(Miola. 141). 이 인용문에서 암시하듯 클레오파트라는 비너스와 연관되어 나타나고 잔인한 파괴행위와 그리고 무분별한 도주와 연관되어 나타난다. 셰익스피어의 클레오파트라를 6월의 암말과 암소에 비유하는 것은 그녀를 여성의 성(sexuality)의 적극적인 원칙들을 재현하는 모순적인 생명체로 묘사하는 것이다. 클레오파트라만이 성적 욕망의 광기로 불타는 것이 아니라 그녀는 안토니 또한 성적 욕망으로 불타도록 만든다.

클레오파트라는 자신이 무대 위에서 명예가 손상당하는 것을 상상해보며 몸서리친다.

> 재치 있는 희극 배우들은 즉석에서 우리들의 신세를 연극으로 꾸며 알렉산드리아의 술잔치 장면을 연출할 테지. 안토니우스는 필시 방탕 속에 빠진 술 취한 모양으로 나올 게고, 어떤 풋내기 소년이 창녀 같은 분장을 하고 클레오파트라를 연기하겠지

> The quick comedians
> Extemporally will stage us, and present
> Our Alexandrian revels: Antony
> Shall be brought drunken forth, and I shall see
> Some squeaking Cleopatra boy my greatness
> I'th'posture of a whore (5.2.216-221)

이 장면은 극중에서 극도의 자의식이 표출되는 순간이기도 하다. 왜냐하면

클레오파트라가 두려워하는 것이 우리가 정확하게 셰익스피어의 극중에서 본 것—취한 안토니와 변덕스러운 클레오파트라—이기 때문이다. 그러므로 어떤 면에서 클레오파트라가 보기를 두려워하는 것은 자신에 대한 진실이다. 자살을 결심하고서 그녀는 명령한다. 그녀는 자신의 마지막 장면을 신과 같은 여왕으로서 연기하며 이는 그들의 뚜렷한 인간적 약점에도 불구하고 안토니와 클레오파트라가 서로 안에서 발견하는 왕족으로서의 위엄이며 이것은 셰익스피어가 우리에게 또한 보여주는 것이다(Dutton, 77). 셰익스피어의 클레오파트라의 자살에 대한 해석은 플루타크의 해석과 판이하게 다르다. 플루타크에서는 클레오파트라가 패전과 안토니와의 사별로 인해 자살한다. 그러나 셰익스피어의 극에서는 클레오파트라는 시저의 승전에서 전시되는 것을 피하기 위해 자살을 선택한다. 클레오파트라는 자신이 로마의 거리에서 풍자 되는 것을 상상할 때 의식(ceremony)의 중요성에 대한 인식을 보여주었다. 프로큘레이우스는 클레오파트라에게 그녀의 자살이 어떻게 시저로 하여금 그의 고상함이 잘 구현되는 것을 세상 사람들이 보는 기회를 앗아갈 것인지를 설명한다(5.2.43-4). 그의 관심사는 오직 시저가 관대하고 자비로운 사람이라는 것을 세상에 증명하는 것이다. 그러나 클레오파트라가 실재로 듣는 것은 그 말 이면에 숨겨진 그의 생각이다. "그녀의 로마에서의 삶은 우리의 승리가운데 영원할 것이다 her life in Rome/ Would be eternal in our triumph(5.2.187)". 그렇다면, 클레오파트라의 자살은 시저로부터 그의 영원한 승리를 앗아가는 역할을 한다. 자신의 죽음을 의식화함으로써 클레오파트라는 하나의 무대를 다른 무대를 가지고 반항하고 자신의 신비로움이 번역되는 것을 방해한 것이다. 이집트 여왕의 의상을 갖춰 입고 왕들의 무덤에서 패전한 안토니의 귀환을 기다리는 클레오파트라는 그녀만의 신비로움과 이국성을 극대화시켜 자신의 이집트성이 훼손되고 조롱당하는 것을 방해한다. 그녀의 자신의 죽음에 대한 의식화는 자신의 다름의 번역할 수 없는 신비로움과 자율성을 최대한 장엄하게 재현하기 위한 기제로서 작용한다.

4. 나가며

엘리자베스 테일러는 자신의 유언에서 두 번 결혼했었던 전 남편인 리차드 버튼의 무덤 옆에 묻히기를 원했다고 한다. 비록 리차드의 아내가 거부해 무산되기는 했지만 말이다. 그녀가 영화 *Cleopatra*에서 리차드와 함께 보여준 클레오파트라의 연기를 보면서 필자는 그들의 사랑의 핵심은 무엇일까를 생각했고 그 계기로 이 글을 쓰게 되었다. 뮤지컬이나 영화에서 주로 다루어지는 주제는 그녀의 민족주의적 성향과 에로스적 측면이다. 필자는 안토니의 클레오파트라에 대한 과도한 사랑이 그녀의 이국성에 기초한 것임을 제시하고자 하였다. 다시 말하자면 그들의 관계의 핵심으로서 안토니의 에로스적 과도함과 클레오파트라의 이집트 여왕으로서의 이국성에 주목하고자 하였다. *Antony and Cleopatra*에는 여행자로서의 안토니의 모습이 부각되어 재현되어 있고 이는 플루타크의 원전에서 중요하게 다루어지지 않았던 모티브이다. 즉, 셰익스피어의 희곡에서는 알렉산더 신화와 헤라큘레스의 신화가 주요 모티브로 등장한다. 서론에서 언급했듯이 알렉산더 신화는 클레오파트라가 알렉산더의 후손 즉 그리스인이라는 점과 알렉산더가 페르시아의 공주 록사나와의 이종족 결합을 함으로써 이종족 결혼을 용인한 점에서 강화되어 나타난다. 혼종 결혼에 대한 유연한 태도와 클레오파트라에 대한 그리스 후손으로서의 긍정적 인식은 셰익스피어의 작품에서 원전과 다르게 부각되어 나타나고 있다. 또한 헤라큘레스의 신화는 영웅적 난잡함을 그 주요 내용으로 하고 있다. 안토니의 클레오파트라에 대한 과도한 사랑은 그의 영웅적 난잡함과 여행자로서의 인간적 모습에 기초하고 있다고 볼 수 있다.

안토니의 "맹목적인 사랑이 도가 지나쳤다"라고 비판적인 발언을 하면서 시작하는 희곡인 『안토니와 클레오파트라』를 특징짓는 것은 안토니의 클레오파트라에 대한 과도한 사랑과 그 사랑의 기초로서의 클레오파트라의 이국성이다. 그의 결단과 용기를 볼 수 있는 마지막 자살 장면에서 그는 로마와 그 가치들을 거부하며, 자신의 뛰는 심장을 클레오파트라에게 바치며, 죽음 후의 클레오파트라와의 해후를 기대하며 새로운 초월을 꿈꾼다. 또한 클레오파트라의 이국성은 안토니가 나일 강의 악어에 대한 레피두스와의 대화에서 보여주듯이 번역과 언어적 차용을 부인하고 있다. 그녀의 신비로움은 '미지의 것'이라고 규정된 그녀만의 이집트 여왕으로서의 고유함과 화려함이며, 그녀는 또한 자살 장면에서 자신의 이집트 여왕으로서의 위엄을 최대한 극대화시켜 자신의 이집트 성이 훼손되고 조롱당하는 것을 저지한다. 그녀의 이국성은 안토니를 사로잡은 무기였던 동시에 자신의 이집트 여왕으로서의 자율성을 최대한 장엄하게 재현시킨 기제였다.

Works Cited

김경혜. 「『안토니와 클레오파트라』에 나타난 페미니즘 전략과 그 한계」. *Shakespeare Review* 42 (2006): 641-69.

윤희억. 「『안토니와 클레오파트라』: 바흐친적 패러디 양식과 다성성의 세계」. *Shakespeare Review* 46 (2010): 755-74.

이경옥. "Eros in *Antony and Cleopatra*: The Impossibility of Grasp".

Shakespeare Review 42 (2006): 561-79.

이용관. 「『안토니와 클레오파트라』에서의 이중파국」. Shakespeare Review 43 (2007): 501-18.

이행수. 「인간본성의 상징으로 본 『안토니와 클레오파트라』」. Shakespeare Review 49 (2013): 481-500.

조윤경. 「셰익스피어의 『안토니와 클레오파트라』와 뮤지컬 <클레오파트라>(2008) 의 비교연구」. Shakespeare Review 45 (2009): 407-28.

_____. 「할리우드 클레오파트라: 클레오파트라의 변신과 오리엔탈리즘 담론」. 2013 ELLAK International Conference Proceedings. 413-26.

Crane, M. T. "Roman World, Egyptian Earth: cognitive difference and empire in Shakespeare's Antony and Cleopatra" in Comparative Drama. 43.1 (2009): 1-18.

Dutton, Richard. William Shakespeare: A Literary Life. London: Macmillan Press Ltd., 1989. 71-87.

Eagleton, Terry. William Shakespeare. Oxford: Blackwell, 1986. 76-89.

Gillies, John. "'The open worlde': the exotic in Shakespeare" in Shakespeare and the Geography of Difference. Cambridge: Cambridge UP, 1994. 112-22.

Havely, C. P. "Imperialism and Antony and Cleopatra" in English Review-Oxford. Vol. 21. no.4. (2011) pp. 12-14.

Kluge, S. "An apology for Antony, morality and pathos in Shakespeare's Antony and Cleopatra" in Orbis Litterarum. 63.4 (2008): 304-34.

Mankiewicz, J. L. Cleopatra. Beverly Hills: Twentieth Century Fox Film Corporation, 1963.

Miola, Robert S. Shakespeare's Rome. Cambridge: Cambridge UP, 1983. 116-63.

Ryle, S. J. "Antony and Cleopatra, Mankiewicz and the sublime object" in Adaptation. 4.1 (2011): 66-107.

Shakespeare, William. Antony and Cleopatra. Ed. M.R. Ridley. London and New York: Routledge, 1954.

3

1
장

Venice, Cosmopolitanism and Nomadism:
The Merchant of Venice and *Death in Venice*

Venice is such an enchanting place to visit and when you hear the place you would automatically be reminded of the name Shylock, and I would like to discuss the place particularly in terms of cosmopolitanisms of a Jewish and a German. The one is Shakespeare's *The Merchant of Venice* and the other is an interesting film, *Death in Venice* (1971). The topic of cosmopolitanism will be examined, for the first play, through the analysis of the representation of Shylock which shows the contrast between civilized Europeans and barbarous savages. For the second film, the cosmopolitan is a German professor who travelled from Munich to Venice because of his health problems. The contradicting idea of nomadism is artistically achieved through the representation of an Italian teenager, Tatsio, who is the unattainable other in the film. Before analyzing the two works, it is necessary to define the terminology of cosmopolitanism. Is it related with the Eurocentric universalism, or with blurring modern notions of the nation-state? In my article, it will be articulated in terms of nomadism, the meaning of which will be analyzed later in the main part. In the *Merchant of Venice* and *Death in Venice,* Venice is the place where contradicting national identity and culture is diffused and coexisted.

The meaning of nomadism is originated from French philosopher Gilles Deleuze's ideology that is to pursue new self denying oneself constantly without being confined by particular values and life styles. The notion was analyzed by Francis Barker in his article on *Coriolanus* in terms of 'nationalism, nomadism, and belonging in Europe'. Cosmopolitanism is closely related with the basic notion of nomadism in the context that geographical boundaries and modern notions of nation state are being blurred by the ideology of world citizenship. *In the Merchant of Venice,* Venice is expected to profit from barbarous people without compromising its integrity as a civilized and Christian state. As Gillies mentioned, the image of the maritime world in the *Merchant of Venice* is not the Venetian reality but Elizabethan ambitions for London. Venetian fantasy is projected because Venice might have represented the idea of a world maritime capital which leading Elizabethan merchants had in mind for London. The representation of Shylock and his usury seems to ironically foreground the eurocentric ideology and white anglo-saxon centered viewpoint. Shylock is one of the different exotic types and there is a focus on ethnicity in his being a Jewish. Like the barbarians, Shakespeare's exotics are innately outsiders. However, the text seems to ambiguously blur the distinction between Antony and Shylock. Even though Antony is represented as an ideal merchant with morals and values, the prejudicial viewpoint about Shylock as a cruel usurer is at the same time interrogated and empathy with Shylock is exquisitely and subversively achieved.

In *Death in Venice*, the professor Aschenbach tries to evade to face with his genuine feeling and senses. At the time of his stay in Venice, contagious disease is raging and he attempts to go back to Munich. However, he comes back just because of Tadzio to Lido hotel in Venice. In the film, the lively beach scenes and all the fruits of orange, strawberries and lemon represents energy and 'life' because he is dying and desperate for life. The figure of Tadzio represents teenager's energy and his beauty is appalling to the German music professor. The professor's personal status as a musician is at risk and his daughter is dead and his body is collapsing suddenly. The music Tadzio is playing is lingering in his mind and being played in his mind several times. His desire is climaxing when he visits a brothel. A young prostitute was playing the piano and the figure of Tadzio is overlapped with the girl, he just pays the money and escapes from the place. After that incident, he murmurs watching Tadzio that "I love you, don't smile like that to anybody else". In the mean time the professor finds out the people are disinfecting Venice and at a dinner party, he is being mocked by a group of musicians when he asks about the situation. When he visits a bank at San Marco square he comes to realize that Asia Cholera is expanding and Venice is vulnerable because of its geographical characteristics. All the Venetians are terrified but they are silent because of summer tourists. In the mean time, he decided to change his appearance by cutting and dying his hair, and doing make-up and putting a pink rose in his suit pocket. He tries to make his appearance young to make himself attractive to Tadzio and he can't be able to leave Venice. At the last scene, with the tragic music of Mahler's Adagietto from the 5th Symphony, he slowly faces with his death. The beach is without people now. In the last scene, he is sitting on a relaxing chair and he is looking at Tadzio walking slowly into the water. The notion of nomadism is prevalent in the representation of an Italian teenager, Tadzio, who is the unattainable other, and also the object of desire and the source of happiness for Aschenbach in the film. Like Shylock, the professor Aschenbach is the other in Venetian society in terms of his ethnicity, and his age. However, for a cosmopolitan German professor, Venice is the place of love and happiness because of

Tadzio's presence in Venice. Tadzio is gorgeously captivating as the object of Aschenbach's obsession and provides him with passion and inspiration. Like Shylock, professor Aschenbach is a cosmopolitan and a nomad who blurred geographical boundaries and attained world citizenship by overcoming his rigid moral and choosing his destiny as at once a pitiful caricature, his make-up melting under the hot Venice sun, and a noble figure who accepts irresistible Tadzio. Whereas the representation of Shylock shows the contrast between civilized Europeans and barbarous savages, the representation of Aschenbach seems to have much more emphasis on the boundaries of age rather than on those of nations. However, the idea of nomadism is artistically achieved in both works respectively through the representation of Shylock both as a cruel usurer and as a character interrogating the Eurocentric ideology and attaining empathy, and through the representation of Aschenbach who is obsessed with the unattainable other and blurred the geographical boundaries. In the *Merchant of Venice* and *Death in Venice,* Venice is the place where contradicting ethnic identity and culture is diffused and coexisted.

Works Cited

Francis Barker. "Nationalism, Nomadism and Belonging in Europe: *Coriolanus*" in 1997.

John Gillies. *Shakespeare and the Geography of Difference*. Cambridge: Cambridge UP, 1994.

Death in Venice. Luchino Visconti, Warner Bros. 1971.

William Shakespeare, *The Merchant of Venice*.

The Merchant of Venice. Michael Radford, Sony Pictures Home Entertainment, 2005.

Blue, Red, and the Representation of the Marginalized Culture in *The Merchant of Venice* and *Blue is the Warmest Color*

Michael Radford's *The Merchant of Venice* was released in 2005. Al Pacino's performance as Shylock is amazing and Jeremy Irons plays the role of Antonio with his partner Joseph Fiennes who plays the role of Bassanio. In the film Jews are represented as being contagious people so they are forced to wear red hats. "The Red" color represents here the significant meaning of "danger" and "disease". In the film, *Blue is the warmest color*, a lesbian couple are depicted as "bizarre" in the beginning and the hair color of the masculine woman is blue. She is, at least in the beginning, depicted as someone abnormal and conspicuous to regular normal people, particularly to the friends of her feminine partner in the film. The color symbol of Red and Blue in these two films represents a "minority" who is marginalized from the centre. The difference between the two films is that the one emphasizes the marginalization of Jewish people, while the other foregrounds the marginalization of gay culture. My article emphasizes the color symbol of Red and Blue by examining the above mentioned two films respectively in terms of race and sexuality.

Red, and Blue

In Michael Radford's *The Merchant of Venice*, Shylock's being Jewish is represented through his wearing of a red hat. It is not certain whether this tradition is based on the factual situation at the time, but the symbol of a red hat is obviously foregrounded in the beginning of the film and the viewer of the film conspicuously grasps the meaning of the symbol.

> Intolerance of the Jews was a fact of 16th century life, even in Venice, the most powerful and liberal city state in Europe. By law the Jews were forced to live in the old walled foundry or 'Geto' area of the city. After sundown the gate was locked and guarded by Christians. In the daytime any man leaving the ghetto had to wear a red hat to mark him as a Jew. The Jews were forbidden to own property. So they practised usury, the lending of money at

interest. This was against Christian law. The sophisticated Venetians would turn a blind eye to it but for the religious fanatics, who hated the Jews, it was another matter.

In the beginning of the film, the above passage is being depicted on the screen and the background scenes are about the Jews wearing red hats and being marked as dangerous and contagious people. Therefore they are segregated and guarded by Christians. The color "red" here obviously represents the danger and disease that Jewish people might have in the Venetian society. In the film, Shylock is wearing a red hat and he is the typical Jew who is one of the outsiders in the fanatical Christian society of Venice. In addition, his being an "outsider" is apparently displayed by the conspicuous color of "red" and he is coded as a "contagious" person. However, the representation of Shylock and his usury in the film reveals to us the contradictory values between the civilized Christian culture and the barbarous Jewish culture. Antonio and the state of Venice is expected to profit from barbarous people without compromising its integrity as a civilized and Christian state. Shylock asserts and inscribes the ideology that is persuasive in the increasingly capitalist marketplace of Venice. Capitalistic ideology is firmly inherent in his mind and he seems to blur the dichotomy between the civilized Christian culture and the uncivilized Jewish culture by interrogating the racial dichotomy and the viewers of the film are led to ask with

Portia "Which is the merchant here? and which the Jew?". The efforts to categorize the Jewish people as contagious and dangerous people are disrupted by the contradictory ideology.

In the BBC culture article, "Sex on Screen: No longer taboo" of 8 January 2014, it is mentioned that "the most talked-about eight minutes in cinema last year were in the French film, *Blue is the Warmest Colour*. The movie's graphic lesbian sex scene was so explicit and prolonged—frankly, it looked exhausting—that Abdellatif Kechiche's three-hour coming-of-age drama could have been dismissed as pornography. And yet, while there was much debate concerning the morality of a 52-year-old male director telling two naked young actresses to contort themselves into human reef knots, the film won the Palme d'Or at the Cannes Film Festival, and went onto garner rave reviews. Most critics accepted that Blue is the Warmest Colour wasn't a blue movie -but an honest, unflinching portrayal of first love." In the film, *Blue is the warmest color*, the masculine woman's hair color is blue and that is impressionable and unforgettable until the end of the film. Emma (masculine woman) has the familial background of high class culture and when she invites Adele (feminine woman) to her house, we notice the paintings of Emma's father and understand that the talents of Emma are inherited from her father. Meanwhile, Adele's parents show the characteristics of the low class culture whose questions to Emma mainly focus on making a living in her future, and Adele has to introduce Emma as just a friend not as a partner. It is intriguing to compare the attitude of Emma's parents who understand and accept their daughter's sexual preferences. Despite their differences in their familial background, Emma and Adele feel strong bonds between them and the first encounter with each other is artistically represented in the film. The blue color of Emma's hair when she first comes across Adele and catches Adele's attention on the road is impressively represented in the film and carved deeply onto the mind of the viewers. The camera closes up on Adele's blushing cheeks and her eyes lingering on the attractive appearance of Emma. Adele is infatuated with Emma at the first sight and the fetishization of each other's body is depicted in the later part of the film. Adele's struggling with the inevitable attractiveness of Emma and her innate prejudice against gay culture and curiosity about gay culture is later developed to her adventurous visit to some gay bars with her male friend.

The notion of marginalized culture is expressed by the color symbol in *The Merchant of Venice* and *Blue is the warmest color*. In *The Merchant of Venice*, Jews are represented as being dangerous and contagious people so they are compelled to wear red hats, whereas a masculine lesbian, Emma, is depicted symbolically by her blue hair. The color blue and red here in those two films are the symbols of abnormality and conspicuous behavior based on the notion of danger and disease. As I mentioned, the color symbol of red and blue in these two films represents a marginalized voice excluded from the centre. The difference between the two films is that the one emphasizes on the marginalization of Jewish people while the other emphasizes on the marginalization of gay culture. Therefore, the color symbol of the two films is fundamentally originated from the dichotomous understanding of European centered culture of Shakespearean period and heterosexual centered culture of 21st century France.

3
장

—

『코리올레이누스』에 나타난
영웅의 몸, 그리고 국가건설

루시우스가 자신의 몸을 로마제국을 위하여 바쳤다고 주장하며 자신의 몸에 난 흉터를 자신의 주장에 대한 증거로서 제시하듯이 코리올레이누스는 로마적인 것을 영웅의 피와 그의 몸에 새겨진 흉터를 숭배함으로써 구현하고 있다. 흥미롭게도 피와 흉터에 대한 과도한 집착이 이 작품의 지속적인 모티프가 되고 있다.

메네니우스. 예, 정당한 보상이라고? 정당하고말고. 한데 어디에 상처를 입었습니까? 아, 두 각하, 안녕하십니까? 마르치우스가 돌아왔습니다. 점점 더 교만하게 굴 명분을 갖게 됐소. 어디를 부상당했습니까?
볼룸니아. 어깨와 왼쪽 팔입니다. 관직에 입후보하려고 단에 서면 두드러지게 드러나는 상처를 평민들에게 보여주게 될 겁니다. 타르퀸을 추방했을 때에도 몸뚱이에 일곱 군데나 상처를 입었습니다.

메네니우스. 또 목에 한 군데, 다리에 두 군데, 내가 알기에도 아홉 군데나
　　되지요.
볼룸니아. 이번 원정이전에 이미 스물다섯 군데에 상처를 입고 있습니다.
메네니우스. 그럼 스물일곱 군데가 되는군요. 그 상처의 하나하나가 적군
　　의 무덤 구멍이었지요 (환호성과 나팔소리가 들린다). 아, 나팔소리가
　　들린다. (2.1.141-155)

우리가 메네니우스와 볼룸니아의 대화에서 알 수 있듯이 코리올레이누스
는 흉터와 상처들의 상징적인 구현으로서 기능하고 있으며 이는 그의 전쟁
에서의 위대한 성취를 보여주는 시그널이다. 국가적 영웅의 신화를 생성하
고 유지시키는 것은 폭력과 군사적인 전쟁에 의한 육체절단이다. 그것이
바로 볼룸니아와 메네니우스가 상처를 말하는데 헌신적이며 그에 대해 열
정적으로 담화하고 있는 이유이다. 이 상처들은 코리올레이누스에게 영사
직을 수행하기에 합당한 자격을 부여하는 지점이며 진정한 증거인 것이다.
볼룸니아는 버질리아를 부추겨 코리올레이누스의 상처에 대한 자신의 만
족스러움을 공감하도록 유도한다: "헥토르에게 젖을 먹이고 있는 헤큐바
왕비의 앞가슴도 그리스 군대의 칼에 찔려 피를 내뿜고 있을 때의 헥토르
의 이마처럼 아름답게 보이지는 않을 거야(1.3.40-43)" 그녀가 여기에서
사용하고 있는 이미지는 흉측하고 충격적이다. 그녀는 우유보다 피가, 가
슴보다 상처가, 그리고 평화로운 수유보다 전쟁이 더 아름답다고 주장한
다. 그녀는 자신의 전사 아들을 자랑스럽게 여기고 있으며 잔혹한 전쟁과
국가주의적 생각에 대한 지지를 다음과 같은 대사에서 표현하고 있다: "나
에게 현재 열두 아들이 있다고 치자. 그 애들이 모두 다 사랑스러워서 너
나 네 남편 마르치우스처럼 귀엽더라도 그중 열 한 명이 나라를 위해 목숨
을 바치는 것이 주색에 빠져서 빈둥거리며 살아가는 한 아들보다 훨씬 더

바람직한 것이 아니겠느냐?(1.3.24-25)" 위대한 군사적 영웅의 남성적 정체성은 자신의 어머니에 의해 영향을 받았고 형성되었으며, 그녀는 자신의 자연적 성 역할을 전복시키며 적극적인 그녀의 삶은 자신의 아들을 통해 대리적으로 성취되고 있다. 그녀는 아들에게 "아! 나의 용사, 너를 만들어 내느라고 나도 수고를 했다(5.3.63-4)"라고 자신의 역할을 상기시킨다. 그녀는 코리올레이누스가 싸우고 피 흘리는 모습을 상상하고 자신의 아들이 전쟁터에서 귀환했을 때 그의 새로운 상처를 세며 아들의 기록을 업데이트한다. 분명히 상처에 대한 집착은 자신의 어머니 볼룸니아와 그의 대리 부친인 메네니우스에게만 국한된 것은 아니다.

> 코미니우스. 그 자신도 온통 피투성이가 되어 있었습니다. 그분의 일거일동은 죽어가는 적의 신음소리에 장단을 맞춰 움직였습니다. 그분은 단신으로 무시무시한 적의 성문 안으로 뛰어들어 선혈로써 그 문에 종횡으로 적의 필멸을 그려놓고 구조도 기다리지 않고 되돌아 와서 구원병을 얻자마자 성난 혹성이 내려앉듯 곧 코리올레스를 함락시켰습니다. (2.2.109-114)

코미니우스는 코리올레이누스의 피투성이 몸을 군사적 용맹스러움과 승리의 절대적 구현으로서 언급한다. 피와 상처가 없었더라면 코리올레이누스의 정체성을 구현하는 것이 절대적으로 불가능했을 것이다. 실재로, 국가적 영웅의 몸은 애국주의 담론의 중심에 위치하고 있으며 국가적 가치로 정의되고 그러한 사명감을 띠고 있다. 바커는 "로마적인 것이 코리올레이누스의 모습에 중점적으로 구현되어 나타난다는 것은 중요한 사실이다. 또한 상처와 피를 부각시킴으로써 그러한 형상화가 근본적으로 이루어지고 있다. 이러한 사실은 로마적인 것의 국가적 가치를 영웅의 몸과 연관시키도록 유도하고 있다"라고 주장한다(Barker, 14). 상징적인 영웅의 몸과 국가적인 가치의 논리 사이에는 형상화의 연관성이 있다는 것을 부인할 수 없다. 코리올레이누스는 전쟁터에서 로마의 가장 최고의 부하이며 평화 시에 가장 진정한 대표자이다. 그는 로마의 가치와 전통, 국가적 논리의 진정한 구현이다. 특히 코리올레이누스는 자신들의 계급의 이익만을 추구하는 서민들과 호민관들과 차별되게 로마의 공격적인 이익추구에 헌신적이다. 그의 몸은 기계 혹은 전쟁엔진으로서 형상화된다. 그의 몸은 기괴할 정도로 침범할 수 없는 그리고 고립된 존재로 묘사되고 있으며 이러한 이미지는 그의 몸을 칼 그 자체로 변신시킨다. 영웅의 몸을 국가적 가치의 화신으로서 형상화하는 것은 로마제국의 공격적인 군사 제국주의를 반영한다. 로마는 코리올족이나 볼시안족과 같은 이웃 부족들을 정복함으로써 팽창하고 있었으며 이러한 제국주의 팽창 시기에 코리올레이누스 같은 전쟁 기계를 필요로 했던 것이다. 그의 침범할 수 없는 몸은 국가의 형성에 필수적이며 그의 육체적인 몸은 영웅의 몸과 국가적 연대의 형상화 사이의 거래를 부각시킨다. 민중들의 코리올레이누스 환영은 너무나 놀라운 것이어서 그것은 국가적 영웅에 대한 열렬한 찬미를 보여준다.

> 브루투스. 저 사람 얘기를 하지 않는 사람이 없군. 시력이 약한 사람은 안경까지 쓰고 그 사나이를 보려고 하는군. 수다스러운 유모는 애기가 자지러지게 우는데도 그 사람 이야기에 정신이 없어. 식모들도 더러운 목덜미에 대마 손수건을 두르고 담장위에 올라서서 그자를 보려고 야단이야. 상점이나 진열장이나 창문이나, 지붕 위나 사람들로 초만원이야. 지붕 꼭대기에 걸터앉은 갖가지 얼굴들이 그를 보려고 정신이 없어. 좀처럼 나오기를 싫어하는 신관들까지도 평민들과 밀거니 밀리거니 하면서 숨을 헐떡거리며 잘 보일 장소를 찾고 있어. 평소에는 얼굴을 가리고 있던 귀부인들까지도 타는 듯한 햇 을 받아서 그 아름다운 볼의 화장이 엉망이 되는데도 개의치 않고 소란이야. 마치 수호신이나 다른 어떤

신인가가 살며시 그자의 육신 속에 숨어들어서 그를 알아볼 수 없는 아름다운 모습으로 만들어 놓기라도 한 듯이 말이오. (2.1.203-19)

이 인용문은 브루투스가 언술한 것으로서 그는 코리올레이누스의 승리에 공감을 느끼지 못하는 인물이다. 비록 그는 코리올레이누스의 인기에 반감을 느끼지만 그는 어쩔 수 없이 다양한 사회 계층의 사람들-평민, 모습을 잘 드러내지 않는 성직자, 그리고 귀족 여성들-의 코리올레이누스에 대한 열렬한 찬미를 묘사할 수밖에 없다. 로마 민중들의 나이, 직업, 성, 옷차림, 그리고 얼굴색의 진정한 다양성에도 불구하고 이들은 모두 하나가 되어 국가적 영웅을 보려고 그리고 그의 승리를 찬미하려고 혈안이 되어 있다. 다시 말하면 그의 은혜로운 자태는 거의 종교적인 모습으로 승화되어 있다.

그러나 로마의 국가적 아이디어를 영웅의 폭력을 당한 몸에 투사함으로써 전사의 몸과 폭력을 우상화하는 것은 지속될 수 없다. 왜냐하면 국가적 화신으로서의 상징적 영웅의 모습은 환상이라는 것이 드러나기 때문이다. 국가적 영웅에 의한 재현의 문제는 메네니우스의 '복부의 비유' 스피치에 명확하게 언술되어 있다.

메네니우스. 자, 내 말을 들어 보세요. 복부는 진지하고 사려 깊고 탄핵자들처럼 경솔하지 않기 때문에 이렇게 대답했죠. "조합원 여러분들, 과연 그렇습니다. 나는 음식물을 먼저 받아들입니다. 그렇지만 그것은 어디까지나 조합원들 전체의 생활을 지탱해 나가기 위한 것입니다. 나는 온몸의 창고이기도 하고 상점이기도 합니다. 그러니 그것을 받아들이는 것은 당연합니다. 여러분들은 미처 생각지 못하셨는지 모르지만 나는 언제나 그것을 여러분들의 혈관을 통해 각 부분으로 보내고 있습니다. 조정이 되는 심장이나 본부가 되는 뇌수, 그 밖에 조합의 모든 부분에, 제일 강한 근육으로부터 가장 약한 혈관에 이르기까지, 골고

루 나에게서 받아간 것으로써 거기에 알맞은 일을 할 수 있는 활력을 얻게 됩니다. 설사 그걸 금방 알 수는 없더라도 말입니다. 여러분. . ." 하고 복부가 대답했지요. 아시겠습니까?

시민 1. 알겠습니다. 그래서요?

메네니우스. "설사 무엇을 공급하는지 금방 알지 못하더라도 언제나 여러 분들 각자에게 음식물중의 알맹이는 되돌려 드리고 나는 단지 껍데기 만을 차지하는 셈입니다. 이와 같은 사실을 증명해 보여 드릴 수 있습 니다" 하고 말했다면 어떻게 하시겠습니까? (1.1.129-145)

메네니우스의 사회에 대한 생각은 합력에 의존하고 있다. 그에 따르면 로 마의 국가적 정체성은 어떤 민주주의적 생각에 의해 형성된 것이 아니다. 그것은 전형으로서의 대표자의 아이디어에 근거하고 있다. 다시 말하면, 로마의 국가적 정체성은 최다 득표수나 연대에 근거한 것이 아니라 합력과 전형으로의 포섭에 근거한 것이다. 2막 3장에서 겸손의 가운을 입은 코리 올레이누스는 시장에서 민중들을 대면한다. 그는 이러한 민중들의 동조를 간청하는 의식을 혐오하는데, 왜냐하면 이는 일정 정도의 쌍방의 상호 존 중과 평등을 전제로 하기 때문이다.

시민 3. 물론 그럴 수 있소. 그렇지만 말뿐이지 우리에게 실천할 권한은 없 잖아. 만일 그자가 우리에게 상처를 보이고 자기의 공훈을 이야기한다 면 우리는 제각기 그 몇 개의 상처에 일일이 혀를 틀어박고 대변을 해 야만 돼. 즉, 그자가 근사한 공훈담을 늘어놓으면 우리도 그럴듯하게 그리고 공정하게 받아들였다고 하지 않으면 안 돼. 은혜를 모르는 것 은 인간이 아니고 괴물이라고 하거든. 그런데 수만 명의 민중들이 모 두 은혜를 저버릴 경우에는 곧 수만 명의 괴물이 생기는 셈인데 우리 는 그 민중의 한 사람이므로 우리도 그 괴물의 패거리가 될 수밖에 없 지. (2.3.4-13)

시민들 중의 한명은 '권력'에 대하여 이야기하며, 민중들이 자신들의 권력을 국가를 위해 명예롭게 봉사한 사람들에게 이양할 때만 권력을 분배해서 가질 수 있다는 자신의 생각을 피력한다. 그는 민주주의는 정치적으로 의식이 있는 개인들에 의해서 완성될 수 있다고 믿는다. 그러나 코리올레이누스는 개인이 자신들의 정치적 권력을 가지고 있으며 그렇게 취급되어야 한다는 생각을 받아들이려고 하지 않는다. 그러므로 그는 극도로 민중들을 경멸하고 그의 존경받는 자아가 자신이 가장 혐오하는 다른 사람들에 의존해야 한다는 사실 때문에 딜레마를 느끼며 고통스러워한다.

> 코리올레이누스. 왜 이런 수직물옷을 걸치고 여기에 서 있어야 한단 말인가. 만나는 족족 이놈 저놈에게 필요 없는 추천을 간청해야 하나. 뭐? 그것이 관습이라고? 관습이 원한다고 무엇이나 한대서야 옛날의 먼지를 털 기회는 영영 없잖아. 그러면 실수는 쌓이고 쌓여서 산더미를 이루겠지. 그리하여 진실은 감히 얼굴을 내밀 틈이 없을 거야. 이런 머저리 흉내를 내기 보다는 차라리 높은 자리와 명예직은 그것을 좋아하는 놈들에게 주어 버리는 게 낫지. 그런데 벌써 절반은 치렀군. 지금까지 참아온 이상 나머지 절반도 치르기로 하지. (2.3.114-122)

코리올레이누스에게는 겸손의 옷을 입고 민중들의 달콤한 동조를 간청하는 것은 '그들과 같은 종류의 사람'이 되는 것을 의미하고 그것은 역겨운 입 냄새를 가진 군중이 되는 것을 의미한다. 그는 개인들의 정치적 권력에 관심이 없으며 민중들의 투표권이 불필요한 것이라고 간주한다. 그는 자기 자신만이 고정불변의 존재라고 믿게 된다. 코리올레이누스는 민중들에게 아첨하는 것은 자신의 승리에 찬 남성성을 훼손하는 것이고 전사의 검이 기생충의 실크처럼 부드럽게 변할 것이라고 믿는다. 부드럽고 의존적인 기생충이 되는 것을 방지하기 위해 그는 전사의 검으로서 자신의 강직함을 유지시켜야 하는 것이다. '전사의 검'과 '기생충의 부드러운 실크' 의 상충되는 이미지는 코리올레이누스의 딜레마의 전조가 된다. 그는 민중들의 승인을 간청하는 것을 마지못해 수행하게 되는데, 왜냐하면 간청하거나 멋진 말로 아첨하는 것은 자신의 약함을 인정하고 타인에게 의존함을 의미하기 때문이다. "당연히 받아야 할 것을 간청해서 받다니 죽는 것이, 굶어 죽는 것이 더 낫겠다"(2.3.112-13). "한 마디라도 달콤한 말을 해서 그들의 자비를 구하지는 않겠다"(3.3.90-91). 간청하는 것은 자신의 남성적인 정체성을 훼손하는 것이고 자신을 여성적으로 만드는 것이다. "좋습니다. 별 도리가 없군요. 나의 기질 같은 것은 아무 데로나 없어져 버려라. 어디 창부의 혼이라도 내 속으로 옮겨와 봐라. 싸움터의 북소리에 어울리던 나의 굵은 목소리는 내시의 가는 목소리나 어린애를 재우는 엄마의 자장가 소리로 변해라"(3.2.110-115). 말로 다 할 수 없는 위험들을 겪고 자신의 국가를 위하여 엄청난 역경을 인내한 후 전쟁터로부터 돌아온 코리올레이누스는 평화적인 시기에는 자신이 아첨꾼과 여성적인 인물이 되도록 요구 받는다는 것을, 그리고 그것은 자신의 남성적 정체성에 상충된다는 것을 발견한다. 그는 이러한 상충되는 면을 받아들일 수가 없고 그리하여 그의 국가에 대한 헌신은 보상받지 못하고 마침내 그는 추방된다. 린다 우드브리지는 이러한 늙은 병사의 모습을 르네상스와 자코비안 드라마의 인물을 예로 들어 보임으로서 언급했다. 바나베 리치는 자신의 책,『군인직을 떠나는 리치』에서 평화를 회복한 시기에 별 볼일 없이 여겨지는 병사의 비애를 쓸쓸하게 표현하였다.

경험은 이제 나에게 가르쳤다. 병사가 된다는 것은 고통과, 고생, 혼란, 동요, 추위, 배고픔, 슬픔, 형편없는 잠자리, 보잘것없는 임금, 불편한 잠자리, 그리고 수많은 재난들과 함께 한다는 것이다. 이 수많은 싸움에서 봉사한 병사가 받게 되는 최고의 보상은 여우의 꼬리로 찰싹 때려주는 것. 나는 그들이 받은 더 이상의 보상을 본 적이 없다. 이제 병사가 되는 것과 반대로, 기쁨과, 즐거움, 위안, 환희, 평화, 조용한 휴식, 맛있는 음식, 내가 다 열거할 수 없는 수천가지의 다른 기쁨들이 있다. 상당한 기간 동안 봉사했으니 자신의 일에 대한 보상으로 자신의 아내의 입술을 즐길 수 있기를.

정직한 병사는 전쟁터에서 돌아와 자신이 고상하고 여성적인 궁정사회에서 극심한 사회적 불이익을 당하게 된다는 것을 발견한다. 코리올레이누스가 로마사회에 대해 느끼는 씁쓸함도 같은 맥락에서 이해될 수 있다. 평화적인 시기는 남성적인 군사적 영웅을 민중들에게 아첨하는 수치스러운 위치에 서도록 위협한다. 나이 든 병사들의 냉소주의와 불만족은 르네상스와 자코비안 문헌과 실재 사회에서 만연해 있었다. 도외시된 군인들은 평화적인 시기의 여성적인 가치에 불만족스러울 수밖에 없었고 그들은 군사의 검에서 부드러운 실크로 자신을 변화시킬 수 없었다. 시시니우스에게는 코리올레이누스의 경직됨과 부드러운 실크의 가치를 받아들이기를 거부하는 것은 폭력이자 우쭐하는 독재로 밖에 보이지 않는다: '그 도시에 사는 사람들을 철거시키고 자신이 민중이 되고자 하는 이 독사 같은 인간이 어디 있느냐?'(3.1.261-3). 여기에 국가적 영웅에 의해 로마의 가치를 대변하려는 생각과 민중들의 힘에 의해 민주주의를 실현하려는 생각이 대치된다.

> 시시니우스. 민중들이 없다면 이 도시는 어떻게 존재한단 말인가?
> 민중들. 맞습니다,
> 　　　민중들이 바로 도시의 주인입니다. (3.1.198-99)

체현의 담론은 민중들의 국가적 정체성에 대한 주장과 코리올레이누스의 국가적 정체성에 대한 단호한 체현의 상호충돌에 의해 의문이 제기된다.

체현된 국가적 영웅이 민중들과 그들의 정치적 목소리들을 수렴할 수 없고 추방되어야 한다는 것은 명확하다. 코리올레이누스가 추방되는 시점에 용사의 몸과 폭력에 대한 집착과 국가주의와 군사주의의 건설은 국가적 체현이 환상이라는 사실에 직면할 수밖에 없다. 비록 그의 흉터와 피와 상처가 로마의 국가주의에 있어 강력한 가치가 되지만 그것들은 부인되어야 한다, 왜냐하면 국가적 영웅의 절대적 '나'는 집단적인 정체성의 자율적인 담론을 받아들일 수가 없기 때문이다. 이러한 진실과 직면하는 것은 딜레마에 직면하는 것이다. 한쪽 측면에는 피와 상처, 그리고 상징적인 영웅에 의한 국가적 가치의 대변이라는 강력한 주제가 있는 반면, 또 다른 측면에는 민중들의 목소리에 의해 발현되는 민중의 민주주의 가치가 있기 때문이다.

로마적인 것이 코리올레이누스의 모습에 괄목할만할 정도로 집중되어 나타나고 있고 그러한 모습이 상처와 피를 부각시킴으로서 재현되어 있다. 로마적 전통의 국가적 아이디어를 건설하는데 폭력의 정치학이 설득력이 있다, 왜냐하면 로마는 다른 이웃 부족을 점령함으로서 자신의 정체성을 확립할 필요가 있었기 때문이다. 이러한 합병과 점령의 시기에, 코리올레이누스 같은 강력한 전사가 국가적 전통을 재현하고 국가를 형성하는데 필수불가결하게 작용한다. 그의 육체적 몸은 영웅의 몸과 국가적 가치의 체현이라는 재현적인 거래로 상징적으로 규정되어 진다. 그렇지만 상징적인 영웅에 의한 국가적 가치의 재현은 민중들의 민주주의적 가치에 의해 발현되는 반대담론에 부딪히게 된다. 폭력의 정치학과 국가주의의 건설은 그 체현의 환상에 직면하게 되고 불가피하게 국가적 영웅의 추방을 목격하게 된다. 우리가 『코리올레이누스』에서 살펴보았듯이 군사적 폭력은 구체적 인간의 몸에 대한 전개로서 재현된다. 이러한 전개는 시민의 무질서에 대한 불안을 불러일으킴으로써 국가적 연대감을 강화하기 위하여 성취되는 것처럼 보인다. 그들의 몸의 절단이나 상처는 무질서에 대한 불안을 부각시키고 그들의 구체적인 인간의 몸에 가해진 폭력을 통하여 국가적 연대감이라는 이데올로기를 고취시킨다. 코리올레이누스의 흉터로 가득한 몸은 능동적인 국가에 대한 봉사로서 그리고 지지물로서 기능한다. 영웅의 몸에는 팽창하는 군사적 제국주의의 기운이 흐른다. 그의 몸은 국가적 아이디어와 로마적 전통의 체현으로서 재현된다. 이러한 영웅의 몸의 영토화는 영국의 영토로서의 엘리자베스 여왕의 재현에서도 유사하게 발견된다. '디칠리 초상화'에서, 엘리자베스의 몸은 영토가 되고, 이러한 맥락에서 민족주의의 이데올로기는 그 자체를 투영시킨다. 자신을 찬미하는 부하들에게 여왕을 멋지게 보여주는 것은 보는 사람들에게 애국심을 고취하도록 전개되며, 엘리자베스 신화는 국가적 질서를 지탱하도록 이용된다. 이러한 영국적 애국주의는 그 당시에 특별히 형성되어 지던 국가적 정체성의 확립을 공고하게 하는 역할을 한다. 군주의 그리고 국가적 영웅의 몸이 영토로서 재현되고 국가적 이데올로기의 중요성으로 깊이 있게 규정되어 있다는 점은 굉장히 흥미로운 사실이다.

Works Cited

Adelman, Janet. "'Anger's My Meat': Feeding, Dependency, and Aggression in *Coriolanus*" in *Representing Shakespeare: New Psychoanalytic Essays*. eds. Murray M. Schwartz and Coppelia Kahn. Baltimore and London: The Johns Hopkins University Press, 1980. 129-149.

Barker, Francis. *The Culture of Violence: Essays on Tragedy and History*. Manchester: Manchester UP, 1993.

_____. "Nationalism, Nomadism and Belonging in Europe: *Coriolanus*." in 1997.

Lemonnier-Texier, Delphine. "The analogy of the Body Politic in Shakespeare's *Coriolanus*: From the Organic Metaphor of Society to the Monstrous Body of the Multitude." *Moreana*. Vol. 43, 168 (2006) 44, 169-170. 107-31.

Sanders, Eve Rachele. "The Body of the Actor in *Coriolanus*." *Shakespeare Quarterly*. 57.4 (2006): 387-412.

4
장
—

Shakespeare and Gender Studies

For approximately the last two decades, gender studies have provided an invaluable discourse for understanding and appreciating Shakespeare's plays and poems. It is only since the mid-1980s that gender studies as a theory has focused on Shakespearean drama. This course will focus on the secondary literature of gender study critiques, trying to define their characteristic concerns and understand their principal approaches to Shakespearean drama. Questions of transvestism and challenging gender boundaries will be central. Questions of sexuality, nation-building, and power will be considered. The course will proceed through three sessions in which critical essays will be carefully compared. In each case the original text will be an obvious reference point but one approached via the essays, rather than directly.

Materials

All the secondary literature that we will be reading are available from the library. Primary texts should be bought or borrowed from the library in the specified editions.

Programme

Session 1: Transvestism and Dissolving Gender Boundary: *Shakespeare in Love (Twelfth Night, As You Like It, The Merchant of Venice)*

Session 2: Erotic Power and Reinterpretation: *Othello (Guess Who's Coming to Dinner, Jungle Fever), Hamlet, The Winter's Tale*

Session 3: Gender and Colonialism: *The Tempest (The Discovery of Guiana, Diario), M Butterfly*

Reading List

Session 1: Transvestism and Dissolving Gender Boundary: *Shakespeare in Love (Twelfth Night, As You Like It, The Merchant of Venice)*

Marc Norman and Tom Stoppard. *Shakespeare in Love: A*

Screenplay. New York: Miramax Film Corp and Universal Studios, 1998.

William Shakespeare. *Twelfth Night.* Ed. J.M. Lothian and T.W. Craik. London and New York: Routledge, 1988.

_____. *As You Like It.* Ed. Agnes Latham. London: Methuen, 1975.

_____. *The Merchant of Venice.* Oxford: Oxford UP, 1993.

Jean Howard. 'Crossdressing, The Theatre, and Gender Struggle in Early Modern England' in *Shakespeare Quarterly* 39 (1988), pp. 418-440.

Lisa Jardine. 'Cultural Confusion and Shakespeare's Learned Heroines' in *Reading Shakespeare Historically,* London: Routledge, 1996, pp. 48-64.

Lisa Jardine. *Still Harping on Daughters.* London & New York: Harvester, 1983.

Marjorie Garber. *Vested Interests: Cross-dressing and Cultural Anxiety.* London: Penguin Books, 1992.

Judith Butler, *Bodies That Matter.* London: Routledge, 1993.

Roy Strong. *The Cult of Elizabethan Portraiture and Pageantry.* London: Thames and Hudson, 1977.

Session 2: Erotic Power and Reinterpretation: *Othello (Guess Who's Coming to Dinner, Jungle Fever), Hamlet, The Winter's Tale*

William Shakespeare. *Othello.* Ed. M. R. Ridley. London & New York: Methuen, 1958.

_____. *Hamlet.* The New Cambridge Shakespeare. Ed. Philip Edwards. Cambridge: Cambridge UP, 1994.

_____. *The Winter's Tale*. Ed. Stephen Orgel. The Oxford
Shakespeare. Oxford: Oxford UP, 1996.

Stanley Kramer. *Guess Who's Coming to Dinner,* 1967.

Spike Lee. *Jungle Fever*. CA: Universal Studios, 1991.

Valerie Traub. "Jewels, Statues, and Corpses: Containment of
Female Erotic Power" *Desire and Anxiety: Circulations of
Sexuality in Shakespearean Drama*. London and New York:
Routledge, 1992. 25-49.

Valerie Wayne. 'Historical Differences: Misogyny and *Othello*' in
The Matter of Difference. ed. Valerie Wayne, London and New
York: Harvester, 1991. pp. 153-79.

C. T. Neely. "Women and Men in *Othello*" in *The Woman's Part:
Feminist Criticism of Shakespeare*. Eds. C. R. Swift Lenz, Gayle
Greene, and C. T. Neely. Chicage: U of Illinois P, 1980. 211-39.

Peter Stallybrass. "Patriarchal Territories: The Body Enclosed" in
*Rewriting the Renaissance: The Discourse of Sexual Difference
in Early Modern Europe*. Eds. M. W. Ferguson et al. Chicago:
U of Chicago Press, 1986. 123-42.

Session 3: Gender and Colonialism: *The Tempest (The Discovery of
Guiana, Diario), M Butterfly*

William Shakespeare. *The Tempest*. World's Classics. Ed. Stephen
Orgel. Oxford and New York: Oxford UP, 1987.

David Henry Hwang. *M Butterfly*. London & New York: A Plume
Book, 1989.

Margarita Zamora. Gender and Discovery in *Reading Columbus*.

Berkeley: University of California Press, 1993. pp. 152-79.

John Gillies. *Shakespeare and The Geography of Difference.* Cambridge: Cambridge UP, 1994. pp. 140-155.

Peter Hulme. *Colonial Encounters: Europe and the native Caribbean, 1492-1797.* London & New York: Routledge, 1986.

Louis Montrose, "The Work of Gender in the Discourse of Discovery" in *New World Encounters*, ed. Stephen Greenblatt, Berkeley: University of California Press, 1993. 177-217.

Abena P. A. Busia. "Silencing Sycorax: On African Colonial Discourse and the Unvoiced Female" in *Cultural Critique* 14 (winter 1989-90). 81-104.

Francis Barker and Peter Hulme. "Nymphs and Reapers Heavily Vanish: the Discursive Con-texts of The Tempest" in *Alternative Shakespeare.* Ed. John Drakakis. London: Routledge, 1985. 191-205.